CENSORING AN IRANIAN LOVE STORY

A novel

SHAHRIAR MANDANIPOUR

TRANSLATED FROM FARSI BY SARA KHALILI

Little, Brown

LITTLE, BROWN

First published in Great Britain in 2009 by Little, Brown

A CIP catalogue record for this book
is available from the British Library.

Hardback ISBN: 978-1-4087-0160-7
C format ISBN: 978-1-4087-0222-2

Printed and bound in Great Britain by
Clays Ltd, St Ives plc

Papers used by Little, Brown are natural, renewable and
recyclable products sourced from well-managed forests and certified in
accordance with the rules of the Forest Stewardship Council.

Mixed Sources
Product group from well-managed
forests and other controlled sources
www.fsc.org Cert no. SGS-COC-004081
© 1996 Forest Stewardship Council
FSC

Little, Brown
An imprint of
Little, Brown Book Group
100 Victoria Embankment
London EC4Y 0DY

An Hachette UK Company
www.hachette.co.uk

www.littlebrown.co.uk

The tale of he who a treasure map found that out some gate should you take leave, there sits a dome, if your back to the dome you turn and your face fronting Mecca, and an arrow you sling, whither the arrow falls a treasure trove lies. He went and arrows he let fly, so much so that he despaired, he did not find. And this news reached the King. Long-range archers arrows let fly, indeed naught was found. When to his Holiness he appealed, unto him it was inspired that we did not bid to pull the bow-string. Arrow in the bow he set, there before him it fell.

SHAMS TABRIZI (d. 1248)

DEATH TO DICTATORSHIP, DEATH TO FREEDOM

In the air of Tehran, the scent of spring blossoms, carbon monoxide and the perfumes and poisons of the tales of *One Thousand and One Nights* ~~sway on top of each other, they~~ whisper together. The city drifts in time.

In front of the main entrance of Tehran University, on Liberty Street, a crowd of students is gathered in political protest. With their fists raised they shout, "Death to captivity!" Across the street, members of the Party of God, with clenched fists and perhaps chains and brass knuckles in their pockets, shout "Death to the Liberal . . ."

The anti-riot police, armed with the most sophisticated paraphernalia, including stun batons purchased from the West, stand facing the students. Both groups try, before they come to blows, to triumph over their opponents by shouting even louder. Drops of sweat ooze from faces and specks of spit spew from mouths. Fists, before pounding on heads, rise without miracle towards the sky.

It is perhaps because of these fists that from the sacred sky of Iran no miracle ever descends. Since one hundred and one years ago – when the first revolution for democracy triumphed in Iran – fists similar to these have risen towards the sky of a country with the greatest number of holy men, with the most prayers, tears, and religious lamentations; and today, I believe, the greatest pleas to God for speeding up the day of resurrection rise from Iran.

A short distance away, on the pavement, with her back to the steel fence lodged in the three-foot-tall stone wall surrounding Tehran University, stands a girl who, unlike most girls in the world but like most girls in Iran, is wearing a black headscarf and a long black coat as a coverall. She possesses a beauty common to all girls in love stories, a beauty that many girls around the world, and in Iran, who read these stories want to possess. If the ghosts of the thousands of poets who died a thousand years ago, seven hundred years ago, or four hundred years ago, and the spirit of those yet to be born – who, unlike the living, in the democracy of death amicably and tolerantly wander the streets of Tehran – see her large black eyes, they will liken them, as is customary of their poetry, to the sad eyes of a gazelle. An old simile for a pair of Oriental eyes that stole Lord Byron's heart, and Arthur Rimbaud's, too . . . But contrary to this clichéd simile, there is a mysterious look in this girl's eyes. It is as if they possess the power to traverse time, the power to pass through the golden walls of harems or perhaps the firewalls of websites and Internet filters.

But the girl does not know that in precisely seven minutes and seven seconds, at the height of the clash between the students, the police, and the members of the Party of God, in the chaos of attacks and escapes, she will be knocked into with great force, she will fall back, her head will hit against a cement edge, and her sad Oriental eyes will for ever close . . .

The girl attracts the attention of mysterious people who, during political demonstrations in Iran, monitor the scene from discreet corners and identify people. They point her out to one another. One of them, from a very professional angle, takes a photograph and films her.

I know **this girl is not a member of any political party, but she is timidly holding a sign that reads**

DEATH TO FREEDOM, DEATH TO CAPTIVITY

It is a strange slogan that I don't believe has ever been seen or heard under the rule of any dictatorial, Communist, populist, or even so-called liberal regime. And I don't believe it will ever be heard under the rule of any future regimes that for now remain nameless.

When they pause to catch their breath in between shouting their slogans, the students seeking freedom and democracy point to the girl and her sign and ask, "Who in the world is she? What is she trying to say?"

The more experienced students, old hands at political protests, respond:

"Completely ignore her. She's an infiltrator. The Party of God has paid her to create distrust and division among us. To defuse the conspiracy, just act as though she doesn't exist."

On the opposite side, the fanatical members of the Party of God also point to the girl and ask, "What's that prissy girl trying to say over there?"

They hear from their leaders:

"The lewd hussy is one of those Communists who have recently come back to life. Their Big Brother in Russia is gaining strength again . . , but the pathetic slobs only have a handful of members in their party. This is how they hope to attract attention . . . Just ignore her. Act as though she doesn't exist."

With their two-way radios, the secret police pass along the girl's location and ask, "What does this mean? We have no instructions for such cases. What should we do with her?"

And they receive instructions:

"Watch her with extreme vigilance and caution. This is most definitely a new conspiracy and a new plot for a velvet revolution orchestrated by American imperialism . . . Keep her under surveillance but do not let her suspect anything. Let her think she doesn't exist."

Nameless shades of rage and hatred, voiceless cries of blood and hope and darkness hang in the air. From one direction, meaning Anatole France Avenue, and from the other direction, meaning Revolution Circle, the police have blocked all car and pedestrian traffic to this section of Liberty Street. In Revolution Circle, there is a logjam of hundreds of cars, anxious and overwrought drivers blow their horns, and among the cars curious people stand peering towards Tehran University. It was right here that more than a quarter of a century ago, on a cloudy winter's day, the people of Tehran for the last time dragged down the metal statue of the Shah sitting astride a horse. Of course in those days, when it came to dragging down metal statues of dictators, American tanks sided with the world's dictators.

The student protesters, aware that they are about to be attacked, break into a heart-rending anthem:

> *My fellow schoolfriend,*
> *you are with me and beside me,*
> *. . . you are my tear and my sigh,*
> *. . . the scars of the lashes of tyranny rest on our bodies,*

3

our uncultured wasteland, all its wild plants weeds,
be it good, be it bad,
dead are the souls of its people,
our hands must tear down these curtains,
who other than you and I can cure our pain . . .

In the lyrics and melody of this anthem lies an age-old Iranian sorrow that brings tears to the girl's eyes . . . She raises her sign even higher. From behind the veil of her tears, the world is transformed into undulating buildings, severed shadows and rippling reflections on water . . . The young girl's isolation and her fear of strangers heighten. She looks up to find some solace in the blue of the sky. She sees a winged horse that, like a white cloud, ignoring the people below, flies by. Terrified, she sees flames rising from the horse's back. The blazing horse disappears behind a high-rise. The girl waits, but the horse does not reappear . . .

Then she imagines that in the midst of the shouts of anger and spite, a muffled voice is calling her name.

"Sara! Sara!"

The girl wipes away her tears and looks around. There are people and shadows moving in every direction. It seems they are afraid of coming close to her.

"Dimwit! Dimwit! I'm talking to you!"

The voice bears the same chill and odour that gust out of a refrigerator that has not been opened in a month. The girl looks behind her. A dark face, with no neck or torso, is suspended in the air. Two of the steel bars in the green fence surrounding Tehran University that have broken out of the stone wall have sectioned the face in three . . . She thinks this face belongs to one of those sprites her grandmother said have parties in the city's public bathhouses at night and that the only way to tell them apart from humans is by their hoofed feet . . .

"Hey! Dimwit! Get rid of that sign and escape! I'm talking to you!"

Again the girl looks behind her. She sees that same fluid, dark face on the other side of the fence. She thinks perhaps someone is squatting down behind the wall and has lifted his head up to the fence.

"Hey! Daydreamer, go home! Today death has it in for you. Go home! . . . Do you understand? It's been half an hour since death fell in

4

love with you. It's sharpening its sickle to stab into your body. Run while you can . . . Do you hear me . . . ?"

No, this face and its cobwebbed voice cannot be real. Sara peeks through the fence and behind the stone wall and sees the figure of a hunchbacked midget dressed in clothes that seem to belong to centuries ago . . . She opens her mouth to ask:

What in the world do you want from me?

But her words choke in her throat. Petrified, she realizes that at this moment, any question and all the words in the world will seem absurd and meaningless. There appear to be no eyeballs in the round eye sockets in that face. They resemble two wells with moonlight reflecting on the dark water at their pit.

"What do you want with my eyes? Think of yourself. You will be killed . . . Do you understand? . . . Run! The fighting will start any minute now."

The scuffle begins. The shouts of slogans and obscenities and the screams of boys and girls being beaten drown in the daily clamour of the city of eleven million.

We skip past this scene because it seems to have nothing to do with a love story. However, if you have paid attention, you will have noticed that I, with that notorious cunning of a writer, have described the scuffle between the police and the students in such a way that I cannot be accused of political bias.

If you ask me who I am, I will say:

I am an Iranian writer tired of writing dark and bitter stories, stories populated by ghosts and dead narrators with predictable endings of death and destruction. I am a writer who at the threshold of fifty has understood that the purportedly real world around us has enough death and destruction and sorrow, and that I did not have the right to add even more defeat and hopelessness to it with my stories. In my stories and novels there are men whom I have created with a body and romantic valour that I do not possess. Similarly, there are women whose bodies and personalities I have reproduced from the body and soul of the woman whom I have seen longingly in my dreams – although I have never had the sincerity to give this fantasy woman a permanent face so that I don't confuse her with certain real women. Between you and me, I have on occasion even cheated on this fantasy woman and imagined and written of her blond hair as black, and once as auburn. At any rate, I hate myself for sending characters that I like, that I have scrupulously created word by word, towards darkness or bloody death at the end of my stories, like Dr Frankenstein.

For these reasons, and for reasons that like other writers I will probably discover later, I, with all my being, want to write a love story. The love story of a girl who has never seen the man who has been in love with her for a year and whom she loves very much. A story with an ending that is a gateway to light. A story that, although it does not have a happy ending like romantic Hollywood movies, still has an ending that will not make my reader afraid of falling in love. And, of course, a story that cannot be labelled as political. My dilemma is that I want to publish my love story in my homeland . . . Unlike in many countries around the world, writing and publishing a love story in my beloved Iran are not easy tasks. Following the victory of one of our last revolutions – during which our shouts for freedom, with the assistance of the Western media, deafened the universe – to make up for two thousand five hundred years of dictatorial rule by kings, an Islamic constitution was written. This new constitution allows the printing and publishing of any and all books and journals, and strictly prohibits their censorship and inspection. Unfortunately, however, our constitution makes no mention of these books and publications being allowed to leave the printers.

In the early days following the revolution, after a book had been printed, its publisher had to present three copies of it to the Ministry of Culture and Islamic Guidance to receive a permit for it to be shipped out of the printers and to be distributed. However, if the ministry deemed the book to be corruptive, the printed copies would remain imprisoned in the printers' dark storage, and its publisher, in addition to having paid printing costs, would either have to pay storage costs, too, or would have to recycle the books into cardboard. This system had driven many publishers to the brink of bankruptcy.

In more recent years, to limit their financial risk, and for books not to remain in storage houses for years and grow mouldy waiting for an exit permit, based on a semi-verbal, semi-formal agreement, prior to actually printing a book, the independent Iranian publisher will voluntarily, with his own two hands and feet, deliver three copies of the manuscript prepared with the latest typesetting and page design software to the Ministry of Culture and Islamic Guidance to receive a permit before the book is actually printed.

In a particular department at this ministry, a man with the alias Porfiry Petrovich (yes, the detective in charge of solving Raskolnikov's murders) is responsible for carefully reading books, in particular novels and short-story collections, and especially love stories. He underlines every word, every sentence, every paragraph, or even every page that is indecent and that endangers public morality and the time-honoured values of society. If there are too many such underlinings, the book will likely be considered unworthy of printing; if there are not that many, the publisher and the writer will be informed that they must simply revise certain words or sentences. For Mr Petrovich this job is not just a vocation; it is a moral and religious responsibility. In other words, a holy profession. He must not allow immoral and corruptive words and phrases to appear before the eyes of simple and innocent people, especially the young, and pollute their pure minds. Sometimes he even tells himself:

"Look here, man! If one word or phrase escapes your pen and provokes a young person, you will share in his sin, or worse, you will be just as guilty as those depraved people who produce pornographic films and photos and illegally distribute them among the public."

From his perspective, writers are generally devious, immoral and faith-less people, some of whom are directly or indirectly agents of Zionism and American imperialism, and they try to deceive him with their tricks and ploys. Given his profound sense of responsibility, while he reads the type-set manuscripts, Mr Petrovich's heart beats wildly. As he advances page by page, slowly the words begin to make strange movements before his eyes. In his mind, among the echoes of the words, he hears mysterious whisperings that put him on his guard. Suspicious, he goes back a few pages and reads more carefully. His face begins to perspire, and his fingers start to tremble as they turn the pages. The more he pays attention, the more devious the criminal words become. They move around; the sen-tences intertwine. Implicit expressions, explicit expressions, innuendos and connotations concealed in shadows begin to parade around in his head and create an uproar. He sees that some fucking words are lending letters to one another to create vulgar words or raunchy images. The sound of the pages turning resembles the sound of a guillotine blade falling. Mr Petrovich hears the hue and cry of the words explode in his ears. He yells:

"Shut the hell up!"

He puts pen to paper to underline the word "dance", but realizes that the writer himself has instead used the expression "rhythmic movement". He pounds his fist on the page. A few of the more cowardly and conservative words quiet down, but amid the racket of the others there is sarcastic laughter. Overwhelmed, Mr Petrovich gets up from behind his desk.

It is because of these emotional tortures that at times examining one book can take as long as a year, or five years, or even twenty-five years.

So it is that many stories, especially love stories, in manoeuvring their way through the Ministry of Culture and Islamic Guidance are either wounded, lose certain limbs, or are with finality put to death.

In the love story I want to write, I will not run into any difficulties as long as in the opening sentences I depict the beauty of spring flowers, the fragrant breeze and the brilliant sun in the blue sky. However, the minute I start to write about the story's man and woman and their actions and conversations, Mr Petrovich's perspiring, irate and reprimanding face will appear before my eyes.

Ask:

What do you mean?

So that I reply:

In this love story, I must have a feminine protagonist and a masculine antagonist, or vice versa. Now surely, with an *Unbearable Lightness of* curiosity you want to ask, Shouldn't there be a man and a woman in an Iranian love story?

Ask, and I shall answer:

Well, in Iran there is a politico-religious presumption that any proximity and discourse between a man and a woman who are neither married nor related is a prologue to deadly sin. Those who commit such prologues to text, and such texts to sin, in addition to retributions that await them in the afterworld, will in this world too be sentenced by Islamic courts to such punishments as imprisonment, the lash and even death. It is to prevent such prologues and deadly sins that in Iran, females and males in schools, factories, offices, buses and wedding parties are kept apart. In other words, they are protected from each other. Of course, several revered clergymen have opined that pedestrian traffic on streets should also be segregated. They know that in the modern world they must present plans founded on scientific research; therefore, based on the findings of their experts, they have presented their plan as such: In the morning, for example, men will be permitted to walk along the pavements on the right side of the streets, and in the afternoon, the women. Conversely, on the pavements flanking the left side of the streets, in the morning women, and in the afternoon men, will be allowed to come and go. As a result, both sexes will have access to shops on both sides. A few of these clergymen even object to and criticize films that have received a screening permit from the Ministry of Culture and Islamic Guidance because in rare scenes the actor and actress playing husband and wife, or brother and sister, are shown alone together in the kitchen or the living room. These gentlemen reason that a man and a woman who are not *mahram* – meaning neither married nor immediate kin – should never be alone together in a room or in any enclosed space.

In response to such criticisms, numerous experts and ministers from the Ministry of Culture and Islamic Guidance, as well as film directors, cinematographers and other crew members involved in film-making have in lengthy and frequent articles and interviews explained, "Gentlemen! Don't worry. In scenes where it appears that an actor and an actress are alone, there are, in fact, behind the scenes, meaning a little farther away from the camera, tens of crew members present – including the director, the assistant director, the stage assistant, the cameraman and his assistants, lighting crew and . . ." Despite these explanations, several of the complaining gentlemen have suggested:

"Let us assume it is so. But the audience only sees a man and a woman alone in a room. And the fact that a man and a woman are alone in a room will lead the audience's imagination to a thousand sins."

I hope this introduction has helped you understand why publishing a love story in Iran is not a simple undertaking . . .

Now ask me how I hope to write and publish a love story, so that I can explain:

I think because I am an experienced writer, I may be able to write my story in such a way that it survives the blade of censorship. In my life as a writer, I have come to learn Iranian and Islamic symbols and metaphors very well. I also have plenty of other tricks up my sleeve that I will not divulge. The truth is that a long time ago, I never really intended to write a love story. But that boy and girl who meet each other near the main entrance of Tehran University and in the chaos of political demonstrations stare lovingly into each other's eyes have convinced me to write their story.

They have known each other for about a year and have shared many words and sentences. But it is on this spring day that the girl for the very first time casts her eyes on that boy's face . . . Don't be surprised by the paradox in my last two sentences. Iran is a land of paradoxes . . . If you ask:

Did they meet on a matchmaking website?

I will emphatically say:

No . . .

And even more emphatically I will suggest that these two characters are far too innocent and fictional to meet on a matchmaking website or on websites where one seeks a sex partner . . . In fact, such websites are banned in Iran. But allow me to tell my story.

As you have realized, the girl's name is Sara. And the boy's name is Dara. Don't ask: I confess, the names are pseudonyms. I don't want the real characters to face any problems for sins or illegal acts that they may commit in the course of my story . . . Of course, selecting Sara and Dara as pseudonyms from among thousands of Iranian names has its own story, which I must tell.

Once upon a time, long ago when I was at primary school, Sara and Dara were two characters in our first-year reading books. Sara was there to introduce the letter S and Dara to introduce the letter D . . . Long ago in Iran, not an Islamic regime but a monarchist regime ruled. From that regime's perspective, there was no problem for Sara and Dara, after having been introduced to schoolchildren, to appear alone in a room in other lessons to talk, for example, about a parrot so that the letter P could be taught. In those bygone days, Sara was illustrated with long black hair and wearing a colourful shirt, skirt and socks, and Dara was drawn wearing a shirt and trousers. They were beautiful, but we schoolchildren used to draw a moustache for Sara and a beard for Dara . . . Years later, I mean, when I was a student at Tehran University, we Iranians grew tired of the monarchist regime and started a revolution. Our reawakening began when the Shah, following the advice of US president Jimmy Carter, claimed that he wanted to give the people of Iran political freedom and freedom of speech and thought, and to demonstrate his goodwill he dismantled the Rastakhiz Party – the only political party in the country, which he himself had created. We shouted "Freedom!" . . . We shouted "Independence!" . . . And a few months after the start of our revolution, to our shouts we added "Islamic Republic!" . . . Across the country we set fire to banks because, according to the covert and overt propaganda of the Communists, banks were symbols of the bloodthirsty regime of bourgeois collaborators. We set fire to cinemas because, according to the covert and overt propaganda of the intellectuals, cinemas were the cause of cultural decay, the spread of Westernization and the increasing influence of American Hollywood culture. We burned down nightclubs, bars and brothels because, according to the covert and overt propaganda of the devout, they were centres of corruption and propagated deadly sins . . . Well, a few years after the revolution's victory, in first-year reading books, there was a headscarf covering Sara's black hair and a long black coverall hiding her colourful clothes. Dara was not old enough to grow a beard, therefore only his father had one. According to our religious teachings, a Muslim man must have a beard and must not shave his face with a razor lest he look like a woman.

If I remember correctly, a few years later Sara and Dara completely disappeared from the reading books, and another girl and boy replaced them – siblings with no recollection of the Shah's corrupt and tyrannical regime . . . Now I think you have come to understand that selecting the names Sara and Dara is an Iranian storytelling trick. Without giving Mr Petrovich an excuse to chastise me, they will remind my Iranian readers of the appearance and disappearance of Sara and Dara from reading books, rather like Mr Clementis, a persona non grata whom Soviet censors airbrushed out of a photograph, yet the hat he had lent to a man posing with him remained on that person's head.

By the time Sara and Dara were being transformed, my daughter was in first grade, and there were nights when my powers would fail and I could not come up with a new story to tell her. I had therefore bought her storybooks with tales that were better than mine because they came with illustrations. One night when I opened *Snow White and the Seven Dwarfs* to read to her, I saw to my horror that Snow White was wearing a headscarf and two thick black lines were covering her bare arms. My little girl asked:

"Why aren't you reading?"

I closed the book and said:

"We don't have a story tonight. Sleep so that you will have a beautiful dream, my girl . . . Sleep, Bārān."

We called our daughter Bārān at home. But her name in her birth certificate is something that neither I nor her mother intended to name our daughter. Hence, the name Bārān too has a story, which I will tell you another night. Now, with your permission, I must return to my love story.

Ask me, given that an encounter between a man and a woman is so unlikely in Iran, how do Sara and Dara meet?

As I said before, although Sara and Dara come face to face for the first time on the fringes of the students' political demonstration, they had in fact started writing their love story a year earlier. And this is the story that I now want to tell you.

Sara is studying Iranian literature at Tehran University. ~~However, in compliance with an unwritten law, teaching contemporary Iranian literature is forbidden in Iranian schools and universities.~~ Like all other students, Sara has to memorize hundreds of verses of poetry and the biographies of poets who died a thousand, seven hundred, four hundred . . . years ago. Even so, Sara likes contemporary Iranian literature because it stimulates her imagination.

This literature creates scenes and words in her mind that she has never dared imagine or utter, and of course, this literature too has not dared write those words and scenes openly and explicitly. In fact, when Sara reads a contemporary story, she reads the white between the lines, and wherever a sentence is left incomplete and ends with three dots like this " . . . ", her mind grows very active and begins to imagine what the eliminated words may be. At times, her imagination goes farther and grows more naked than the words the writer had in mind. If she is as clever as an intelligence agent and has the power to decipher the codes that lie in the shadows of the petrified phrases and in the hidden whispers of the conservative words of Iran's contemporary literature, she will find the very things she likes. Sara loves these three dots because they allow her to be a writer, too . . . But she never borrows any contemporary literature from her college library or the central library of Tehran University. Even if she wanted to, I don't think she would find any books by writers such as me.

Ask me why, so that I can explain.

I hope that, in countries where people are proud of their democracies and live confident of a secure future, no one ever has to worry about the books they borrow from a library. I pray that whenever they want, without fear of the future, they can at least read *The Jungle* by Upton Sinclair or the dull and artless *The Iron Heel*, a bad work by a relatively good writer who drank too much whisky and wanted to replace American democracy with *Animal Farm* democracy.

As I was saying, we Iranians, having lived under the dictatorial rule of kings for two thousand five hundred years, have expertly learned that we should never leave any records or documents behind. We are forever fearful that the future will bear even harsher political circumstances, and hence we must be extremely vigilant about our lives and the footprints that linger in our wake. It is for this reason that records of our history are often limited to the travelogues of Westerners and reports by Western spies. Sara knows that the circulation system at Tehran University library is computerized, and that any book she borrows can someday be used as evidence against her and she could be expelled. Of course, circumstances in my dear Iran still allow a few crumbs of freedom, but Sara prefers to borrow her favourite books from a public library and has become a member of the one in her neighbourhood. Exactly a year before the political demonstration I told you about, on a spring day – and in most old Iranian love stories there is a beautiful spring day with the song of nightingales and other pleasant-sounding birds resonating from sentences – Sara appears at the public library. The small reading room in this library has been divided into two sections by the library catalogues so that the boys and girls seated at the tables cannot see each other.

Now you probably want to ask, What are the boys and girls supposed to do if they need to discuss a school project or exchange ideas?

If you ask one more question like this, I will be forced to say:

Madam! Sir! Why can't you imagine any culture other than your own? What kind of a question is this? Clearly girls and boys in Iran have no school-related discussions and no need to exchange educational information. Like everywhere else in the world, discussing Derrida's "Différance", debating the Planck wall or chaos theory and the butterfly effect are consciously or unconsciously excuses for a girl and a boy to establish a private relationship that will end in sin. For this very reason, if they speak to one another on university grounds, they will receive a written warning from the Disciplinary Committee. They are not only prohibited from talking to one another in libraries, but they cannot even climb over the Planck wall with the language of their eyes to exchange information . . . So please let me continue with my story.

Sara walked towards the librarian's desk . . . With this sentence the love story I want to write and hand over to Mr Petrovich continues.

Sara asked the librarian:

"Do you have *The Blind Owl*?"

The librarian firmly replied:

"No, miss. We don't have *The Blind Owl* at this library."

Sara did not give up.

"Of course I know you don't have *The Blind Owl* on the shelves. I meant, if it is among the books you have removed from the shelves, could you make an exception and lend it to me for a few days . . .? I study literature and I have to read *The Blind Owl* for an important project."

The librarian, this time more sternly, said:

"Miss! I told you we don't have these banned books; ~~and by the way, you're the idiot, not me. I know there is no way they would give you a project on *The Blind Owl* at the university~~."

Sara, having given up on getting her hands on a copy of *The Blind Owl*, walked out of the public library. She didn't notice that in her wake a young man walked out from the protected men's section and at some distance followed her all the way home. Consequently, the next day when she saw the same young man near her house, she did not recognize him. The young man was selling second-hand books, which he had laid out on a few sheets of newspaper spread on the pavement. Surely the paperback edition of *The Blind Owl* was among his books. But Sara, proud of her beauty and accustomed to ignoring the people around her, walked to the university without stopping. The neighbourhood butcher was skinning a green baby dragon hanging on a hook suspended from the ceiling . . .

The next day, the same young man was sitting in exactly the same spot. Of course he had fewer books. The same was true of the days that followed.

In Iran, book lovers distrustful of the entire world sometimes think that the street pedlars who sell banned or rare books are agents assigned to identify and track readers.

On the seventh day, Sara finally stopped at the pedlar's spread and browsed through the books and, suddenly, she saw *The Blind Owl*. She asked its price. Contrary to the general practice of selling rare or banned books at a much higher price than the list price on the back cover, the young man asked for very little money. And in a trembling voice he added:

". . . The price of one Winston cigarette, miss. On the condition that you read it carefully. Please cherish this book . . . Read it very carefully, much more carefully than you would other books . . . Carefully, accurately . . ."

No street pedlar or bookseller had ever spoken to Sara in this manner. She thought, Here's another one of those mentally disturbed people whose numbers are growing in Iran. She happily bought the book and put it in her handbag. The book was transmitting a mysterious energy to her. During her first class at the university, while the professor was busy explaining and explicating a lengthy poem composed seven hundred years ago that was replete with complex and unfamiliar Arabic words, Sara opened the book under her desk and started to read that surrealist story, which in Iran is famously believed to make its young readers lose hope in life and commit suicide – the same way that years ago its writer, Sadeq Hedayat, committed suicide in Paris. However, aside from the strange power of the opiate and carnal words, the book seemed to hold another secret, a secret that Sara thought she had seen in the book pedlar's eyes. That day, Sara went home from the university far more quickly than usual. She closed the door to her room, ~~lay down on her bed,~~ and began reading the book from the beginning.

I guess by now you have realized that the crossed-out words in the text are my own doing. And you must know that such fanciful eccentricity is not postmodernism or Heideggerism. In fact . . .

And by now you have surely grasped the significance of ". . ." in Iran's contemporary literature.

On page seven, Sara noticed several purple dots. She paid no attention to them and continued reading voraciously. *The Blind Owl* is a novel that begins with the nightmarish incidents in the life of an Iranian artist who paints on ewers. One day the artist goes to the storage alcove in his house to fetch a bottle of old wine that he has inherited from his mother – an Indian dancer who danced with a Nag serpent in a Linga temple. As he reaches for the wine, he sees a hole in the wall to the wasteland behind the house. He sees a stream. There is an old, bent man sitting under a willow tree, and on the opposite side of the stream there is a beautiful woman, as beautiful as the women in Iranian miniatures, leaning forward and holding a single black lily out towards the old man. The next day, the artist realizes that in fact there is no hole in the wall of the storage alcove. But he has fallen in love with that ethereal woman, and now spends his days wandering across the wasteland around his secluded house searching for her, for the stream, and for the willow tree . . . **On page seventeen, Sara thinks that whoever the previous owner of this book was had either not valued it or was a book abuser to have marked and defiled its pages with purple dots** . . . And the blind owl who cannot get that ethereal woman out of his mind continues to search for her. One night, returning from a disappointing search, he sees the woman sitting next to the front door of his house. He takes her home and gives her some of that old wine. A wine that we learn is laced with poison from the fangs of a Nag serpent. The woman dies with a taunting look in her eyes, leaving the mysterious image of her gaze for ever etched on the artist's mind. The blind owl cuts up her body, which is surrounded by golden bees, and puts the pieces in a suitcase. Outside, it is as if the world has been transformed into a nightmare. In the dark, an old man with a rickety horse-drawn hearse is waiting for him. The cart travels to the ancient ruins of the city of Rey. While burying the suitcase there, they discover a centuries-old clay pot with the mysterious eyes of a woman painted on it . . . The same image that the blind owl will for the rest of his life paint on clay ewers . . .

On page sixty-six Sara realized that the purple dots were not random, and that in fact they had been placed with great precision under certain letters in certain words. She went back to the first dots on the first page of the book. They appeared under the letters S, a, r, a, H, e, l, l, o. It did not take her long to realize that the first four letters spelled her name and the rest spelled the word "hello" . . . The mystifying tale of _The Blind Owl_ had a maddening lure, but Sara had fallen captive to the marked letters on the pages of the book. She turned page after page and carefully found them. She wrote them all down on a sheet of paper and began connecting them together. At times she would connect one or two letters too many, and at times too few . . . But finally,

eight hours later, the complete letter lay before her.

Hello Sara,

As I mark these purple dots, I pray that you will discover my secret code. That day when you were asking the librarian for *The Blind Owl*, I was there. For a long time now, whenever you go to the library, I am there, too. The card catalogues don't allow me to see your face, but from between their legs I can see your shoes. I know all your shoes very well. I have given each pair a name. For example, your brown shoes that have a scratch on them, perhaps from a barbed wire or the thorn of a rosebush, are Rainy, because you wear them on rainy days. That library doesn't have *The Blind Owl*. It doesn't have many of the other great novels either. According to the new librarian, they have weeded out all the immoral novels from the shelves. I had a small library of my own at home which I treasured. But then I started selling books near your house so that I could give you *The Blind Owl*. To make sure people believed I was really a street pedlar, I had to sell many of my books. I sold my *One Hundred Years of Solitude*, I sold *Anna Karenina*, *The Great Gatsby*, and *Slaughterhouse-Five* . . . They even bought Italo Calvino's *Invisible Cities* from me. I sold the collected poems of Lorca, Neruda and Forough. But I put such a high price on *The Blind Owl* that people laughed at me. If this letter is of no value to you, at least value this book. To break free from our hypocrisy, its writer fled to Paris and committed suicide there. I wish I was as powerful a writer as he was, so that I could write a beautiful and extraordinary letter to you. If I could write a letter to you that no man in love has ever written, I would want nothing more of my life, and death would be easy for me . . . Please don't be scared. Just as I have been in love with you for a very long time and you have never noticed me, trust that you will never sense my presence unless you yourself allow it. Next Thursday, when you go to the public library, borrow *The Little Prince* if you like . . .

Sara tried to remember the young man's face, or at least his voice. But strangely, she had no image of him in her head. It was as though a hand had erased it.

Sara borrowed *The Little Prince*. In her first reading she didn't grasp much of the beautiful story because her entire attention was focused on breaking the code of the letter contained in the book. That letter read:

Hello Sara,

Why have you started to turn around suddenly and look behind you ever since you read my letter? You will never recognize me among the people on the street. I have studied make-up. The day you bought the book from me I had really changed my face.

I am always very far from you. But following you, even at a distance, gives me the pleasure of knowing that I breathe the air you have exhaled. Sometimes – of course, not often – I walk towards you from the opposite side of the street so that I can catch a glimpse of your face, to see whether you are happy or sad. I know all the expressions of your face. I can even tell by the way your long, beautiful fingers hold your books whether you are tired or full of energy. Those nights when I wander the streets, I sometimes pass by your big house. Don't worry, I don't stop. Not even for a second. I just walk by and look up at your window. I don't like its heavy curtains. Why do you keep them drawn most of the time? Open them. Let the moon shine into your room. The ultramarine moonlight will create a beautiful new colour on the walls. At night, when the light is turned on in your room and I know you are there, your room becomes my star. But this one star is different from all the other stars in the sky for me because there I have a red rose that is different from all the other red roses in the world for me, and with all my heart I wish it happiness. I learned this from *The Little Prince.* Now that I have someone in my life for whom I wish happiness with all my being, even if I am never to be a part of that happiness, my life has found a beautiful new meaning. Now I can at last cope with people. I have even grown to like them, because I think among them there are people whom you like and who make you happy . . . It doesn't matter who I am and what my name is. I used to be a student at Tehran University, too. I studied film-making. But I was expelled. As for my name, just pretend it is Dara. It is an alias that the writer who will one day write about my life will conjure up without giving it much thought. They will not hire me at any company or factory. I cover my expenses with the little money I earn painting houses. Whenever I paint a wall, I first write your name on it in ultramarine blue, and then I cover it with the colour the wall is supposed to be. Just last month, I was painting a newly built house and the contractor turned up unexpectedly. He saw how all the walls had *Sara* written on them . . . We had an argument. He fired me . . . I will write the next letter in Bram Stoker's *Dracula.* The people who decide which books belong in libraries sometimes miss a few, or maybe they don't understand these types of books. If you would like to write back, mark the letters in this book in blue ink. If not, in the *Dracula* letter I will let you know which book will have my next letter . . .

Sara had to wait two weeks to borrow *Dracula* because someone had already checked it out of the library. She read the third letter, but she didn't write back. Whoever was writing these letters really meant what he said, and moved so ghostlike on the fringes of Sara's life that despite her curiosity she couldn't guess his identity. Sometimes, after walking home along her usual route from the university or library, she would run up to her room and from the narrow opening in the heavy curtains she would look out to see who was following her. Pedestrians, young and old, walked by, but none of them showed any interest in her window . . . For seven consecutive nights Sara sat by the window and peered out at the street. But to no avail.

Sara liked the story of Dracula.

Hello Sara,

I really like your trainers, the ones with the blue stripes. Your beautiful stride has a wonderful weightlessness to it when you wear them. I have named them Shirin Walking on Water, and sometimes I call them Ophelia. Has anything changed at the university that they now allow you to wear colourful shoes? Sometimes when I follow you down the street, I try to step in your footsteps.

~~I wish I had the powers of Count Dracula. Not so that I could come up to your bedroom at night and suck your blood, but so that I could protect you for the rest of your life without you ever knowing.~~

The supervisor at the public library has grown suspicious of me. He threatened that if I don't watch myself, he will call the patrols from the Campaign Against Social Corruption and they will arrest me. I didn't react to any of his insults. I was so angry my blood was boiling, but I even managed to apologize to him. ~~If I were a Dracula I would have drunk his blood.~~ So now when you leave the library, I wait awhile, and then I run to catch up with you somewhere near your home. I wish I could come to your class at the university and just sit in a corner and watch you. But at the university they consider people like me to be vulgar and filthy monsters. In Francis Ford Coppola's film version of *Dracula*, which you can easily find on the black market, there is a scene in which Dracula, in love, turns Mina's teardrops into emeralds in the palm of his hand. Even if I was once a hateful beast, even if I was once a Dracula, I have

19

changed since I got to know you. I found a strand of your hair in the pages of *The Little Prince*. I don't believe it was there on purpose, but it is now my treasure . . . This single strand of black hair means the world to me. You are my Shirin. I only wish I were your Farhad. I wish I had a mountain to carve into a castle for you with nothing but a pickaxe. Borrow *Khosrow and Shirin*.

In many Iranian mystical poems, some of which date back almost a thousand years, the Sufi poet – most classical Iranian poets were Sufis – speaks of an earthly heavenly beloved, a beloved who can be a woman and yet is a representation of God. He uses many words to liken his beloved's beauties to nature, fruits and flowers; of course not directly, but by using familiar similes. It starts with her figure, which is often likened to a cypress tree. To understand this Iranian simile, do not bring to mind the extreme tallness of a cypress tree; instead look at the wideness of its bottom and the narrowness of its top. Then our poet will compare his beloved's eyes to narcissus flowers, or to the eyes of a gazelle, and if they are Oriental eyes, he will compare them to almonds. Her eyebrows he will compare to bows that let fly the arrows of her eyelashes towards her lover's heart. Her lips, if they are thin, he will compare to a narrow wisp often woven of silk, and if they are plump, he will compare them to rubies that of course are as sweet as sugar. Then the poet will liken his beloved's breasts to pomegranates. The Iranian Sufi poet does not normally travel any farther down and self-censors the rest of his similes, allowing the reader's imagination to travel south on its own. The few who have dared travel below their beloved's breasts have again used the language of nature and erotic foods. Evidently, in those days Iranians were not familiar with the banana, or with the orchid or, for that matter, with the flower in the film *The Wall*. About nine centuries ago Nizami, a great Iranian poet, created two beautiful yet strange scenes in a famous romantic poem called *Khosrow and Shirin*. This narrative in verse is the love story of Khosrow, one of the greatest kings of Persia, and an Armenian princess named Shirin. Shirin has undressed and is bathing in a pond. Khosrow is out hunting and by chance arrives at the pond and starts ogling Shirin from behind the bushes:

A bride he saw as ripe as the full moon . . .

. . .

In cerulean water like a flower she sat,
in cerulean silk up to her navel wrapped.
. . .

From that flower's substance the entire pond,
an almond blossom an almond at its heart.
. . .

To each side her tresses she combed,
violets crowning a blossom she combed.
. . .

She a treasure chest its treasure pure gold,
her wavy tresses a snake upon the chest coiled.
. . .

From the gatekeeper's hand has fallen the garden-gate key,
her pomegranate breasts in the garden revealed.
. . .

Unaware of the king's gaze that jasmine lingered,
for the view of her narcissus the hyacinth hindered.
. . .

When the moon from the dark cloud emerged,
Shirin's eyes the king discerned.
. . .

But this that pool of sugar saw no means,
than her hair like the night to spread upon the mist.
. . .

In this romance, as in all romances, there are many incidents and events that impede Shirin and Khosrow from meeting each other and from being alone together, away from the eyes of the fiercely devout who behaved much like modern-day censors.

Finally, however, Shirin arrives in Madayen, her beloved's capital city . . .

In those days, Madayen was the wealthiest and the most splendid capital city in the world. Remnants of the massive arched roof of its royal palace can still be found in Iraq – I mean, that country that was once part of the Persian Empire and that today, because of the unrelenting war there, those Americans whose knowledge of geography is not very good no longer mistake for Iran.

A long time has passed since Shirin and Khosrow met and fell in love, but they still haven't done anything. On their long-awaited wedding night, Shirin lectures Khosrow: After all the wine you have drunk in your life, on this one night do not drink. However, by early afternoon, from the intense excitement of consummating their marriage, Khosrow starts to drink. By nightfall, completely drunk, he waits for Shirin to walk through the doors of the nuptial chamber bathed, made-up, perfumed and wearing a negligee that the trend-setting Victoria's Secret has yet to dream up . . . Imagine the nuptial chamber, not with your own strong and scientific imagination, but with the unscientific and idiotic imagination of a film such as Oliver Stone's *Alexander*. Imagine the chamber with an Egyptian-Arabic-Indian-Iranian-Chinese decor, with a bed that has so much gold or so many emeralds or diamonds strewn on it that there is no room to lie down. In one corner there is an Indian Shiva, somewhere else there is the figure of Ra, the Egyptian deity, and in yet another corner smoke rises from a Chinese incense burner. And there, in the middle of the bed, lies Khosrow, the emperor of Persia, all sprawled out. I cannot find an Iranian imagery for Khosrow; therefore, like those Hollywood movies that jumble everything together, I will compare him to Ganesha, the Hindu patron of arts and sciences and the god of intellect and wisdom whom I like very much. Ganesha has an elephant's head and a human body. He loves sweets, and in Farsi the name Shirin means "sweet". But I have chosen this simile because Ganesha's trunk is likely to bear similarities to Khosrow's manly trunk.

Regardless of the elephant's trunk, when Shirin realizes that Khosrow is drunk on this historic night, out of mischief she sends her stepmother into the nuptial chamber instead of going in herself. The description of the old woman is thus:

Like a wolf, not a young wolf but an old one, with a pair of sagging breasts that resemble two sheepskin sacs, an old hump on her back, her face as wrinkled as an Indian walnut, her mouth as wide as a grave and with only a couple of yellow teeth in it and no eyelashes on her eyes . . . The old woman enters the room. Khosrow, drunk, is taken aback. What is this? How did pretty Shirin suddenly turn into this? He concludes that it is because of his inebriated state that he sees Shirin like this, and he gets his hooks into her. The old woman screams out in pain, Shirin save me! Shirin enters the room and Khosrow realizes his mistake.

Here, the poet again offers a lengthy description of Shirin's beauties. He compares her body to all sorts of flowers and all sorts of rare sweets and foods. Of course, from the standpoint of literary ingenuity and poetic creativity, the descriptions are truly rich and beautiful.

The poet writes that Shirin's lips and teeth are of the same essence as love. Her lips have never seen teeth, nor have her teeth ever seen lips. This half-couplet offers one example of the ambiguities of Iranian literature because one can derive various interpretations from it. Perhaps Shirin's lips are so plump and protruding that they do not touch her teeth. Or perhaps they are, as we say in Farsi, like a finely tapered braid and so thin that no teeth could bite into them. In other words, this half-couplet could imply that no man has ever bitten Shirin's lips, or that her lips have never touched a man's teeth, or even that her teeth have never bitten a man's lips. Do you think there is any better way to describe a woman's virginity than to suggest that she has never experienced a stolen kiss?

In olden days and current times, when Iranian men search for a spouse, they search for a woman whose lips have never touched teeth and whose teeth have never touched lips. And when they seek a lover, they want someone with extensive experience in biting. Unfortunately, oftentimes either they don't find her or they end up with her opposite . . .

In subsequent verses Shirin's body is progressively thus described:

Her face resembling flowers . . . The front and back of her body akin to soft white ermine, and her fingers reminiscent of ten elongated ermine tails . . . Her body, milk and honey; her eyebrows, arches stretching as far as her earlobes; and the curve of her double chin draped down to her shoulders.

Given the information the poet offers, we know that Shirin is from Armenia, and given that Iranian men generally prefer fair-skinned blondes, women from Armenia – which at times was and at times was not part of Iran – were and remain symbols of beauty. However, given the similes I have described, this Shirin is definitely not this century's fashion.

In any case, the old woman escapes from the room and Shirin appears before Khosrow. Now Khosrow's eyes widen at the sight of all that beauty and sex appeal. This, in fact, is the story's climax. *Khosrow and Shirin* is made up of six thousand five hundred verses. Approximately four-fifths of it recounts how Khosrow heard praise of Shirin's beauty and desired her, how Shirin travelled to Iran from Armenia, how they met, how they fell in love and how eager they were to fall into each other's arms. The verses also relate how an innocent man named Farhad, ill treated and poor, who did not possess the position, power, or sexual wherewithal of the emperor Khosrow, falls in love with Shirin, how the romantic affair turns into a love triangle, how Farhad, in demonstrating the magnitude of his love for Shirin – or perhaps to exhibit his manly prowess – begins to carve a passageway in a massive mountain with only a pickaxe. Which one of her two lovers do you think Shirin should have picked: the sleeping drunk or the mountain-carver?

Throughout these verses, numerous obstacles and incidents and even separations bar Khosrow and Shirin from lying in each other's arms. But after all is said and done, like all lovers across the world, be they in Mogadishu or Sarajevo, in Tehran or Baghdad or Paris, at last Khosrow and Shirin come together on that long-awaited night and they start planting flowers and drinking milk sweetened with honey . . . In other words, the poet has composed five thousand two hundred verses and developed scores of incidents before Khosrow and Shirin finally join in the nuptial chamber and make love.

Can you guess what happens on this night?

In a half-couplet, the poet suggests that when Khosrow perceives Shirin's sensuality, he turns into a beast that has seen the new moon – or, were we to find metaphors consistent with Anglo-Saxon culture, he turns into a werewolf who has seen the full moon.

Guess!

Please do not refer to your own personal experiences.

I suspect you have guessed wrong. No, Khosrow does not attack Shirin. Instead he flops down on the bed and falls asleep. Yes, precisely at that tender and fateful moment . . .

Now I'm thinking that perhaps one reason Macedonian, Arab, Turk, Mongol, Afghan and English invaders could so easily and effectively occupy the magnificent empires of Iran was exactly this. Our kings had the habit of falling asleep precisely at tender and fateful moments, moments when they had to be men, to be strong, to be hard, and to occupy something small and sweet, and by the time they woke up, all was lost, and not only their kingdom but their wives, slaves and sisters had been occupied.

Fortunately, however, at least in Khosrow and Shirin's story, the king does not wake up to the angry face of a Macedonian or a Mongol or an Afghan. Instead he sees his Shirin sleeping beside him like a flower; and at last, he begins the much-delayed labour.

In an old Iranian text, about four hundred years ago, at a time when censorship was still not so powerful and institutionalized, in describing a scene of 66, an Iranian writer used weaponry and warfare metaphors quite successfully. He wrote: He raised the meaty mace and pounded it against the tallow shield.

However, Nizami, that delicate-natured poet, did not favour such violence. Instead he depicted scenes of lovemaking in this manner. Khosrow loses patience and begins to kiss and fondle Shirin. In other words, he begins to lick sweets and suck candy. Beside these comparisons, like the slow-motion replays of scored goals in sports matches, the poet again compares these actions to planting and gardening:

> At first he began gathering flowers,
> like blooms on that face laughter blossoms.
> . . .

Then together, the poet and Khosrow begin picking fruits:

> Of apple and jasmine sugar-plums he made,
> at times with pomegranates and narcissus he played.
> . . .

I assume you can discern the body parts that apple and jasmine represent. To increase your knowledge of fruitology, I reiterate that in Iranian literature, pomegranates are generally used to talk of, or not to talk of, small firm breasts that fit in one hand. Narcissus is generally a reference to beautiful eyes, but I doubt that Khosrow, at the height of his excitement, can be bothered to play with Shirin's eyes. Therefore, narcissus could be a simile for Shirin's orchid.

The replay of the scored goal sometimes extends to wildlife:

> Now and then the white falcon the king's grasp fled,
> now and then the pheasant upon his chest perched.

25

> *Now and then such pleasure came from flight,*
> *that the dove prevailed upon the hawk.*

These verses are a work of genius in depicting a sex scene in which the woman is active.

> *The doe and the lion together travailed,*
> *upon her at last the lion prevailed.*

Then comes the act of plunging into the jewellery store:

> *Wondrously to the treasure-trove's depth he went,*
> *with his ruby her agate seal he rent.*

Meaning Khosrow tore the agate seal of Shirin's virginity.

Then again we come to a description of Shirin's food products, and we read of a boneless date, which means a seedless one, that penetrates her. No, it is not over yet. The account of their lovemaking now becomes slightly more human, and in very poetic, beautiful and perfectly rhyming words we read that a body has coiled around a body and a soul has reached a soul. No, it is still not over yet. In fact, it is time for the sea and scuba-diving:

> *An oyster cradled upon a coral horn,*
> *now water and fire together conjoin.*

And at last it is over:

> *From fire and water's colourful scheme,*
> *with cinnabar and quicksilver the nuptial chamber teemed.*

Meaning there is silver and cinnabar-coloured water everywhere. The garden-trekking, zoo-travelling, fruit-picking, and scuba-diving of the two lovers takes an entire day and night, and then the two sleep for an entire day and night . . .

This too is another discovery of why invaders could occupy our country so easily. When the king spends twenty-four hours in the flower bed, the garden, the zoo and underwater, and then he sleeps for twenty-four hours, when does he ever find time to run the country?

I hope that after this rather lengthy example, you have come to understand why censorship is so complicated in Iran, and why Iranian literature, which is quite rich, is so difficult to translate and to read.

Reading six thousand five hundred verses can take a long time, but Sara quickly finished the book. Contrary to her expectations, Dara's letter in this book was very short.

Sara, you probably love Khosrow, a wealthy king, handsome, frivolous and yet also a strong and brave man who has won many battles and wreaked havoc on the Romans. I don't think you could love Farhad. A sincere, timid and poor lover who kills himself when he loses hope of ever having Shirin. Yet he never cheated on his love in order to forget . . . But I think Khosrow and Farhad are two sides of the same coin. They complement each other. It is when the two are joined that they create a true lover . . .

The next book was Milan Kundera's *The Unbearable Lightness of Being*. It was impossible for this politico-erotic novel to be among the books at the library. But **Sara, following the instructions given to her in the letter, found it hidden behind a stack of dusty books by Avicenna, the legendary tenth-century Iranian philosopher and physician. She first deciphered the letter, and after reading it several times, she read the novel. She read ravenously, and of course in many places she became terribly stressed.** Many scenes in the book had been censored and replaced with the infamous ellipses.

Two months have passed since Sara read that first novel, and now the curtains in her room are always open, except for times when she wants to change her clothes. The image of a beautiful girl sitting at the window of a beautiful house is a romantic and male-attracting scene throughout the world. As a result, Sara found a few new admirers. As soon as they saw her at the window, they would line up on the

pavement opposite her house and stare at her. But Sara was sure Dara was not among them, because they were all so boorish-looking. Some of them were even vulgar; they would whistle at her, or they would make funny gestures with their hands, eyes and lips. Sara's father, a traditional man who took great care of his daughter's untouched flower, had become extremely angry by the constant presence of the young men, and had made up his mind to call the police. However, three days later, the pestering admirers had all disappeared.

Sara was growing more restless and curious by the day to see Dara. Of course, she herself had labelled her emotions as mere curiosity. She had created a vague image of his face in her mind, and with the aid of her imagination she would add features to this hazy image, and this further fanned the flames of her curiosity.

In the next letter she read:

Don't worry about those pests. They don't even dare walk past your house any more. But you shouldn't spend too much time sitting at the window either. Not that I don't like it, but I'm afraid your next admirer may be a thug. My left eye is still bruised from one of them punching me . . . Why don't you write to me? Haven't I convinced you that you can trust me? What trouble could you get into if you only encode a few words to me? The letter won't even be in your handwriting, and you can completely deny it whenever you want . . .

A bruised left eye was a good clue. But she didn't find Dara. Instead, she saw several women with bruised eyes or cheeks from the beatings of their husbands' fists.

She had completely given up hope when one day, near her house, she suddenly felt her heart explode and her knees weaken. It was walking towards her. A left eye with a conspicuous black bruise under it. Excited and embarrassed, Sara looked the other way. She even considered turning around and changing course. However, when she managed to regain her composure, she turned and looked at the young man's face again. She recognized him. He was one of the pestering admirers who used to stand in front of her house. He would hold his thumb and pinky up against his ear mimicking a telephone, and then he would point to the wall behind him where in red paint he had written his mobile phone number and drawn a broken heart next to it. Sara was shocked and disappointed. She worried that this ugly, vulgar and undignified man was the Dara of her dreams. The pestering admirer saw Sara, too. But he quickly turned around and with long and rapid strides walked in the opposite direction. In effect, he ran away. Sara breathed a sigh of relief. She was now certain that the man was not Dara. In that last moment before he turned around, Sara noticed the young man's right eye. It too had a bruise under it.

Hello Sara,

Thank you for writing that two-sentence letter. I am truly honoured. But it really did me in. By the time I searched every single page of *War and Peace* to find the fifty-nine letters you marked, my eyes were all swollen. Even Natasha wasn't as mischievous as you. To make sure no one discovers your letter, even though it is very unlikely, I rubbed out the dots and returned the book to the library; just the way all the dots from the letters I have sent to you have been rubbed out. Life isn't so pleasant these days. I may not be able to write to you or to even see you any more. ~~I used to be in prison. I was released on the condition that I would not leave the city. Once a week I have to go and show myself and sign. These days, the more I swear that I am no longer involved in political activities, the more they suspect me. I have even confessed that I have fallen in love, and now detest any and all ideologies but . . .~~ As always, I wish you happiness . . .

This was the last letter Sara decoded from the pages of Ibsen's *An Enemy of the People*. This book too had been carefully hidden for her behind a stack of dusty books. Sara no longer saw a sign or a dot from Dara . . .

Dara disappeared.

Something was lost in Sara's life. She felt lonelier than ever before. She read more novels and stories than ever before. She told herself that Dara had read them too, or was reading them now. Unlike in the past, she looked at the faces of the people on the street; she felt she liked them because one of them may have spoken to Dara or perhaps knew him. She especially looked at the faces of the street pedlars, but she saw no sign of familiarity in their eyes. Sometimes she thought Dara may have had some sort of a physical handicap. Sometimes she thought Dara had tricked her: anyone else would have shown himself to her at least

once . . . Until at last, on that spring day, in front of the main entrance of Tehran University, on the fringes of the impassioned student demonstrations, Dara introduced himself to her and their adventure began . . .

Years before Sara and Dara's first meeting, I had the honour of meeting Mr Petrovich. In those days I was a young writer who in his solitude had spent years carefully reading novels and stories. I had even extracted the styles and techniques of all sorts of classical and modern writers from their books and had noted them on index cards. I had then concluded that every writer must have his own particular worldview and philosophy. I therefore read as many books on philosophy as I could. To analyse my characters successfully, I read the equivalent of a university degree in psychology. I had Freud and Jung and their followers in one hand, and Pavlov and his followers in the other, until I arrived at American psychology. Next, I told myself that a great writer will never become a great writer if he is not well versed in world history and politics. Therefore, as a social and literary responsibility, and despite my family's trepidations, I chose political science as my field of study at the university.

Before I left Shiraz for Tehran and Tehran University, my father, who was a wealthy, self-made man, pulled me aside and said:

"Look, son, there's no future for you in political science. The best jobs for political science graduates are at the Ministry of Foreign Affairs. But positions like ambassadorships and director generals and whatever else belong to the relatives of the Shah and his royal court. They won't even make you a mere clerk."

My father was absolutely right, and that is why I disagreed with him. He went on to say:

"What's more, if you study political science, because you are a very emotional person, there is a good chance you will end up joining some anti-government political group, you'll become a Communist, an urban guerrilla, and you'll end up having to deal with the secret police. By the time they're finished with you, if you have not been executed or sentenced to life in prison because of the hot baked potatoes and the Coca-Cola bottles they have shoved up your arse, you'll be walking funny for the rest of your life . . . Go to America, study engineering or medicine and become the pride of your family and your country."

At the time, I could not tell my father that I did not want to become a Communist, nor did I want to be an ambassador . . . Therefore, against his advice, I went and studied political science. I wanted to go as far as a doctorate degree, but first came the revolution, then the war, and I who wanted to become a great writer told myself that many of the world's great writers have experienced war, and so I signed up for military service and volunteered to go to the front. The first outcome of the Iran-Iraq War was millions of dead and disabled; the second outcome was that soon after peace was established, we realized that we were two Muslim countries and therefore brothers. It seems the war also wanted to offer the world another great writer, and for this reason, after eighteen months, it sent me back to my hometown, Shiraz, alive and well. And I, who even in the trenches had spent my time reading novels from the farthest reaches of the world – *The Soul Enchanted*, *David Copperfield*, *Moulin Rouge*, *Resurrection* and . . . and . . . and had not stopped the exercise of writing, was fully armed and ready to write my first masterpieces and to present them to the world.

Ask me:

Was all this self-adulation, as with other big-headed writers, just to claim that you are a great writer?

And I will answer:

You are wrong again. No, I didn't say all this to suggest that I am a great writer. I said it all to explain why I have *not* become a great writer. In other words, I want to say that I was just another young man with *Great Expectations* of my future as a writer. In 1990, I was thrilled to learn that on the advice of Hooshang Golshiri, one of Iran's great writers, a reputable private publisher had agreed to publish the second collection of my short stories, titled *The Eighth Day of the Earth*. Every day I sat waiting for the telephone to ring so that I could hear my publisher's voice tell me that my book had been printed. I waited for almost a year, until one day I finally heard his voice on the telephone.

"Shahriar! We're screwed! I'm ruined . . . The Ministry of Culture and Islamic Guidance has complained of thirteen separate points in your book – all sexy words and phrases . . . You have to come to Tehran. What a mistake I made investing in a young writer. My capital . . . I'm ruined!"

I kept thinking, When did I ever write sexy stories? I could not come up with an answer, so I quickly got on the bus and headed for Tehran. The six-hundred-mile road between Shiraz and Tehran passes by the two-thousand-five-hundred-year-old ruins of Persepolis; it passes by Isfahan, one of the most beautiful cities in Iran which some five hundred years ago served as the capital city of the Safavid Dynasty; it passes by the religious city of Qom, which is the centre for educating and producing clergymen, and it passes by two great deserts as well. During the night, when the two opium-addicted bus drivers would change shifts somewhere in the divide between the two deserts, I had ample time to calculate how many pages of the book had to be replaced in order to revise thirteen sentences on thirteen different pages. I concluded that approximately one hundred and ninety thousand pages had to be replaced.

You will likely say:

Don't ridicule us! Like all bad writers, some of whom even become bestsellers, you too take your readers for fools! What is this? You who claim to have prepared and armed yourself to become a great writer, didn't you know anything about mathematics?

As a matter of fact, not only had I studied mathematics, but I had even hammered into my head *The Meaning of Einstein's Theory of Relativity* by Russell. It is you who lack knowledge of mathematics . . . Look here! These were the early post-revolution days when publishers would request a permit for a book to leave the printers after it had actually been printed, and three thousand copies of this sinister book had been printed and bound and were waiting for their exit permit from the printers. My publisher had explained that to change one word or one sentence on one page, sixteen pages of a book had to be replaced because books are printed in sixteen-page forms. Now let's assume that to revise thirteen sexy phrases, four sixteen-page forms had to be extracted from the book.

Four multiplied by sixteen makes sixty-four. Now sixty-four multiplied by three thousand.

It is your turn to calculate. Even without accounting for the cost of ink and the salaries of the printers' employees, figure out how much oil must be extracted from the belly of my beloved motherland and sold, and its oil dollars sent to Brazil to purchase paper, and how many trees in Brazil have to be sacrificed to make all this paper.

A book for which so much damage is inflicted on nature, whether a masterpiece or rubbish, is a murderer.

Now I understand why I was inspired to name the book *The Eighth Day of the Earth*. And now I understand that if God had not stopped to rest after he created the world, and had instead taken on the toil of writing stories and novels himself, there wouldn't be so much damage done to the beauties of the nature he created.

In any case, on an autumn day when the air in Tehran was a mixture of carbon monoxide, the scent of rain and the fleeting perfume of a girl who years later would be named Sara, I, with all my ambition, climbed on the back of my publisher's dilapidated motorcycle and together we headed for the Ministry of Culture and Islamic Guidance. The rain had just stopped. Mud and slime flew at us from the wheels of passing cars. We rode past Tehran University. There were no demonstrations in front of its main entrance because by then all anti-government students had been purged and the preferred students had already enrolled. Of course, much later, they too would become opponents of the government.

On our perilous journey through the terrifying jungle of Tehran's traffic, my publisher was thinking that if, instead of publishing literature and supporting stupid young storytellers, he had published guidebooks for wise young people on passing university entrance exams, especially for the engineering and medical schools, he would have been rich by now, and instead of riding this ten-year-old Yamaha, he would be driving a brand-new Mercedes. And I was telling myself that if, instead of all this labour for literature, I had listened to my father and studied engineering or medicine in the United States, instead of riding this dilapidated motorcycle, I would be driving a Porsche, and I would have stopped in front of this publisher's bookstore and, just to make him happy, I would have bought precious yet unpopular books for my private library. But the truth is, I was ashamed. It was no small sin that in an Islamic country thirteen sexy phrases had been discovered in a one-hundred-and-forty-page book. At last, with such thoughts of *Fathers and Sons* and *Crime and Punishment,* in an office in the grand and majestic headquarters of the Ministry of Culture and Islamic Guidance, like two Joseph Ks we sat facing Mr Petrovich.

Mr Petrovich, part detective, part criminal court judge and quite imposing, was sitting behind a large desk. He was about thirty-five years old, with sharp eyes and a closely trimmed beard. He ordered his secretary to find and bring the file for *The Eighth Day of the Earth*. During the thirty minutes it took to produce it, Mr Petrovich was discussing advancements in print technology in the West and the unbelievable speed of new

33

printing machines with a bearded middle-aged man sitting in an armchair next to his desk. The middle-aged man's composure suggested that he was someone important and someone whom Mr Petrovich held in high regard. At the time, I foolishly hoped that the man would leave before the file containing the sexy phrases lay open on that desk. Luckily, he did not. Mr Petrovich handed a sheet of paper to my publisher with a list of page numbers and lines that were problematic. Then, like a father who has seen his newborn child for the first time, I laid eyes on my book. However, just like the dark-skinned father who suddenly sees that his child is white, I too was shocked. My book had no cover.

The first sentence that was underlined as sexy and provocative was this:

"My eyes shift from her face to her neck and then move farther down, and I am disgusted by the feelings her breasts do not awaken in me . . ."

You probably think the sentence is obviously sexy. Ask me if the breasts are naked, and I will say no. The sentence is in a short story entitled "Thursday's Sara", I mean, it was. In the story, a young officer, wounded at war and paralysed from the waist down, as he does all his other days and nights, lies on a bed in his mother's house. It is raining and his sad fiancée who has come to visit him is standing beside the window drawing lines on the fogged-up glass. The man's spinal cord has been severed and he has told his fiancée that it is over between them. But his fiancée, a nurse at a mental hospital, continues to visit him every Thursday and talks to him about a girl named Sara – Sara's first appearance in my stories. Sara is a lively, emotional and playful girl who can awaken the courage to fall in love in any man. But it seems Sara has no memory. Every Thursday, the nurse recounts one of Sara's escapades for her paralysed fiancé. At the end of my story, the young man suspects that if Sara really exists, she exists only in his fiancée's fantasies, and that, in fact, the young woman is only articulating her own lost dreams . . .

It is in such a setting that the man looks at his fiancée's face, neck and torso.

The argument between Mr Petrovich and me began. I said:

"Sir! What is sexy about this sentence? It is just the opposite. The man is paralysed. He has lost his manhood. That is why the sight of his fiancée's breasts disgust him . . . Please pay attention to the word 'disgust'. Who in the world is going to be aroused by reading this sad story and the description of a feeling of disgust?"

Mr Petrovich had his own reasoning and was particularly sensitive to the word "breast".

The next sentence, in another story, was something like this:

". . . Suddenly the woman, as though she had gone mad from thirst and the hellish heat, wildly ripped off her clothes and poured the remaining water in the ewer – their only reserve for the next few days – over her head. Her husband, weak with dehydration, was sprawled out in the corner of the hut. Passively, he watched as the drops of water trickled down the wrinkles and lines on the woman's pale thighs and plunged to the thirsty earth . . ."

With a look of reproach Mr Petrovich said:

"What about this? It is truly a vile and filthy scene."

And I, as though defending the rights of the woman in Hawthorne's *The Scarlet Letter,* with passion and literary conjecture, actually legal conjecture, in defence of every single word of that story, said:

"My esteemed sir, you have read the story. There is a drought. There is a shortage of water in this southern village. Misery and death have befallen the people. One night the villagers all have the same nightmare, a nightmare as black as tar; and it happens on the night when the American coup d'état succeeds in Tehran, and Mossadeq is arrested for the crime of nationalizing oil and the Shah is supposed to return to the country. What's more, the woman in the story is at least sixty years old . . ."

I apologize to all the beautiful sixty-year-old ladies. In those days, there were no Internet sites to post photographs of the ten sexiest Hollywood stars over fifty.

Tirelessly I argued.

"Sir, imagine the wrinkles on dehydrated skin, the white lines underneath withered skin, the filth and grime of not having bathed for months . . . Greasy, gross . . . What is so sexy about all this? The only beautiful woman in the story, as you have read, has been compared to a flower with absolutely no description of her face or figure."

Unconvinced, Mr Petrovich said:

"I just don't understand why you writers insist on depicting such filthy scenes and presenting them to the reader's imagination."

"Sir! It is not about insisting. It is life. Believe me, to make a story believable, its characters have to be portrayed, otherwise the reader will not find them credible . . . You yourself have read how the location of the village is described in detail. Its surrounding deserts have been illustrated in many sentences, even the animals and the men."

"Well, I never said we are against descriptions. What we say is that you should describe the beauties of nature, the glory of the sky and the galaxy, meaning all the beauties that God has created. Writing of such images you will be blessed in the hereafter as well, because if your readers are intelligent, from your writings they will discover the greatness of God and their faith will be strengthened."

I blurted out:

"Sir, it isn't the writer's fault if there are also ugly things and unbathed women in the world . . . By the way, aren't they also God's creations?"

Mr Petrovich glared at me. His knotted eyebrows were saying, You're getting too big for your boots. His angry eyes were saying, You're running away with yourself.

But perhaps because I was a young writer and he didn't want to drive me towards the anti-revolution camp, he masked his anger and continued.

"Well, in this section, if you had not described the woman's body, your story would not have suffered at all."

"It certainly would have suffered. I think the scene where the water drips onto the dirt is good literary imaging. I think stories are written so that such images can be created."

"As a matter of fact, these lengthy illustrations make the story dull and boring. In a story, events have to take place one after the other. For example, you should have just written, 'She empties the ewer over her head'."

"That's not possible, sir. Then the reader will wonder whether the woman has gone mad."

"Well, in your story you want to show that the woman has in fact gone mad."

"Sir, these two madnesses are completely different. In a weak story, characters go mad without logic and literary sense, in which case it will seem as if all the bones in the story are broken. To write a good story, we have to try to make sure that even characters who go mad have a rational reason for it . . ."

Mr Petrovich walked out of the room and returned with a glass of water filled with ice. To quell the flames of his rage, he drank it all in one gulp. Mr Petrovich is not alone; many of us Iranians are terribly angered when someone teaches us something we don't know. But my excitement and passion in defending my stories were so great that I didn't realize I was being offensive. Our argument dragged on to other phrases in the book. In those too there was either the word "breast" or words used to describe the beauty or ugliness of the lips, arms or thighs of a woman . . . By then my face was drenched with sweat and I was swearing to God and to the Prophet that for a reader familiar with these stories, such descriptions would not be sexually arousing at all, and that if someone is looking to be aroused, he is far better off looking elsewhere. I mean, instead of reading the word "breast", he can just go out into the street where there are plenty of breasts and thighs . . .

After an hour of heated discussion, neither I nor Mr Petrovich had been convinced. Finally, Mr Petrovich, who perhaps still wanted to avoid breaking the heart of a young writer, fed up and exhausted, said:

"No. No matter what I say, you come up with ten justifications for it."

And without any apparent forethought he blurted out:

"As an impartial observer, let's ask this gentleman's opinion."

And he offered my book with the underlined sentences to the dignified gentleman.

"As a fair-minded reader, you be the judge."

The dignified gentleman began pensively reading those thirteen notorious lines . . . Ten minutes . . . fifteen minutes went by. My heart was pounding in my chest. I knew the moment of the verdict was at hand. Drops of sweat, like drops of water dripping off a wrinkled thigh, dripped onto the floor. My publisher was still sitting there, quiet and meek, and the dignified gentleman had gone back yet one more time to reread from the very first instance . . . Twenty-three minutes . . . I couldn't figure out what he was doing with the breasts and thighs of my story . . . And all the while, Mr Petrovich sat there looking at me with an air of victory. The ice in his glass melted . . . Half an hour . . . Finally the dignified gentleman spoke.

"What can I say . . . It is not easy to judge . . . In any case, perhaps . . . I don't know . . . Perhaps for men of our age it would not be arousing, but for the young . . . What can I say?!"

Impulsively, I said:

"Dear sir, you are still young. Were you really aroused by those sentences?"

This was one of those rare moments in my life when I was shrewdly clever . . . It was obvious that the dignified gentleman, even if he had

been aroused, could not confess to three men that he was sexually stimu-
lated by reading a few sentences. Hence he said:

"No."

And I in turn said to Mr Petrovich:

"You see, sir . . ."

Now in an environment awash with mutual understanding, our discussion continued for another twenty minutes. Mr Petrovich agreed to forgo
censoring several sentences. I did not want to give in on the others, but
my publisher whispered that I had gone far enough and that I should not
make him any angrier and any more tired.

We left the Ministry of Culture and Islamic Guidance. I climbed up
behind my publisher on his motorcycle and we rode off. Small drops of
water from the wrinkled thighs of the clouds above Tehran rained on our
faces. The drivers of hundreds of polluting motorcycles and cars were
blowing their horns, cutting one another up and cursing at one another.
On the crowded streets people were going about their daily headaches and
responsibilities. No one paid any attention to the noisy passage of one of
the greatest and most honoured publishers and one of the future's greatest
writers of their country. In those days, many middle-class and working-
class people were forced to take on two jobs just to make ends meet, and
they hardly gave a damn if in some scene, in some story, a man's gaze
moved across his fiancée's breasts or not, or whether the man's manhood
was intact or not, or even whether his fiancée had any breasts or not. And
for this reason, the pithy three-thousand print run of books was shrinking
even further. But still, I felt as though I had lost some part of my soul, as
though parts of my body had been stripped naked, stared at and severed.

I said to my publisher:

"Mr Petrovich forgave us three breasts and two thighs."

He did not answer, and to escape the traffic he turned into a side
street. Perhaps he was wondering why, instead of publishing troublesome
books by young writers, he didn't publish instructive books on religion or
books on the writs and principles of Islam in laymen's language that millions of people seeking government jobs and admission to universities
would buy to prepare for the multiple-choice questions of the Islamic
selection process . . .

If that is indeed what he was thinking, then I would have had to be thinking: in addition to the millions of job seekers and university applicants,

thousands of Communist Tudeh Party followers purchase these books and memorize them far more scrupulously than any non-Communist, so that they can infiltrate government offices and universities.

We rode past a beautiful modern high-rise building with elements of ancient Greek and seventeenth-century Iranian architecture. The motorcycle's groans suddenly stopped. The startled publisher cursed at the raindrops. We climbed down. He started fiddling with the spark plugs.

Next to the front stairs of the building with its postmodern façade, a street pedlar wearing clothes reminiscent of eight hundred years ago was sitting on the pavement with a box in front of him. We Iranians are used to such characters. In their boxes they have magic for sale. Talismans for rendering the enemy mute . . . Potions to pour in front of a foe's door so that the sound of laughter will never again emanate from it . . . Snake's eggs to make someone fall in love . . . Hyena's pussy to be mixed with the bones of a hundred-year-old cadaver and fed to a husband so that he does not fancy taking another wife . . . Scraps of paper with spells written on them in strange script to be steeped in water as a cure for the ailing . . . Rings for becoming rich . . . The pedlar raised his head. Our eyes met. I thought, One day I will write your story too. And I heard his voice somewhere deep in my ear, Write! I also have Indian elephant's testicle powder dissolved in syrupy Ganesha potion. Any writer who drinks it will win the Nobel Prize . . . If you win it, write in your story that the potions, talismans and spells of medicine man Jafar ibn-Jafri are more potent than those of all other medicine men . . .

Miraculously, the motorcycle engine started. We climbed back on. We were moving away from the witchcraft-selling medicine man. I turned around and stared at the path of his dark gaze and said to my publisher, "It didn't turn out too badly . . . Three breasts and two thighs . . ."

My publisher still didn't express any joy. We passed in front of a hospital affiliated with Tehran University. Above its main entrance, on a huge thirty-foot-by-six-foot banner, in large, beautiful calligraphy, was written

MEDICAL SEMINAR ON THE CAUSES AND PREVENTIONS
OF BREAST CANCER

Let us return to Tehran University . . .

~~The students are still being beaten up . . .~~

No, this sentence will not appeal to Mr Petrovich at all. What's more, from the standpoint of Iranian literature, it is not at all exciting because in my country, since the founding of the first university, getting beaten up and thrown in jail have always been among the required credits for students . . . Therefore, this is how I will transition back to my story. Let us together return to that beautiful spring day on Liberty Street . . .

The efforts of the anti-riot police to disperse the students continue. There are exactly three minutes and three seconds left until the moment when Sara will be thrown to the ground and her head will hit against a cement edge. To escape the terrifying face of that timeless hunchback, she moves a few steps closer to the conflict, not knowing that she has moved a few steps closer to the location of her death. Sara, her eyes still brimming with tears, raises her sign with its strange slogan even higher, and by doing so attracts even greater attention and graver danger. In Iran, any action, innovation or even non-cliché art that is not based on our traditions or on our so-called modern traditions attracts the greatest threats, attacks and hatred from all fronts. **It is at this very moment that Sara again hears:**

"Sara! Leave this place . . ."

Aggravated by the pestering hunchback, Sara once more peers behind the fence. There is nothing there but the trunks of the old sycamore and cypress trees of the university campus . . . Then she hears:

"I'm Dara . . ."

Sara looks to her left and sees a young man standing three steps away leaning against the short stone wall and looking in the opposite direction from her. Dara, without turning to face her, says:

"What are you doing? Everyone here belongs to some political group. They're looking out for one another. You on your own are in more danger than anyone else . . ."

Now our love story is slowly approaching its first incident.

Dara continues to talk to Sara in a way that no one will notice.

"Please throw away your sign. Let's leave this place."

Sara, confused, her eyes brimming with tears, still has not clearly seen Dara's face. She sees him pass in front of her. She realizes that as he walks by he takes the sign from her hand and throws it behind the university fence. And then she hears:

"Please follow me at a distance . . ."

Mesmerized, Sara begins to walk ten steps behind Dara. She's not scared of losing him in the crowd; she is certain he is keeping an eye on her. They leave behind the anger and chaos of Liberty Street. The dust of decay from flying carpets hovers in the sky above Tehran . . .

Finally, Dara stops in front of the ruins of a cinema that, years ago, during the days of the revolution, was burned down. Sara involuntarily stops next to him. Dara has a brand-new beautiful handkerchief that his late grandmother had given him as a keepsake. He doesn't know why he always carries it with him. And all I know is that this handkerchief will play a key role in my story, just like Chekhov's gun hanging on the wall. The edge of the white silk handkerchief is embroidered with delicate red roses. Sara dries her eyes with it, and in this magnificent moment, for the very first time, she sees Dara's face . . . which in our story is a kind and gentle face. A high forehead, thick eyebrows, large black eyes, thirsty curved lips, teeth as lustrous as pearls from Bahrain and ebony-coloured hair with locks tousled on his brow.

I am teasing you. My story's Dara doesn't look like this at all. If you are really interested in picturing his face, then set your imagination in motion. As a hint, I can tell you that in this novel Dara has a hazy face.

~~And for the very first time in this universe, their eyes meet.~~

It is right here that I, the writer, run into a few snags. In all probability, at this very moment Mr Petrovich's exactitude has heightened, and he will immediately underline the phrase "their eyes meet". My second problem is that even in front of the ruins of a cinema that is not playing any romantic film, a few blocks away from which political demonstrations are under way, an Iranian boy and girl cannot simply stand in the street and stare into each other's eyes; chances are the patrol from the Campaign Against Social Corruption will arrest them.

My one hundred and first problem – I still don't know what the third to the hundredth problems are – is that Sara and Dara are not familiar with those opening lines of dialogue between a man and a woman that throughout the world and in all love stories are identical and equally tedious. Even if they are familiar with Danielle Steel's novels and their Iranian equivalents, at this moment those clichéd discourses seem dull and idiotic . . . You may not believe me, but it is true that many of Danielle Steel's novels have been translated into Farsi, and together with their Iranian imitations are reprinted tens of times in large print runs. I really would like to meet Danielle Steel some day and, straight off, ask her, What have you done for Mr Petrovich to issue permits so generously for your novels to leave the printers – of course, after having deleted the kissing scenes? What if Mr Petrovich is smart enough to know that such novels breed tame citizens who never question anything? Or did you perhaps buy a talisman for stirring benevolence in his heart from Jafar ibn-Jafri?

Sara wants to complain:

Where did you suddenly disappear to?

But she doesn't. And I write:

In this strange moment, every word, every sentence, seems hollow and absurd . . .

From the late Henry James, may God rest his soul, I know that to heighten the dramatic energy of my story, I have to limit its perspective to either Sara or Dara. But then to respect narrative candour, I will have to write of the secret thoughts and desires of that character. Should I fall into this trap, I will also fall prey to Mr Petrovich. On the other hand, I really don't want to portray my story's character as cold, or to conceal his or her emotions in the vein of Hemingway and his American successors. So what am I to do? In your opinion, what can one do with words that are at times idiotic when writing a simple scene of a young man and woman looking into each other's eyes in some street in Tehran? Let's leave it up to these old words and see what they themselves will write.

Suddenly, a bolt of lightning flashes from Sara's black eyes and sets fire to the wheat fields of Dara's soul . . .

I did say words sometimes become dim-witted. Since Madame Bovary's death, such sentences seem rather inane.

Let us write:

Four pupils like four black mirrors facing each other . . .

Four windows open onto each other's darkness . . .

But where in the world is there something called a nose between two mirrors or two windows? We therefore have to forgo such clichés and nose-y portrayals. I will write:

In want for words, two pairs of pupils together darken a long silence.

I think if we Iranian writers continue such exhausting exercises, at long last our syphilis-stricken dream of winning a Nobel Prize might become reality. I should remember to tell that fortunate writer, or unfortunate writer, because in Iran he or she will surely be accused of collaborating with Western intelligence services, to make sure and thank Mr Petrovich when addressing the Nobel Committee.

Anyway, perforce, Sara and Dara, start to walk side by side . . .

In step with the united steps of the two characters of our story, destiny changes. **In the chaos of the clash between the students, the police, and government sympathizers, the frail figure of the hunchback midget receives a hard blow from a person who is either beating an escape or rushing to strike. The midget falls to the ground, his small head smashes against a cement edge, and his eyes for ever close . . .**

BĀRĀN AND DANIEL

In this segment of the story, I come to think that selecting the name Dara for the antagonist was a big mistake. I have just remembered that Dara was not only the name of the character in first-year reading books, but it was also the name of one of Iran's kings. It could therefore make Mr Petrovich wary of my entire story, and with his conspiracy-seeking eyes he may scour every word and sentence, thinking that I am a monarchist. However, given that my story has advanced tens of pages, I cannot simply use the find-and-replace function in Microsoft Word to change the name of my story's character. For quite some time now, I have come to know him as Dara. Changing his name at this point would be similar to your brother or husband or boyfriend suddenly asking you to delete his old name and to start calling him by a new name, simply because he doesn't want you to think he is a monarchist. In that case, your problem will be simpler than mine, because your brother or husband or boyfriend has a real existence, and with this real existence he can enforce the censoring of his old name and its replacement with his new one. However, from the start of this story, I have seen Dara in the shape of the word "Dara", I have grown attached to him, and it is with this name that I have developed his character. If, based on the Sinbad Theory, I change his name at this point, I will also have to change his character. For a writer, this is akin to committing cold-blooded premeditated murder. Yes, it is true that my writings are dark, and that because of the darkness in my mind I have sent several of my stories' characters to death and destruction. But these days, with all my being, as a will and last testament, I want to write a bright love story in which there is no sorrow, no one dies, no hearts suffer, not even the tip of a pencil breaks.

It is here that I must recount the story of naming my daughter. Even if you don't ask, I will tell you.

When my daughter was born I wanted to name her Bārān (Rain). In fact, to find this unique and rare name, I had reflected and researched for more than a month. I had told myself that the daughter of a young man who wants one day to become one of the greatest writers of his country, even of the world, should have a name that is Iranian, beautiful, literary, rare, a symbol of life and reflective of the particular creative taste of her parents . . , But when I went to the General Register Office to get her birth certificate, I was told that I could not name my daughter Bārān. I asked:

"Why can't I name my daughter Bārān?"

The young bearded administrator in charge of birth certificates looked at me as though he were looking at some idiot who had given no thought to the future and fate of his daughter and said:

"I have never heard of anyone naming their daughter Bārān."

"But I want to name my daughter Bārān."

He scoffed:

"My good man, who in their right mind names an innocent child Bārān? In a few years, when your daughter goes to school, she will stand out, her classmates have never heard of anyone named Bārān, they will make fun of her. They will tease her, and say your father must have been a cloud . . . Do you get it, Papa Cloud?"

"Sir! Bārān has a romantic and beautiful nuance. In our desert country rain is a divine gift. Allow me to name my daughter Bārān. I am sure that from now on many people will name their daughters Bārān."

By now he was angry. He roared:

"No! I will not . . . We have prepared a list of beautiful, meaningful Islamic names. Look through the list and find a proper name for the poor child."

He put a list of hundreds of names in front of me. Most of them were Arab names. Feeling obstinate, and of course not daring to express my anger, I blurted out:

"Sir, can I name her Roja?"

He knotted his eyebrows that were thicker than his beard.

I said:

"The name is popular in northern Iran. Roja means the 'morning star'."

He agreed.

In those days, Communist parties were still active in Iran, and they often named their artistic groups and the bands that played their revolutionary anthems Roja or the Red Star . . . It seems the world's Communists have taken full ownership of stars, similar to Muslims and the crescent moon . . . Still, my daughter's name did not become Roja as easily as that. A month later when I went back to pick up her birth certificate, I saw that instead of "Roja" they had mistakenly, or intentionally, written "Raja", which is not only an Arab name but a man's name. The law in Iran requires that to change a name one must petition the court. We were forced to hire an attorney, and a year later, when the court agreed to the correction of my daughter's name, she finally became Roja. I have never in my life been a Communist, not only because I was born to a bourgeois family, but also because I have read books such as *Animal Farm* . . .

Likewise, I have never been Jewish. Years later, when once again I went to the General Register Office for my son's birth certificate, the administrator in charge snidely said:

"You shouldn't have rushed! You might as well have waited for your golden-wee-wee'd boy to turn one before you came for his birth certificate."

He was right. My wife and I had spent three months debating, researching and even arguing to come up with a beautiful, unique and literary name for our son. At home we called our daughter Bārān, so it would have been nice for our son's name to rhyme with Bārān. At last, like an inspiration, the name Māhān had come to me. And I told the administrator that I wanted to name my son Māhān . . . He knotted his eyebrows that were thicker than his beard . . . and said that he would not allow it. I asked why. He said:

"First of all, Māhān is an obsolete name. Second, his classmates will make fun of him at school."

Then he faked a scholarly mien and added:

"Third, Māhān is plural."

By then I was a known writer, and to develop a pure and unique prose I had practised thousands of pages of story-writing, and I had read thousands of pages of old Farsi texts and tens of books on Farsi grammar and linguistics. Still, with modesty I said:

46

"My dear brother! First of all, Māhān is the name of a green and lush place in the desert in eastern Iran."

"Aren't you ashamed of yourself? Years from now, kids in school will make fun of this poor innocent child, taunting him that his father was probably Papa Desert."

"Second, in the Farsi language *ān* does not imply a plural form. Māhān means 'like the moon'."

He suddenly grew angry and growled:

"Don't give me all this hot air. Go and get a permission slip from the director of the General Register Office for me to name your kid Māhān."

This time I was determined to insist on my rights as a father and had no intention of giving up that easily. I got into my car, drove past the tomb of our world-renowned poet who died seven hundred years ago and headed for the other side of town and the Central Office of the General Register. I waited for three hours until I was finally given permission to see the director general. Angry and determined to reclaim my rights, I stepped into his office. But the second I saw him sitting behind his large desk, and before he had even raised his head to see my non-Islamic appearance, I quickly turned round and walked out. I drove back to the opposite side of town and back to the administrator in charge of issuing birth certificates. This time, obstinately yet with censored anger, I asked:

"Brother, can I name him Daniel?"

To my surprise I heard:

"Why not? Daniel is the name of a prophet."

I think that, despite his exceptionally Islamic appearance – long beard and collarless shirt – the administrator did not participate in Friday prayers and street demonstrations, because he should have known that at all Friday prayers and in all street demonstrations, after the slogans of Death to America, Death to the Soviet Union, Death to England and Death to France, in a much louder voice participants shouted, Death to Israel . . . It had slipped his mind that we are strong supporters of the Palestinian people and that our country has been in some sort of an undeclared war against Israel . . . And that is how one of my children ended up with a Communist name and the other with a Jewish name. I am glad I did not have a third child because I don't know which one of the names favoured by our enemies he or she would have ended up with.

Ask me: ·

Does this chapter have anything to do with your love story and censorship?

It most certainly does. In fact, for you to discern fully the symbols and metaphors of my story, I am forced to introduce you to yet another form of censorship – sociocultural censorship – which in Iran has a history of more than two thousand years . . . It is a phenomenon in comparison to which the scissor blades of Moharram Ali Khan seem like delicate jasmine petals.

Now you must want to ask, Who in the world is Moharram Ali Khan?

That's strange! You are familiar with the likes of Damocles and his sword; King Arthur's master swordsman Sir Lancelot; Josef Ignace Guillotin; Josef Mengele, the doctor at Auschwitz who with his scalpel conducted medical experiments on the prisoners; and even with murderers such as the one in *The Silence of the Lambs* who skinned people and sewed their skin into clothes, but you don't know who Moharram Ali Khan is?

In the 1930s, Moharram Ali Khan was responsible for censoring newspapers published in Tehran. Armed with his weapon of choice, a pair of scissors that resembled the jaws of a Nag serpent, he would turn up every morning and every evening before the newspapers went to press. He would carefully study the columns prepared for layout, and wherever he found a sentence or sentences that were contrary to the interests of the king, the government, the governor, or even small government departments, he would with great dexterity surgically remove them . . .

CENSORED TESTICLES

The sky above Tehran is filled with smoke from the factories in the outskirts of town and from the purple fires of alchemists in the tales of *One Thousand and One Nights*. Motorcycles that double as express taxis intricately weave their lone passenger through deadlocked traffic. In the street the scent of Clinique Happy lingers in the air in the wake of a beautiful woman clad in a coverall and head-scarf . . . Sara and Dara, in the shadow of a postmodern high-rise building, approach a street pedlar. The man's clothes are a blend of traditional Arab, Afghani and Turkish garb . . . The government of the Islamic Republic has coined this year the Year of Progress and Blossoming. Therefore, this year we Iranians have a five-month-long spring. Consequently, Sara and Dara have ample time to carry on with their romance in this season. **Seeing a handsome couple, in a voice that seems to come from the pit of a magic lantern, the street pedlar says:**

"A talisman for bliss . . . A spell for love and compassion . . ."

Sara and Dara sit in front of his box and rifle through the small dark bottles, colourful powders, locks, plaques and rusted metal talismans with strange designs etched on them.

Sara asks:

"Do you have a talisman for hate?"

Dara says:

"A talisman to free the mind, so that someone is not in your thoughts night and day . . ."

The spellbinding gleam in the old man's eyes darkens. His eyes fill with sorrow, the sorrow of an aged lover remembering a love *Gone with the Wind* . . . He digs into his deep pockets and pulls out a roll of thin yellow paper. He tears off a piece. From his breast pocket he produces a Parker fountain pen and starts to draw strange signs. The ink spreads on the paper and makes the signs look even more ominous . . . Sara takes the magic paper.

"After the spell works, I ask that you tell your friends that the potions, talismans and spells of medicine man Jafar ibn-Jafri are more potent than those of all other medicine men . . ."

Sara asks:

"How much should I pay you?"

"If I take money from you the magic of the spell will be undone."

The magic seller turns to Dara. He stares into his eyes. Then, with the anguish of a father taking his son to the sacrifice altar, he says:

"Master! You have ninety-five tumans in your pocket. Offer it to me as a gift."

Dara reaches into his pocket and takes out a few crumpled notes and a coin. He counts them and stares at the old man in amazement. The old man kisses the notes as he would a holy object, he touches them to his forehead and closes his eyes . . . A few steps away, Dara tells Sara:

"Actually, I am the one who needs that spell. Let me have it so that I can be free of the agony of thinking of you day and night."

Sara, with a mysterious smile on her lips, says:

"Why are you so sure that I am not the same way, and that now that I have seen you I won't get even worse . . . I have dropped most of my university courses this term . . ."

They are now crossing a bridge over a motorway. The river of cars, taking no notice of them, courses beneath their feet.

Dara says:

"I wish I had a car. In a car there is less risk of being caught."

"Do you really want to stop thinking of me?"

"Were you telling the truth when you said I have been on your mind?"

They are now two-thirds of the way across the bridge. Sara stops. She takes the magic paper from her pocket and holds it out towards Dara.

"What shall we do? Shall we get rid of it?"

Dara takes the other end of the paper and pulls. The paper rips in

two. They each tear their half into pieces . . . The drivers passing under the bridge will never guess what spell the tiny pieces of paper falling on their cars like yellow snow have undone . . .

Mr Petrovich will say:

You really are a bad writer . . . This is a nice scene. On a bridge, a young couple bid each other farewell. After their morally wrong correspondence, on the first day of their encounter, the wisest thing they could do was exactly what came to their minds, to part and never think of each other again . . . If you separate them on this very bridge, it will turn out to be a nice story. Imagine. One walks to the left of the bridge, the other to the right . . . and neither one turns to look at the other.

I will say:

Sir, the parting of a young couple on a bridge isn't as free of danger as you might think. Bridges are not endless. Even the longest bridges in the world, from the right and the left, lead to streets and neighbourhoods. In these streets and neighbourhoods there are plenty of girls and boys and men and women. In fact, it is possible for our beautiful Sara to get trapped by one of those gangs that have recently been kidnapping girls, or by one of their good-looking members who makes an innocent girl fall in love with him and takes her home, and there they film the lovemaking or rape scene and sell copies of it on the black market. You are probably not aware that the most provocative American and Japanese porno films are sold on the black market for two or three thousand tumans, but these Iranian films, even though they are poorly made, with no lighting and with the girl not being a real blonde, are bought and sold for twelve thousand tumans. On the other side of the bridge, too, how do we know that Dara, who is a good-looking young man, in whose eyes the sorrow of love has left a romantic look, does not walk into a street where a bad girl falls in love with him. Please allow this innocent girl and boy to walk together.

My predicament, however, is that Sara and Dara cannot walk together for very long. The patrols from the Campaign Against Social Corruption, armed with Kalashnikovs, could arrive at any moment and arrest them.

You will probably say:

Well, they can claim to be brother and sister.

I will reply:

No, they cannot.

Ask me why and I will explain:

If they claim to be siblings or even cousins, two patrols, a man and a woman, will take each of them aside and interrogate them separately. They will ask, for example, what their grandfather's or brother-in-law's name is. If Sara and Dara have previously exchanged these sorts of details, the questions will then extend to the colour and brand of the fridge in their house, their neighbour's last name and similar basic questions. If their answers do not match, Sara and Dara will be taken to the detention centre for the socially corrupt. There they will join homeless addicts, pimps, prostitutes and other morally depraved people. In one of my stories, I led my protagonist and antagonist to a cemetery as their meeting place. They sat on the grave of the boy's mother and quietly talked. At the time, the anti-corruption officers' imagination did not extend to a girl and a boy taking advantage of the grave of an unsuspecting and helpless dead mother to set the stage for their sin.

Dara asks:

"What colour is the fridge in your house?"

"Why do you ask?"

"I don't know. I don't even know how it popped into my head . . . Tell me, what kind of flowers and trees do you have in your front yard?"

"We have geraniums, violets and an apple tree. Why?"

Sara does not receive an answer. She thinks what a secretive character and complicated mind Dara has. Having a secretive character, being complicated and quiet, are good characteristics to have to pique a girl's curiosity and interest. Of course, only up until marriage.

Now Sara and Dara are passing in front of Qajar Optician's. The store's decor is no less stylish than the most fashionable boutiques in Paris.

Sara says:

"I have to buy a pair of large sunglasses."

The store owner, Agha Mohammad, with a beardless face and feminine mannerisms, greets them.

Several centuries and many years ago, Agha Mohammad of the Qajar Dynasty was one of Iran's warrior kings. After the conquest of an Iranian town, in one fell swoop he commanded that the eyes of the townspeople be censored from their sockets and piled up in the town square.

Sara tries on several pairs of designer sunglasses, most of which are knock-offs made in China, and walks out with a pair of large Ray-Bans covering her black eyes. Agha Mohammad follows her with his eyes as she passes in front of the store window and sighs:

"What a shame for those beautiful eyes ~~and that tantalizing face~~ to be hidden behind those glasses."

In his youth, Agha Mohammad was held hostage in the court of another Iranian king who ordered Agha Mohammad's testicles be deleted from his body with a pair of special scissors.

If you ask me why I have recounted this historic detail, which seems unrelated to our story, I will immediately respond:

Clearly you are still not as familiar with Iranian symbols as you should be . . . My dears! The point of this historic detail is to remind you that in Iran, scissors had uses other than their common utility and other than cutting out excess sentences from newspapers and manuscripts . . .

Sara and Dara arrive at an Internet café.

Ask me if there are Internet cafés in Tehran.

Of course there are. What image do you have of Iran? Are you like that person I once met at the literary festival in Stavanger, Norway, who after my long-winded talk on modern and postmodern literature in Iran asked:

"Have you heard of the Internet in Iran?"

Or like my son's schoolfriend in Providence, Rhode Island, who asked him:

"You don't have cars in Iran, you ride camels; why do you want to make a nuclear bomb?"

Faced with such questions, many Iranians quickly point to the past glories of our land and explain that Iran is Persia, and they remind you that our country has more than two thousand five hundred years of history and civilization. But since I am a writer and have a bit of an imagination, I will not make this mistake because I know that after my explanations you will say, Well, yes, you had a great empire with all this history and a civilization replete with culture, science and architecture. Something, however, must have gone very wrong for you to have fallen on such pitiful times that today the Russians are building your nuclear power plant. If these Russians knew how to build a reactor, their Chernobyl wouldn't have gone bust.

In response to this comment I will steadfastly keep my silence. Not because you are right but because in Iran, as an Iranian, especially as a journalist or a writer or even a nuclear scientist, I am not allowed to express my opinions of our government's nuclear energy policies. As it is, with this love story alone, I will have enough headaches to deal with.

Then come and let me take you, together with our protagonist and antagonist, to an Iranian Internet café.

Here too I prefer not to write that Sara and Dara's eyes secretly meet. However, I am now obliged, as is customary in all love stories, to describe Sara and her feminine beauties. Otherwise, neither you nor Mr Petrovich will read my story . . . Aside from her large black eyes, the first striking feature in Sara's face is her luscious lips that are perpetually smouldering as though from thirst. Well, if I write such a sentence, Mr Petrovich will immediately demand that it be deleted.

I therefore write:

Sara's lips resemble plump, ripe cherries with their delicate skin about to split from the heat of the sun.

So far our story has not progressed badly, although critic-approving tension has yet to build. Our next predicament surfaces in the dialogue that follows.

Sara says:

"They hit really hard with those batons."

Dara says:

"Some of the batons give an electric shock. They paralyse you for a while."

Ask:

Well, what is wrong with this?

I will answer:

These lines are appalling. I don't mean politically . . . Don't you get it? If you live in a country where its fourteen-hundred-year-old language contains thousands of symbols, metaphors and similes that in addition to their mystical meanings and interpretations also whisper of amorous and sexual connotations, and if you are someone who, from the crack of dawn until dusk, has the job of vigilantly reading stories and poems lest there be sexually suggestive symbols and metaphors in them, then surely your mind will instinctively suspect every letter for fear that its connotations may together commit a sin in the shadows of the reader's mind.

Now you've grasped the quandary of our story. Yes, the difficulty is with the name and the shape of a baton . . . Sara and Dara must therefore talk about something else. But I cannot even have one say to the other:

Let's talk about something else . .

Because "thing", with its inherent ambiguity, can be interpreted as the most vile and libellous word in the Farsi language. In interpreting words for their sexual undertones, the Farsi language is exceptionally rich and clever. Yet I cannot put my pathetic protagonist and antagonist in an Internet café with no dialogue and no action. Let us picture them.

Sara wants to stir her hot chocolate, but she drops her spoon on the floor. Dara takes his spoon out of his teacup and offers it to her . . .

Not a bad scene for enriching a simple communication. Although this too could be labelled a sexual metaphor.

Ask me how, and I will say:

Years ago, in a friend's novel, a motorcyclist runs out of fuel on a dirt road in the desert. For miles around, there is no woman in sight, not even a peasant. Finally, the driver of a pick-up truck stops to help . . . The sentence underlined by Mr Petrovich for deletion was this: "The motorcyclist inserts a plastic hose in the fuel tank of the pick-up truck and sucks on it. As soon as petrol begins to flow, he inserts the hose in his motorcycle's fuel tank . . ." If I and my novelist friend and all Iranian writers had put our heads together, we would never have consciously recognized the subtext of this modern, sexually explicit, petrol-related, motorized scene. It is thus that the late Roland Barthes's theory of the Death of the Author is, in my dear homeland, subconsciously practised. We may therefore have to forgo the lending-of-the-spoon scene. To have the two characters of my story finally say something to each other, I give them a few watered-down lines.

Sara says:

"The beauty of spring saddens me . . . Unlike spring, autumn is an unassuming and humble season that quickly makes friends and grows dear."

She adds:

"I wish I were seventy years old."

Then together they declare:

"Yes, I like autumn . . ."

By concurrently uttering this simple, romantic and harmless sentence, the two are transformed into the happy-go-lucky characters of cheap romance novels. But I know that such characters belong in nineteenth-century Paris, not in the city of Tehran. I am therefore convinced that their fate will be similar to that of William Shakespeare's disaster-prone lovers, eternally entangled in a convoluted and ill-fated tragedy.

Ask me, How could such romantic simplicity in the twenty-first century lead to a complicated tragedy?

I will answer:

You see, at twenty-two and thirtysomething, Sara and Dara are both virgins. Sara's virginity is a foregone conclusion, because according to Iranian values (traditional and intellectual), a girl who is neither married nor a virgin cannot possibly fall in love; she has been deceived by false love, has lost her virginity and must therefore become a woman of ill repute. Should her father or her educated brothers, who night and day chase after their non-virgin girlfriends, ever discover her secret, they will either drive her to suicide, or if they are truly fanatical, kill her. The law of the land gives them the right to protect their honour . . . Dara's virginity, too, should not be a surprise. A few months after the Islamic revolution triumphed, all the brothels across Iran that had not already been burned down were shut down, and it was ordered that the shameful word "prostitute" be deleted from the Farsi-language lexicon and replaced by the phrase "vulnerable lady". Well, a few madams were executed and a large number of vulnerable ladies were left abandoned on the streets. Now, influenced by German law and culture, you want to say:

Then the likes of Dara have access to the vulnerable ladies on the streets, and at the age of thirtysomething they should no longer be virgins.

Have the courage to say it like a brave Berliner for me to respond:

First of all, since the vulnerable ladies began working on the streets, their rates have gone up. Second, in Iran, one condition for being able to make vulnerable ladies vulnerable is at least to have an empty house somewhere. Third, if you are arrested while making a vulnerable lady vulnerable, if you are married, your punishment will be death by stoning and if you are single, you will receive approximately eighty lashes, the same as what that vulnerable lady will receive . . . But none of these is the reason for Dara's virginity. His problem is that he cannot even make contact with a vulnerable lady.

Ask:

Why . . .?

I will answer:

Because Dara is interested in reading stories and novels. I don't know about your country, but in mine a good number of people who are readers cannot sleep with prostitutes. They find shame and disgrace in such an act . . .

Of course, blushing with embarrassment, Dara wants me to censor this segment of the story to his benefit. Very well . . . But how can I convey this vital piece of information about the characters of my story to my readers? It is here that the fine art of Iranian storytelling must step in and create a cipher that, after the publication of the book, will be quickly deciphered by the clever Iranian reader.

I hesitate to write: "No butterfly has ever transferred pollen from the blossom of sin from Dara's body to Sara's body . . ." It is too scientific, too old, and it reminds us of the bedlam of the butterfly effect. I will therefore write:

The perspiration of *vessāl* (union, realization, attainment) **has yet to seep from the pores of their bodies' imagination . . .**

The word *vessāl*, in the ages-old Iranian literature, has many explicit and implicit religious, mystic, amorous and sexual connotations and hence is not really translatable. A Sufi, after much self-discipline and worship can "attain", or *vessāl*, with God. A lover who has suffered can after years "unite", or *vessāl*, with his beloved. A story writer too can "achieve", or *vessāl*, a good story. I therefore don't think Mr Petrovich will be too exacting when it comes to this word. Though I suspect that the words "perspiration" and "pores" will likely make our readers sweat, and the word "imagination" will direct them to other implicit suggestions.

It is at this very moment that the ghost of the dead poet sitting in a corner at the Internet café notices Sara's eyes glancing anxiously towards the window, and he is inspired to compose a new simile: two carnivorous black flowers lying in wait for plucked-winged butterflies, for ethereal bees, lewd bees . . .

Sara opens her mouth to speak an important sentence revealing a terrifying and diabolical secret. But just like Nathaniel Hawthorne's Faith in "Young Goodman Brown", who at the moment of bidding farewell to her beloved chooses to remain silent, so does Sara. Dara too has a never-asked question on his mind, but he too keeps silent. And thus, an ominous fate awaits their love.

Like a good girl, Sara starts to drink her hot chocolate. Like a good boy, Dara sips his tea.

~~Sara says:~~

~~"It's very hot."~~

~~Dara says:~~

~~"Mine, too."~~

Before I can decide on the word "hot", a boy with hair similar to the gothic hairstyles of some American teenagers and wearing a Linkin Park t-shirt bursts into the Internet café and in a muffled voice warns:

"The patrols!"

The boy works for the owner of the Internet café as a lookout. The boys and girls quickly separate and rearrange the tables and chairs. The girls pull their scarves down over their highlighted hair, the boys hide their necklaces under their t-shirts. By the time two patrols walk in, the girls are huddled together at one end of the café, the boys are gathered at the opposite end, and they are all staring intently at their computer screens. Sara and Dara, lacking experience, sensed the danger at the very last minute and separated. The patrols carefully inspect each computer screen. Fortunately, everyone has been browsing educational websites, websites with beautiful pictures of nature and websites of government-sponsored newspapers. In Iran millions of Internet sites containing very immoral materials are filtered out by expensive software programs purchased from a very moral American company. Among these, political anti-revolution websites and even the websites of Voice of America and the sponsored Radio Farda are filtered out. Of course, the man responsible for this Internet censorship is not Mr Petrovich. All Mr Petrovich knows about computers is that they are machines that in Iran usually make terrible mistakes. For example, they once printed one million tumans instead of ten thousand tumans on his electricity bill, a mistake that took months of trudging through government bureaus to correct.

Today the girls and boys are lucky. The patrols only arrest the Linkin Park fan on the charge of exhibiting a Western appearance. But Sara is not feeling well. This is her first brush with such an experience. Colour has drained from her face, and she keeps imagining her father clutching at his ailing heart and suffering a heart attack after hearing of her arrest in the company of a young man. If you have detected any similarities between Sara's father and Mr Petrovich, I emphatically deny them.

Besides, Sara must soon return home; her mother is undoubtedly worried. Even though news of incidents such as student protesters being beaten up in front of the university is not broadcast by the media, they quickly spread throughout the city by word of mouth. Sara and Dara exchange email addresses and bid the first scene of our story farewell.

Meanwhile, one of Sara's classmates wakes up in her shabby rented room in a building near Tehran University. She had known there would be demonstrations at the university and had found it more prudent to stay at home. She is a bookish student and doesn't want any trouble. All she wants is to get her degree as quickly as possible, return to her small town, find a job and help support her elderly parents who work two shifts a day . . . To prepare for her next exam, she was forced to stay up until four in the morning to memorize one hundred verses of poetry from one thousand years ago in their proper order. Exhausted, she opens her heavy eyelids. The first thing she remembers is that the night before she had forgotten to lock the door. She glances towards her small stereo – her only valuable possession – and, relieved to see it still there, she looks over at the door. Her eyes fill with horror.

A hunchback midget is sitting on the floor, leaning against the door with his legs spread apart. His head is hanging down on his chest, and his lifeless eyes are fixed on his thighs.

THE BOTTOMLESS WELL

In the next scene of our story, **it is midnight. A crescent moon, ~~resembling the Joker's sneering lips,~~ shines in the brown sky above Tehran. Sara, in her room, ~~under the sheets,~~ is whispering** quietly and having a computer chat with Dara. **Because she has no prior experience, she is especially cautious. ~~Although she may later become more daring.~~ Her parents are both well educated, but they are terrified that an evil hand may pluck their beautiful, sheltered flower. As a result, they strictly monitor her relationships.** Mr Petrovich will probably appreciate this segment, and he may pardon one of our story's future censor-worthy sentences.

Dara too is in his room whispering.

Ask me what they are whispering about, and I will say:

They are discussing "A Cliff Somewhere", a story by Shahriar Mandanipour.

Dara says:

"It is a cowardly story. Even if the man and woman cannot walk together in the street, even if they are too scared to sit in a café and talk, now that they are on top of a mountain, why don't they talk openly to each other? There are no patrols from the Campaign Against Social Corruption and no informers to call them."

Sara says:

"Remember that they are sitting beside an old, perhaps ancient, well."

"I haven't forgotten. The well actually exists on top of a mountain in Shiraz."

"A well that the townspeople believe is bottomless."

"Sara, I know all this. My question is, why do a man and a woman who were once in love now constantly talk in codes and metaphors? They can talk frankly about their problems. For example, the man can say that he realizes they are no longer in love. They were together for a certain period of time and used each other's bodies as much as they could, they secretly made love wherever they could. Maybe that is why their love was ruined."

"But that is not the point. The point is whether that well is really bottomless or not. The writer wants to tell you and me, his readers, that the physical relationship between a man and a woman is like that well. Perhaps at times it has a bottom, and perhaps at times no matter what you throw in it you will never hear it hit the bottom."

"No, you've misunderstood. Their problem is that they have gone too far in their physical relationship, so far that when making love they even bring images of other people to their bed. This is reaching the bottom of the well. But what I'm questioning is why the writer dragged this poor couple to the top of a mountain, if even there he has not had the guts to put frank and honest words in their mouths. There on top of the mountain, instead of talking, the two sit and throw stones in the well and try to hear them land at the bottom . . . Who in the world does that?"

"Well, if they spoke openly, the story would not have received a publishing permit."

"Excellent. That's why I say it's a cowardly story. The writer has played tricks to pass censorship. I don't like a writer who plays tricks. A writer who can trick the censorship apparatus can trick his readers, too."

"But if they had not sat next to that well, if they had not talked as though they did not need to say much, then there wouldn't be a story."

"Do you think it is a story?"

"I don't know. But it has somehow become mysterious. It makes me think."

If you think I am going to fit this dialogue into my love story, you are wrong. But the self-censorship is not because Dara did not like my story; it is because I don't want to give away a story that I happen to like and that I hope will one day receive a reprint permit. Therefore, I write

Dara says:

"I believe people in love don't need words, letters and conversations. They simply look at each other and read each other's thoughts. Just that."

Sara likes what Dara has said. She thinks the same way. The world's

lovers may have created the most captivating and the greatest number of stories in the world, but they have no need for words.

How about the need to meet? Precisely my problem. My lovers have to meet somewhere in order to read each other's eyes and mind.

In any case, Sara and Dara's innocent conversation leads to a discussion of film, Dara's favourite medium of art. Sara has no access to the black market for DVDs and videotapes, and has therefore not seen many films. **Dara reveals a small part of his life's secret to Sara.**

"It was because of film that I lost everything, even my future."

Sara knows that to learn the secrets of this strange man's life she has to be patient and to do away with superficial curiosities. Their conversation leads to films that they have recently seen on national television.

Just last night, after an entire month of advertising, a very old production of *Othello* was aired on Channel 2.

Dara asks:

"But did you see Desdemona in the movie at all?"

"Just in the last scene. They showed her dead body on the bed for a few seconds."

"I guess she was wearing a sleeveless low-cut dress in all the other scenes."

Dara has guessed correctly. And that is precisely why I will not only make no mention of my Sara's long black hair, but I will not even describe her without her headscarf and coverall – just like Iranian films that show women wearing a headscarf at all times, even in their homes. However, if one day an Iranian writer decides to describe the black cascade of his Sara's hair, the best trick is that same defamiliarization envisioned by Russian formalists. The writer can, without mentioning the word "hair", write: "Rippling, nightlike strands that flow from the living marble and that the black wind ushers towards the light . . ."

Dara talks to Sara about the happy times he had at the university and explains that because no company or business will hire him, he still lives with his parents . . . Sara explains that she is in her final year of studying literature at the university. Because she is familiar with the life of her author – me – she knows that with a degree in literature she shouldn't have high hopes of finding a job either. In Iran, whenever someone asked me about my job and I replied that I was a writer, they would immediately say, "I mean your job. What do you do?" This is because unlike Mr Petrovich and his superiors, ninety-nine point nine per cent of Iranians do not perceive literature as serious work.

Sara and Dara talk about chaste and saintly love, a love untainted by earthly lusts and desires. Together they voice the expression "Platonic love". It doesn't matter. Like many Iranians, they don't know that in his philosophy of Platonic love Plato was mostly concerned with well-proportioned young boys. The misunderstanding is due to errors made in translating Plato's writings, much the same way that another one of his works has been attributed to Aristotle and has been incorporated as such in the teachings at seminaries.

I don't know what the connection is between Plato and apples, but **Sara is now talking about the apple tree in the garden at her parents' house that is now, for the second time this season, full of blossoms.**

She wants me to give her a romantic sentence to speak. A sentence about the flight of the apple blossoms and their dance in the spring breeze of Tehran. But for different reasons, both Dara and I disagree with such a sentence.

Dara says bitterly:

"I really don't like apples. One of my recurring nightmares is that I bite into a red apple and realize that my teeth are left behind in it."

Dara's dislike of apples bears no association with the archetypal forbidden fruit, and I have told him time and time again that I am sick of using repetitive symbols, especially symbols that since the early days of Eve have all too often been manhandled. But my own opposition to the white apple blossoms dancing is more pragmatic than this. I remember years ago, in a story written by one of my friends, Mr Petrovich censored the sentence "The leaves fall dancing from the trees" because the word "dancing" is deemed vulgar and is forbidden.

It is now one o'clock in the morning. Sara says goodbye to Dara and quickly goes to sleep to have beautiful dreams . . .

Earlier than her, many people in Tehran, this city that once had one of the most beautiful and light-filled aerial views in the world, hoping for beautiful dreams, have turned out their lights and gone to sleep. The new government has decreed that all restaurants and food sellers must close at eleven o'clock at night so that citizens do not stay up late unnecessarily and harm their health. I remind you that for people in Iran the only night-time entertainment is to roam around the streets and to eat. Those who are wealthy go to restaurants, and the middle classes and below go to hamburger places. For a family or a few friends going out for a hamburger, by the time they make their way through the traffic from one end of town to the other to a hamburger place that looks like McDonald's, it takes three or four hours and kills the tedious evening. (Have you noticed the contrast between the philosophy underlying the concept of the hamburger in the West and the course of action required for eating a hamburger in Iran?) Now ask the question that is on your mind. Don't be timid. Ask.

And I will answer:

Fortunately, McDonald's does not exist in Iran. The daring ingenuity of the person who installed an M on the neon sign of his hamburger place lasted all of one day. On the second day, a group of people raided his eatery, burned it down and proclaimed that McDonald's was a symbol of the globe-devouring, McDonald's-eating America. The incident took place years before Mr Morgan Spurlock's experience in *Super Size Me*. You are therefore free to think that these people were concerned about Iranians gaining weight. Given this reasoning, we can be grateful for restaurants and food sellers having to close at eleven o'clock.

What do you suppose the imposed closing hour of restaurants has to do with literature?

Actually, there is a very subtle connection. What else is there to do for people who have nothing in particular to occupy their time with from seven to eleven in the evening? People who, incidentally, are too tired and stressed to engage in the task of increasing the Muslim population of the world, as has been implicitly suggested by the government. Yes, reading and taking refuge in Iranian literature await them.

By enforcing the directive to close restaurants, the government is in fact supporting literature . . . Mr Petrovich straight away disagrees with our conclusion.

"It is impossible for the government of Iran to support a corrupt and immoral literature that merely has its eyes on the West and its decadent sexual freedoms. Don't kid yourself . . ."

Mr Petrovich is right. To occupy the Iranian population's leisure time, the government has invested, and continues to invest, in television programmes and film series that, more often than not, portray writers, poets, and intellectuals as wimpy, bungling, unprincipled crooks and addicts, much in the same manner that Western spies are always portrayed as well-dressed men wearing ties. Perhaps the banning of ties in Iran – which I will elaborate on later – was because they can be perceived as an arrow pointing to a man's lower organ.

The clock hands in Tehran have just killed the hour of two in the morning. Sara is deep in sweet sleep. She is dreaming of the romantic poem *Khosrow and Shirin*. She sees herself standing beside a beautiful pond. The pond is like a mirror. Sara sees her reflection on the water. She is wearing a magnificent white dress, ~~like a princess's dress,~~ and around her beautiful neck a string of pearls glistens like the moon. Sara looks around to make sure no man is hiding behind the bushes ogling her. Then she slowly steps into the pond. When she is waist-deep in the water, the folds of her skirt, like the petals of a water lily, float and spread around h... She wades deeper into the pond. It is as if the water is purifying her body. Now the pearls on her necklace are floating around her neck, and their lustre has intensified. Their shimmer brightens the water and deepens Sara's delight. ~~With every step that she takes, she first sees the determined three-dimensional darts of her breasts, then the beautiful oval of her knees and her shapely calves~~ . . . Her pleasure is short-lived. She feels the weight of lecherous eyes on her shoulders. With a deep sense of foreboding she looks back at the dark bushes; fireflies are flickering around them. Suddenly ~~she feels the water directly touching the nakedness of her body~~, she sees her white dress, like a blossoming water lily, float towards the opposite shore. She reaches out to it. But the dress floats beyond her reach. She takes a step forward. The water reaches her thirsty lips, but her dress has floated even farther away. Panicked, with her hand reaching out towards her dress, she takes a long step forward. Contrary to her expectation, her foot does not reach the pond floor. It is as though a dragon has opened up its jaws underneath her. She is sucked into a bottomless abyss. She looks up. The silvery surface of the pond is moving away from her. Terrified, she realizes that the end of her dream has reached the beginning of her death. She feels the gaping maw and the repulsive stroke of the dragon's tongue against her calves . . . She struggles to pull herself up. The surface of the pond has changed to a murky green. As if she has inhaled flames, the cavities of her nostrils burn all the way up into her forehead. She can no longer hold the air caged in her lungs. She hears the sound of the bubbles bursting out. The dragon's scorching tongue is coiled around her body . . . Her eyes grow dark.

In that final moment when she has surrendered to drowning, she feels her head break the surface of the water on the other side of the world. She opens her burning eyes. She sees herself chest-deep in the sea. Around her in the water there are fully dressed women wearing headscarves. Shocked and terrified, they stare at her. A wave strikes against Sara's back. Seawater flows down her shoulders ~~and onto her hardened breasts that like the noses of two ships want to slice their way through the sea . . . The wave ebbs and the water sinks below Sara's breasts. The women point their fingers at her and scream in horror. Sara covers her floating breasts with her hands. Only then does she realize that she is in the women's section of the sea. Not far away, on either side, the area is closed off by green tarpaulin screens. The sun and salt water have corroded the fabric and it has ripped in several places. The rushing waves pull the torn sections back and forth, and half a mile away she can see fat and hairy bodies in the men's section of the sea.~~

I am pleased with the last sentences of this scene. While writing them, I reached a state of mind that I have named "the first lovemaking of writer and words". Every writer has met with his words time and again. They have had frequent conversations. They have even flirted with each other. But there are those rare moments when the shadows and the naked bodies of the writer and the words, in one time frame of the story, in one setting of the story, are coupled. They become two lovers who have long known each other and who in their clandestine meetings have frequently concealed their longing for one another. And now, for the first time, the writer and the words begin a strange lovemaking, like two ambisexual creatures that have created a new composition.

I am certain Mr Petrovich cannot find fault with Sara's Freudian nightmare, but he will surely dislike the scene where she emerges from the sea. Therefore, with my own hand, I have crossed out the scene to which I have briefly made love . . .

Do not pity me, dear reader! Wherever you are in this world, if you are lying in your bed in a high-rise building in New York and reading before sleep, do not pity me. If on a pleasant sunny day you are sitting in the Bois de Boulogne in Paris and reading, do not pity me. If in a bookstore, searching for a book to offer your lover, you have by chance opened this book and are reading these lines, do not pity me. Even if you have just ended your first carefree lovemaking with your new lover, and he has been lulled into serene sleep, and beside his bed you have found and opened this book, you have no right to pity Sara, Dara or me! Because the scenes and sentences that I cannot publish in my book, I will write in my mind, and given that until now no one has been able to read my thoughts and fantasies to punish me for them, I will make love to these words in the same way that Dara lives for the magic of cinema and falls in love and for his beloved he dreams up romantic novelties . . .

How?

This is just the story I now want to tell.

While Sara is swimming in the pond and the sea, on the other side of town, Dara is lying on his bed drowned in manly thoughts. To communicate his forbidden thoughts to my reader, stream of consciousness is the best trick. This time, however, I have not chosen this narrative ploy to meet the requirements of the story's form. Instead, I want to write seemingly confused lines, sentences without verbs, phrases in different tenses, all surfacing from the zigzagging of memory, and I want to write them in such a way that the images they produce, like Russian Matryoshka dolls, fit snugly inside one another. With this method, I hope to tiptoe softly around the walls of Mr Petrovich's cleverness and arrive at the wide-open plains of my reader's imagination and intelligence. Dara is contemplating Sara's white ankles – a sockless feminine ankle that peeks out from below trousers worn under a coverall is the sexiest image one can perceive in the streets of Tehran. On each of Sara's white ankles Dara has seen two cerulean veins that start below the ankles' projection, and after their rise and descent on the other side, they come together to create a pale purple vein that disappears under the hem of her trousers. Like two narrow streams that, after travelling a winding and twisting course, somewhere on the map meet, and their course often continues beyond the edge of the map.

Then, in Dara's stream of consciousness, I write

Step by step, white, reflection of light from the whiteness of two ankles on the blackness of the asphalt . . . Step by step, white, two cerulean veins on the whiteness of ankles, inspiration for the inventors

of script among the reed beds cradled by the Tigris and Euphrates . . . The flight of a dry autumn leaf alongside two cerulean rivers that remind autumn of the greenness of spring . . . Two rivers part and give birth . . . Two connected lines in the palm of my hand, one the line of my life, one the line of my death, one the line of my solitude, one the line of your solitude, Sara . . . And I fall upon the shores of a copper-coloured pond. On the far side, a flamingo with crimson flames licking beneath its wings stands on one leg and dreams of migrating. On the horizon I see the dark cylinder of the Tower of Babel against the light, erect and solid it has risen towards the sky, and from its peak a cream-coloured cloud pours down, the fountain of blind men's fantasies, the fountain of inspiration for flamingos that migrate with purgatories beneath their wings . . . Sara . . . Sara . . .

After I write these lines, Dara's perspiring and provoked stream of consciousness cuts to an image of gruelling march exercises at the military base. To the sound of masculine heaves, muscular, booted legs rise in unison, and with the power that raised and ruined the Tower of Babel and the towers of Metropolis, they pound against the belly of Mother Earth. Now, **Dara's mind, in *Remembrance of Things Past*, travels to a childhood memory of his grandmother. The old woman tells a seven-year-old Dara to stick his fingers in his ears.**

"What do you hear, my boy?"

"It sounds like the wind . . ."

"No, press your fingers deeper into your ears. Listen! What do you hear?"

"It sounds like the roar of fire."

"Excellent! This roaring fire is that same hell into which we descend for our sins. There are snakes there as long as streets from fear of which sinners take refuge with the dragons. Pits filled with boiling pungent water, our bodies blister, we burn to a crisp."

Suddenly Dara feels a burning sensation in his hand. He jerks his arm away from its proximity to Sara's bare arm which he has seen in his mind's eye. Dara's stream of consciousness continues, and here I must be able to write with even greater creativity than James Joyce, because the last effort made by Joyce, his Iranian translator and his publisher to obtain a publishing permit for the Farsi translation of *Ulysses* met with failure. At the time, Mr Petrovich, who tried to be lenient with Iranian writers and translators and wanted somehow to work out their problems, suggested that the stream of consciousness voiced by Molly, the female character who has visions of adultery, be printed in Italian in the Farsi translation. Thus, not only would the book not suffer heavy censorship, but the Iranian reader would not suffer sexual provocation . . . In Italian, not in English, because Italian is not a widely known language in Iran, and curious readers would not be able to find a dictionary quickly to translate the sentences and become sexually aroused.

Still, I have too many problems of my own to worry about Joyce's publishing predicaments in Iran. One of my current problems is that **in his room, as on so many other nights, Dara is suffering from insomnia. Sara's voice still echoes in his ears and in his thoughts.** He remains in a dreadful struggle with himself, so that other than Sara's ankles, he imagines the rest of her body only in a coverall and headscarf. Not only because his sexual abstinence will otherwise be compromised, but because **he believes that if he imagines Sara in any way other than what she herself has allowed, he will have betrayed her . . . and he finally concludes that to avoid being unfaithful to Sara's image, he must try to drive her out of his mind. Therefore, as on so many other sleepless nights, Dara lies down on his back and stares at the white ceiling. If he can slowly forget the weight of his body, if he can concentrate, if he can stop himself from blinking even when his eyes begin to fill with tears, after about an hour, little by little, magical colours will begin to emerge on the white of the ceiling like water stains, they will connect, and a full-colour image will appear before his eyes.** The image of a blind Al Pacino dancing with that beautiful stranger in *Scent of a Woman*. The scene has always brought tears to Dara's eyes. Years ago, one of his dreams was to see this film, and his other favourite films, on a large screen with surround-sound so that he could enjoy the full frame of the film and the director's work. Yet, in the past twenty years, *Dances with Wolves* has been one of the very few American films that has been screened in cinemas in Iran. Of course, after having been censored. Therefore, it is impossible for Dara to see the beautiful dance of a blind man with a stunning woman on a cinema screen. However, one of Dara's secrets is that he doesn't need to go to the cinema ever again. For him, the magic of cinema, not the magic that you see on IMAX screens around the world but the real magic of cinema, started several years ago. It started when he served seven months in solitary confinement.

Most likely you have no concept of the agony and horror of a solitary prison cell, and by no means do I want to reproach you for this. In fact, I want to congratulate you for having led such a civilized life that you have no understanding of what solitary confinement is like. Anyhow, as I write these sentences, I find it likely that at some point in time I will be confined to a solitary cell for having written them. I don't know whether I can find a way to survive and not to break in a windowless cell so small that one cannot sleep with outstretched legs.

Dara was arrested for hiring out and selling videotapes of banned and immoral films.

Now you may say:

So your story's Dara is not as squeaky clean and as upstanding a character as you have described, because he used to deal in porn films.

You are wrong. Dara was hiring out and selling copies of cinematic masterpieces, and only films by his favourite directors such as John Ford, Hitchcock, Orson Welles, Antonioni, Bergman, Kubrick, Polanski, Oliver Stone, Jarmusch, David Lynch and . . .

Now ask:

Do you really mean to tell us Dara was thrown into solitary confinement for selling and hiring out artistic masterpieces of the cinema?

So that I can answer:

No. In my beloved land no one is sentenced to solitary confinement for distributing banned films, unless he is believed to be an agent of the CIA or MI6 and on a mission to destabilize the moral, cultural and religious values of Iranian society, and particularly if he has previously been implicated in anti-revolution activities. Please don't say anything. I know the plot has become more snarled. We must therefore visit the past. As I mentioned earlier, the story is that, years ago, Dara was arrested for being a member of a leftist political party, and he was sentenced to two years in prison. While in prison, he had signed several sworn statements that after his release he would no longer participate in any political or anti-revolution activities. On his second day of freedom, Dara visited the Fine Arts College of Tehran University to see what his status as a student was. Prior to his arrest, he had completed all the required credits for film direction. To earn his degree, he had only to hand in his thesis, a comparative and semiotic study of *The Trial*, directed by Orson Welles, and *The Trial*, written by Franz Kafka.

At the college, no file or record belonging to a former student named Dara M. can be found. After searching for some time, the impatient, newly hired clerk returns to his desk, looks suspiciously at Dara, and asks:

"What did you say your name was?"

"Dara . . . Dara M. . . . brother."

In those days, it was quite common and highly advisable for a man to be addressed as "brother" and a woman as "sister", instead of "sir" or "madam".

The clerk behaves as though he is dealing with a deranged lunatic.

"Are you sure that is your name?"

"Yes, brother."

"What kind of a name is Dara? You should go to the General Register Office tomorrow and change it. They have a list of all the good names there. In case you don't already know, Dara was the name of a tyrant, pagan, idolater king who used to attack Arabia and capture Muslims seven hundred years ago. He used to pierce a hole in their shoulders and run a rope through it so that they wouldn't escape."

Dara, trying to mask his anger, says:

"First of all, Dara was king about two thousand years ago. Second, at the time, the Prophet of Islam had not even been born. Third, Dara was not a pagan, and as a matter of fact Alexander, who attacked Iran and brought about Dara's death, is the one who was the idolater. Fourth, the king who pierced holes in the Arabs' shoulders was Shapour. And if only he had not done so, the Arabs would have escaped, tasted freedom and later a group of them would not have created the Baath Party and Al Qaeda . . ."

Dara stops himself. The new clerk is glaring at him with a look that suggests:

Kid, your words are bigger than your mouth.

Still, Dara continues. "Fifth, when I was born, the name Dara was in first-year reading books."

The clerk bursts into laughter:

"So, little Dara, you're still in the first year. Why are you here saying you were a university student? Get out of here and don't bother me again."

Dara protests:

"Sir, why are you making fun of me? I was a student at this college two years ago."

71

The clerk raises his voice:

"Listen, boy, you dimwit, how many times do I have to tell you, we did not and do not have a student named Dara M. I spent a lot of time looking for your name in the computer system, and then I searched through all the archived files."

He shows Dara his dust-covered hands. From his pocket, Dara pulls out his transcripts, all with excellent marks, and shows them to the clerk.

The clerk glances at the documents and throws them down on his desk.

"I will do you a favour and ignore these scraps of paper."

"Brother, I don't need you to do me any favours. These are documents that this very college gave to me."

"Now I'm sure you've lost your mind. Look here, I can simply call security and have them arrest you."

"On what charge?"

"On the charge of forging confidential university documents."

"But these documents are authentic. Look, they have the seal and signature of the university principal."

The clerk carefully examines the seal and signature of the university principal.

"Forget it! The brother who used to be the university principal was dismissed last year, and now he sells tickets at some cinema. Go and see him, maybe he'll give you a job."

"Then you agree that these documents are not forgeries?"

"Don't insist that I agree. If I do, I will have to call university security to come and arrest you."

"On what charge?"

"Theft. Do you know how long the prison sentence is for stealing government documents?"

"You mean to suggest that I stole my transcripts from the university archives?"

"Yes. Precisely."

"Well, if I stole these transcripts from the university archives, then I must have been a student here."

"No, you were not, because we only trust the documents that we ourselves have."

"If I accept that I stole my transcripts from the university, then you must accept that I was a student here."

"Who do you think you are to tell me what I should or should not accept?"

"First of all, I'm not telling, I'm truly asking. Second, I am a nobody, I'm not even a human being, I am these scraps of paper that prove I was a student here."

The clerk pounds his fist on his desk.

"No, you were not. According to our documents you were not."

"Then put it in writing and give it to me."

"I can't do that. If I do, starting tomorrow there will be a thousand nutcases like you queuing up here asking for affidavits that they were not students here."

Dara finally loses his temper and yells:

"I will file a complaint. I will go to the university principal and file a complaint."

"Go and see any idiot you want."

Their quarrel escalates. Now Dara is yelling like a madman and flailing his arms. Two other newly employed clerks come to their colleague's aid and, not so politely and not so impolitely, they throw Dara out of the building. Confused, shaking with anger, ready to cry from despair, Dara sits next to the box trees of Tehran University. He is sitting exactly where, years later, a hunchback midget will fall and hit his head against a cement edge . . . Dara watches the students walking out of the old college buildings of Tehran University with envy. He doesn't know Mr Petrovich, otherwise he would have recognized him among the doctoral students of literature, who, with his Chinese-made Samsonite briefcase, wearing telltale facial stubble and a white untucked shirt, haughtily distances himself from the undergraduate students.

And Dara sees Jafar ibn-Jafri, hefty tomes in hand, heading towards the College of Physics. A smile of recognition appears on the man's lips, but he quickly regrets this and turns away from Dara. Dara sighs.

"What should I do? What should I do?"

He is starting to think that perhaps he was never a university student, and that all the sweet memories he has are fantasies from his prison days. But just as he begins to doubt even his own name and wants to head home to see whether he has only imagined their house, too, someone

73

calls his name from the other side of the box trees. Dara peeks behind the trees and sees one of the old college employees sitting there. Trying to keep his voice down, and without looking at Dara, the old employee hurriedly says:

"Don't look at me, boy. Sit right there with your back turned to me and just listen."

Dara sits back down and listens to the old employee whisper.

"You dimwit! What did you come here for? You've been expelled from the university. Don't make unnecessary trouble for yourself. Go home and think of something else to do with your future."

Dara bursts into tears.

"But I studied here for six years. All my marks were excellent."

"Whatever . . . I took a risk out of sympathy and came here to give you some advice . . . Don't cry, you're a man. Men don't cry. Get up and go home; and don't tell anyone I talked to you. Many of the old employees were purged. My file is on the purging committee's desk, too. Go and be strong, boy . . . Goodbye."

Dara followed the old employee's advice and decided to be strong and not be a burden to his family. He set out to look for work. But month after month as he grew stronger, he realized more and more that finding a job was impossible. Hoping to find work in his favourite field of study, he naively applied to the television stations, but as soon as they found out that he used to be a political prisoner they politely showed him the door. Dara applied to the film-making studios, hoping that perhaps they would give him a job on one of their productions, those very films that he considered mundane and moronic. (In those days, the creative directors of Iranian cinema were restricted to their homes and barred from working.) After the film production companies, Dara headed for the advertising agencies, those very agencies that he had in the past deemed to be the make-up artists for the vulgar face of the bourgeoisie. By now he was no longer a Communist, nor was he a socialist or a liberal. In other words, he had successfully become a man with no political convictions.

Even at home, when his mother would complain about the rising cost of life's necessities, Dara would say:

"Mother! You too? All this is a rumour spread by the anti-revolutionaries. According to government statistics, inflation in Iran is only five per cent, which is quite normal."

74

Of course, without his mother noticing, he would try to eat less bread and rice.

In any case, when Dara gave up hope of ever finding a proper job, he thought of turning to the illegal occupation of selling and hiring out films. At the time, cinemas that had survived the torchings of the early days of the revolution were facing bankruptcy because screening Western films was banned, and the state-operated television stations, other than a few mind-numbing series and chat shows on morality and ethics, kept rerunning a handful of old films. Even if they wanted to broadcast new films, they couldn't. The station managers, as well as we, the Iranian population, had newly discovered that there are very few films in the world that do not feature women, and fewer yet in which women adhere to the Islamic dress code.

As a result, while VCRs and videotapes were banned, a significant number of Iranians owned a decrepit Sony T7 or a newer VCR model. From Dara's point of view, his work was neither illegal nor immoral because unlike the underground networks that dealt in American action films, porn films and trashy films made in India and Hong Kong, he only sold and hired out copies of the world's cinematic masterpieces. The problem, however, was that he had very few clients interested in his films, and their numbers were dwindling by the day. Apparently, tastes were changing, and some Iranians were growing particularly fond of a certain genre of shoddy Iranian films made before the revolution. During the Shah's regime, these films were often made in only a week and featured characters that were, by and large, thugs, lowlifes and prostitutes, and they generally featured scenes of the thugs drinking in cheap nightclubs with half-naked fat women singing and dancing, followed by a brawl between the drunken thugs. Often, a dancing girl or prostitute would fall in love with the knife-wielding thug and would regret her profession. Then the chivalrous thug would beat the mean thugs to a pulp and take the dancer or prostitute to a holy place and pour the water of repentance over her head and they would get married and live happily ever after.

It was under such circumstances that Dara believed his work to be a truly valuable cultural endeavour, and he was sure that if he were ever arrested, as soon as the officers saw his inventory of films, they would actually commend him. But one night as he was leaving a client's home on foot, a patrol car from the Campaign Against Social Corruption pulled up next to him. The officers searched his bag and discovered seven videotapes. *The Trial, One Flew Over the Cuckoo's Nest, Z, Blowup*, the uncensored version of Tarkovsky's *The Mirror*, Bahram Beizai's *Downpour* and the animated *Snow White and the Seven Dwarfs*.

If Dara, during his interrogation at the bureau of the Campaign Against Social Corruption, had cooperated, expressed regret and written down the names and addresses of all his clients on the investigation report, he would have been sentenced to only a few months in prison, or sixty or seventy lashes or just a monetary fine. Contrary to his assumptions, the interrogator was not a harsh man. He was a young man, about the same age as Dara, who wore prescription glasses with very thick lenses. In a dark, dank room, he sat behind a rusty metal desk covered with dents. Dara stood in front of the desk. The interrogator looked into his innocent eyes with kindness and curiosity and in a gentle voice said:

"I don't believe you are a corrupt person."

Dara equally gently replied:

"Brother, in this world everyone claims to be the best human being. But only God knows who is good, who is bad . . . I have studied a little."

Even more gently the interrogator said:

"In my line of work I come across all sorts of people. From illiterates and louts to university graduates and professors. Once they even arrested someone who had two doctorate degrees, economics and – I don't know – management of something or other."

"Well, brother, there are no jobs out there."

"I think if an illiterate person who grew up on the streets and who cannot tell right from wrong gets into distributing vile films, he is less guilty than the educated person who does it."

"You are absolutely right. I completely agree with you."

Dara saw the young interrogator's eyes fill with sorrow, and he heard a telltale voice of deep-rooted pain.

"Everyone says the same thing. When you are arrested, you are all immediately sorry and ask for forgiveness."

"But I was being sincere."

"I don't want to insult you and others like you. But I just don't understand why you get involved in such filthy rackets. When you walk out of here, you simply serve your sentence and go on with your lives. But what about the likes of me? I cannot stop thinking of why people commit such

crimes and sins. I feel sorry for you. This very night I will see your innocent face in my dreams, and I will have to get up and pray for you."

The young interrogator's face now resembled that of a tortured saint.
Dara said:

"Thank you for your sympathy."

"Are you mocking me?"

"No . . . Not at all."

"I sensed it in your voice. You were being sarcastic."

"I swear I wasn't. I am truly grateful. But I find it very strange that
someone like you, here . . ."

"It is exactly people like me who should be here. Here, this department, organizations similar to ours, have the most sensitive responsibility.
If we can eradicate social corruption, we can claim that the revolution has
successfully turned its final corner. We can then show our revolution to
the entire world and invite the people of the world, especially the corrupt
Westerners, to follow our lead."

The young interrogator's eyes were brimming with tears, and he was
pressing his hands against his temples. In the same sad and suffering
voice he asked:

"Then why? Why do you do such things? How can you swallow food
that was bought with ill-gotten gains . . . How does your conscience allow
you to sleep at night when you know that with your vile tapes you have
corrupted the pure and innocent souls of hundreds of youths?"

"But brother, my conscience is clear, at least as far as what I have done.
I don't corrupt anyone's soul. Quite the opposite, I allow my clients to see
excellence. I teach them that there is still beauty in this world. The
beauty of art, creativity . . ."

Wide-eyed, the young interrogator stared at Dara:

"What do you mean? You just said that you agreed with me."

"I say it again. I too believe that people who hire out out worthless
films are doing a bad thing. But I rent out films by Altman, Forman,
Kubrick and Welles."

"These people, where are they from?"

"They're Americans . . . Have you ever seen Orson Welles's *The Trial*?"

"No."

"You have to see it, brother. You have to see it . . . The film is based on
Kafka's novel *The Trial*."

"Where is Kafka from?"

"He was from Czechoslovakia."

"You mean he was a Communist?"

"No . . . He was Jewish."

"So he was a Zionist?"

"No, he was just a Jew."

"Well, Marx was Jewish, too."

"No, Kafka was an artist. His novel is a literary masterpiece. In most cases when cinema has wanted to adapt a literary masterpiece to film it has failed, except . . ."

Dara, who had a tendency of becoming quite excited whenever there was talk of film and cinema, had forgotten where and in what situation he was. He passionately continued the discussion.

"In rare cases . . . I consider Orson Welles's *The Trial* to be one of the masterpieces of cinema that has gone unappreciated. It is even better than *Citizen Kane*. *The Trial* is very rich in semiology. Whenever there is a discussion of this film, to prove that the codes of cinematic language are different from those of literary language, I use the example of the American version of *War and Peace*. The film has completely failed. I will never forget, the minute I laid eyes on Mel Ferrer as Prince Andrei, I burst out laughing. The guy doesn't have the dignity and majesty of Prince Andrei at all."

"Are you a monarchist?"

"Not at all. Allow me to finish."

"Go ahead. I'm listening."

"I mean, the art of cinema can be even more powerful and more beautiful than literature."

"We believe this, too. Our enemies know very well how effective and destructive cinema can be. The Americans have tested this, and they have learned that they cannot bring our revolution to its knees with coups d'état and wars, so they have resorted to exporting filthy films to weaken the will and faith of our youth."

"I agree with you. I completely agree. But . . . Am I giving you a headache?"

"No, not at all. Speak. Your comments are new to me. I have never come across anyone like you in this place."

"Don't you realize that some people are starting to like those trashy films that were made before the revolution? Well, why do you think that is?"

The young interrogator was avidly listening to Dara. He said:

"Tell me. I find this interesting."

Dara was gasping from the excitement of the discourse and the stifling dank air in the room. He continued:

"Whenever I hear one of my compatriots praising a corny Iranian or Indian film, I am angered to the point of madness."

The young interrogator interrupted him:

"I see you are very angry."

"I am sorry, brother. But to tell you the truth, I am furious."

"Go ahead, throw a punch, kick."

"Excuse me?"

"If it's going to calm you down, take your anger out on this desk. I don't want you to speak in anger . . . In Islam it is a sin to speak in anger."

With a kick Dara added another dent to the many dents in the desk and actually felt his rage and angst over his arrest subside. Calmly, he continued,

"Well, you have to allow the likes of me to continue our work and to introduce the art of cinema to people. The language of cinema has its own distinct codes. People have to learn these codes. Once they do, they will completely relate to the language of cinema."

It was here that the young interrogator's eyes sparkled.

"Codes? There are codes in films?"

"Yes. Much work has been done on the science of semiotics, on the semiology of film, and on imagery codes in general."

"Do you know these codes?"

"Somewhat. To the extent that my education allows, I try to recognize them."

"I knew from the start that you were different from the regular dealers of filthy films. I suspected you were a well-read intellectual and a smart person. What did you study?"

"I studied cinema to postgraduate level."

"You mean you've got a master's?"

"No . . . They didn't give me my degree."

"Why?"

Dara truthfully confessed that he had previously committed political errors and that he had even spent some time as a political prisoner.

The young interrogator was again pressing his hands against his temples. Instead of the glint of curiosity, again the fog of sorrow floated in his eyes. But patiently he encouraged Dara to continue, and for another two hours he listened to his arguments and reasonings and took notes. Finally, when Dara grew silent from exhaustion and sat down on the floor next to his desk, the young interrogator got up and respectfully shook his hand. With Dara's file under his arm, he paused at the door and said:

"I have learned some interesting things from you. Thank you . . . I will pray for you."

Dara was sure the interrogator had left the room to arrange his release. But in the middle of the night two officers came and blindfolded him and transferred him to the special prison for political detainees.

In fact, by confessing to his political past, together with the strange films they had taken from him as evidence and his comments about codes in the language of cinema, Dara had made matters worse. Anyone in the young interrogator's place would have been equally suspicious that Dara was in fact playing the same role that Radio Free Europe had played from behind the Iron Curtain – and, even more important, that by deciphering codes hidden in certain films he was also involved in undercover activities.

Dara was transferred to a high-security prison and thrown into a small, solitary confinement cell so that he would come to his senses and reveal the names of his contact or contacts at that spy agency and divulge the so-called codes. Time in a small cell is more pitiless and painful than any instrument of torture. The agony of solitary confinement is not that time seems to pass extremely slowly, it is that it seems not to pass at all. Dara could not tell night from day. He had lost the comfort and pleasure of the passage of time. After a while, which for the people outside was two months, he realized that he was dancing like Zorba the Greek up the stairway to insanity. He constantly talked to himself and could not tell whether this was good or bad for his mental stability.

Sometimes tears would well up in his eyes, and the desire to weep would lump up in his throat, but a mysterious energy would stop him from giving in to the tears. This energy had perhaps permeated the walls of his cell from the resistance of past prisoners, and it was now reflecting itself on him. Now and again, he would recall memories his father had shared with him about his own time in prison – which I will tell you about later. Dara would think about the tricks his father and others in his cell block would use to strengthen their spirits, although they were not all that useful to Dara, because each prisoner, much like his unique fingerprint, has his own individual resistance and breaking point.

Sometime later, he noticed that on one of the cement walls, the wall to the right, he could see strange shapes formed by the configuration of the small pores and the tiny grains of sand. A sheep with dragon's wings, a heart pierced with a spoon instead of an arrow, the face of a man whose eyes were two female genitals, a pair of scissors with its blades curved in the shape of smiling lips, and, most interesting and familiar of all, a figure that looked a lot like Dopey, the youngest dwarf in *Snow White and the Seven Dwarfs*.

Searching for these images became a good pastime for Dara. The problem, however, was that they did not last. If he focused too much on them, they would fade away. The moment he would wake up, he would look to where he had seen the last one, but he would not find it. The cold and cruel cement would have regained its imageless quality. The pictures appeared at their own will. But it seemed as if their appearance and disappearance had some particular sequence and time interval. Thus, the cement images became Dara's clock and calendar. If to escape the silence and timelessness of the cell he had previously wished that they would come and even wake him up from his sleep for another round of intense interrogation with the same old questions and the same old answers, he now wished that they would somehow forget about him altogether. In the next phase, he tried to bring the appearance of the images under his control. Now, without fearing the progression of insanity, he comfortably spoke to the cement wall. To remain focused during the course of the conversation, he even etched an ear and a mouth on the wall with his fingernail. He reached a stage that when he spoke to the ear, images would appear in the periphery of his field of vision. At one point, he didn't know whether it was day or night; he suddenly thought that the mouth resembled the toothless mouth of Steve McQueen in *Papillon*. It was the mouth of a man who has aged prematurely but who has triumphantly survived solitary confinement, and now that they have released him, a strange smile has formed on his creased lips. Remembering Papillon's superhuman resistance strengthened Dara's will. He reached a point when he could complete the missing features around the ear and mouth and see Steve McQueen's face. Then he decided to see a more pleasant image from the magical world of cinema, and a sequence of superimposed kisses from *Cinema Paradiso* appeared before his eyes. Dara didn't know whether this irony was rooted in his own subconscious or in the subconscious of the cement. But he knew he was committing a sin and that he might, under these very difficult circumstances, lose God's benevolence and forgiveness.

In fact, even when Dara was a Communist, unlike some Communists, he had not been able to erase God from deep within his heart. In those days, when he read the *Manifesto* over and over again so that its words would be etched on his brain cells, he felt that from somewhere deep in his soul a whisper of shame rose and echoed in his ear, in that same place where Grandmother had told him to stuff his fingers . . . But in those days of discovering the pleasures of rebelliousness and defiance, he could not understand from where this whisper rose and because of whom. Until at last, during his first prison term, Dara discovered that all that time he had been ashamed of himself before God, his childhood companion. And just as every night he would remove the pus-encrusted bandages from his feet and inspect the infected whip wounds on his soles, and just as hour by hour he would hunt fleas from his underarms or pubic hair, and because he did not have the heart to kill them he would send them off to the prison guards from under the cell door, he set aside the philosophical theory of materialism and began talking to his God. In the early days of his rediscovered faith, Dara did not allow himself to take advantage of God's mercy and compassion. He believed that if under those difficult circumstances he asked anything of God, his belief would in fact be insincere and, like so many others, he would be foolishly attempting to deceive a God that is all-knowing. But many months later, when he felt that, just as for the prophet Jonah in the stomach of a great fish, God had forgiven him, too, he asked God to do something so that they would release him. And now, too, during his second term in prison, he was ashamed of seeing images of censored kisses from *Cinema Paradiso* and wanted God to do something so that he would stop seeing them.

At last, his visual creativity grew so strong that he would first make a white cinema screen appear on the cement wall and then the moving pictures of a scene from a film. The first scene he watched in full cinematic clarity and brilliance – having begged for absolution from God, the most creative director in the world – was the scene in which Stan Laurel clenches his fist, stuffs tobacco in it as if it were a pipe, lights it, and sucks on his raised thumb and blows smoke out of his mouth. By remaking this scene, Dara laughed for the first time during his solitary confinement. Hearing Dara's laughter, the prison guard most probably thought this prisoner too had gone completely insane, and from then on he no longer threw Dara's food in front of him; instead, with respect and kindness he gently put it on the floor in front of the cell door. Dara's interrogator too had changed his behaviour towards him. Not because he thought Dara had gone mad, but because he saw that this prisoner, with perseverance, with no hesitation or weakness, and, most important, with no duplicity, had stuck to his initial statement and refused to confess to being a spy . . . Now, Dara could even will the scene of the film he was watching to run in slow motion, and if he felt like watching one of the classics, such as *Casablanca,* he could watch it in full colour. Yet his love of cinema was so true that he would immediately feel that by colourizing the film he had cheated on his lover.

One day he watched a seven-hour version of *Titanic.* Don't rush to tell me that no such version exists. I know. Dara knew it too. What is interesting is that Dara had never even seen James Cameron's *Titanic.* He had only read news of its production and a synopsis of its screenplay, accompanied by two hazy close-ups of the leading actors, in a film magazine. They had even printed a black stripe over Kate Winslet's neck. But Dara's willpower and abilities were greater than those of any Hollywood producer. With an investment of lengthy meditations, he was able to screen his own *Titanic* on the cement wall.

Producing *Titanic* did not bring Dara fame and Oscars, but it did bring him something far more important. At the very moment when his film's two lovers bid each other eternal farewell, Dara realized that he had never fallen in love. Yes, it was true that he was, and had been, in love with cinema, and it was true that in his solitary cell he could even make love to cinema whenever he wanted to without having to tolerate the headaches and consequences of making love to a woman. But at that moment he realized that something had always been missing in his life: love, in its true sense, for a woman. Therefore, he earnestly asked his

God that should he one day be released from this prison, to bestow upon him the gift of love . . . And the miracle happened far sooner than he expected. Dara's interrogator finally accepted the fact that he was not a CIA agent. One day, which Dara only later realized was day, the guards opened the door to his cell and politely asked him to walk out. Dara, who really did not want to part with his cell and its magic wall, did not budge. After all, he was watching Hitchcock's *Vertigo*. The guards were forced to drag a kicking and screaming Dara out of the cell and out of the prison. Confused and disoriented by the natural sunlight, Dara walked home. His mother cried out as soon as she saw him and held him in her arms. Dara wept on her shoulder not knowing whether these were tears of joy or sorrow. That day, when he saw his face in the mirror, he was horrified. His skin had turned the colour of camphor, and his cheeks were so hollowed that his beautiful Aryan nose protruded like the beak of a bald eagle. A month later he had chosen painting as a vocation and had joined the public library . . . It was there that he saw Sara for the first time . . .

On the day Dara saw Sara and thought this was the girl he should fall in love with, back in Shiraz, I was afflicted with a familiar attack of discovering my own loneliness. From time to time I suffer this emotional attack, especially when I am happy, when I have succeeded at something, and on those rare occasions when I am pleased with myself. Immediately, a gentle, soothing sorrow engulfs my entire being. In truth, I have always seen myself as a lonely person, even though I have very good friends, even though I have a kind family. The attack of discovering one's loneliness is different from the common feelings of loneliness . . . Although my work is to grapple with words, I have no words with which to describe and explain this feeling. Perhaps I write stories to show that in life there are moments, emotions, and events that cannot be explained with words.

On that autumn day, I headed for the old garden estates of Shiraz. It was drizzling. There were hardly any passers-by in the narrow, winding alleys between the mud walls surrounding the gardens. The winds of previous days had piled the dry leaves at the foot of the walls, and now the rain was weighing them down. The poet who died seven hundred years ago was standing at the end of the alley sending inspiration for one of his most beautiful *ghazal*s to himself seven hundred years back.

They have closed the tavern door O God do not approve,
for they open the door to deceit and hypocrisy . . .

Then he held his thirsty mouth open to the sky to drink the dust of
centuries-old grapevines in the drops of rain. With no need for words we
waved to each other. I retraced my steps. Years ago this poet had inspired
me to write one of my rare love stories. In that story, I wrote of the dust of
his body scattered across the city of Shiraz, and I wrote that he believes
the more people can create true and lasting love, the more his dust will
gather and he will come to acquire form and colour. Lucky him and lucky
those who can fall in love.

I was deep in such thoughts when I realized I was walking along Zand
Avenue. The crowded pavements of one of Shiraz's oldest avenues can
exaggerate as well as console one's sense of loneliness. After every rain,
ghosts of the perfumes of roses that blossomed and withered seven hundred years ago, and ghosts of the aromas of wines that poets drank in
secret seven hundred years ago, are released in the air in Shiraz. One side
of the street is lined with stores that sell cheap clothes made in China,
and the other side with maple trees. Their leafless branches reach up to
the clouds like nerves, and ghosts of their winged samaras twirl as they
rain down on the street.

Suddenly I see Mr Petrovich walking towards me. Years have passed
since I first met him. He must have come to Shiraz on holiday. I try to
hide behind the pedestrians, but he sees me and walks towards me.

"How are you? You look like a drenched mouse . . . What are you doing
here?"

"I'm well. I was just out for a walk."

"I noticed you were deep in thought. Has something happened?"

"No, not at all. I was just thinking."

"What were you thinking about?"

"About how wonderful it would be if we could not think at all."

Mr Petrovich stares into my eyes. I freeze. I feel he is capable of reading people's minds. He says:

"It's been a while since I heard anything about that love story you
wanted to write."

I didn't know that, years later, I would attempt to write a love story, but
he knew. I say:

"I haven't decided to write a love story yet. I am sometimes tempted, but I won't find the courage for some time."

"Why?"

"As you know, writing a love story is as difficult as starting a love affair and holding on to it."

"You surprise me. You are comfortable sharing your feelings with me."

"I surprise myself, too. I always censor myself with others, but when it comes to you, something makes me pour my heart out."

The two jagged blades of his eyes take aim at me.

"Look, this isn't all some kind of pantomime, is it? You haven't got some trick up your sleeve, have you?"

"I don't think so."

Women in black coveralls and men wearing dark, shabby clothes and muddy shoes pass by. High above the street, a flying carpet, drop by drop, melts in the rain. Turquoise and ochre-coloured raindrops fall onto the city. The carpet shrinks and flies away.

Mr Petrovich, in that persistently suspicious tone, says:

"I am familiar with the temperament of you writers. I know you are fragile and sensitive. That's why the cursed devil targets you more than it does ordinary people. He tries to tempt and deceive you into writing things that are not in your best interests. I wonder if you realize that I only want what is best for the likes of you?"

"Thank you for your concern."

"Are you mocking me?"

"No . . . not at all."

"I sensed sarcasm in your voice."

"No. I truly am grateful. But I do find it strange that someone like you . . ."

"Well, people like me need a holiday too, once in a while. We can't sit in a room all our lives reading rubbish books."

What is left of my energy to speak is rapidly draining. A long silence prevails. As always, I try to avoid meeting Mr Petrovich's eyes.

"I honestly feel some sort of friendly intimacy towards you. I sense you are thinking of writing things that you shouldn't write, and that if you do, writing them will not have been in your best interests. It's like thinking of killing someone when you have no rational reason for doing so. Be careful not to kill your innocence by thinking of forbidden things."

"I am sure I have killed the desire to kill in my soul by killing plenty of fictitious characters."

"In this world of reckoning and retribution, there are all sorts of killings. Remember, thinking of sin is itself a sin. You writers should know that if the thought of writing a sinful story enters your mind, your sin is far greater than that of an ordinary person, because your sin infects the minds of your readers, and the more readers you have, the greater your sin. Do you understand?"

"I understand, brother . . ."

To change the subject, in a voice that seems to come from the pit of a well, I say:

"While in Shiraz, be sure to visit the Vakil Bazaar. If you can manage not to forget that it was built hundreds of years ago, in some corner you will see a pedlar who sells talismans and spells for making wishes come true. You can ask him for a spell that would stop all Iranian writers from ever thinking of a sinful scene. If you buy this spell, it will not only ease your mind, but it will also ease the minds of us writers."

"What delicacies does this Shiraz of yours have that one can take back as gifts?"

"Well, just as pomegranates from Saveh are famous, or almonds from wherever and corals from some sea, before the revolution, wine from Shiraz was famous. But after the revolution, well . . . Now they make Shiraz wine in Australia and California."

"Where did you get such accurate information? Don't tell me you've been – "

"No, not at all . . . One of my friends told me . . . I'm sorry, brother, I'm not feeling well. If you don't mind, I have to return home."

Shiraz, too, is a city that oscillates in time; its past seasons, even its past hundreds of years, mirror on its present time. I walk away. For a long time I feel the weight of Mr Petrovich's eyes on the back of my neck. I turn round and look back. He is still standing there, watching me. This time, his fluid shape-shifting face has a short brow, an Arab nose, Mongol eyes and thick, greasy lips that look as if he has just eaten fat-laden mutton stew.

I'D RATHER BE A SPARROW THAN A SNAKE

The next scene of our story begins in a cinema. ~~After ten late-night computer chats and several emails,~~ **Sara and Dara have planned to meet. They saw each other only for ten minutes in the brightly lit hall and are now sitting in the dark.** In the film Sara and Dara have chosen to see, there are no images of the modern life of Iranian urbanites. Instead, like many arty Iranian films that receive golden awards from reputable film festivals around the world, the film portrays misery, poverty and despair in Iran. In the forty-fourth minute of the film, finally, for the first time, Dara's right forearm and Sara's left forearm are positioned on their shared armrest. A few minutes later, the armrest begins to shake.

Ask me whether this is the climax of my story, so that I can say:

No . . . What is going through your mind?

The shaking armrest has nothing to do with those actions that take place in dark cinemas in the West. Sara and Dara's arms have started to shake from a mysterious force, from some sort of telepathy. It is the same force that drove the cavemen of the Lascaux caves in France to carve magical images on the cave walls. It is perhaps the same force that can trigger the fuse of a suicide bomber in Baghdad . . .

Now you know that you are not dealing with an ordinary love story. So don't ask and let me tell you:

One of the sexiest scenes I have ever seen belongs to a film made in Iran after the Islamic revolution. In one scene, the man and woman find a small bird in the street, a sparrow that has fallen. They take the sparrow to a café, and they sit facing each other at a small table. The woman is as usual wearing a headscarf and a coverall. The man is wearing a long-sleeved shirt. In Iran it is forbidden for men to wear short sleeves. The woman begins stroking the sparrow. Then the man reaches out from across the table and, ever so carefully, so that his fingers do not come into contact with the woman's hand, strokes the sparrow's head and neck. In turn, one stroke from the woman, one stroke from the man . . . Meanwhile, they talk about their daily problems and about sparrows.

If you ask Dara, he can explain the thousandfold process of making a film in Iran. First, a permit to make the film must be obtained. Therefore, the screenplay is delivered to the Ministry of Culture and Islamic Guidance to determine whether it is suitable to be made into a film or not. Then the competency of the screenplay writer, the competency of the director, the competency of the actors and other participants must be determined and approved by the ministry. After these stages, which can sometimes take up to a year or even longer, the switch is flicked and the film can be shot. But the ordeal is not over yet. After editing, the film must again be delivered to the Ministry of Culture and Islamic Guidance for the responsible parties to watch carefully. They will either categorically forbid it from being played on screens or, if the film-maker is lucky, they will issue orders for certain scenes to be revised or cut for it to receive a screening permit. In the final stage, the esteemed responsible parties will even determine which cinemas the film can be shown at – in cinemas in the provinces, in cinemas with tolerable seats, functional projectors and speakers that allow the audience to actually understand the dialogue between the characters, or in run-down cinemas with wooden or metal seats, with audio systems that play sound mixes of their own composition, and that reek of natural odours emanating from their bathrooms.

I think at the time the sparrow film was made, the person responsible for issuing screening permits was that famed blind censor.

Don't smile. I am completely serious. During our thousands of years of history, we Iranians have always sought to make the impossible possible. During a particular period when the censorship imposed on films and television programmes was at its most severe, the censor responsible for the state-operated Channel 3 was a blind man. To determine whether films or television programmes should be aired or archived, one or several people would sit with this blind man and describe the scenes to him. Shot by shot. It was he who would decide whether a particular scene was appropriate for broadcast or not.

Here I must divulge one of Dara's secrets. He has participated in two of these meetings.

How?

Well, some of us Iranians like to do contradictory things. In the morning we walk down the street shouting, "Long live Mossadeq, Iran's nationalist prime minister." In the afternoon we walk up that same street shouting, "Death to Mossadeq, the turncoat traitor." And just as effortlessly, we help the architects of Operation Ajax, who have given up all hope, watch in total disbelief as their failed coup d'état succeeds at the hands of a group of Iranians . . . In a recurrence of this Iranian contradiction-making enterprise, after the Islamic revolution a large number of skilled professionals were dismissed from their jobs because it seemed they were not committed to the revolution. To replace them, people who were committed to the revolution but who were not skilled were hired. The plan was that in several years, with the strength of their commitment, they too would become skilled. But many of the new employees were so committed that they never became skilled. Much later, a small number of these people decided secretly to exploit the skills of the dismissed skilled professionals. By coincidence, Dara became party to one of these secret operations. One evening when he had finished painting a house and had received his pay, he decided to treat himself to a water pipe at a café. While smoking it, he was listening to two young men discuss a sparrow-caressing scene in an Iranian film. As was his habit, he could not hold his tongue, and joined in the discussion by offering a sharp critique of the film from the perspective of the famed film theoretician Robin Wood. The two young men, who did not understand much of what he was saying, were observing his enthusiasm and soaring excitement in mocking silence. When Dara finished his argument, one of them turned to the other and asked:

"Hey, Upchuck Essi, did you delight in the gentleman's pomposities?"

"The gentleman is a cinema guru. He's way brainier than us with our Ph Ds. he must be John Wayne's cousin."

"And his mum is Sophia Loren."

Dara finally realized they were making fun of him. He turned away, and his eyes met a pair of eyes with a strange look in them. The man, together with a burly companion who had the appearance of a bodyguard, was sitting at the next table.

He said:

"Brother, you seem to know a thing or two about cinema."

"A little."

"Come to the television station tomorrow, Channel 3. I have work for you."

"Sir! They will not let me into the television station building. My name is on the blacklist."

"What is your name?"

"Dara M."

"Come tomorrow morning at eleven and tell the guard your name is M. Dara. From now on that is what your name will be at the television station . . . Don't forget! If you slip up and give them your real name, I'll get into trouble. As of this minute you are my expert on cinematic affairs."

The man got up, gesturing for his bodyguard to pay for M. Dara's water pipe as well. He put his hand on the bodyguard's shoulder and Dara, with his jaw hanging, watched them leave. Upchuck Essi turned to his friend and said:

"You see! Didn't I tell you John Wayne is the gentleman's cousin? He pulled a few strings and got him a job . . . And look at us miserable wretches. Jackie Chan won't even hire us as the slobs who get beaten to a pulp."

Now let us picture together a meeting of the blind censorship supervisor and his group of seeing expert consultants. In this meeting they have to make a decision about an American anti-American film – which these days is not hard to find. The film was recently hunted down by television station detectives after an exhaustive worldwide search. It is scheduled to be broadcast on a public holiday when television stations become charitable and air feature films. The meeting takes place in a small private screening room with magnificent furniture and a very expensive sound system.

Before the private screening, the expert consultant on matters offensive to morality says:

"Sir, I am totally against broadcasting this film."

He is asked why. He responds:

"Because the word 'dance' appears in the title. 'Dance' is a vulgar and obscene word."

Dara, as the expert on cinematic affairs, says:

"But the title of this film is *Dances with Wolves*. There is nothing wrong with dancing with wolves."

The expert on matters offensive to morality says:

"Dancing is dancing. Do you think Iranians will think of dancing with wolves when they see or hear the word 'dances'? They will immediately think of Arabic belly-dancing. The Westernized ones will think of the tango, and the minute they think of dancing, they will start dancing . . . The burden of their sin is on your shoulders, brother."

The expert on anti-American affairs says:

"But in this film they show how wonderful and civilized the Indians were and how savage the Americans were. We have to broadcast this film so that the people of Iran realize that, without us, the Americans will either massacre them or banish them to parched wastelands in America."

The blind censorship supervisor, whom we will call Mr X, says:

"It seems you have all watched this film many times without me. Now play it and tell me what you see."

They play the film. Shot by shot they have to press PAUSE and explain every detail of the film and every action of its characters. They even describe facial expressions and hand gestures.

Mr X who, unlike his experts, is well versed in English, has no difficulty understanding the film's dialogue; his problem is with the sound effects.

"What was that sound?"

They explain that it was the howling of a wolf.

"Are you sure? I've heard that sound in some of the dirty sexy films. Brutish men howl like that. Look carefully deep into the scene and see if there is some filthy action going on somewhere in the background."

They rewind and watch carefully. No, fortunately there is nothing going on in the background. They continue playing the film and describing it to Mr X, until the film's first woman appears on the screen. With the first shot of the woman, the expert on matters offensive to morality yells:

"Cut! Cut! You can't show this part."

Mr X asks:

"Hey! Tell me, what's on the screen?"

"Sir, a woman has entered the scene whose hair is completely revealed."

"That's not a problem. Seeing the hair of a non-Muslim woman is not a problem."

"Sir, that's not all. All the Indians are naked from the waist up."

The expert on cinematic affairs says:

"Well, that's how the Indians used to dress. They can't show Indians wearing Arab clothes."

Mr X asks:

"What else do you see?"

The expert on matters offensive to morality, who has become quite agitated, says:

"Sir, ask your cinematic affairs expert. In my opinion the protrusion of her breasts is fairly noticeable."

Mr X says:

"If they are not bare, then there is no problem."

"They are not bare. But what about the Indian men? They have painted their faces in strange colours, and the way they flaunt their long hair and bare arms is scary."

Mr X says:

"Well, there's nothing wrong with the audience being scared."

"But sir, it's not the Indians that scare me. Our wives and other people's wives will see this film, too. Don't you think that seeing the bodies of these burly Indians may . . ."

Mr X says:

"We have broadcast several Italian westerns, and as far as I have been told the Italian Indians were also half naked and no one has complained. So, it is not a problem."

The expert on matters offensive to morality shouts:

"Sir! What's not a problem? These rousing Indians are a problem from the tops of their heads to the tips of their toes."

Mr X shouts back:

"My man, I said it is not a problem. Stop being so highly-strung."

Then he asks cleverly:

"Let's see. How tall are you?"

The expert on cinematic affairs gleefully butts in:

"Sir, he is about four feet tall and has a really big belly."

The screening continues.

The scene in which the Indian husband and wife are making love is cut.

The expert on matters offensive to morality shouts:

"Pause! Sir, pause the film."

Mr X, who is himself holding the remote control, presses the pause button.

"Don't argue with each other. Just tell me what you see."

"Sir, the woman is standing in a pond and she is holding up her skirt. It is as if Shirin is bathing in the pond and we are ogling her like Khosrow, that wine-guzzling philanderer."

"Well, all women hold their skirts up when they go in the water. It's not like she is wearing a bikini."

"But we can see her naked calves."

"How about farther up? Can you see her knees?"

"Yes, sir. What's more, some parts of her thighs are also exposed."

"Well, cut those out."

The kissing scene is also cut, so is the one revealing the actress's midriff. Dara, who is now angry, says:

"Sir, in this condition the film is completely meaningless. In the next scene, when the man and the woman talk intimately with each other, the audience will wonder what happened, when did this woman become so friendly with Kevin Costner?"

Mr X, a bitter smile on his face, says:

"The audience of such films is smart enough to know what has happened. If they can imagine what has happened in the shots we have cut, then the film has worked without us having aired unethical scenes."

The expert on matters offensive to morality says:

"Sir, in dubbing the film we can make them siblings who long ago lost each other and who have now found one another. In that case, we can show scenes of their conversations together."

The expert on cinematic affairs objects:

"Sir! But there is a scene in which the couple gets married according to Indian traditions. Hand in hand they are sent to their Indian tent, and the Indian women ululate the same way our women do at weddings."

The expert on matters offensive to morality responds:

"This too has a solution. In dubbing the film we can have one of the Indians say that this is an old Indian tradition whereby brothers and sisters who lost each other years ago and who have now found each other are made brother and sister again."

Mr X says:

"Cut this scene."

With these pauses, plays, rewinds and arguments, seven hours have now passed, and time continues to pass until in the middle of one scene the expert on matters offensive to morality suddenly shouts:

"Cut! Cut! They kissed. They kissed each other."

Arguments ensue on what should be done with the scene. The expert on matters offensive to morality says:

"I wish they had kissed like brother and sister. In that case, if we portray them as siblings, the audience will find it completely acceptable."

Mr X says:

"In that case, if the director were to see our dubbed version he would surely approve, because if they are siblings, and if they have found each other after many years, the film becomes far more dramatic."

Shaking with rage, Dara growls:

"Then his film would become just like Bollywood films, or Iranian films."

Frustrated, Mr X says:

"Fine . . . Cut this out too, but don't cut the previous scene where they are bringing their heads together. This way the audience will think they want to whisper an important secret about the wolves or the Indians to each other."

The screening continues without any further problems, and everyone breathes a sigh of relief that ño other censor-worthy scenes have been discovered.

It was around the same time that while watching a film on television we would suddenly see that, contrary to the tenets of film-making, and contrary to the most basic principles of cinematography, a mid-range shot would abruptly change to a close-up. A hazy, staticky, faded close-up. It took a while for us to realize that this only happens when the actress enters the scene. After much research, we learned that to avoid having to cut films by some forty-five minutes, and because eliminating certain scenes would render a film completely meaningless, those in charge of censoring television programmes had, with the use of state-of-the-art technology, found an artistic-cinematic solution. If in an important scene the actress was dressed in a sleeveless shirt or a short skirt, they would refilm shots of her face in close-up and insert these images into the film. If you ever have occasion to see one of these adulterated or overhauled versions, on my behalf please tell the director, whose eyes are most certainly wide with surprise:

"What did you expect? Stop kicking and screaming and thank God. Isn't this better than having the arms, legs and breasts of your film cut out with a pair of scissors?"

It is under such circumstances that the Olympian inspiration for that creative scene of the couple stroking a sparrow came to the makers of that film. Another interesting point about that film is that the sparrow is its best actor, because it made no attempt at escaping the clutches of the man and woman, and it never complained about its torturous circumstances. Just imagine yourself as a helpless sparrow in the hands of a couple who desperately desire each other but who have never even touched. And now, perforce, fully dressed and in a public place, they are sitting across from each other, and they take turns stroking you. Time drags on, hidden hormones begin to secrete, and they keep stroking you; and the director, who probably likes his inspiration for this artistic scene very much, calls for multiple takes. If any of us were in that sparrow's position, in the clutches of a highly provoked couple, I doubt we would be left with a single bone intact . . .

Sara and Dara, still in the cinema, are sitting with their arms close together. With no sparrow to stroke, they have little else to do but watch that artistic Iranian film. **The film is about a young girl and boy in love. The boy has asked for the girl's hand in marriage, and the girl's father has told him that because he does not have a house of his own, he will not consent. Now there has been an earthquake, and all the houses have been destroyed, and the boy is again hopeful that because everyone is now homeless, perhaps the girl's father will agree to their marriage. Sara and Dara are so captivated by the scenes of Abbas Kiarostami's film and the sadness and suffering of the young couple that they forget this is the first time they have sat so close to one another. During the final scenes of the movie, they even have tears in their eyes.**

After leaving the cinema, they walk together in silence for a long time. Then Sara notices that Dara is deliberately walking in step with her, as though they are marching together.

Sara smiles and points to Dara's feet and asks:

"Why are you doing this?"

"I don't know. Ask my feet."

"Why is your voice trembling?"

"Ask my heart."

With this sentence, Sara's heart begins to beat rapidly.

Dara asks:

"What should we do now?"

"I don't know, ask our fate."

"Where is our fate?"

"I don't know, ask our destiny."

Dara thinks, I pray our destiny is not in the hands of a gutless, miserable, censored writer . . . Unconsciously, and unlike lovers throughout the world, they avoid strolling along quiet streets and beautiful tree-lined alleys. Walking down a crowded street, sheltered by pedestrians, lessens the danger of being seen and arrested. But not for one moment during this innocent stroll can Sara forget the fear of arrest. Last year, when one of her classmates returned to the university after a month-long absence and in an awful emotional state, she told Sara that a month earlier she and her boyfriend were arrested while watching sparrows in a quiet park. On the very first night of her arrest, they had taken her to the medical examiner to see whether she was still a virgin or not. Then they had called her parents. After her release, before which she had to pledge in writing never to commit such misdeeds again, she was faced with her mother's incessant tears and her fanatical father's and brothers' relentless reprimands. Everyone, even relatives, would scold her for having brought shame on the family. Sara's friend, with tearful eyes, had confided in her that she had not been allowed to come to the university or even to leave the house. However, her broken emotional state and humiliation were so profound that she didn't want anyone to see her anyway. During that one month, her father and brothers had put such pressure on her that she was eventually forced to reveal her boyfriend's address. When the boy was released after twenty days of detention, they had cornered him in an alley together with her roughneck uncle, and beaten him up. Sara's friend had learned such a lesson from her romantic tryst that from then on she was even afraid of inadvertently coming close to a boy in the street. Of course, time helped her forget the torment and humiliation of the incident, especially after she bought a nightingale in a cage from a pet shop without knowing why and passed the dreary afternoon hours watching it, listening to it and trying to caress it.

Sara, like all people who in the first days of their friendship share

sweet memories of their past, begins to share with Dara memories of her friend from her primary and high-school years.

"We became friends on the very first day of primary school. When we turned nine, they told us they wanted to have a celebration for us. On the day they celebrated our puberty, we wouldn't have been able to go up on that stage if we didn't have each other. A month earlier they had told us when the celebration would be held. Our mothers had bought white dresses and white headscarves for us. At school they had given us a pair of wings that we would pin to our backs to look like angels. Everything was beautiful. We were two nine-year-old girls who were suddenly told they were like angels. But on the morning before the event, our teacher started telling us things we couldn't understand. She told us that after the celebration of our puberty we would become women, and that we should start living like women. She told us that we must now start saying our daily prayers properly and in full. Up to that point, everything was fine; I always liked to pray and at the end of my prayers I'd ask God for an A-plus in my exams. But the lady teacher started telling us things about our bodies and womanhood that scared us. She talked about our bodies bleeding. But she didn't say from where. She said we would find out later. Every morning when we woke up, my friend and I would check our arms and legs to see if we had bled . . . It was a daily nightmare. She even told us that after the celebration we would be old enough and woman enough to have husbands . . . It was not a good day. I thought that after we finished singing and flapping our wings like angels on the school stage, they would grab me outside the school and take me to the house of an ugly, burly man for me to marry him . . . I was so scared."

Sara was right to be scared, because although educated Iranians realized years ago that we should talk to our children and teach them about sex and sexuality, in our schools and our homes we still censor this critical subject. We postpone it month after month and year after year until a time when, if a boy asks his father, How did you come to have me, and his father, influenced by Western cartoons, says, Well, one night Mr Stork brought you in a bundle and left you at the door, his son will immediately say, You saddo, you mean to tell me that you never did it with Mum? Not even once?

I myself had this problem. My son was growing older month by month and getting closer to the age of puberty. Although I had brought him up and treated him like a friend, every time I came to teach him about sex I would suffer some sort of ineptness and even embarrassment. I was constantly looking for an excuse to open up the conversation with him, but as long as my innocent son waited for me to teach him about the stork and the night and the like, I didn't. Until, as luck would have it, in the heart of Berlin, nature and wildlife literally initiated my son's sex education, perhaps in the fiercest manner and perhaps in the most natural way.

How? The heart of Berlin and wildlife . . . ?!

Yes; and it was of course not in the days of the Nazis. In fact, it was the year 2000. I had been invited to Berlin for a literary event, and had taken my son with me. In those days, in addition to Spielberg's dinosaurs, my son was also fascinated with wildlife. He constantly drew pictures of sharks and black panthers. I don't know whether these two animals have any connection or relevance to a twelve-year-old boy approaching puberty or not. In any case, one day we headed out and went to the spectacular Berlin zoo. It was a beautiful and memorable day for both of us. We were having a wonderful time looking at the different animals. We would make up jokes about them, and my son would film them so that he could show the film to his classmates. Then we heard the lions roar. We were drawn in their direction. The lioness was behaving rather strangely. She was rolling around on the ground and moaning in an odd way. We thought she was suffering from a stomach ache and concluded that the zookeepers must not be taking good care of the poor animals.

My son asked:

"What's wrong with the lion?"

Like an experienced vet I said:

"The poor thing clearly has wind."

But suddenly, before the stunned eyes of father and son, the lion with all its majesty meandered over, climbed up on the lioness's back and got busy humping.

My son asked:

"What is he doing?"

I looked at my son from the corner of my eyes. His eyes had grown exceptionally round. I mumbled:

"For now, just watch. I will tell you later."

My son wanted to film the scene, but fortunately the camera's battery was completely drained after the long filming of the black leopard. I say "fortunately" for two reasons. First, because similar to Japanese tourists who become so involved in filming and taking photographs that they in fact do not see anything, my son would have missed the real scene. Second, taking a tape of the utterly unveiled mating of two lions back to Iran was definitely not a wise thing to do. If as usual the film was inspected at Customs, we could be arrested for importing a pornographic film, a rare one at that, and sent to where Dara used to be.

It was after watching this scene that I finally lost my inhibitions and put aside the two thousand-five-hundred-year-old self-censorship and delivered a completely scientific lecture about sex to my son. He kept nodding pensively, and once in a while he would say:

"Hmm . . ."

Now that years have passed since that day, and I have with great joy bought an electric razor for him, I sometimes wonder, What if this boy who learned his first lesson in sex by watching a lion in action wants to undertake all such endeavours like a lion?

Far away from the lions, in sharing her memories, Sara has reached her early high-school years.

"During my first year in high school it became fashionable for girls to wear shoes in colours other than black. It was a nice fashion. They went well with our black coveralls and headscarves. One after the other, girls started wearing colourful shoes, until one day the physical education teacher announced on the loudspeaker that wearing colourful shoes to school was forbidden because it was a very vulgar thing to do. As usual, the next morning she was standing at the school entrance with the principal. They used to search our bags every day to make sure we didn't have pictures of actors. That day, they not only didn't allow girls wearing a little make-up to enter the school, but they were making the girls wearing colourful shoes go back home and change their shoes.

"Some time passed, and my friend and I suddenly came to think that, although we may not be allowed to wear colourful shoes, colourful shoelaces were not forbidden; and one day we both went to school with red and green shoelaces. Our schoolfriends kept pointing out our shoes to one another in surprise. During the last period, one of them went and told the physical education teacher, and she came and took us to the head teacher's office. First, she gave us a long lecture about how we were provoking the wolves that sit outside the school and prey on naive girls like us, and then she told us that we must not wear coloured shoelaces any more. We said, 'But, miss, you never said they were banned.' She said, 'Well I'm saying it now . . .' What was interesting was that as of the next day we saw girls on the street wearing black shoes with green or yellow shoelaces. It was as if we were all inspired at the same time . . . You know! That in itself was some sort of a protest. It was some sort of a struggle to make ourselves look pretty."

Dara confesses:

"You Iranian women have always been more creative and courageous than us men."

Sara laughs and says:

"But that isn't the entire story. One day I have to tell you about the time we put different coloured buttons on our black coveralls."

As though she has suddenly remembered something, Sara stops laughing and anxiously looks around. Pity that it isn't possible, but if Dara could see her bedroom, he would see thick and thin lines in different colours painted on its walls, like formless drawings by children before they become trapped by shapes and when they simply and freely like colours.

Involuntarily, they both stop in front of a street pedlar's collection of books spread out on the pavement. Tehran is again lost in time. It is not clear whether the sun is rising or setting above the city. Sara jokingly asks the old man with long white hair:

"Sir, do you have *The Blind Owl*?"

Sitting on a stack of books, the old man bitterly answers:

"Oh, lady! Why are you looking for *The Blind Owl*? We are all blind owls."

"God forbid! Don't be so morbid."

The old man stares obstinately into Sara's eyes. His pleasant face is familiar to Dara. His books are a strange combination of old and new thrown haphazardly on the ground. Planck's book on quantum physics, Khayyám's *Rubaiyat*, Stephen Hawking's *A Brief History of Time*, *Bees and Refuting Marx's Theories*, the biography of that mercenary Saddam Hussein, *One Thousand and One Nights*, *Modern Iranian Poetry*, Moamar Qaddafi's *The Green Book*, Popper's *Open Society and Its Enemies*, Sternberg's *The Psychology of Love*, *Eichmann: His Life and Crimes*, *The Three Musketeers*, *Seven Effective Ways to Quit Opium*, Borges's *Labyrinths*, *The Islamic Guide to Sex*, *Zen*, Simone de Beauvoir's *The Second Sex*, Rumi's

Ghazals, Existentialism, Palestine, Seven Ways to Summon Ghosts, One Hundred Years of Solitude, Baudelaire's *The Flowers of Evil* . . .

Seeing the translation of Baudelaire's poetry, Dara suddenly remembers who the old man is. He is shocked. He did not expect to see Iran's great romantic poet in such a state. Before the revolution, in literary and women's magazines that were now bought and sold in secret, Dara had seen the poet's special sections and his photograph – a sad-looking man with long, dishevelled hair, a cigarette between his fingers, his forehead resting on his hand, his eyes staring at a point away from the camera – and next to his large photograph his ~~erotic~~ love poems~~, all in praise of the bodies of his multitude of lovers who had all thought they would be his last. After the revolution, none of his books had received a permit to be printed or reprinted~~.

Dara asks:

"Are you not Mr N V Wine?"

This was the poet's pseudonym.

The old man, still staring at Sara's face ~~appraisingly and~~ with admiration, angrily replies:

"I used to be . . . Now, I rue the day I ever wrote poetry."

On the crowded street people are drawn to the brightly lit shop windows and the wares of all the other pedlars except this one.

The old poet turns to Sara and says:

"If you are interested in old handwritten books, I have an edition from five hundred, six hundred, seven hundred years ago. It is from my own personal library. I'll sell it to you for next to nothing."

He gets up from the stack of books. Only then do Sara and Dara see that some fifteen tomes with old gold-hammered leather bindings have made up his seat. The books emit an ancient and lost echo.

The old man invites Sara to his side. He opens one of the handwritten volumes and hands it to her ~~in such a way that his fingers brush against hers. Dara sees the old man's caressing hand reluctantly, longingly, separate from Sara's hand~~ . . . The book's pages are made of Samarkand paper that, with the passage of time has turned yellow and brittle, and each page is embellished with gold paisley illuminations. Sara carefully leafs through the book. A full-page miniature drawing appears before her eyes. Rare shades of azure, vermilion and ochre shine on her face and the tiny beads of sweat above her lip.

"Beautiful young lady, this handwritten narrative in verse of *Khosrow and Shirin* dates back to five hundred and thirty-eight years ago . . . Do you know *Khosrow and Shirin*?"

Mesmerized, Sara can only nod.

~~The old man, pretending to want to look at the miniature, brings his head close to that part of Sara's neck visible from beneath the knot of her headscarf and inhales deeply. Sara hears the sound of that long breath, but she does not pull back.~~

Surprised, Dara says:

"If this book is authentic, it is worth ten or twenty million tumans. Perhaps much, much more . . ."

The old poet, ~~still intoxicated by the scent of Sara's body and~~ angry at Dara's interruptions, without looking at him growls:

"I have never in my life owned anything fake. If I find the person who truly wants this book, I will sell it to him or her for a pittance. Girl, do you want it?"

Sara stares into the old man's eyes. It is the first time Dara has seen such a look in her eyes. He freezes in horror. In those large black eyes, respect, ancient bewitchment, ~~desire,~~ the last gaze of a sacrificial lamb, greed, the rage of a woman raped and other unknown emotions have created an alchemy.

Dara pleads:

"Sara, let's go."

Sara, still staring into the old man's eyes, says:

"Why are you giving away your precious possession?"

The poet says bitterly:

"~~This country no longer needs poets and books.~~ Just tell me, do you want it, ~~pretty~~ girl?"

It seems the handwritten book is transmitting an irresistible magical power to Sara's body.

"Yes . . . How much do you want for it?"

"I don't want money."

"Then what do you want?"

And still their eyes remain locked.

Dara shouts:

"Sara!"

"Are you sure you want it?"

"I said yes. What do I have to give for it?"

The old man looks at the lock of hair that has escaped Sara's head-scarf . . . and whispers:

"Your headscarf . . . Right now."

Sara slams the book shut. A halo of golden dust envelops her hands.

"Here?"

"Right here, right now . . . If you don't have the guts, get out of here."

Sara looks at the people on the street, at the shops and at an infuriated Dara. This is the most *Indecent Proposal* to make to an Iranian girl like Sara on a street of the Islamic Republic. Without seeing, without touching, one can speculate that at this very moment sweat is simmering between Sara's breasts and along her inner thighs.

"Do you understand what you are asking? Aren't you ashamed of yourself?"

"Even if I were to be ashamed, a girl like you shouldn't be. Will you take it off or not?"

"I will be disgraced."

"That is exactly what I want. Now make up your mind."

Dara begs:

"No, Sara . . . No."

Sara puts the book under her arm and raises her hand towards the knot of her headscarf. Now, there is belligerence in her eyes. The old man looks into those eyes with a lust risen from the grave.

"No, Sara. Don't even think about it! Don't ruin us!"

In one swift move Sara rips the scarf from her head and throws it at the old man. Among the passers-by on that crowded street, the few who are looking their way see with disbelieving eyes the black lustre of unleashed hair with a sense of déjà vu in the restlessness of their lacklustre days. Petrified, Dara looks around. If the police or the patrols from the Campaign Against Social Corruption see this girl who has dared to remove her headscarf on the street, they will quickly and brutally throw her in their car and take her away. Sara, as though spellbound, clutching the book to her chest, still makes no move to leave. The number of people who have noticed her gradually increases. Men with lecherous looks and euphoric smiles circle around them; a few make rude remarks. Dara looks at the old man with loathing, but the old poet no longer sees him, or anyone else. He is holding the headscarf to his nose. And at last, drained and overcome by a wave of delirium, he sits down on his stack of handwritten books,

Dara yells:

"Sara, let's go!"

He steps on the books spread on the ground and grabs Sara who, like a paralysed rabbit is standing there, staring at the wolves circling her.

"You stupid girl! What have you done?"

Dara grabs hold of Sara's sleeve and drags her behind him. With his arm and shoulders he cuts through the circle of men half running, taking Sara with him. Surrounded by those men, at least they were safe from the eyes of the patrols driving by. Now the passers-by are shocked at the sight of the two of them in that state. Frightened, a few even make way for them. In the inferno of his mind Dara searches for an escape. He has an idea. He opens the book and puts it on Sara's head and yells at her to hold it there. Running, they leave behind the men who are seeing them off with vulgar jibes. They reach a women's clothes shop. Dara shoves Sara inside.

A few of the loafers who have seen Sara without a headscarf walk over to the store and peer through the window. But Dara's face is so full of rage and his fists so uncompromising that the men are forced to go on their way. In Iran it is forbidden for men to enter shops that, among other things, sell ladies' underwear, even if the man is a customer's husband. Of course, some of these shops sell extremely sexy underwear illicitly that even sex shops in Amsterdam do not offer. Dara, like a sentry, stands waiting at the door until his Sara walks out wearing a new headscarf. Her eyes have a look more mystifying than ever, but at least one can see the blaze of victory in them. She shifts the handwritten book under her arm and asks briskly:

"Well, what should we do now?"

Dara does not answer. If one of his fanatic ancestors were there instead of him, with his eyes blinded with blood, he would now be gnawing at his thick, double-hilted moustache with wrath and pondering ways in which to behead the woman who has so squandered his honour. However, not only does Dara not have a thick double-hilted moustache, he even shaves his rather sparse beard. As a result, the extent of his anger is to bark back:

"Nothing. You have to go home."

He hails a taxi for her. Sara is still so intoxicated by the handwritten book that she pays no attention to Dara's anger. He slams the car door shut and shouts through the window,

"If you love me, burn it."

"In your dreams."

Well. You, who have read this Iranian love story up to this point, know very well that I cannot include the scene in which Sara takes off her headscarf and the ensuing events in my story and hand it over to Mr Petrovich. The censorship apparatus will most certainly stamp the scene as provoking and injurious to public chastity. Even worse, there is also the possibility of a political interpretation of the scene. An interpretation that was not in my conscious mind, but now that I put myself in Mr Petrovich's shoes and read the story from his perspective, I do see it.

The political accusation will be that this scene openly encourages Iranian girls to take off their headscarves on the street. And worse, that it does not show the girl who has committed this vulgar act being arrested, punished and sitting in prison regretting her actions. Even worse yet, with the assistance of her stupid boyfriend, the girl happily returns home.

Graver than this politico-headscarfy interpretation is that I, the writer, may be accused of alluding to one of the popular slogans of the early years of the revolution. The slogan that members of the Party of God shouted while facing a demonstration by a group of Iranian women opposed to wearing headscarves and chadors: "Headscarves or head slaps!"

The demonstration was broken up, but the battle cry lived on, and contrary to the libertarian slogans popular in those days, the wearing of headscarves and chadors became mandatory in Iran.

What's more, Sara's descarfing scene can be found guilty of showing support for the anti-hijab measures taken by a former dictator king.

How?

Ask, so that I can explain.

Once upon a time in Iran, some seventy years ago, a dictator king who wanted to dictate over a country so that it would become more like Western countries, banned the Islamic form of dress, or hijab, and ordered Iranian ladies to take off their headscarves and chadors. Following this decree, the police would stop women who had come out onto the street wearing headscarves and chadors and they would beat them over the head with batons so that they would take off their hijab.

As an Iranian man, I am ashamed of myself because on neither occasion was I able to take any action in defence of my grandmother, mother, sister, wife and daughter.

Therefore, I cannot have Sara running around the streets of Tehran with no headscarf. But I really like this scene. If I were a sapless Iranian writer, I would write the scene like this:

The old womanizing poet who terribly regrets his past escapades and has repented, now wants to spend the final years of his life in purity and beauty with an old love. Therefore, stammering bashfully, he tells Sara:

"This handwritten book is worthless compared to my love for you. I will burn all my wicked poems, and to you I will dedicate all the innocent romantic masterpieces that I shall write, eulogizing our love. For you I will compose all the world's red roses, all the world's sparrows, all the world's Ferraris. You shall have it all. Yours will be the joy of my repentance. Let us get married so that you can then take off your headscarf for me."

Dara shouts:

"No, Sara! Don't ruin us!"

Sara, blushing, with her eyes cast down, asks:

"Do you really like my scarf that much?"

The poet, blushing, with his eyes cast down, replies:

"More than you can imagine. I am not like those ignoble Iranian men. I will give my life for your scarf. I will give my life to write one verse on the hidden beauty of your hair. I will die and in my coffin, from the perfume of your hair, I shall come to life again."

"If I become your wife, will you buy me a silk scarf with tassels on it?"

"I will buy all the scarves in the world for you."

Signs of consent begin to appear on Sara's mesmerized face. She feels deeply the poet's poetic, hairy, mystical, headscarfy, handwritten love. She feels that it would be impossible for her to find another man as sensitive and another love as pure. Looking appraisingly at the poet's face, it seems to her that the tragic wrinkles of his ageing beauty are fading away. Sara opens her lips to say yes to that handsome, besotted, mystic poet.

Dara shouts:

"Sara! Sara! What about me?"

I shout:

"Sara! Sara! What about my love story?"

And with the power of my pen, I shut Sara's mouth.

The only solution that comes to my mind is to rely on my readers' intelligence and imagination. Therefore, the final sentences of this scene will be these.

Dara shouts:

"Sara!"

"Are you sure you want it?"

"I already said I do. What do you want in return?"

The old man looks at Sara's headscarf, and under his breath, in a way that in this world only Sara can hear, he whispers . . .

Half an hour later, walking side by side in silence, Sara and Dara arrive at the beautiful Vanak Circle that somehow resembles Trafalgar Square, in London. I want the time in my story to be a romantic autumn afternoon, but unfortunately the President of Iran has at this very moment, in a revolutionary speech, proclaimed that on this hot afternoon he has hot news for the people of Iran – *We have resumed our efforts at enriching uranium.* **Sara shifts the handwritten book under her arm and asks briskly:**

"Well, what should we do now?"

In utter rage Dara roars:

"Nothing. You have to go home."

He hails a taxi for her. Finding an empty taxi in Tehran is not an easy task. When a taxi driver picks up a passenger who has yelled his destination in through the side window of his twenty-year-old car, he will slow down in front of other passengers for them also to yell their destination in through the side window. If their route matches that of the first passenger, he will let them in – at times cramming as many as six people in the car. But I, in support of Dara, send an empty taxi their way. **Dara pays an extra fee, hires it exclusively and ushers Sara into the car. Sara is still so intoxicated by the handwritten book that she pays no attention to Dara's anger. Dara slams the car door shut and through the window shouts:**

"If you love me, burn it."

"In your dreams."

I LOVE YOU BUT I NEVER WANT
TO SEE YOU AGAIN

Dara starts walking towards his house. As he nears his poor neighbourhood, his anger slowly turns into bitter sorrow. He has resolved to use his iron will, a remnant of his prison days, to rid himself of *The Agony and the Ecstasy* of Sara. He repeats to himself the title of this chapter which I have put in his head: I love you but I never want to see you again . . .

However, at precisely eleven o'clock that night, he adds another imprint of his fist to the wall of his room ~~and thinks, I don't give a damn about that intelligence agent who may be tapping my telephone~~. Aware that Sara's parents are asleep at this hour, he dials her telephone number and tells her that he has fallen even more deeply in love with her because she is different from all the other girls in the world. They arrange to meet three days later. After half an hour of exchanging ideas about where in Tehran it would be safest for them to meet, they finally say goodnight so that Sara, who feels tired, can go to sleep.

How? It's obvious. With the five-hundred-year-old handwritten book in her arms.

The three days that remain until another romantic rendezvous pass like three hundred years for Dara. They have arranged to meet in a mosque. In its front yard, where the colour of the turquoise tiles of the inscriptions prays upon the water of the shallow pool, they will have the opportunity to talk quietly for a short while. They both believe that the spiritual environment will help keep their love pure. But they are both shocked when they arrive at the mosque. There are cheap flyers giving notice of a death taped to the walls. Below the beautiful sentence "From God we come and to God we shall return", there is a picture of someone familiar to them: the old lovesick poet. Inside, a modest memorial service is under way with only a handful of old men and women present. Sara goes to the women's section of the mosque and Dara to the men's. Separated, they will not have to worry about seeing each other's tears.

When entering the mosque, neither Sara nor Dara saw the ghost of the poet who, with the sorrow of having remained incomplete and the agony of the poems he had not composed, was standing beside the old shallow pool. But the moment the poet laid eyes on Sara, his sad lips curved into a smile. He quickly moved to her side and at very close proximity accompanied her as far as the women's entrance. His ghost is not allowed to enter that section.

Sara, together with the poet's old sister, begins to weep. Dara, together with the poet's closest friend, a long-forgotten writer whose works never received a reprint permit after the revolution, with tearful eyes stares at some distant point. He regrets that four days earlier, at the height of his anger, he had wanted to kill that cheeky poet, and he is ashamed that, having seen his picture on the death notice, for a few seconds he had felt joy deep in his heart. He therefore allows the tears seeking absolution to flow from his eyes.

Up in the pulpit, the preacher preaches about the seven stages of hell. Fire, pits filled with foul-smelling boiling liquids, women who have violated the Islamic dress code hanging by their hair, snakes with bites so painful that fearing them hell's residents take refuge with the venomous vipers and other infinite horrors. Then he proceeds to describe the beauties of heaven. Streams of milk and honey, fruit trees that bend their branches down to heaven-dwellers who crave their fruit, beautiful heavenly nymphs with skin so translucent that their insides can be seen. The lot of every male heaven-dweller is seven thousand of these nymphs ~~who are all virgins and who after every sexual encounter become virgins again, and each sexual encounter lasts approximately three earth days~~ . . . Then the preacher begins to talk about the deceased poet. Of course, he mispronounces his name and makes no mention of his pseudonym.

An hour later, having cried sufficiently, Dara and Sara leave the mosque. With no particular destination in mind, they begin to walk. Subconsciously, they are scared of going to an Internet café, and they don't feel like seeing yet another film abounding with misery. ~~The problem is, when a young boy and girl walk together, at times their arms come into contact. For two virgins, such contacts are both pleasurable and frustrating.~~

Every half-mile they ask each other, "Well, where should we go?" or, "What should we do?" and they find no answers to their questions. At the very moment of hopelessness when they both despair, and for being together they see no solution other than to part ways, in the interest of my story I am forced to inspire Dara. I whisper in his ear, "Boy! Look to your right. What do you see?"

"A hospital."

"Well, this hospital has an A & E department. Do you get it?"

Dara looks at me sheepishly. I say:

"You really deserve to be a virgin at thirtysomething. Go to the A & E, sit comfortably in a couple of chairs, and talk . . . Do you get it?"

He looks at me with such surprise it is as if he is looking at Bacchus. I say:

"This is one of the few benefits of having a writer for a friend. It will never occur to the police or the patrols that a young couple would take advantage of an A & E like this."

Dara does not wait around to hear more. The two rush into the hospital. I write:

Seeing a hospital sign, Dara suddenly changes their course in that direction.

Sara says:

"Why here?"

"Be clever, my dear."

The two sit next to each other in A & E. Tehran's morning and evening newspapers, even the English-language _Tehran Times_, are arranged on the coffee table in front of them. They each pick up a newspaper and open it.

Sara says:

"You don't look like someone who would know such tricks. ~~Maybe you have lots of experience with girls.~~"

"No . . . I saw the hospital sign and was suddenly inspired."

It doesn't matter. I, being a writer in whose country copyright laws do not exist, am very much accustomed to others passing off my ideas as their own. I have absolutely no problem with them doing so. But I just don't understand why, as soon as they do such things, they suddenly become my enemy, so much so that they wish for my existence to be censored from the pages of time. What troubles me more is that there are a few writers who, on the outside, are opposed to the regime but who secretly collaborate with Mr Petrovich and read some of the more complicated books to expose their concealed scenes and inferences. I worry that they will tell Mr Petrovich. By handing two newspapers to his story's characters, this guy is suggesting to his readers that the newspapers published by the Islamic Republic are worthless, and that they are only good for this girl and boy to use as a cover for their transgressions. Consequently, in the final edit of my story, I will probably do away with Sara and Dara holding newspapers, hoping that Mr Petrovich will like their innocence and creativity in taking refuge in an emergency room, and not censor the scene.

Now I must explain the setting of my story. Hospital emergency rooms in Iran are places that perhaps even the art of cinema cannot justly portray. For you to have some concept of an Iranian emergency room, let me say only that the annual average number of people killed in road accidents in Iran is ten times greater than the number of Americans killed to date in the second war with Iraq. Therefore, **as Sara and Dara sit in that hospital, the doors to the A & E constantly open and the casualties of main roads, motorways and streets, and the casualties of hundreds of other locations and accidents, are rushed in. Typically, they are drenched in blood; they scream in pain and their stretchers are being pushed by family members or friends who, in typical Middle Eastern fashion, often wail and scream louder than the injured or dying person. And they all pass in front of Sara and Dara. Other emergency-room patients lie moaning on stretchers parked along the hallways because there are very few A & E personnel and they don't have the strength and energy to tend to everyone. Tired and stressed, they too are forced to shout as they talk to each other or when they ask each other for assistance.**

Please set your imagination in motion. First, imagine that you are one of the world's greatest writers. Then, imagine how, given all your writing skills, you can move your love story along in that horrifying setting . . .

I have learned from experience that if I put myself and my story's characters in a predicament, if I can tolerate their reprimands, after a while I can come up with a good narrative solution. The scene in A & E is one of these predicaments. Now, after three days of thinking about how I should advance my story, I have come up with an idea. To compare the brightness of your mind with the darkness of the mind of an Iranian writer, you should first tell me what your plan is for this segment of the story and then ask me about mine.

And I will say:

Dara opens his mouth to speak a candid and unambiguous sentence to Sara. A sentence that more or less all the world's lovers speak. That same sentence that all the world's lovers count the seconds to hear from their own lips and from the lips of their beloved. You know what that sentence is, so tell Dara that, with the same make-believe seriousness, looking as if he is reading news of the most critical nature in that censored newspaper, he should turn the page and suddenly say:

"Sara! I am so in love with you."

Sara, looking very serious, as if she is reading news of the most critical nature, in the shelter of the newspaper turns to Dara, stares into his eyes and with her eyes she answers:

" . . ."

This time, I have no fear of Mr Petrovich's censorship because this segment of the story takes place in my imagination. In this world of imagination, away from Mr Petrovich's eyes, I want to invite you to inspire Sara to tell Dara anything you like – of course, only if you succeed in your efforts at preserving your freedoms.

The doors to A & E open and four men, two of them pushing a stretcher and the other two escorting it, walk in. One of the most beautiful and delicate women in the world is lying on the stretcher. I said one of the most beautiful women in the world because the most beautiful woman in the world does not exist in the world; although, when many men in the world want to tame a woman, they magnanimously call her the most beautiful. **But what is most strange about the newly arrived group is not the woman's beauty. It is that the four men accompanying her are wearing clothes reminiscent of outfits worn by Iranian commanders one thousand five hundred years ago. They are wearing shields and helmets adorned with shining stripes of what looks like gold, and the hilts of their swords sparkle from gems that resemble rubies and diamonds.**

They could be actors in a play about the lost Persian Empire. Perhaps during the show or the rehearsal the actress had an accident, and they have brought her to A & E still dressed in their costumes. On entering A & E, the injured woman's conveyors and companions have completely lost their composure and look overwhelmed. It is obvious that they don't know what to do. The tormented eyes of the woman lying on the stretcher find Sara's from among the multitude of lecherous male eyes ogling her, and appeal for help. She is terribly embarrassed in front of the four men accompanying her and cannot cry out from her feminine pain. ~~The centre of the silk sheet covering the woman is stained with blood.~~ To stifle her groans, she gnashes her bloodless lips between her teeth. Sara walks over to her. They whisper to each other. Then Sara pulls herself away and nervously runs around the A & E department until she finds a female nurse. Together they push the stretcher into a room and close the door.

Dara pounds his fist on his knee. He is not sure whether he should think, Just my luck or be happy that Sara has rushed to someone's aid. He hears mocking laughter. He looks round and sees the man who sells talismans and spells sitting a few seats away, laughing at him. Dara turns away from the magic pedlar and stares at the closed door of the room Sara is in. Smelling of incense, Jafar ibn-Jafri walks over and sits next to him.

"I see you have not used my magic spell."

Dara asks:

"Do you also have someone sick or injured here?"

"Yes and no. I mean, almost like you."

A rare smile of understanding and sympathy forms on his lips. He whispers:

"The person who led you here did not have the brains to know that he should send young lovers to beautiful places and gardens, and not into the thick of blood and pain."

Dara shrugs and says:

"It was my own ingenuity."

And again he looks at the closed door of the room. The magic seller says:

"You won't be seeing your friend again for some time. The injured lady is holding her hand and begging her not to leave her alone."

He scoffs and, pointing to the door, continues, "It is a violent world. Some brides end up with excessive bleeding."

The four commanders who, contrary to their warriorlike appearance, look scared and ill at ease, are standing in a corner whispering. The A & E security guard walks up to them and points to the exit. They try to ignore him. The security guard gets angry. He calls his colleague, and together they throw the four men out. The magic pedlar laughs out loud. Half an hour later, Sara walks out of the room. There is a drop of blood on her hand; she asks Dara for a handkerchief. Dara again gives Sara his grandmother's handkerchief. The bloodstain spreads on the handkerchief like one of the delicate red flowers embroidered on its edge.

"What is it?"

Sara is about to cry.

"You men! Did you see how delicate she was? That savage groom has . . ."

She covers her face with her hands.

"Well, what happened? Will she recover?"

"They can't stop the bleeding. They're calling a specialist – Dr Farhad."

Dara is very sensitive to hearing Sara speak the name of another man.

"Who's Dr Farhad?"

"Don't you know him? Many people in Tehran know him. He is one of the best specialists and surgeons. Some of the students who are beaten up and are afraid of being arrested at the hospital go to his office, and he treats their wounds free of charge and gives them medicine."

Sara goes back into the room. Half an hour later, a tall, slim, tired-looking man rushes into A & E. The admitting nurse shows him the room. It is the first time Dara, and we, see Dr Farhad, but I don't think it will be our last encounter with him. Medicine-man Jafar ibn-Jafri points to the closed door.

"Did you see him? It was Physician Farhad."

"Do you know him?"

"Yes. We are in some ways professional rivals. He takes business away from me. He has opened up a clinic in a run-down neighbourhood, and three days a week he sees poor patients free of charge. These days, dimwits like him are hard to find. But although he hates me, I don't hate him. I even like him. There will come a day when he, too, will be my customer . . . No matter how many diseases he can cure, there is one that he cannot. He will come to me to buy anti-love medicine."

Suddenly, Sara walks out of the room frowning and, ignoring the talisman seller, says:

"Let's go."

Outside it has started drizzling. The four commanders are still standing warily in a corner, waiting. Sara walks over to them.

"Are you here with that bride?"

All four nod.

"Are you related to the bride or the groom?"

Confused and embarrassed, they look at one another.

"Don't tell me you are just the guard officers on duty!"

They nod.

"Tell Khosrow for me that he is more savage than a wild beast."

Sara's face has darkened with hatred and rage, and her lower lip is cut from the bites of her teeth. She walks away. Burning with curiosity, Dara cannot hold his tongue, and a few steps away he asks:

"Khosrow? How do you know the groom?"

"Their wedding was last night. The girl told me . . . Her name is Shirin. You disgusting men. It's between you and me now!"

Sara starts walking faster towards her home. A shocked Dara can barely keep up.

To tell you the truth, I too am shocked. I am thinking, What if King Khosrow's lovemaking with his bride Shirin was not as our great poet Nizami has described, ever so romantic, ever so soft, as soft as flower petals and stamens . . . I am shocked and terrified to think that Nizami too may have been afraid of censorship, and has offered an account contrary to reality.

The raindrops over Tehran bring with them the dust of nearby deserts and the soot of dilapidated cars; with them they bring to earth the drifting dust of flying carpets and the dust of the bodies of emperors; and with them the dust of Adam and Eve and grapes that were never picked from vines pours onto the asphalt . . . Dara, still in disbelief, is thinking of timeless and placeless names and events, when for the second time that day he is caught off guard. Sara, still with anger in her voice, says:

"I'm very late. I should have been home by now. Mr Sinbad is coming to our house."

"Mr Sinbad? Who in the world is Mr Sinbad?"

"My suitor. He insists that we get married while it is still spring and go to Spain for our honeymoon."

Dara stops. Sara walks away.

THE BEARD

At eight in the evening, in front of Sara's house, Sinbad climbs out of his latest-model BMW. He has been relentlessly pursuing Sara's hand in marriage for some time now. Sara's parents are very much in favour of the marriage because Sinbad is a self-made man. Unlike most crude yet wealthy bazaar merchants, he is a handsome thirty-seven-year-old. And unlike most crude yet wealthy bazaar merchants, he can speak a foreign language, and Chinese at that. How it is that without any university education Sinbad can speak Chinese is a story unto itself that I may tell you later. But, in the vein of classic novels, allow me, at the first appearance of this character in our story, to introduce him to the greatest extent possible.

As a schoolboy, Sinbad dreamed of becoming a doctor or an engineer so that he could selflessly serve his country. However, tides did not turn in his favour. His father died when he was still in the first year and reading lessons on Sara and Dara. He grew up in poverty and finished high school with great difficulty. At the time of the revolution, Sinbad was a clerk issuing birth certificates at a General Register Office in Shiraz. However, just as the revolution changed many things in the land of Iran, it very quickly changed Sinbad's life, too. The first change occurred on his face.

Ask me what I mean, for me to say:

In the year following the revolution's victory, Sinbad still did not have a positive outlook on the reformations that were taking place. His father's death and a life with no resources and no support had made him conservative and apathetic. He had not taken part in any of the anti-Shah demonstrations in which the majority of the people of Iran had participated. He used to say, "Who cares if the secret police arrest political activists and torture them? Who cares if oppositionists say there is no freedom of speech in the country, or that there is censorship? I know I can say whatever comes to my mind. Now if what comes to their mind is forbidden, then it's their own fault. Let us live our lives. I am content. I know that I will receive my salary at the start of the month, and I know that until the end of the month my mother and I will not go hungry and the landlord will not evict us. Of course, my salary isn't as high as I would like it to be, but my boss has promised that in a few years I will earn enough money even to save some for a trip. Let us live our lives . . ." And thus he had lived. He was always afraid that someone would become upset with him. He was afraid that people would think he didn't have a good opinion of them or that he disliked them, and he was afraid of being asked his opinion on even the most mundane issues. He believed that whatever there was in the world was meant to be, and that people who fell on hard times were people who had ignorantly tried to change all that was well entrenched in the world.

Even after the revolution, when day-by-day Western values were coming under greater attack, Sinbad would go to work with a closely shaven face and a well-pressed suit. In those days, there were two different fashions at work. The young leftists who belonged to various guerrilla factions wore Chinese-collared shirts and green military overcoats made in Korea (the ones made in the United States were better, but they were expensive), and among the revolutionary Muslims, the women wore black chadors or headscarves and long black coveralls, and the men sported some sort of a pieced-together Islamic look.

Unlike his colleagues, Sinbad, who made every effort to perform his duties as diligently as he had in the past, did not give up wearing a tie, that is, until the day he heard it being referred to as "the noose of civilization" on a radio show. Then he thought this piece of fabric did not have enough value for him to tie it around his neck and in an evolving society to portray himself as having been lassoed. By now some of his colleagues, especially those who had religious leanings from before the revolution, no longer tucked their shirts in and instead let them hang casually out of their trousers. (The same fashion that, years later, would become all the rage in the West.) These colleagues no longer shaved because beards had become the symbol of a revolutionary Muslim. Some of them had grown full beards, while others only had stubble. (The same fashion that, years later, would become all the rage in the West.) The darker the trousers and the more grease-stained the shirt, the more revolutionary the man. Consequently, bright and happy colours were rapidly fading from the streets of Iran.

Sinbad's colleagues, the truly devout who had actively participated in the dangerous days of the revolution, as well as those who only after the revolution's success had turned into revolutionaries, often participated in the daily street demonstrations against the revolution's present and future enemies. But Sinbad, although he no longer wore ties and had, after some time, conceded to letting his wrinkled shirt hang out of his trousers, didn't like to participate in these events. He thought he should focus instead on performing his daily duties. But, day by day, the harder he worked, the more he fell behind with his work. The first problem was that the responsibilities of his colleagues, who together with the new directors and vice-presidents participated in the daily street demonstrations, had fallen on his shoulders. The second problem was that the number of newborns was strangely and mysteriously on the rise and, consequently, so was the number of applications for birth certificates. It was during this time that on radio and television programmes certain revolutionary individuals would announce that, after extensive research, they had concluded that advertisements sponsored by the previous regime claiming that families with only two or three children live better lives were an imperialist conspiracy. These revolutionary individuals would pound their fists on the table and say, "By advertising conjectures such as Malthus's theory, imperialists were conspiring to reduce the Muslim population of the world."

In any case, the situation got so bad that Sinbad was at the office working until eight o'clock at night, and when he would finally feel faint with hunger, he would take the remainder of his colleagues' work home and attempt to finish it all by two or three in the morning. Still, he did not complain. That is, until the day one of the vice-presidents summoned him to his office and warned that if he continued to fall behind in his duties, it would become obvious that he was opposed to the revolution, and he would be purged. Sinbad wanted to shout in protest, but he realized that speaking his mind would only make matters worse. That day, for the very first time in many years, Sinbad took a few hours off during the day and went out. Alone, he went to a neighbourhood where the old gardens of Shiraz still stood. Oblivious to the drizzling rain, he walked along the winding alleys between the walled gardens. He was so lost in his thoughts that he did not see the ghost of the poet who had died seven hundred years ago. The poet was holding his face up to the sky with his mouth wide open to drink the rain. When he saw Sinbad he waved to him, but Sinbad did not notice. The poet offered him the ghost of a goblet of wine. Sinbad did not notice this either, and walked past him. The dreary rain was still falling on the ghosts of rains that had fallen seven hundred years ago, and the poet watched with compassion as Sinbad walked away. And that is why the poet did not see the other ghosts approaching him. In one startling moment they attacked him, the goblet fell from his hand and with no resistance he surrendered to the *shahneh*s. The *shahneh*s were constables under the command of a heartless and bigoted ruler who in the early thirteenth century had occupied Shiraz, the city of poetry, roses, wine and heavenly consumption. He had beheaded the previous ruler and had transformed Shiraz into a spiritless and sombre city. The task of these *shahneh*s was seemingly that of sheriffs, but after a while their occupation changed to patrolling the city streets, arresting people who did not adhere to Islamic dress, locating secret taverns, breaking wine casks and taking the wine-drinkers to be flogged. One of the *shahneh*s smelled the poet's breath and yelled triumphantly:

"He's been drinking . . . He's been drinking wine."

A second one shouted:

"So we finally have him."

The third one, who obviously had it in for the poet, grabbed him by the lapels and roared in his face:

"I've been after you for two years, but you kept evading my trap. Tomorrow I will treat you to eighty lashes in the town square."

The poet, a sly smile on his lips, said:

"Of course I've been drinking. But only sacred wine."

And at this very moment, inspiration for one of his most beautiful and most famous *ghazal*s – the one that captivated Goethe – came to him.

> *They have closed the tavern door O God do not approve,*
> *for they open the door to deceit and hypocrisy . . .*

The poet glanced at his goblet that lay on the ground. One of the *shahneh*s noticed the direction of his gaze and picked up the goblet as evidence.

He smelled it. His expression changed. Surprised, he smelled the goblet again. He groaned:

"It smells of rose water."

One by one they smelled the goblet. There was no mistake. It smelled of the Shiraz rose.

The most resentful among them said:

"That's not a problem. We'll pour some wine in it and throw in a full decanter, too. Let's take him."

And they dragged the poet's ghost away.

Sinbad did not see this either.

The next day, his colleagues saw him fresh from a good night's sleep, with a neatly shaven face and wearing a suit, walking beside them in the street demonstration. He was raising his fist in the air more enthusiastically and shouting more passionately than they were. Death to America, Death to Britain, Death to France, Death to Russia, Death to Israel, Death to Communists, Death to Hypocrites, Death to Liberals . . .

However, as the demonstrators blocked the traffic and advanced street by street, Sinbad grew more and more convinced that certain people were giving him angry looks. He reasoned that it was because they were a really angry crowd, but he could not understand why some of them kept knocking into him as if to force him onto the pavement and into the crowd of onlookers . . . Finally, he was driven out from among the demonstrators with a big and disturbing "why" on his mind.

The next day he joined a demonstration against improper Islamic dress, but he was forced out in the same manner as the day before.

Two days later, in the afternoon, a disciple of the poet who died seven hundred years ago, with a handwritten copy of the poet's latest *ghazal* hidden in his Sufi's robe, saw Sinbad again strolling along the same winding alleys between the old walled gardens. He was deep in thought, and kept asking himself a question. The disciple who, intoxicated by the beauty of that *ghazal,* was rushing to deliver it to another disciple, looked around cautiously and then held the piece of leather on which the *ghazal* was written in front of Sinbad's eyes. Sinbad did not see him and went on his way. When the sun was setting behind the smog and the screams and laughter of the yet-unborn children of the city, Sinbad, tired and depressed, had still not found an answer to his big "why". On the way back to his house in a poor neighbourhood of the city, in a long and narrow alley, he saw a pedlar selling talismans, spells and magic powders. It had been years since Sinbad had seen such street pedlars. The man was wearing clothes that were a mix of Arab, Afghani, and Indian, and as though he had been expecting Sinbad, with his large luminous eyes he watched him approach.

When Sinbad was close enough, the pedlar bellowed:

"Talismans for good fortune . . . Potions for compassion . . . Incantations for wishes . . ."

Sinbad knelt down in front of the pedlar's wooden box. But just as he came to speak and to ask what he should do, from the man's unmoving lips he heard:

"I know who you are . . . With a whip made of your own skin you flog yourself."

"Help me . . . A talisman, a spell . . . Something . . . No matter what the cost. I will beg and borrow to pay for it . . . Help me."

The magic seller raised the glass lid of his box and began rummaging through the talismans, the small vials of colourful powders and the scraps of paper with spells written on them. All the while, he was mumbling:

"I have a talisman that will stir your love in the heart of the one you love, I have padlock powder for women who have horny husbands – mix it in their tea and make them drink it, the man will be locked and he will no longer think of taking a second wife . . . I have an incantation that, if you repeat it one thousand times, any incurable patient will be cured. But . . ."

He took his hand out of the box.

"But what?"

"Now I am sure, I have nothing for you."

"Search! Search some more. You must have something."

"I don't need to search, because the spell that would grant you your wish is just what I told you."

"How could that be? My problem is no more complicated than the ones you mentioned."

"It is and it isn't."

"You are lying. You are obviously one of those phoney swindling prayer pedlars."

A sly smile appeared on the magic seller's lips.

"I am and I am not."

"For the love of God, help me. I don't know what to do. Give me a talisman with problem-solving powers."

"You already have your problem-solving talisman . . . It's on your face. I have nothing else to give you."

Sinbad got up angrily.

"Mad, miserable wretch! Gather your stuff and get out of this neighbourhood."

The magic seller sighed.

"Go where? I have always been here."

"If I see you around here one more time, you'll be sorry."

Sinbad kicked the old man's box and walked away. This was the first time in his cautious and conservative life that he had had the courage to express his anger towards someone.

All that night he had nightmares of events that were taking place centuries ago . . . He dreams that he is a Sufi eight hundred years back, shouting in Baghdad's bazaar, "*An-al-hagh,* I am God." Fanatic Muslims seize him and accuse him of being an apostate for claiming to be God and throw him in prison. And he, in his cryptlike cell, continues to shout, "*An-al-hagh.*" From a dark corner of the prison a prisoner asks him, "What is love?" and he replies, "Today you behold and tomorrow you behold and the day after you behold," and he knows that today they will stone him and tomorrow they will hang him and the day after that they will burn his corpse and spread his ashes on the Tigris River. He dreams that in the massacre of the city of Kerman, his head, with eyes wide open, is sitting at the peak of a pyramid of heads and he is looking on as the invading soldiers rape the women. He dreams that in the city of Neyshabur, a short Mongol officiously commands, "You are going to stand right there, and you are not going to think of running away, until I bring my sword to kill you." He does think of running away, but he doesn't have the nerve to go through with it. And he sees the Mongol walking towards him . . . He dreams that his face is among the faces of the sentries on the stone reliefs at Persepolis, all of whom have stood in formation holding their spears for two thousand five hundred years. From the corner of his eye he sees the Indian soldiers who serve the British Empire aim their rifles at his eye, and at the eyes of the other sentries, for target practice. He sees the smoke from the nozzles, he hears the sound of the bullets being fired and he is jolted awake.

It was morning. Later, when he was shaving, he remembered what the talisman pedlar had said. He stared at his face. It wasn't a bad face. It was a handsome face. But there was no sign of a spell on it. Sinbad looked in his mouth; perhaps something there would give him inspiration. With his finger he pushed up the tip of his nose to look inside his nostrils . . . No, he saw nothing strange there either. He cursed the magic seller and left for the office. As on all previous days, his colleagues were either busy debating politics or were getting ready to go to some demonstration against something or other. Among the debaters, two groups were often more impassioned than the rest – they were also louder – the Communists, consisting of ten people belonging to seven different political factions, and the die-hard supporters of the Islamic regime who were far greater in number. Sinbad started to work.

Countless mothers and fathers, most of whom brought their newborn with them, would come to request birth certificates with all sorts of different and at times strange names for their child. Sinbad would record their information in a book, along with the chosen name, and he would ask them to return in two months to pick up their child's birth certificate. The parents would complain:

"Sir, how long could it possibly take to write a couple of names on a birth certificate for us to have to wait two months?"

Sinbad would meekly glance over at his colleagues who were busy arguing, and he would explain all the various steps that he would have to take to issue a birth certificate.

Sometimes the parents, clutching their newborn, would join the debaters and start arguing about the crimes and treasons committed by the Shah's regime, by American imperialism, by Russia, Britain, France, Germany and China. Sometimes one of the die-hard Communists would reach boiling point and shout, "According to Marx . . ." and from the opposite side others would shout back in unison, "Death to communism which says there is no God." It was in the midst of all this commotion that Sinbad would at times make strange mistakes. For instance, on a boy's birth certificate he would write a girl's name, or vice versa. That morning, he was double-checking a birth certificate when, with a spark of inspiration, he suddenly realized that, ever since the revolution, the number of birth-certificate applications for newborns with names of Iranian kings and emperors was decreasing and, conversely, the number of applications for newborns with religious names and Arabic names that have no relation to religious figures was increasing. In a gesture of surprise, as is common around the world, he raised his hand to his face. He realized that he had not shaved that morning. He found it strange that he would forget an age-old habit. Even stranger was that he seemed to have some vague memory of soaping his face and shaving that morning, and then looking at himself in the mirror searching for a spell . . .

The next applicants did not give Sinbad more time to think. It was two in the afternoon when he noticed his colleague, Ms Roxanna, staring at him in surprise. Ms Roxanna was the only woman in their office, and further to the decree forbidding female government employees from wearing make-up, she obstinately came to work every morning wearing make-up, even more make-up than she used to wear before the revolution. The lady was among the very few employees who treated Sinbad with respect, and Sinbad had started thinking that perhaps he was in love with her. The only reason he had not proposed to Roxanna was that he was sure that any day now she would be purged as an anti-revolutionary and a corrupt element. Sinbad knew that, given his meagre salary and the soaring inflation, he had to marry a woman who had a job.

At three in the afternoon, Roxanna again stared at him. But there was no longer any respect or surprise in her eyes. Instead, there was fear. Sinbad rushed to the bathroom and looked at his face in the mirror. He was shocked. Not only had he not shaved that morning, but it seemed he had not shaved for the past three days. Yet Sinbad's surprise was nowhere as great as his surprise, and even horror, the next morning when he stood in front of the mirror. At the sight of a stranger's face looking at him, he screamed and leaped back. A bearded man was looking back at him from the mirror. Sinbad ran his hand over his face, and for the first time in his life he felt the softness of his beard. A full, beautiful, adult beard. The soft hair flowed down neatly, as if it had been blow-dried. The beard had given his face a spiritual and innocent quality. Sinbad examined it more closely. He was experiencing an unfamiliar pleasure. He enjoyed the touch of this alien feature and found his new face interesting to look at, yet he reached for the razor and shaved off the beard and left for the office.

He was in no mood for work that day, but there were so many applicants and so much to do that he didn't even have time to scratch his beard. Ms Roxanna's looks of surprise and fear persisted, and it seemed as if looks of reproach had been added to them. Sinbad thought, The hussy! She acts as if I owe her something. To hell with her. Good thing I didn't propose marriage. Obviously she's one of those foul-tempered demanding women who treat their husbands like slaves and constantly look for excuses to henpeck and drive them mad. Therefore, the last time their eyes met, he did not quickly look away. In fact, with impudence and even anger he stared back at her with a look of What's your problem, hussy? And he held his glare until Roxanna grew embarrassed and looked away.

At two o'clock that afternoon, Mr P. tapped him on the shoulder and asked him to go for a walk. Mr P. was one of those rare people who, prior to the revolution, openly demonstrated his religious inclinations. Even back then, unlike his colleagues, he never wore ties, always had stubble on his chin, and whenever he came face to face with a woman wearing make-up and dressed in Western fashion, he would become terribly uncomfortable. He would blush, sweat, struggle not to look at the woman's face and would turn away. He had once explained to a colleague why he would not even lower his head and look down. "These women . . . One doesn't know what to do . . . Some of them wear such short skirts and sandals without socks that no matter how low you hang your head you can still see part of their legs . . . I get embarrassed instead of them."

During the early months of the revolution, P. organized and led a strike by that bureau's employees, and for this he was arrested and thrown in prison. After the revolution triumphed, he was released along with other political detainees – some of whom had spent more than thirty years in the Shah's prisons – and he returned to his workplace a hero.

Sinbad walked in step with P., who was being very quiet and mysterious. He couldn't figure out what this important person who always ignored him could possibly want with him. He was scared. He thought P. probably wanted to tell him he was being purged. He had prepared to defend himself if such a remark was made and to complain that they should fire Ms Roxanna instead.

A group of a hundred people were walking down the street, hurling their fists at the sky and shouting, "Death to the monarchist, death to the Communist, death to the hypocrite, death to the counter-revolution."

P., in a voice that now sounded sad, said:

"I see you've stopped shaving."

Sinbad ran his hand over his face. He realized that contrary to what he had thought, he had again not shaved. He now had a five-day beard. He did not answer.

"It's very good. Islam disapproves of men shaving their faces and look-ing like women."

"I know."

"I know you know . . . My concern is something else."

"I have always tried to be a good employee. If there is any shortcoming in my work, please tell me and I will certainly rectify it. If you take my job away from me, I will be ruined. I have an old mother who worked as a ser-vant in rich people's homes to raise me, and now she is bedridden."

"No one wants to fire you. My concern is that your growing a beard is a hypocrisy and a pretence. In my opinion, in Islam hypocrisy is a far greater sin than shaving. This is what I wanted to tell you."

Sinbad looked at P.'s sad face in surprise; P. was looking somewhere far away.

"These days everyone is a die-hard Muslim. Mr Kingslave has changed his name to Pious. The man who I do not claim was an infor-mant of the Shah's secret service, but who we know was a member of the Shah-ordained Rastakhiz Party, has grown a beard and is now more devout than the likes of me. He goes to the director general every day and with half-truths and half-lies he badmouths our colleagues, he slan-ders them and, to show that he is a revolutionary, he recommends that some of them be purged. It was he who made the director general suspect you, even though we all know how very responsible you are . . . I am struggling to make sure such people do not get ahead and sidetrack the revolution."

Sinbad said angrily:

"I'm not one of these people. I just want to do my job, collect my salary, and live my life . . . Why are you telling me all this? You should go and stop people like Mr Pious instead."

"I just wanted to tell you that we are all Muslims but if you, from the bottom of your heart, do not believe in practising some of the instructions of Islam, then take it easy with your appearance. Let it be your heart that guides you, with purity of purpose, not to shave your beard. If you pre-serve the purity of your heart, you will be showing God greater love. Hypocrisy will distance you from God."

"Why are you so sure that what you are saying is itself not a hypocrisy?"

Shocked by this question, P. stood motionless. He looked into Sinbad's eyes. Tears welled up, and he looked down.

"You are right. No one can be completely sure . . . Hypocrisy has many faces and many shades . . . Throughout history, all the calamities that have befallen us Iranians have been because of this hypocrisy . . ."

Seeing P.'s vulnerability, Sinbad felt sorry for him. He thanked him and returned to the office.

That afternoon, as Sinbad was walking home, very far from the office, he heard Mr Pious calling him from behind.

"How are you, my fellow colleague . . . I haven't heard from you in a while."

"Well, you are very busy."

"My brother, me? Busy? Well, yes, the director general has put some new responsibilities on my shoulders. My duty is to the revolution; I must bear the weight. Otherwise, I am that same old friend of my fellow colleagues."

"What are you doing around these parts? Your house is at the nice end of town."

"My man, what do you mean, nice? I inherited that ramshackle hut we live in from my father . . . But I was born and brought up in this neighbourhood. I was on my way to my aunt's house when I ran into you. How are you?"

"I'm fine. All is well."

Pious stared at Sinbad with his sharp, perceptive eyes. Then his tone changed.

"I saw you walking with P. this afternoon. I wanted to tell you to be very careful of him. Don't be fooled by his innocent appearance. He is one of those slippery snakes. A long time ago he pulled all our colleagues' files from the archives and studied them. He has made a long list of people to be purged, and he goes to the director general every day and insists that they are anti-revolution elements and must be dismissed."

"There is nothing in my file for me to be worried about. I have always done my job, and I have nothing to do with anyone's good or evil deeds."

"Do you really think it's difficult for them to frame someone? He can easily tell them that you used to be an undercover agent for the secret police . . . As a matter of fact, given the current situation, the likes of you, alone and not having the support of any group or faction should be even more afraid. We are friends and colleagues. We have to look out for each other."

Earnestly, Sinbad said:

"In any case, I too have worked hard for the revolution, and I don't want it to suffer in any way."

Mr Pious thanked him for his goodwill and said:

"I know. What's important is for us to look out for each other and to be united. One of these days we'll get Mr P. fired from the bureau. Then you will understand that I have supported you and wished you well by warning you not to go down the well with his rotten rope."

Sinbad thanked this newfound friend, and Mr Pious, as a gesture of his sincerity, patted him on the back and said goodbye. Sinbad arrived home feeling more tired and helpless than ever before. He warmed up his mother's food, put it in front of her and sat cross-legged in the corner of the room to watch television.

In the television programme, one of the revolutionaries who had lived in France for many years and who had returned to the homeland after the revolution was talking passionately about the government's plan to change Western names. He was explaining that the heads of the Ministry of Arts and Culture – which was later renamed the Ministry of Culture and Islamic Guidance – had organized a committee and issued a warning to factories that made products with Western names and to shops and especially boutiques that had Western names on their signs. Meanwhile, the committee was taking immediate action to delete the names of streets such as Shah Street, Roosevelt Street, Elizabeth Boulevard, Kennedy Circle, and would instead select Iranian names for them. Suddenly, a spark of inspiration flashed in Sinbad's mind. Excited, he got up and started to pace around the small room . . . Yes, this was it. To prove what a good employee he was, to show what a creative and productive mind he had, for everyone to understand that he had never had any fondness for that monarchist regime, he must present the General Register Office with a revolutionary plan that would play a fundamental role in the lives of future generations of Iranians. Given that he had always been a responsible and hardworking employee, he was surprised that he had not thought of this sooner. He quickly stacked up all the paper he had at home in front of him. He divided each sheet into two columns. The column on the right for recommended and suitable revolutionary names, the opposite column for rotten and vulgar anti-revolutionary names. In the introduction to his plan he wrote: "It is obvious and apparent that a name plays an essential role in the formation of its owner's character and his or her future happiness." Sinbad's mind had become very active, and it quickly reminded him of different names. Of course, in his proposed plan, which he would have to present to the director general, he would need to point out that the suitable revolutionary names should only be suggested and recommended to parents who apply for their newborn's birth certificate and that there should be no coercion whatsoever. The rationale behind his plan was that because the Iranian people are extremely logical and steer clear of sentimentality, they would eagerly and wholeheartedly embrace the recommended names and would abstain from selecting anti-revolutionary names for their children. The random few who might not adhere to this revolutionary plan would have proved themselves to be spies and anti-revolution elements, and their punishment would be left up to the courts.

Although Sinbad was very happy to have come up with such an original plan, he was only just grasping the magnitude of his real problem. Yes, his beard. On the one hand, his beard was his saving angel, but on the other, it had got out of control and overly ambitious. Every man's beard grows an average of 0.02 of an inch per day, but Sinbad's beard was growing an average of 0.1 of an inch per hour. Some time later, he would come to realize that its rate of growth depended entirely on his state of mind. In other words, sometimes his beard would grow by as much as 0.3 of an inch per hour. Of course, solving this problem was not as difficult as it first appeared. When Sinbad at last came to accept his beard's eagerness and energy to grow, it was probably the beard itself that inspired him with a solution: to carry a pair of scissors in his pocket at all times, and to find a quiet place every hour to trim it. Of course, because Sinbad did not, and does not, have any connection to literature, censorship and the symbol of censorship, he will never know what bitter irony a pair of scissors in one pocket will put in his other pocket.

Anyway, Sinbad worked on his plan for a week, and after preparing two alphabetical lists of good names for men and women using the world's latest scientific methods, and two alphabetical lists of bad names for men and women that should be deleted from the cultural consciousness and the present-day memory of Iranians, he delivered them to the director general's secretary. And thus, his rise began.

Just as you have guessed, it was Mr P. who was purged. Do I need to remind you that purging, or cleansing, is a form of censorship? As a writer who is at times more ill fated and wretched than *Les Misérables*'s Jean Val-jean, I believe that at the time I consented to the deletion of one word from one story, I also consented to the deletion of one human being from his workplace or from his life. Since Mr P. has been censored, I can no longer help him to have an important role in our love story. Therefore, let us with absolute cruelty no longer think of him.

When I visited the General Register Office for my daughter's birth certificate, Mr Sinbad had already occupied the seat of vice-president for public and cultural affairs. His innovative and revolutionary list of permitted and prohibited names had been distributed to all the General Register Offices throughout the country, and his plan was being implemented everywhere. But his rise did not end here. One day when Sinbad wanted to write a note in pencil, the tip of his pencil broke at the slightest pressure against the paper. It was a new pencil in a nice colour. Sinbad sharpened its tip, but just as he was taking the pencil out of the pencil sharpener, its new tip broke and stayed behind under the pencil sharpener's blade. Sinbad removed the broken tip with some difficulty and sharpened the pencil again, and the same thing happened again and again until Sinbad was left holding a one-inch pencil without a tip. He took another pencil of the same make and examined it. Yes, as you have suspected, it was made in China. In Iranian graphic arts, in addition to a pair of scissors, a pencil or a fountain pen with a broken tip is a symbol of censorship and restraints on the freedom of speech. However, in total contrast to this symbol, that tipless pencil sparked a second great inspiration of Sinbad's life in his mind. Without a doubt, the merchant who had imported these cheap pencils from China and sold them at a high price in the Iranian market – which is under US embargo – had made huge profits. Think about it. How precious a commodity pencils must be in a country with a population that has in two decades increased from thirty million to sixty million, with at least seventeen million students in schools and universities . . . That night, Sinbad wrote another ingenious plan and delivered it to the director general of the General Register Office. According to this plan, he would go on an all-expenses-paid mission to China to research the covert revolutionary techniques used by the Chinese to increase their population and the Red techniques used in their Cultural Revolution to delete the names and symbols of tyrannical Chinese emperors. Sinbad received the month-long assignment and headed for materialist China, whose relationship with Muslim countries was improving day by day. Well, where do you think the best place in China is to do scientific research on deleting counter-revolutionary symbols and methods of population increase? Obviously, Chinese pencil factories.

Ask me what I mean and, by the way, also ask me how all of these labyrinthine tales relate to a simple love story. And I will say:

As a matter of fact, the tales are very much related to our love story. Just as a pencil can freely write the words of a nauseating love story replete with veiled sexual undertones as a service to a corrupt counter-revolutionary culture, it can also be the instrument with which the sentences of that same story are crossed out. In the same way that a pencil in the hands of a corrupt-minded writer or spy or traitor can transfer words that, consciously or subconsciously, carry the viruses of a decadent Western culture, it can also, with the sharpness of its tip, like the needle of a syringe, inject the vaccine against the same anti-revolution microbes in the population's veins. On the other hand, think about it: what a highly consumed commodity pencils must be in a country where thousands of writers and poets write to become the greatest writer or poet in the world and, facing them, thousands of people read what they have written to cross out instances of their immorality.

When Sinbad returned to Iran from his fact-finding mission, in his pocket he had a small contract to import high-quality Chinese pencils to offset the presence of illicit Western pencils. In two years and seven months, through his government position and the friends he had made in the Customs department and the marketplace, Sinbad became the largest importer of handsome Chinese pencils. He resigned from his government job to make room for other creative young people to rise. He relocated his import-export business to Tehran and spent all his energy, ingenuity and experience on importing pencils that did not write at all, and therefore did not burden anyone with the inconvenience of having to cross out and delete any words.

In the process of this revolutionary service, Sinbad amassed a large fortune. His annual income was far more than the seventy-five million dollars that Mr Bush's political machine had once earmarked for changing Iran's political regime. Sometimes, in the company of his merchant friends,

Sinbad would quip, "I can earmark seven hundred and fifty million dollars for changing the American political regime." But our story's Sara has yet to make a decision about marrying Sinbad and spending her honeymoon in Paris or at his villa in Spain. This is one of our story's dilemmas. Sara, just like a decent and virtuous young lady who of course has never worn colourful shoes, who of course has never sewn colourful buttons on her coverall, and who of course has never highlighted her fringe so that she can let it fall out from under her headscarf to lead Iranian men and boys astray, is sitting next to her parents and drinking premium Indian tea with Sinbad.

As soon as we begin this scene in our love story, Sinbad goes to the bathroom to trim his beard down to the same length as it was when he first arrived at Sara's house. I take advantage of this brief interruption to think about how I can find Mr Petrovich, and how I can make him tell me what his opinion of Dara's name is.

Sinbad returns from the bathroom.

Sara's mother, delighted by the honour of having him present in their home, resumes her coquettish verbosity.

"Oh dear, you haven't touched your pastry. If you don't like these pastries, there is an excellent pastry shop nearby. My husband can quickly go and buy some more."

Sinbad, glancing at a silent Sara, puts the pastry in his mouth, and pretending to brush the crumbs off his jacket he brushes away some of the trimmed beard.

Sara's mother asks:

"May I pour you another cup of tea?"

"Please. What a wonderful tea this is. It is very fragrant and full of flavour."

"As you know, these days the market is full of adulterated tea. Even if you put two or three handfuls of it in the teapot, it still has no colour or flavour."

"Is it Iranian tea?"

"Absolutely not . . . What a question! Iranian tea? All our life we have only bought fine foreign tea. The one you are drinking is a Two-Sword-labelled premium Indian-English tea. My husband buys it on the black market."

Sara, angry and disappointed by her mother's bragging, coughs

deliberately. Her mother gets up, not because she has taken her daughter's warning seriously, but to bring the box of the Two-Sword-labelled premium Indian-English tea as proof of her claims.

Sinbad says:

"My good lady, Iranian tea is most certainly a good tea, but it has lost in the advertising arena and its name has been tarnished. When I was a vice-president at the bureau, I ordered that only Iranian tea be brewed and served there. I even tried to make sure that the employees didn't drink non-Iranian tea at home."

While speaking these words, Sinbad tries to memorize the name and address of the producer of the Two-Sword-labelled premium Indian-English tea printed on the box. He's thinking that he may also be clever at importing tea. There are many common factors between pencils and tea and, of course, there are no common factors between Sinbad and those charlatan merchants who sell third-rate Iranian tea, packaged in boxes with Indian writing and the Two-Sword label printed on them, at exorbitant prices on the black market.

Sinbad says:

"Miss Sara, why are you so quiet tonight?"

Since Sinbad's arrival, Sara constantly sees Dara's innocent face in front of her. But once in a while she does feel like taking a peek at Sinbad's face and his beautiful beard. Of all the features on Sinbad's face, Sara likes his eyes the most. From these eyes, the agony of years of poverty, deprivation and toil have not yet been erased. Sinbad, in their only private conversation in this house, has candidly poured his heart out about his childhood and about growing up without a father, and he has told her that he is not one of those nouveau riche people blinded by wealth.

Sara says:

"I was thinking."

"Can you share some of your thoughts with me?"

"As a matter of fact, I wanted to ask your opinion. Surely you are aware that a few days ago there were demonstrations and clashes in front of the university."

"I did hear something about it."

"What do you think of those students?"

Sara's parents both begin to cough.

Sara tells them:

"Please don't cut me off with your coughs."

This is the first time Sara has dared address her parents in this manner.

Deep in my ear I hear Mr Petrovich's voice.

"You see! This rudeness is the result of Sara's forbidden and clandestine love affair. You see what sin does to people's personalities? This is only the beginning. If your story continues like this, this ignorant girl will wreck and ruin her life with her own hands. Give her a stern warning."

But instead, **Sara's mother has dragged her husband to the kitchen to give him a stern warning.**

"How many times have I told you not to buy these cheap pastries? You have embarrassed us. Run out and buy a box of the finest pastries, and I'll see how I can shut Sara up. This ignorant girl will wreck and ruin her life, and ours, with her own hands."

Laughing, she returns to the living room and says:

"Oh dear, Mr Sinbad, don't touch that pastry. Sara's father has just gone out to buy pastries that you would like."

Sinbad obediently puts the pastry back on his plate but continues his conversation with Sara.

"For this reason, I think if I were a student, I too would participate in the demonstrations. I truly respect them. They are the assets of the revolution. If you are one of these students, then on my behalf, please . . ."

Sara's mother quickly interrupts him.

"Sir, what are you saying? My daughter is by no means part of that group of misguided students."

Dolefully, Sara says:

"In fact, this time my mother is correct. I am not one of them."

"In any case, if you ever talk to them, tell them that many of the country's leaders are aware of the problems and issues that have angered them and that they too are distressed. But for the time being, given that we are in the throes of an outwardly cold yet fiery war with the United States, Britain, France, Germany and Israel, it is not wise or prudent for them to create disturbances and provide publicity hype for the Western media and the opponents of the revolution living abroad."

I am positive Mr Petrovich will like this sentence.

~~But Sara, contrary to my wishes and expectations, says:~~

~~"For years everyone has been told to keep quiet, not to criticize, not to object, with the same excuses of war and conflict with worldwide imperialism and the opponents of the revolution . . ."~~

I, without Sara's permission, cross out this sentence, and to avoid having to write the rest of her comments, I leave their house. Outside, I see Sara's father who, instead of running to the pastry shop, is standing frozen in place with a petrified look on his face. Right next to the front door a hunchback midget is sitting on the ground, leaning against the wall with his legs spread apart and his lifeless eyes fixed on his thighs. Scared that someone may walk by and see the corpse next to the front door of his house, Sara's father looks frantically around. I tap him on the shoulder and point to Sinbad's car that shines like a diamond parked among all the old dilapidated cars. Sara's father understands that because Sinbad is a wealthy and influential man, he can easily get rid of the midget.

It doesn't take too much effort for a writer to open the boot of a car belonging to a character in his story. Incidentally, since the age of sixteen, I have longed to have a late-model BMW, and I confess that I, like many others, have a BMW complex. In any case, it takes me all of five seconds to take a screwdriver out of my pocket and break the lock on the boot. I leave the boot open, and as I walk away, with that same screwdriver I scratch an end-to-end line along the side of the car. I whistle as I go so that Sara's father can do the sensible thing without the inconvenience of a witness. Even if Dara still doesn't know why he always carries his grandmother's silk handkerchief in his pocket, I now understand why, this morning, I involuntarily put a screwdriver in my pocket as I left the house.

Now I have something important to do. I must somehow cross paths with Mr Petrovich. Just last night, as I was writing, I put my head down on my desk to rest my eyes a little. There was a large poster of Dostoyevsky on the wall behind me. In this famous painting of the writer's bust, Dostoyevsky's glazed and insanity-stricken eyes stare at some point outside the painting's frame. I, with my eyes closed, was struggling to see Dara's sad face after he hears about Sara's suitor. Suddenly, I thought I heard the sound of a glass object grinding inside a dry and gritty cavity. I swung around and saw that Dostoyevsky's eyes had turned towards my handwritten pages and were reading what I had written from over my shoulder. But those eyes were neither glazed nor tortured, and they seemed more familiar than Dostoyevsky's eyes. I froze; I realized that the eyes belonged to none other than Ivan Karamazov's Grand Inquisitor in *The Brothers Karamazov*; in other words, that same high priest and investigator at the trial of Jesus who, with the most precise scholastic reasoning, somehow accuses Jesus of sedition and sentences him to death.

If only all the horrors in the world were this simple and unimaginative. No, those were not the eyes of the Grand Inquisitor. Drained, I slumped back in my chair. I turned the pages of my story over and said:

"How are you, Mr Petrovich?"

I woke up. I looked at my watch. My eyes had closed for just a few seconds. I was relieved that the scene was only a fleeting nightmare. But my joy was short-lived. I noticed that the cigarette I had been holding was stubbed out and lay crushed in the ashtray. I never stub out my cigarettes because they usually burn to the end sitting in the ashtray and snuff out, or I extinguish them gently and with respect. Just then I remembered that on the border of sleep and wakefulness, I had sensed someone behind me. He had leaned forward and in a fatherly manner had taken the cigarette from between my fingers, and while reading the last page of my story and its crossed-out sentences, he had crushed it in the ashtray with disgust . . .

That night, after scratching Sinbad's car, I walked quickly to a state-run cultural centre where, as an exception, they had allowed an Iranian poet to give a lecture. As I had expected, Mr Petrovich was there. He was sitting in the back row, and with eyes that could read deep into people's minds he was staring at the face of Iran's olden-day poet. The poet's speech was about censorship. For five minutes, in a gentle and edifying tone, he spoke about the harms of censorship, and then he announced that he had recently made a great discovery. A discovery that would see contemporary Iranian literature rapidly gain fame throughout the world, get translated into different languages, produce bestsellers and, at last, secure the Nobel Prize, if not for him, then for another Iranian poet or writer. This great poet's discovery was that censorship drives a poet or a writer to abstain from superficiality and instead to delve into the layers and depths of love and relationships and achieve a level of creativity that Western poets and writers cannot even dream of.

I had opted to sit where I was sure to be in Mr Petrovich's field of vision. Towards the end of the lecture, when I felt the weight of his eyes on the back of my neck, I knew my plan had worked. After the lecture, I casually left the hall. Tehran had again lost track of time, and the ghosts of winters past had laid siege to the city – it was snowing. Large snow-flakes, not blackened by soot, filled the footprints of passers-by who had passed by on the fallen snow, and I knew that soon they would fill my footprints too. Have you ever listened to the sound of your footsteps on snow? Isn't it mysterious? Isn't there a measure of crushing and being crushed in it?

I had been walking for scarcely ten minutes when I heard Mr Petrovich call me from behind.

"Where are you going?"

By now my hair had turned whiter than forty-nine years warranted, and consequently, the snow that covered it made little change in my appearance. Yet it seemed as though time had left Mr Petrovich untouched, except for his eyes, which had become sharper and more chastising. I stood still while he caught up with me.

"I don't know, I was just walking. Maybe there is a sandwich shop open and I can have some dinner."

"Then you must have been making fun of the government directive that forces cafés and restaurants to close at eleven o'clock."

I admire Mr Petrovich's ability to read people's hidden thoughts. It is an ability far superior to the sorrow writers feel when, incredulously, they manage to read a few seconds of the hidden thoughts of the one they love.

I said:

"You said it, not me."

He laughed.

"Forget it, Mr Writer! Wise up! You who consider yourself to be so clever because you can divert people's thoughts away from subjects that you don't like, and towards subjects that you do like, should put all your cleverness to work when you are with me. Don't make pointless comments and don't tell stupid lies . . . Tell me, why did you come to the cultural centre tonight? I know you don't like the poet. Did you want to see me?"

Only then did I realize what a cold and dark night it was.

Most of the streetlamps were out, and most of the windows were dark. There were only the sounds of our feet and the *whish* of the falling snow.

"How is your story coming along?"

"Sometimes it moves along, sometimes it falls down. When it falls, I fall with it."

"Last week I was having lunch with a friend who works at one of the sensitive ministries, and our talk dragged on to you writers. Have you heard the latest joke about writers?"

I couldn't hide my delight at learning that Mr Petrovich is keen on jokes, too. In the light from a window, I saw a torn piece of carpet on the pavement. The snow was coating its shades of azure and crimson.

"It has often happened, and will often happen, that one of you, thinking he is smarter than us, secretly writes something or hides an innuendo in his writings, and then he is thrilled, thinking that he has pulled a fast one. Up to this point it isn't funny. What's funny is that we know all along what he has done or is doing, but we don't react, we let him do what he wants. In other words, we let him assume we are stupid. Sometimes, without his knowledge, we even help him put his plan into action . . . Which one of us do you think is smarter in this intelligence contest?"

"But the writer doesn't have anything to hide because in the end, all he wants is to have his work published. I think writers are the most naked people in the world."

"Stop it, stop it . . . You want to play mind games with me, too? There are some writers who send their writings overseas, supposedly in secret, to have them published under cowardly pseudonyms in periodicals and on websites opposed to the revolution; there are others who pretend to write a harmless love story, and by taking advantage of the innocence of love, they hide political inferences behind symbols and metaphors. But I am talking about writers who are even more clever."

I realized that although Mr Petrovich is still as mistrusting of literature as he was in bygone years, his knowledge has broadened.

I said:

"In my opinion, if a writer has any objective other than writing a beautiful story, he will not become a good writer."

"Excellent. That is exactly what my argument is. I say, sit down and write nice stories, stories that will make your country proud. Tell me, do you want to give a lecture about your thoughts on this subject at the cultural centre? We can invite a large crowd, and the next day nice critiques of your theory will appear in newspapers and magazines. You'll become famous."

"No. Not at all. First of all, the moment I voice my opinion, some of the ideologically predisposed political activists will start rumours that you have paid me off to encourage writers to write shallow, non-protesting, non-committed stories. Second, I think a perfect and beautiful story is the most dangerous story."

"I think you are a really stupid writer."

"Thank you. I use the term 'dimwit' to describe myself."

"Look here. There is a place where a large number of literature experts – real experts, not these second-string critics – are busy working seriously and meticulously. They know all of you better than you know yourselves. Even more important, they have thoroughly researched your private lives and the style, syntax and structure of your stories, and they have input their findings into special software that we purchased from a Western country. If you write a story and publish it under a pseudonym, the next day the expert responsible for your work will be able to determine that it is your work, from its words, style and structure. If he doesn't want to go to too much trouble, he will simply input some information in the computer program, such as a few key words, and extract your name."

I was biting my lips for fear that in my incredible state of shock I would make a sound. It was snowing more heavily, and the cold wind gusting from the end of the street was beating the snowflakes against my face. Mr Petrovich chuckled sarcastically and continued:

"Now you are probably thinking how important and precious you writers must be for such an elaborate system to have been set up for you."

"No . . . Quite the opposite. I am sorry, but I am actually amused that all these experts, systems and software are for a bunch of miserable writers and poets, ninety per cent of whom are completely preoccupied with how they are going to feed their family and come up with tomorrow's rent."

"You see! You see! Then when I call you stupid, you take offence; you make fun of me and say that I should call you dimwit . . . Dimwit! These experts are only working on your works as an exercise. The main stage of their work will be to examine and identify works by the famous and important writers of the world . . . Forget it. All I meant to say is that, after all these years, you still don't know your best critic. If he were to publish his reviews and critiques of your work, you would very quickly become famous. Who knows, you may even win the Nobel Prize. Do you want me to arrange a meeting with him?"

My heart sank. I said:

"No, please. I am not after fame at all. Honestly, I write mostly for my own pleasure."

"Wasn't it only two weeks ago that you were telling your friend on the telephone that if you get the one-million-dollar reward for the Nobel Prize, the first thing you will do is buy a Porsche and drive along the mountain roads in Italy?"

My knees gave way and I fell. It was a good opportunity to catch my breath and collect my thoughts. I said:

"Ah, this damned snow . . . I'm sorry. I slipped."

Looming over me, Mr Petrovich stared at me for a while and then reached down to help me get up. I said:

"Sir, my friend and I were making fun of those people who are dying to win the Nobel Prize. First of all, I love BMWs, not Porsches. Second, ever since I saw how jealous people scratch BMWs with screwdrivers, I have been thinking that it is better for me to fantasize about having a Harley-Davidson instead."

"An American motorcycle?"

"Harley-Davidson is American?"

"Oh, come on."

"So I'll exchange it for a Yamaha."

We were crossing the bridge where Sara and Dara had torn up the spell for hatred. By then I was covered with snow and freezing. But as usual, Mr Petrovich was striding along looking dignified and stately. I could see the snowflakes changing direction as soon as they reached his proximity. The end of the bridge was swallowed up in fog. I asked:

"Do you think Dara is a good name for a fictitious character?"

"It depends on the character. Is he the protagonist, antagonist, or narrator? But if you are looking for a name that in translation would be pronounceable for a foreign reader, then why don't you name him Daniel?"

My knees froze. A few feet away, suspended in the air, menacing clusters of fog were waiting. There was a hint of purple somewhere deep inside them. I wanted to turn round and walk away without saying goodbye. But Mr Petrovich's presence had robbed me of all power of will and strength of anger. The bitter chill crept up my sides and in between my teeth. We entered the fog clusters. Now there was again only the sound of our feet and the *whish* of the snow still falling. A shadow darker than the night approached us, a frail and haggard figure. It blocked our way. He looked first at Mr Petrovich, and then he fixed his eyes, two cubes of very old ice, on my eyes. It was him! The same man from beneath whose cloak many of the world's writers have emerged: Gogol's Akaky Akakievich.

He asked:

"Have you seen the thief who stole my cloak?"

BITTER WATER

On this snowy night, Dara is sitting at the window of his room feeling sad. He feels he is a small pile of snow that Sara with her beautiful hands has delicately and compassionately made into a small snowman, which she has caressed, and which then, squish, she has crushed under her foot. Hearing the sound of the snowman being squashed, Dara angrily punches the wall and swears at himself.

~~"You fucking dimwit!"~~

Just here, I come face to face with another problem in writing my love story. In stories that go to the Ministry of Culture and Islamic Guidance to receive publishing permits, there should be no foul language uttered by the characters, especially popular swear words associated with the primary sexual organs and auxiliary sexual organs. Now imagine that, in one of your stories, you have a foul-mouthed thug, and you want to develop this character. Let's suppose you have reached a scene in Iran in which the thug character has grabbed a polite character by the collar and is picking a fight with him. What would you do?

In an age when every day stressed and troubled people in all corners of the world get into fights over small and petty issues and shout vulgarities at each other, and bystanders become their censors, characters in Iranian stories, in the most critical moments, in climaxes such as fights and brawls, and even on occasions when they are killing each other, can only go so far as: *Rude idiot . . . Grass . . . Moron . . . Cheeky . . . I'm going to slap you . . .* This in direct contrast to American films in which, during similarly critical climaxes, or even in the course of revelries and romantic interludes, words such as *Shit . . . Arsehole . . . Bastard . . .* and *Fuck you . . .* fly from the lips of characters to the farthest limits of the cinema screen. I know polite American television channels have found an effective method of censoring these foul words even when dealing with rap songs. It is that bleep sound that suddenly pops up in the middle of what the character or the rapper is saying. These bleeps may be effective in films, and they may render rap songs more acceptable, but they are not a solution for us Iranian writers. How in the world can we put a high-pitched bleep in the mouths of characters in our stories?

Please do not tell me that those three infamous dots ". . ." will solve the problem.

No, they will not . . . Ask me why and I will say:

The use of these three dots is very dangerous to any story. In fact, it is like gaining access to nuclear energy with which one can either produce electricity to light streetlamps so that ghosts from the stories of Gogol and Bram Stoker, and ghosts from the *One Thousand and One Nights*, cannot go roaming around so easily, or use it to build a nuclear bomb. Readers, however, are generally not interested in lighting lamps on streets inhabited by ghosts. I mean, the moment a reader, especially an Iranian one, sees these three villainous dots, a reaction similar to the chain reaction triggered by nuclear fission of the uranium atom takes place in his mind, and it results in the release of terrifying nuclear energy. When readers see these three dots, control of their imagination is no longer in the hands of the writer, nor is it in the hands of Mr Petrovich. For example, it is possible that at some point Sinbad will discover the existence of our love story's Dara and will realize that Dara's love is what is keeping Sara from saying yes to his marriage proposal. One night, Sinbad could grab Dara in a dark corner of his neighbourhood, throw him against the wall and say:

"Hey chicken! Get out of Sara's life or I will have you sent to where even the Angel of Death won't find you."

Dara could sneer and say:

". . ."

And the writer's intended words would be "to my balls", but the rude reader could interpret the three dots as "tell my balls to go and play squash with your arse," which in Iran, even for homosexuals, would be a vulgar insult . . . Or Dara could tell Sara:

"Open your . . . and . . ."

The deleted sentence would be:

"Open your thirsty lips and suppress my desire."

Meaning, for example, let your lips tell me that our heavenly love

145

should not turn into pure lust. However, the reader's nuclear-enriched imagination will reconstruct the sentence as such:

"Open your thirsty thighs and with your pink scissors circumcise me once again!"

Or the reverse, Dara could write to Sara:

"In the glow of the candle, hand . . . shadow . . . flames . . ."

The romantic reader could assume the sentence to be:

"In the glow of the candle, I will wrap my hand around the shadow of your waist, I will dance the tango with you, desiring the blue of the Mediterranean I shall kiss the shadow of your wine-stained lips, I will become a shadow, I will dissolve in your shadow, we shall fly to the Mediterranean where on the beach, on the golden sand, we shall light a fire with our celestial love, and in the blaze of its flames our shadows will part, we will find physical form, we will become two red roses with our stems intertwined, our thorns piercing each other, dancing in the breeze."

And Stalin could read the same three dots as:

"In the glow of the candle, I write by hand the draft of the anti-government communiqué as shadows of spies lurk behind the window, and tomorrow the flames of the people's rage and hatred shall reduce this tyrannical regime to ashes, and on the bloody eve of victory I know what I must do with you dissenting writers and poets, traitors to the doctrine of the revolution."

It is thus that Iranian writers have become the most polite, the most impolite, the most romantic, the most pornographic, the most political, the most socialist realist and the most postmodern writers in the world. I just don't know in which school of story-writing I should categorize Iranian stories in which thugs, similar to the gravedigger in *Hamlet*, speak literary and philosophical words.

Therefore, when Dara swears at himself with the same words that I have uttered in front of Mr Petrovich, I cross out ~~"fucking dimwit"~~ and I write:

Dara punches the wall and says to himself:

"You idiot!"

He is only then realizing that Sara is a very complicated person. But still he cannot believe that she would conceal the existence of her suitor from him. The first thought that crosses the mind of a man in love, such as Dara, is that his beloved has duped him, and now, to make

her wealthy suitor jealous and to push him to set a wedding date soon, she is talking about this poor lovelorn man and they are laughing at him . . .

The truth is that I too am surprised that Sara, this character that I have created, has suddenly become so complicated. But I tell myself, "You are a nobody in this world. According to all the religious books, Eve managed to surprise all the angels and Satan, too."

In any case, while anxiously waiting for Sara's telephone call so that he could at least hear an explanation from her own lips, quietly so that his parents would not wake up, Dara went downstairs from his bedroom on the second floor. This old house has a small front yard surrounded by high walls. In the corner of the yard there is a small flower bed in which an old jasmine bush has grown thick and run deep roots. Ignoring the cold and the falling snow, Dara knelt down beside the jasmine bush and quickly dug through the snow and dirt and pulled out a package wrapped in plastic. Back in his room, he unwrapped the package and took out a bottle half filled with a colourless liquid.

Right here, as if on a dark, snowy night I have walked into a dead-end alley and have run head first into the dead-end wall, I run into another problem.

What successful love story do you know of in which the abandoned and tormented lover who has learned of the presence of a wealthy suitor in his beloved's life does not knock back a few drinks to console himself? Mr Petrovich, however, does not under any circumstances allow characters in Iranian stories to drink alcohol – just like all those characters in dubbed foreign films screened in Iran who only order milk or orange juice in bars, and we see bartenders bring them gold-coloured milk or burgundy orange juice.

Mr X asks:

"What colour is it?"

The expert on matters offensive to morality says:

"It is some shade of brownish gold . . . some sort of burnt gold . . . It's hard to tell. It seems this damned whisky has a unique colour."

The scene in *Scent of a Woman* in which Al Pacino playing Lieutenant Colonel Frank Slade has taken his drink from the flight attendant and has raised it to his lips is frozen on the screen, and the debate continues.

The expert on matters offensive to morality says:

"Sir, I told you from the start that this film is not worth deliberating over. It is filled with unethical teachings and vulgar language from start to finish."

The expert on cinematic affairs angrily objects.

"Don't prejudge the film like this."

The expert on matters offensive to morality continues with his protests.

"The guy keeps saying don't prejudge, don't prejudge. My good man! Can't you see that this film is riddled with problems? And it all starts with its title – *Scent of a Woman*. We can call it *Scent of Eve*. This way it will have some religious undertones."

"Do you even know what you are saying? Your suggestion will only make the problem twofold. It will be an insult to Eve as well."

"Boo! Boo! Brother, what insult? Have you forgotten the hell Eve put us through?"

The expert on cinematic affairs who has completely lost his temper yells:

"Please stop! This film is about the tenderness of the human soul, it is about the fact that this miserable blind man . . ."

He stops himself the instant he realizes what a horrible thing he has said. But it is too late. Mr X orders him to be thrown out of the room.

The screening continues with no rash decisions about the film's continued existence. Shot by shot all is described to Mr X, and scene by scene they proceed. Finally, they reach the scene in which Al Pacino sits behind the wheel of a Ferrari and wants to drive around the streets of New York.

The expert on matters offensive to morality says snidely:

"These American directors have lost their minds. How could this blind arsehole . . ."

He immediately realizes that he is repeating the same insult as the expert on cinematic affairs. He corrects himself.

"If I were in his place, instead of driving a Ferrari, I would sit at the helm of a Topolof aeroplane and gallivant around the sky."

Mr X says:

"In that case you wouldn't be gallivanting for long. Don't you know that every year two or three of our Topolofs crash?"

The expert on anti-American affairs says:

"It would have been a great film if this lieutenant colonel had sat at the helm of an aeroplane and crashed it into a skyscraper. Like that . . ."

The expert on cinematic affairs, who could not give up watching a good film on the big screen and has all the while continued watching from the narrow opening of the door, can't hold his tongue and blurts out:

"As a matter of fact, if those guys had seen this film, perhaps they would never have killed themselves and so many other innocent people."

To ingratiate himself, the expert on matters offensive to morality shouts:

"Sir! Did you see, sir? This guy didn't leave . . . He's been watching through the door."

Fed up, Mr X says:

"You've only just noticed him? I could hear his breathing all along. Come in and stop all these irrelevant arguments. Let's see what happens in the film."

And the lieutenant colonel, shouting "Hoo-ha," drives through the intersections. Mr X, motionless, barely breathing, eyes closed, is sitting on the edge of his seat with his ear turned to the speaker as if it is he who is sitting next to the lieutenant colonel and relishing the speed of the Ferrari instead of that young boy.

Thus, the Ferrari scene, with no pauses and no explanations, continues up to the point when a police officer stops the lieutenant colonel and asks for his driving licence. Mr X leans back in his seat. A green halo has suddenly appeared around his head. With the air of a holy man he speaks out:

"I think none of you has really understood this film. This film is about the art of seeing. The art of seeing things that are hidden behind the things you see that you don't see. In a way, this film is in praise of the art of cinema and cinema's angle of view in that, amid the profusion of clichéd, blind, and paper-thin lives of seemingly seeing people, it can focus on a different life and a strange character . . . And then with the art of cinema, to show how blind all the drivers, police officers, family members and head teachers are. But in this film, even this different life and this strange character are not what is important. This film is showing us the cinematic art of seeing. If I were this film's director, I would have named the film *Scent of Cinema,* or *Scent of Art* . . . Play the film again from the beginning and all of you get out, I want to watch it alone."

We return to our story and the bitter discussion of alcoholic beverages.

I remind you that, in general, we Iranians have an affinity for surprising the world. Centuries ago, it was one of our people, a great scientist, who discovered alcohol. And now it is we who have contrived thousands of rules, laws and means of deterrence to prevent the consumption of alcohol, to such an extent that the toil, trouble and cost of implementing these laws are far greater than the harm done to society by a bunch of drinking non-believers. We may some day do the same with respect to enriching uranium.

It is in this fashion that, seven hundred years ago, the poet whose ghost we saw at the Internet café time and again used the word "wine" in his poems. In Mr Petrovich's estimation, that poet's wine is a mystical and heavenly wine, and in today's corrupt world, the likes of me do not deserve to have our stories' characters drink mystical wine. But this is not all that important to me. What is important is that in Iranian stories, even the most vile, the most malicious and the most non-believing characters are not allowed to have a drink or two to show how wicked they are, not even if they are members of the Iranian Mafia. Not even if they are thugs, professional racketeers or cut-throats fettered neither by Islam nor by any other human and moral principles. It is thus that characters in Iranian stories not only have no weaknesses and flaws, but year after year they become more saintly.

Therefore, I will only write:

Dara feels thirsty. He feels he cannot bear the weight of sorrow and of that big "why" in temperance. He grabs the half-filled glass next to him and gulps it down to the last drop.

His bitter mouth needs no accompanying taste. In fact, he savours this scorching bitterness; it resembles the bitterness of his existence . . . Like the slithering of molten lava from a volcano between mountain rocks and its sinking into the sea, hot and bitter, Dara feels that phantasmal liquid slide down his oesophagus and wash into his stomach.

If the intelligent Iranian reader asks me, How did this half-filled glass appear in your story, I will not say, You have turned out to be just like Mr Petrovich. I have a different answer to offer.

You intelligent readers only single out and nit-pick stories by Iranian writers. Why is it that when you read the story of "Young Goodman Brown", you don't criticize its writer and ask him how the devil, dressed in those strange clothes, suddenly appears before Goodman in the forest? Or when Gabriel García Márquez writes that flowers rain on Macondo, why don't you pounce on him and ask how all those flowers appeared in the sky in his story? Or for that matter, why don't you ask how it is possible that Dr Jekyll turns into Mr Hyde after he gulps down that bizarre liquid? Now be a little charitable and imagine that this half-full glass was placed next to Dara by that devil in the forest, or by Mr Hyde.

On the other hand, even the least-intelligent Iranian reader, after reading the last sentence I have written about that scorching bitterness, will realize that Dara is drinking home-made or Russian vodka purchased on the black market. Of course, Mr Petrovich will realize this, too, but I accept this risk because it is with this glass of vodka that I can express the extent of Dara's despondency.

To escape his bitter thoughts and suspicions, Dara turns on the decrepit television set in his room and surfs the four channels, desperately hoping that, other than lessons on morality, one of them is broadcasting a programme in which he can find some comfort. Finally, on the last channel, he finds a tolerable folk music programme. Unlike some Iranians, Dara does not have enough money to buy a second-hand Japanese receiver for some thirty dollars, a satellite dish manufactured in underground Iranian workshops for ten dollars, and an original Iranian cover to hide the dish for yet another ten dollars. When rumours spread that the police use helicopters to identify houses with satellite dishes and raid those homes, the creative and ingenious Iranian mind, which in general is shrewder and quicker to react when it comes to unlawful matters, was quickly activated, and it created the means for hiding large satellite dishes. Because of the summer heat, most Iranian houses have large water-cooled air-conditioners on their flat rooftops that during the winter months are protected by tarpaulin covers. Therefore, square wooden frames have been built in the same dimensions as the air conditioners and are placed over the satellite dishes, and specially designed tarpaulin covers are draped over them to make them look like air-conditioning units. Of course, air-conditioning units that remain covered even during the hot summer months . . . Sometime later, satellite-dish owners realized that many of the channels had been jammed, especially those broadcast from overseas by Iranians opposed to the revolution. Again the pioneering Iranian mind, the same mind that built a remarkable car named Peykan, was set in motion and found the means of countering the government-inflicted jams. It was a simple device that had an empty can of beans as its most complicated component. Of course, it was later rumoured that the police had purchased highly advanced electronic instruments from Europe that accurately trace houses that receive corruptive and anti-revolution satellite airwaves, and they raid those homes. Unfortunately, the ingenuity of us Iranians still does not match the technological advancements of profit-seeking multinational corporations in the West. Until it does, people who have satellite dishes have found no other solution than to resort to an ancient Iranian scheme; to shrug their shoulders and say:

" . . ."

While listening to the mournful sound of a sitar, during moments when his eyes can see straight, Dara sees the head and shoulders of a man wearing a hat made of long wriggling fur and a Turkmen fur coat on the television screen. Like all Iranian traditional musicians, the man is most likely sitting cross-legged on the floor. As is their custom, he has closed his eyes and gently moves his shoulders to the rhythm of the music. But at this moment of half-consciousness, this familiar image seems strange to Dara. The camera does not under any circumstances move below the man's shoulders, and when the man raises his arms even slightly, the camera quickly moves up. Because of the movements of his head and shoulders, because of the intoxicated or gratified manner in which he has closed his eyes, Dara imagines that the man is engaged in an unbecoming and rude act with his hands. The truth is that years after the revolution, generally speaking, all forms of music were banned, as was ownership of musical instruments. However, there came a time when it was decided that traditional Iranian music, which has two-thousand-year-old roots, should be more or less allowed. This decision came under strong opposition by many fanatics, yet once in a while, from the crooks and curves of our television sets, we the people of Iran would hear the melody of our heart-rending traditional music. Still, the heads of government-run television stations deemed it unethical to show musical instruments and strictly censored these images. After some time, television cameramen developed such expertise in their vocation that they could film any musician without his instrument ever appearing in the frame. That is why musicians often look like they are in the process of committing an act compared to which the unethical playing of a musical instrument seems innocent.

Dara does not know whether to laugh or to cry at his discovery of this imagery.

An hour later, he opens the window in his room. It is still snowing, but because of the particular state he is in, Dara does not feel the cold at all. He takes a fistful of snow from the window ledge and makes a small snowball. Gently and delicately he makes the ball perfectly round. He caresses it, and then with a silent cry he pitilessly hurls it at Tehran.

It is among my powers as a writer to fly this snowball above the streets and buildings of the city until it finds, and arrives at, this moment in my story.

Outside Sara's house, Sinbad sees the scratch on his car. He looks around angrily and swears out loud.

"Fuck whoever scratched my car!"

But you are wrong. That snowball that is coming and coming does not come to hit him smack on the head.

Ask:

Then where does the snowball go?

For me to answer:

In my dear country, so many strange things happen that I do not need to resort to such wishy-washy ploys of magical realism. By the way, during the past quarter of a century, so many divine and non-divine disasters, including earthquakes, torrential rains and invasions by legions of frogs, bombs, missiles and fighter jets have befallen the people of Iran that they truly have no need for the crashing of a snowball. Of course, I only say this because I really don't know when and where that dangerous snowball will land.

Therefore, **in no danger at all and without noticing the broken lock on the boot of his BMW, Sinbad utters an unvulgar censure at whoever scratched his car and starts the engine. Half a mile down the street, he notices that the boot is open. He pulls over, gets out of** the car and discovers the gift that someone has left for him in the boot . . .

Seeing that innocent and broken hunchback midget in the boot, a succession of obscenities bursts out of Sinbad's mouth.

" . . ."

Please fill in the three dots yourself. I don't like to write swear words that somehow reflect on me, too.

At midnight, Dara at last sees the blinking icon on his computer screen inviting him for a chat.

Dara, who is having a difficult time distinguishing the keys on the keyboard and is constantly correcting his misspellings, writes:

"Why?"

"Why what?"

"Why didn't you tell me you have a suitor?"

"Because you never asked."

As far as I can remember, I have from the start written the Sara of my story with a sad and sober personality. I cannot figure out at what point in the story she developed such a sense of humour.

Dara writes:

"I am in no mood for jokes."

"I'm not joking."

"I have suffered enough torture in my life."

"I know."

"Don't torture me."

"I love you."

"You are lying."

"Yes."

"Who is this guy?"

"I don't know where he first saw me, but one day my father said he had met a very important and wealthy gentleman while waiting in a queue to buy subsidized rice. They quickly became friends and Father invited him home for tea. I was suspicious from the start and found it strange that this gentleman, with all his wealth, would stand in a queue for three hours to buy subsidized rice. The third time he came to our house he proposed to me, and I knew I had guessed correctly – all along his intention had been to meet me. Tonight was the seventh time he came over. My parents insist that I accept his proposal, but I have

not given him an answer . . . Please don't ask me what I want to do. I don't know."

Dara ~~drunkenly~~ wrote:

"What am I to you?"

"You mean you don't know?"

"No."

"The Dara I know is not this stupid."

"Your love has made me stupid."

"Your love too has made me so stupid that I still have not said yes to Mr Sinbad so that seven days later I can fly with him to Spain."

"His name is Sinbad?"

"Did you expect it to be Aladdin? You are Aladdin. Except you have no magic lamp and no flying carpet to take me to Spain with."

"It seems you really like Spain."

"I have always liked Spain. Spain has Lorca."

"It has Buñuel, too."

"It also has self-righteous lovers who kidnap brides from weddings."

"So you want to say yes to him?"

"To Lorca?"

"No. To Sinbad."

"What do you think?"

Here, I am confronted with the question that if we Iranian writers cannot be expected to write a beautiful love story because of Mr Petrovich's presence, then why is it that in countries where love stories are not censored so few good ones have been written during the past several decades? Could it be that today's world no longer grants writers inspiration for love stories?

Dara wrote:

"I think you want to marry him."

"So who are you in the middle of all of this?"

"A snowman. A plaything."

"What if it is you who sees me as a toy to be played with?"

"In this world, only those who have the means can play . . . I have nothing, I am not a player."

After writing this sentence, Dara angrily turns off his computer.

It was thus that Sara and Dara had their first row. Dara thought, It was all a game. They are right to say that no woman should ever be trusted. She wanted me so that she could make her Sinbad jealous . . . I was stabbed in the back again. Dara swore that he would no longer give Sara even a word's worth of his thoughts. And Sara thought, I will no longer give him even a word's worth of my thoughts. He was interrogating me. As if he owns me. They're right to say that if you let them, men will actually believe they own you.

I sometimes think Sara sneaks peeks at the sentences I write about Dara and his thoughts. If my suspicions are correct, somehow I will have to agree with Dara that I should not trust the female characters of my stories. In any case, in this segment I needed narrative tension. Tell me, is it even possible for a love story not to have a row between the two lovers? Or have you ever seen a love in which there has been no jealousy and misunderstanding? If you know of such a love, please let me know so that I can go and fall in love with that love and write about it. I am certain that it will turn out to be a beautiful love story, and perhaps because of it there will be one less suicide bomber.

Five nights have passed since Sara and Dara's screamless and shoutless row. During this time, they have not contacted each other at all. On the fifth night, Sara for the very first time accepts Sinbad's invitation to dinner. Promptly at eight in the evening, Sinbad pulls up in front of Sara's house in his BMW. Sara walks out. Behind her, her parents appear in the doorway and wave at Sinbad. Sinbad waves back. From the doorway, Sara's mother yells:

"Be careful. Don't drive too fast."

Both Sinbad and Sara understand the underlying meaning and the hidden warning of this sentence.

As does Mr Petrovich.

Sara's father, still waving, yells:

"Sara, tell Mr Sinbad all about the excellent grades you have received this term."

Both Sara and Sinbad understand the underlying meaning and the hidden advice of this sentence.

Sara walks up to Sinbad to shake hands with him. But Sinbad does not extend his hand. He says:

"It is not proper for you and I to shake hands before we get married."

Sinbad truly believes in the religious principle that a man and woman who are not married and who are not immediate relatives should not shake hands. But even if Sinbad did not want to abide by this important principle, the experience of that film director who won the Palme d'Or award at the Cannes Film Festival has been an important lesson for him.

If you are curious, ask:

What in the world is the story of this Iranian film director?

For me to answer:

Several years ago, when on the night of the awards ceremony this Iranian director's name was announced and he was invited to go and receive his Golden Palm, up on the stage he came face to face with none other than Catherine Deneuve, who even at her present age is beautiful and enchanting.

Catherine Deneuve held out her hand to shake hands with the Iranian director. The Iranian director, in observance of social courtesy, shook her hand. Then Catherine Deneuve, as is customary, kissed him on the cheek. That night the happy Iranian director either did or did not go back to his hotel room. In any case, the next day he was told that he had been harshly criticized in a few government-owned newspapers in Iran for having shaken hands with a woman outside the circle of immediate kin and, even worse, for having made his cheeks available to the lips of a woman who in her films has revealed her naked body. The criticisms were growing stronger by the day, and it was claimed that this director makes films to the liking of Westerners and intentionally portrays the Iranian public as miserable, destitute and suicidal, and that he has humiliated Iran. The rebukes had their effect. On the night that the now famous director was returning to Iran, a group of fervent Muslims gathered at the airport in Tehran so that, instead of welcoming him with flowers for having achieved this international honour for their country, they could punish him with punches and kicks and perhaps shove a totally Iranian palm up his arse.

However, the ending of this story, unlike most Iranian stories, is a happy one. The Iranian police, aware that if this director was beaten up the next day the media worldwide would make fun of Iran, secretly took him out of the airport and escorted him home. As a result of this rescue mission, a few years later this director invited Juliette Binoche, the beautiful French actress with hidden sparrowlike charms, to Iran. Ms Binoche gladly accepted the invitation and arrived in Tehran wearing a coverall and a headscarf, and she gave tens of photographs to Iranian photographers as gifts. The chance that the lady has read André Malraux's *Anti-Memoirs* is far less than the chance that you, my dear readers, have read it. In this book Malraux has an amazing and even maddening description of the Lascaux caves in France and the paintings by prehistoric men on their walls. He so expertly illustrates the fantastical paintings that we the readers truly see the prehistoric hunters shooting their arrows at the mammoths, and we fall captive to the magic of those drawings and Malraux's words. In another section of the book, Malraux describes the occasion of a speech he gave in one of the French colonies. In this scene, Malraux, as France's Minister of Culture and not as a writer active in the Resistance movement to free France from the yoke of the Nazis, stands facing the outcry of those opposed to French colonialism and stubbornly continues delivering his speech. Then, from here and there, arrows are shot at him. But the French Malraux is brave enough to ignore the deadly arrows and to finish his speech. Therefore, when the French transform a great writer such as Malraux into a Minister of Culture, it should not come as any great surprise to see Juliette Binoche don a headscarf and coverall and get introduced in the Iranian media as an actress's actress.

With the aid of your intellect, connect these two illustrations of Malraux with my remarks about Ms Binoche's trip to Iran and draw your own special conclusion.

Where were we?

Sinbad apologizes for not shaking hands with the headscarf-clad Sara. Just then, Sara sees the end-to-end scratch on Sinbad's BMW.

"Oh! Who did this?"

"I don't know. The night I came to your house some obsessed moron did it."

"You see all kinds of people in this day and age . . . It looks really bad."

Sinbad sighs and thinks, I wish this were my only problem that night.

Given that she knows Dara wanders around her house, Sara thinks this must be his handiwork. She thinks, I didn't know Dara was this obsessed.

Sinbad takes Sara to a revolving restaurant on the top floor of a high-rise office building. People like Sinbad who belong to the nouveau riche class of Iranian society and, because of their government-granted import monopolies, have amassed wealth that no Western industrialist could ever dream of have no fear of the patrols from the Campaign Against Social Corruption. Even if they commit murder and are arrested, with a single telephone call to a government official their record will be cleared. At most, they will be obliged to pay blood money to the victim's family, which will be no more than a few hours' income for them. Therefore, they do as they wish, of course, while fully adhering to the codes of Islamic dress and appearance. **After the recent snow and rain, Tehran's chronically smoggy air is clean, and from the floor-to-ceiling windows the lights of the city's tall and short buildings and the river of headlights along its streets can be seen. To start, Sara orders a real orange juice-coloured orange juice and Sinbad orders a Coca-Cola also in its original colour.**

Sinbad says:

"Until a few months ago, this restaurant only had a few customers because it is so expensive. But ever since it was rumoured that some of the waiters serve bottles of mineral water filled with vodka to special clients, every night there are ten new customers."

"Do they really bring it to the tables?"

"Bring what? Orange juice?"

Sara laughs.

"Oh, stop playing with me! I mean what you mentioned."

"No, dear, it's just a rumour."

But apparently the rumour is so widespread that the poor waiters look really frustrated and sweaty. Each time they pass by certain tables, the customers stare at them and wink . . .

Sara says:

"Maybe the owner started the rumour himself to attract more customers."

"I hope not because they will shut down the restaurant, and we won't be able to come here any more."

So far, Sinbad has not revealed to me when and how he learned his subtle and witty approach to women. Like all Iranians, he too always has a few new jokes about government leaders up his sleeve, and makes Sara really laugh.

The restaurant slowly turns – of course, with the occasional clanking of its worn-out engine, which is probably among the items embargoed by the United States and which cannot be purchased on the black market as easily as one can purchase centrifuges for enriching uranium. Now the snow-covered Damavand Peak in the north of Tehran is in Sara's view. Not the poet who died seven hundred years ago, but the poet who died some one hundred years ago, has likened this conic volcanic peak to a beast in chains above Tehran.

Sinbad is talking about the beauties of his villa on top of a tall hill facing the turquoise Mediterranean Sea. Sara sees herself standing next to the pool of that villa, looking out at the horizon across the sea. From somewhere, like a film score, a guitar is playing Fernando Sor's Étude 22. A white bird, with the blue of the sea reflecting under its wings, flies close by. ~~The wind blows in Sara's long hair. It caresses the naked skin of her arms and thighs. And from the other side, from deep within the young flesh of her body, the pleasant and suppressed sense of freedom and intoxication flows towards the pores of her skin.~~ But ~~at the height of this euphoric sensation,~~ Sara feels she is missing something. Suddenly she knows what; it is floating in the sky above the Mediterranean. A white cloud that looks just like Dara's head . . . Sara fixes her eyes on Dara's cloudy eyes and feels how much she wants him to be standing there beside her on that hilltop.

Sinbad walks out of the glittering white villa and asks her a question. The villa disappears. A frustrated waiter walks by.

"Did you say something?"

Sinbad stares intently at Sara's face.

"I asked you what you were thinking about."

I am beginning to suspect that perhaps Sinbad keeps company with Mr Petrovich, because he is constantly asking Sara what she is thinking.

"Nothing."

"Stop it, girl. It's impossible for someone not to think about anything . . . Tell me. I promise I will not tell your parents."

"I was thinking of one of Lorca's poems."

"Is this Lorca Kurdish?"

"No."

"His name sounds Kurdish."

"He is Spanish. I really like his poems. They are filled with sun and love and blood."

"I'll go and buy all his books tomorrow, I want to learn and like everything you like."

"You won't find any of them."

"Why?"

"For years translations of his poetry have not received a reprint permit."

"No problem. I have friends at the Ministry of Culture and Islamic Guidance. If this Mr Lorca writes an application letter, I could perhaps speak to my friends and get the reprint permit for his books."

Sara smiles and turns to the window. Now she sees the southern part of Tehran with its tight clusters of light from the small beehive-like houses of the poor and its patches of dark from the immigrant villagers' hovels. Near the horizon a few flames from Tehran's oil refinery lick towards the sky.

At eleven o'clock, Sinbad takes Sara home. The streets of Tehran are slowly emptying of their maddening traffic. On one of these streets, Dr Farhad is driving back from the free clinic he runs in the poor section of town. Unlike other nights when he would return home tired but with a deep sense of satisfaction, tonight his entire body is stiff with fear and drenched in sweat. The corpse of that hunchback midget is in the boot of his old car. Someone had secretly left the corpse in the waiting room at his clinic and run off. Dr Farhad knows that no one, not even the clever Iranian detectives, will believe his innocence. These are terrifying and breathtaking moments for the noble doctor. He can, at any moment, run into a police checkpoint.

I am not suggesting that the police at checkpoints on Tehran's streets are searching for the hunchback's corpse. However, in the process of searching all the exposed and concealed parts of a car, they sometimes ask the driver to get out and they smell his breath; if he has consumed any alcohol they can arrest him, and if the driver has not consumed any alcohol, but happens to have a woman in the car with no documents proving his immediate kinship with her, they can arrest him, and if he has no woman in the car, but they discover cassette tapes or CDs of forbidden Western music, they can arrest him, and if . . .

Let us see how Dr Farhad plans to rid himself of that corpse.

Dr Farhad is convinced that he must get the corpse to the northern part of Tehran. He doesn't want to create any problems for the poor people who live in the southern part of the city – they have neither the means to hire a lawyer nor any contacts in the judicial system. From fear, his heart at times pounds like mad and at times, nearing a complete freeze, it slows down. As if one of his patients has suffered a heart attack on the operating table, his brain frantically considers hundreds of probabilities and possibilities, hoping to find a suitable place to dispose of the corpse that has been bestowed upon him. At this very instant, a brilliant idea sparks in his mind. He remembers one of his close friends, Dr D. . . .

I will tell you in secret that Dr Farhad does not want to leave the hunchback at the front door of a dedicated doctor like himself and run away. He remembers that last year Dr D., who specializes in surgery, wanted to publish a book on prostate surgery – the fruit of his years of experience – but a man called Mr Petrovich did not issue a publishing permit for the book because of one fundamental problem: the image of a pair of surgical scissors on the cover.

As you can see, our story is at a crossroads. One road leads to Dr D.'s house and the other to Mr Petrovich's office. In the censor-approved text, we have ignited a spark in Dr Farhad's mind, and we have sent him in the direction of Dr D.'s house, but in our confidential pretend text, Dr Farhad decides instead to drive his old car to the Ministry of Culture and Islamic Guidance. Unfortunately, our story's events do not unfold as easily as this.

Dr Farhad is driving along the dimly lit Bahar Street. Suddenly, he sees the tail-lights of two cars standing in the middle of the road some two hundred feet ahead, and he sees the shadows of checkpoint officers. He stops breathing. With eyes half blinded by fear, he looks at both sides of the street hoping to find a road or an alley he can turn onto. But the checkpoint police have been wisely hand-picked. For a moment he considers turning the steering wheel and going back, but that would be a grave mistake. If he is lucky and the police don't riddle his car tyres with bullets, they will immediately pursue him, and his car is not a red Ferrari in which he can have any hopes of escaping.

It is too late for any thought or action. He reaches the checkpoint and stops. On the poorly lit street, two officers armed with machine guns are standing on the lookout. Three other officers have taken the driver of the car in front out of his car, two of them are searching under the car seats, and the third one is carefully inspecting the boot. Dr Farhad desperately whispers:

"It's over . . . I have reached the end point of my life . . . It's all over."

And he sees himself: On one side of destiny, like many Iranian specialists he has migrated to the United States and is now driving his red Ferrari from a large and expensive hospital in Los Angeles, in which he is a major shareholder, to his villa on Mulholland Drive . . . On the other side of destiny, he sees himself in a prison uniform, sitting in a small cement cell with ten murderers, smugglers and addicts, who in general do not look kindly upon doctors and who are now sneering at him with toothless mouths and waiting for the prison lights to go out.

Dr Farhad feels the glaring eyes of one of the machine-gun-toting officers on him and smiles bitterly at his fate.

But come, let us help him. This selfless doctor, even at this daunting moment of peripeteia, is worried about the critical condition of one of his poor patients whom he is scheduled to operate on tomorrow. A patient named P., who spent seven years of his life as a volunteer on the front lines of the war with Iraq, who still has a piece of shrapnel from an Iraqi mortar shell lodged near his spinal cord and who will become paralysed if he is not operated on.

What do you think we can do to help Dr Farhad? Give me the time it takes for the next three dots to think of something.

. . .

No, even after these three dots I still cannot think of a way out. Help me. I need a spark of inspiration, a blow to shake the dust of time from my numbed mind . . .

Something hits me on the back of my head. I stifle a cry behind my tightly pursed lips for fear that it will attract the attention of the checkpoint officers. I run my hand against the back of my head. A bit of snow comes into my hand, and the rest of it streams down under my collar. I look up at the sky. It is not snowing.

Please don't ask. We don't have time. Just push your hand down on the horn of Dr Farhad's car. Just that. Do it.

A hideous and congested honk echoes in the street. The machine-gun-toting officer who from the street has been observing the doctor's nervous behaviour walks up to his car. Suspicious, he says snidely:

"You seem to be in a big hurry."

The doctor wipes the sweat off his forehead with the back of his hand and says:

"Yes . . . I'm in a hurry."

Just then, a spark flashes in Dr Farhad's mind. He takes out his medical identity card and shows it to the officer.

"I'm a surgeon. I have an accident victim in A & E. If I don't get there quickly, he will die."

In the beam of the headlights, the officer carefully examines the identity card, then he walks over to his commanding officer who is searching the boot of the car ahead. They exchange a few words. He returns and gives the identity card back to the doctor.

Still suspicious, he asks:

"You don't have any illegal stuff in the car, do you?"

"Only my medical bag . . . Please let me go, my patient will die."

"You're not lying to me, are you?"

"What lie?"

"The patient you say is dying, where is he hurt?"

"They have only told me that he has been in a bad accident. I suspect his ribs have broken and punctured his lungs . . ."

He is short of breath; he feels the sharpness of his own ribs against his lungs. With great effort he moans:

"May I?"

"Go."

Dr Farhad puts the car in gear, but the commanding officer has just walked over and is scrutinizing his face.

He says:

"Stop right there."

Dr Farhad gives up.

"Aren't you Dr Farhad?"

"I think so."

"Did you have a patient named Bibi Attri?"

"Yes. I operated on her myself. It was one of my more difficult surgeries."

The commanding officer turns to his colleague:

"Don't let the doctor leave until I come back."

The doctor feels the sharp blades of all his scalpels on his body. In the rear-view mirror he sees the rotating emergency lights of a patrol car go on. "It's all over. They're taking me to jail." The patrol car pulls up next to his car. The commanding officer yells from the car window,

"Bibi Attri is my aunt. You operated on her free of charge. Thank God, she feels better than I do. Which hospital are you going to?"

With what's left of his energy, Dr Farhad blurts out the name of a hospital.

"I will escort you. Follow me."

At the commanding officer's gesture, the other officers quickly pull aside the street barricades. Dr Farhad puts his foot on the accelerator and at high speed follows the siren and the revolving red lights, which to him are as beautiful as arctic twilight.

A few minutes later he pulls up in front of a hospital. He waves to the commanding officer and rushes in. When he has made sure that the patrol car has left, he will come out and head for his destination.

Mr Petrovich will sceptically ask:

"Let's see, is Dr Farhad driving along Bahar Street? But Bahar Street is not on the way to Dr D.'s house."

I will say:

"He has been so terrified and shaken that he has probably taken a wrong turn somewhere. He will realize it himself and find his way."

"But I don't like this part of your story. You are teaching people how to con the checkpoint officers . . . By the way, you can rest assured that the commanding officer who escorted Dr Farhad will be arrested tomorrow and tried for collaborating with the counter-revolution."

And Dr Farhad, at the end of Bahar Street, is still wondering how and why the horn of his car, which is more than twenty years old, had miraculously honked.

On the tenth night after their row, Dara concludes that he has perhaps been angry with Sara for no good reason, that he has really insulted her and has spoken to her as though he were interrogating her, or as though he owns her.

Sara too has concluded that Dara had not really insulted her, that he had simply asked a few questions, and that these sorts of questions are normal when you love someone, and they are not at all meant as an interrogation or a claim of ownership.

Until tonight, Dara had preferred to spend very little time with Sara on the telephone. ~~Because of his past political activities and imprisonment, he thought it possible that his telephone would occasionally be tapped, and he therefore considered email and computer chats to be safer.~~ But on this night, instead of reading lifeless written words, with his entire being he wants to hear Sara's voice. Therefore, heroically, at seven o'clock he dials Sara's telephone number. The line is busy. He thinks:

It's obvious. She is talking to Sinbad about their trip to Spain. It's really over. I will not call her again.

But at that very moment Sara had been dialling Dara's number. She thinks:

It didn't take him long to find himself some other plaything. It's really over. I will not call him again.

Exactly thirty minutes later, they concurrently dial each other's telephone numbers again. The lines are busy. Sara thinks:

See! I was right.

Dara has the same thought.

Of course, these concurrences rarely happen in the so-called real world, but in the world of fiction, where censorship peers at every high and low, they can easily occur.

Here I come face to face with another one of my story's problems. No, it is not Mr Petrovich who complains; instead, certain intellectuals and critics from my favourite country will grab me by the collar.

Ask, Why? For me to answer:

Well, if I write that Sara dials Dara's number first, there is a chance that some hard-line Iranian feminists, who bear no resemblance to Iran's true activist feminists and who scare me very much, will pull their headscarves down over their uncombed hair that they have not washed in a week, and they will say:

"See! Despite all your cunning, you finally revealed your male chauvinism, Mr Writer. By forcing Sara to call Dara first, you are suggesting that women are weaker than men and that they belittle themselves. Hurry up and delete this sentence from your story."

Yet, if I write that Dara calls Sara first, it is possible that some seemingly hard-line political activists will criticize me and say·

"In other words, you are saying that a political activist and a former political prisoner who has survived the torture of solitary confinement is so helpless before a woman that he cannot resist her for even ten days. You have been paid off by the government to write that political activists are weak and to tarnish the legend of their resistance. Hurry up and delete this sentence from your story."

As you may have guessed, I am introducing you to another world of censorship, one that is even more powerful than Mr Petrovich and all the employees and bureaus of his ministry.

Now, in your opinion, should Sara call Dara first, or should Dara call Sara first?

We Iranian writers know how to get out of such binds. For example:

A third person who is sitting in a reputable government office and is assigned to monitoring and recording Sara and Dara's telephone conversations can connect the two lines at the same time. Perhaps he feels sorry for them; perhaps he wants them to have their talk so that his work will be done and he can go home, or perhaps he likes the blushing conversations of these young lovers.

They both press the earpiece against their ear and the mouthpiece against their mouth . . . They hear each other breathe. At this moment, all words seem absurd. With hearts in which the revolving red lights of an ambulance or a police car pulsate, each waits for the other to find and to utter the first word.

"Hello."

"Hello."

Then, again, a long silence . . . The sound of breaths . . . Breaths converse . . . The excitement of the breaths heightens . . . They seem to hear the sound of sweat seeping from the pores of each other's skin . . . From the perforations in the receivers, the clicking sound of thousands of conversations connecting and disconnecting . . . A long sigh . . . Its response, a longer sigh . . . Unsteady breaths . . . A climaxing moan . . .

Drenched in sweat, they concurrently hang up the telephone.

Don't ask.

Years ago, in one of my dark stories with a sad ending, to depict the intense and maddening love of a man and a woman, I needed to write a literary, creative and fresh description of their lovemaking. Because of Mr Petrovich's exactitude, I could not write of their actual lovemaking. And for how long can writers continue to write words such as:

The man said:

"Shall we go?"

The woman replied:

"Let's go."

And for how long can we write, "The man and the woman walked into the room and closed the door . . ." with no further explanation. Another problem was that I absolutely did not want to describe a lovemaking scene in a way that would make my story verge on the pornographic and perhaps become a bestseller. I believe that any artificial or even trendy element that is added to the tragedy of a story is a betrayal of literature. For this reason, I wanted with all my love of words and my love of their explicit and implicit connotations to create sentences in which the words too would make love. I worked for hours on this scene, but whatever I wrote screamed of being denied a publishing permit. When I had at last given up hope and was deciding to force the two lovers to part rather than make love, I suddenly remembered a word that I had read in old texts of Farsi literature – *khanjeh*. That was it – the key to my problem. It was a word that centuries ago had become obsolete. Its meaning: lustful groans during sexual intercourse. From a literary perspective, the aggressive sound of *kh,* that in continuation of its intonation couples with the mysterious sound of *j,* was exactly what I wanted. Every writer, even if he has never been some sort of a Don Juan in real life, after years of writing comes to understand that sometimes one word does the work of tens of compliments and hundreds of clever enticements.

In any case, to set the stage for this word and to protect it from the blade of censorship, I wrote of the man's stream of consciousness during their lovemaking. Complicated sentences, a labyrinth of associations and recollections of past memories. The man's eyes on the narrow strip of sun that from the small opening in the curtain is shining in on the carpet and like a blade has divided it in two. The recollection of his hand being slapped by the head teacher of the primary school . . . The man's eyes on the naked lightbulb hanging from the ceiling of his bedroom and his rediscovery of it . . . Memories of a cold winter morning when breaths turned to steam . . . The blending of breaths . . . The protracted sound of a horn blowing as a car sped down the road . . . And finally I wrote: *khanjeh*s.

I assumed that Mr Petrovich would not be patient or proficient enough to find an old and rare dictionary to look up the definition of the word *khanjeh*. I assumed that even if he does look up the word, because it is now obsolete and lacks any fresh and sexy connotation, he might perhaps have allowed it to live in my story. Some time later, a critic who was not all that pleased with me wrote and published a review of the story. In it he explained the definition of *khanjeh*.

Why give such a complicated example? In one of my stories, of which I will not expose too much lest it be refused a publishing permit in my beloved land, to tell my reader that the story's husband and wife are making love, I wrote that the woman is sleeping face-up on the bed; her husband enters the room; after the argument they have had the previous week, it is now time to make up. A bright Iranian morning is coursing outside their small house. From the window, the woman can see a small section of the blue sky and a patch of cloud that is floating like a kite and is the same shade of white as the milk with which she once breast-fed her daughter . . . Then in the woman's angle of view, the window frame begins to move. It moves up and down but the sky and the white cloud remain motionless. Then the woman turns her eyes away from the window and sees the hollow of her husband's ear. I also wrote a description of the ear, its grooves and the darkness in its cavity. Of course, very briefly because I knew that in the throes of excitement, movement and pleasure, no woman, not even Virginia Woolf, would have the concentration to observe the minute details of an ear . . .

Perhaps as a small point in creative-writing lessons, it may be interesting to note that prior to writing this scene I had no personal experience or knowledge of how a woman sees a ceiling and a window when she is lying under an eager and invading body and repetitive movement and pressure are exerted on her. I wanted to know if, when force is applied to the middle section of a woman's body and moves her, does the window frame in her vision also move? Therefore, I lay down on my office floor and tried to imagine myself as that woman, and I started to rock my body up and down and focused my eyes on the window and the cloud.

There is no need for you to undergo this scientific experiment. After all, one of the advantages of reading stories is that the experiences of the characters and the writer are transferred to the reader. Therefore, I will tell you that the conclusion was disappointing. Lying down on my back, no matter how much I swayed my body, I realized that the window relative to the sky, and the patch of cloud relative to the window, did not appear to move.

But in my story I really needed that window to move in the woman's vision. I told myself, What do I care if in reality the window doesn't move; it moves in my story. And boldly I wrote that it did. It is in such cases that fictional reality parts from the reality of the world out there. Nabokov has, in his brilliant lectures and lessons on literature, said, "Literature was born on the day when a boy came crying wolf, wolf, and there was no wolf behind him."

But this is simple. I would say that the best stories are those in which the lying shepherd boy, or the writer, comes crying wolf, wolf, and a wolf that was not there appears behind him.

Therefore, the window still moves and the earth *e pur si muove* and Gregor Samsa still wakes up to find he has turned into a cockroach.

Mr Petrovich will say:

"Do you really think that if writers write about the wolf it will appear behind them?"

"It depends. If they write really well and creatively, somehow some sort of a wolf will appear behind them and before the eyes of the reader."

"But this is very dangerous. What you are saying is that writers can write about hundreds of anti-regime guerrilla groups and thousands of counter-revolutionaries, spies and renegades, and they will all appear."

I have to kick myself really hard. What have I done? I have not only made matters worse for myself and my colleagues, but . . .

"In reality, you story-writers are like Aaron, who made a golden calf and misled the Israelites. You deserve whatever trouble comes your way."

"Sometimes your imagination works harder than any writer's."

"Don't try to fool me. In other words, you can write in your story that at night I fall asleep and dream that I am dead and I wake up to see that in reality too I am dead. I must write a new report and a new plan of action concerning you writers."

"No. No. You should only write a story."

"You have a story in which a lonely office worker returns to his rented room and sees the corpse of a stranger in his bed. What did you mean by this corpse?"

"Just a corpse."

"You have portrayed that poor office worker as cowardly, conservative and calculating. A man who, in my opinion, is a model citizen, someone who tries to do his job well, who does not interfere and meddle in matters that do not concern him, who always carries his identity card in his pocket and who does not do anything that would have him crossing paths with the police. And you have put a stranger's corpse in his bed. Why? To punish him? To say that cowardly people all have a corpse in their home? But it is you who is the coward."

"Yes. Well, I saw this corpse in my own bed first, and then I wrote the story."

"So you confess that you have committed murder, too. What did you do with the corpse? Where did you dump it?"

During a semi-brave midnight telephone conversation, ~~when the desire to hear the voice of one's beloved has stifled all fears and precautions,~~ Sara asks Dara:

"Was it you who scratched Sinbad's car?"

"No . . . I find it shameful even to look at such cars."

"How are you feeling?"

"Bad."

"Why?"

"You know."

"Do you miss me?"

"You know."

~~**"Then why don't you make plans to meet me?"**~~

~~**"I'm not sure you will have time for me in between all your other dates."**~~

~~**"Let's meet somewhere tomorrow afternoon. I've got a class, but I won't go."**~~

~~**"Where can we go? I see how you are always terrified of being arrested when we are together. I hate myself for having put you in such a difficult position."**~~

~~**"It doesn't matter. These fears and excitements are somehow sweet.**~~

It's some sort of an adventure in my monotonous life. I like it."

"Where?"

"Three o'clock, Vanak Circle."

"No, it's a popular stomping ground full of patrols . . . Let's go to the Museum of Antiquities."

No, it doesn't work. This segment of Sara and Dara's conversation is not real at all. Given Dara's political past and the possible wiretapping of his telephone, they will plan their meeting differently.

Sara says:

"I was really missing *The Blind Owl* today. I read it again. I discovered new things in it."

"What?"

"Chapter seven, the scene on the third page, is a masterpiece of symbolism. It illustrates fear in a very succinct and real way. I think it is more powerful than Kafka."

"The pages that follow are also powerful."

"No, the scene he has developed on this page, is the peak of his strength. Do you remember we talked about Hedayat's nostalgia for ancient Iran? I think he has reflected all his nostalgia on this page. It is as if he has pressed all the pieces in the Museum of Antiquities like a cluster of grapes and has dripped their syrup on this one page. Read it again and you'll see what I mean. Chapter seven, page three."

Deciphering the code in this dialogue is as follows:

"I missed you a lot today. I went over all my memories of you. I want to see you again."

"When?"

"On the seventh day, at three o'clock."

"Can we meet at a later hour?"

"No. At this time. We'll meet at the Museum of Antiquities which we have discussed. Do you understand what I'm saying? On the seventh day at three o'clock."

Of course, *The Blind Owl* does not have a chapter seven.

"Now, tell me the truth, did you scratch Sinbad's car?"

"No."

"I wish it were you who'd scratched it because then I would know you really love me."

Sara's statement and the repetition of the car-scratching subject are starting to worry me. In my mind, without the aid of any time machine, I can see the future.

Mr Petrovich will throw the typeset manuscript of my story on his desk, he will stare at me for a long moment with his probing and condemning eyes and finally he will say:

"Hmm . . . One other instance is added to the list of your book's immoral teachings. You encourage your readers to go and scratch innocent people's cars. Instead, Sara could say, I am happy to hear that it wasn't you who scratched the car because if you had said it was you, I swear I would despise you so much that I would scratch out your name and all my memories of you . . . It is a beautiful literary sentence, isn't it? I have used the metaphor of scratching very well, haven't I?"

"What can I say . . . The truth is that all this scratching is making me sick."

Mr Petrovich will stand up. In a dry and formal tone he will say:

"I have to be at a very important meeting in a few minutes. I advise you to work on your story very carefully, both with respect to these minor details and to the major problems it has."

In that future that has now become my present, I walk out of the Ministry of Culture and Islamic Guidance. My head is about to explode. I begin to walk aimlessly. All I know is that . . . I don't know anything, and I don't know at all what I should do. I tell myself, "You are not all that different from Dostoyevsky's *Idiot*, except that you are more naive. If instead of all those years when you spent the hopes and dreams of your adolescence, youth and middle age writing stories, if instead of all that danger you put yourself into to experience life and to write better stories, if . . . if . . . if instead of all this foolishness you had spent only a little time on your father's assets, you would have been a wealthy man by now, and instead of writing a miserable love story, you could have invited not only Sara but any other beautiful woman to your villa in Spain and at night you could have read love stories by French writers to her . . ."

Lost and confused, tears have welled up in my eyes. I can't see my surroundings very well. All I know is that I am on a narrow and crowded street. I am pushed and shoved by people rushing by. Sometimes they call me names.

I wipe away the tears that are not permitted to flow and see that I am on the old Lalehzar Street. I think, What an excellent and appropriate setting!

I trip over the wares of a street pedlar. If it were any other street pedlar, he would have sent a few vulgar obscenities my way, but the man who sells talismans and magic smirks and says:

"For your troubles and pains I have problem-solving spells . . . You are really blind."

"Yes. I am really blind."

I walk away. From the realization that I have been really blind all my life, tears again fill my eyes. But a few steps farther, I discover that from behind the veil of tears, Lalehzar is a timeless street. The street that eighty years ago was in a way Tehran's Broadway, and a place for entertainment and shopping for the wealthy and the aristocrats, is now a strange and compelling setting for a scene in a story. I tell myself, "This street, with its old stores where the poor now shop, with its old theatres, with its burned-down cinemas and its street pedlars, is a really safe place for Dara and Sara to go for a walk!"

I no longer need to pull the curtain of tears away from my eyes. I tell myself:

"Hey, you! Blind or seeing, yes, you are an idiot. An idiot for writing stories. But you like this idiocy . . ."

THE BRONZE MAN

We Iranians take great pride in the empires we have built. If you read our extraordinary history, our country has been occupied time and again, we have been massacred time and again, our cities have been reduced to dust, and then, with diplomacy, intelligence, cunning and patience, we have introduced our invaders, who were often from savage tribes, to our culture and, as the saying goes, we have made human beings out of them.

The problem with us Iranians, however, is that because we have all these past glories, it is no longer very important for us to make a name for ourselves and to be of benefit to the world today. It seems we don't care at all how the world will judge our current circumstances.

At the Museum of Antiquities, side by side but without their arms brushing against each other, Sara and Dara are strolling along and looking at the beautiful, majestic artefacts of ancient Iran; they are ~~exchanging private words and~~ **talking to each other.** Here too they are careful of their actions because they know museums have guards who, instead of guarding priceless and rare artefacts, pay more attention to the conduct of the visitors. Regardless, this place is far safer than the streets and parks.

Sara and Dara are spellbound by the gold plates, jewel-encrusted arms, inscriptions and golden ornaments that are at least two thousand years old. They gaze silently at each item and forget their own conversation.

Finally, they arrive at the statue of the bronze man. The statue of a commander from the Parthian Dynasty. The dynasty that revived the Persian Empire by overthrowing the government that Alexander had

instituted after his conquest of Persia. The bronze man, with his mysterious bronze colour, with his heroic stature, wearing a metal costume that still bears the fineries of aristocratic Parthian dress, stares at them with his unique Aryan eyes. He stands as confident of his own eternal existence as did the statues in the museum of Baghdad before it was pillaged. Awestruck, Sara stands staring at the majesty of that statue. Dara dolefully whispers:

"His arms!"

The arms of the statue are broken off below the elbows, but his bearing is so stately that it seems he holds all the power in the world in his hands.

Sara whispers:

"This is what they call a real man."

"What does he have?"

"If he falls in love, he will trust his love."

"His hands . . ."

"Yes, his hands . . ."

"At least we still have these. Those scoundrel Western archaeologists have taken the bulk of our ancient treasures, and they are now in museums in London, Paris and New York."

~~"Perhaps it is for the best. At least there they are safe. No one will steal them."~~

Sara is referring to the disappearance of one of the two gold treasury tablets that were discovered beneath the foundations of the palace at Persepolis during an excavation. The story of Persepolis's construction was engraved on them, and now only one remains in Iran. The fact that at the command of Darius, ruler of a great empire in the fourth century BC, a documented account of his palace's construction was buried in its foundations is itself intriguing. It is said that at the height of his power, Darius wisely realized that his empire would one day be plundered by invaders and destroyed by fire. He had therefore hidden the two tablets for a professor named Ernest Hertzfeld.

But this is only part of the story. At one point, news of the disappearance of one of the gold tablets from the Museum of Antiquities spread throughout our country. Some time later, newspapers reported that a museum manager had been arrested and accused of its theft. Later, it was reported that the thief had confessed that he had melted the gold tablet and had sold the gold for four thousand dollars.

I don't know about my fellow countrymen's sentiments, but in my heart, I hope that the confession was a lie and that the tablet was sold to one of countless Iranian antique dealers and taken out of the country, and that years from now it will resurface in some private collection. For me, an Iranian who loves his country, this may be a bitter hope, but sadly it is one that may be more attainable than any other.

Dara says:

"This bronze man is the symbol of us Iranians . . . The world has cut off our hands."

"Perhaps we cut them off ourselves."

"No. We are a great nation. We have a rich culture."

"We had."

"I really don't like you being so anti-Iranian. If you think like this, you will end up like those Iranians who prospered in this country, used its opportunities, and when they made a name for themselves, went to the West and put their brains to work in the service of Westerners."

"Maybe this country drove them out."

"Even if what you say is true, they should have stayed and taught this country not to sacrifice its good Isaacs."

"Have you yourself ever managed to teach this to an Iranian?"

"How could I teach anyone anything when before I even became an Abraham they battered and beat me?"

I'm not sure whether you will make out the Iranian metaphors of this dialogue. But all I can say is that other than a US attack on Iran – which the American media stir up whenever they are short of headlines – there have been hundreds of other major attacks on Iran, and each time one of our empires suffered a defeat, the gates to its fortresses were opened to its enemies from the inside, with no Trojan horse involved. I don't mean there are many traitors among us. What I mean is that there is no short-age of opportunists among us. These opportunists, with innocent smiles, have pushed the best offspring of Iran towards destruction – people who could truly save the country from plunging down the cliff of backwardness. And following their assassination or suicide while exiled in the West, the rest of us Iranians, even those of us who benefited from the even-handed and reformist actions of those people, have not uttered a single word in protest, and have in fact tried to justify that their deaths or suicides were deserved.

This subject is somewhat complicated, and unfortunately there is no more room in my love story to dedicate to it. Let us go and see Sara and Dara at the museum.

Sara asks:

"Do you think this bronze man was ever in love?"

"If he weren't in love he would not have survived for two thousand years. Perhaps I will turn into a mud statue after I die."

After leaving the security of the museum walls, Sara's anxiety returns. On these occasions the poor girl starts to sweat and feels nauseated. They begin rehearsing some of the personal information that they have memorized in case they are arrested and interrogated.

Dara asks:

"What is my aunt's name?"

"Roya."

"What is her son's name?"

"Rostam."

"Where is their house?"

"Liberty Street."

"How many rooms do we have in our house?"

"One living room downstairs and two bedrooms upstairs."

"What flower do we have in our garden?"

"Jasmine."

"What brand is our washing machine?"

Sara cannot remember.

"Think! You'll remember."

Sara cannot remember. Dara teases:

"Then you were lying when you said you are one of the top students at the university. Is this how you memorize your lessons?"

Sara asks:

"What brand is it?"

"None. We don't have a washing machine."

Sara, pretending to be angry, jabs Dara with her elbow. Suddenly scared, they look around to make sure no one is watching them.

And now they are walking along the narrow and busy Lalehzar Street. The streets here are always swarming with people. The small shops and pedlars, with their wares spread out on the ground every few feet, attract not only people with limited means but loafers and idlers as well.

More important, though, are the black marketeers who stand alone and cater to their clientele. They have an uncanny sixth sense – envied by writers – with which they can tell by looking at the face of a passer-by whether he is looking for black-market merchandise or not and, if so, exactly what he is looking for. After pinpointing a potential customer, as that person walks past them they whisper in his ear. For example

"Atashpareh's latest album has arrived."

(That would be a minx called Fireball.)

Or:

"Wet . . .?"

Meaning alcohol.

Or:

"Dry . . .?"

Which most probably means opium.

The inventory of black-market goods could include

– Grocery coupons. (Families of seven or more who cannot afford to buy groceries even at the relatively low government prices sell their coupons on the black market so that families who do have money can use them in addition to their own coupons.)

– Foreign cigarettes, drugs, alcohol.

– Hard-to-find medications. (Iranian doctors, the likes of Dr Farhad, know that certain medications cannot be found in pharmacies. Therefore, to prevent their gravely ill patients from having to wander around, when writing a prescription they will also tell them where on the black market they can find that medicine.)

– CDs or cassette tapes of banned music, particularly Los Angeles music. Don't misunderstand, I don't mean West Coast music. I am referring to a genre of so-called Iranian pop that is produced in great quantity and shameful quality in Los Angeles and smuggled into Iran. This hub of Iranian music production, right under Hollywood's nose, was spontaneously established after the Islamic Revolution. A throng of good and bad singers, musicians, composers and songwriters, who along with thousands of other Iranians had secretly escaped or legally migrated to the United States, started producing music for the state of California, which in just a few years had one hundred thousand Iranians added to its population. In Iran, on the other hand, where in the early post-revolution years the population had dropped by a few million (but further to recommendations by certain government officials had started passionately and tirelessly reproducing by night so as to benefit from extra grocery coupons meant for families of seven or more), music was declared forbidden. At the time, Iranian radio and television channels broadcast revolutionary anthems day and night. Yet a small group of Iranians was eager to listen to music. Therefore, a few entrepreneurs started copying Los Angeles-made music onto cassette tapes and sold them on the black market in Iran. Later, CDs were added to the offerings.

Iran is one of the very few countries in the world that has music and films (especially Hollywood movies) favoured by segments of its society produced overseas and delivered to its shores with no capital investment of its own, no shipping and insurance costs, and no copyright.

On the crowded pavement of Lalehzar Street, Sara and Dara see a seemingly blind man trip over the box of the magic pedlar. The pedlar scoffs.

"For your troubles and pains I have problem-solving spells . . . You really are blind."

Sara and Dara walk past this dialogue. They arrive in front of a very old theatre that has been shut down. Years before the revolution, Iranian plays such as *Khosrow and Shirin* used to be staged here. Notices of death, smiling pictures of candidates running for the Tehran City Council, all of whom claim they will make Iran the world's mightiest country, and advertisements for preparatory classes for college entrance exams are glued to the old theatre doors. As Sara and Dara walk past the theatre, a young man whispers to them:

"Copies of *Brokeback Mountain* have arrived. Five hundred tumans."

Dara's steps weaken. Sara says:

"No, it's too risky. Don't stop."

The young man follows them, and as he walks past them he brings his head close to Dara's ear and whispers:

"I have the cool bedroom film of the series actress. Twelve thousand tumans."

Sara and Dara slow down to put some distance between themselves and the black marketeer. Sara asks:

"What did he have?"

"The filthiest film in the world. The boyfriend of an actress who plays in an Iranian television series has filmed their lovemaking and has circulated the tape."

"Aah! That poor girl."

"Yes. That poor girl . . . She committed suicide."

For a few minutes they walk in silence. Towards the end of Lalehzar Street Sara asks:

"I hope you're not like that boyfriend."

"~~As if you and I are making love day and night.~~ As if you and I are in the same room day and night."

And then Dara adds:

"Not even in my dreams would I allow myself to touch you."

At this moment, the two who are walking side by side like strangers turn and stare into each other's eyes. In each other's eyes they read many unspoken and unthinkable words~~, words of repressed yearnings and desires. And in each other's eyes they see images of forbidden words, words such as "kiss", "pomegranate", "milk and honey", and "oyster".~~ . . .

It is fortunate, and rare, that as they stare into each other's eyes and stroll along that street, there are no street pedlar's wares in their path. Yet it seems that great desire also reawakens bitterness and pain.

Dara asks sarcastically:

"What news of His Excellency, your gentleman suitor?"

"His Excellency is well. So?"

~~"How can you be with me and at the same time lead that man on?"~~

~~Sara does not answer. It is now that, according to romance novels, black clouds fill the beautiful blue sky.~~

~~Dara again asks:~~

~~"How can you?"~~

~~Sara replies:~~

~~"How can you keep silent when they have forced this headscarf on my head?"~~

With these words Dara is delivered a powerful punch in the mouth. For an entire thirty-seven minutes they walk in total silence until they finally arrive at a public park. Dara, with bloodshot eyes, asks Sara to keep herself busy for a few minutes by looking in the shop windows on the other side of the street until he goes somewhere and returns. No matter how many times Sara asks him what has happened, she receives no response other than his hurry to leave. Dara, half running, enters the park. He has to get to a toilet.

No, don't misunderstand. He really does have to pee. He has needed to pee ever since they were at the museum, but that punch in the mouth from Sara has made it worse. In the dire state of almost losing control, with many apologies to the people standing in the queue, he rushes into a cubicle and shuts the steel door. On the top part of the door, meaning the upper third of the Rule of Thirds in visual arts, a large uneven hole has been cut out so that if someone is standing in the cubicle and pissing or doing something else, his head can be seen from the outside. In Iran, from a purely religious point of view, pissing while standing up is as unbecoming as participating in certain activities that take place in the toilets of bars and clubs in the West.

Dara, completely drained, returns. He finds Sara on the other side of the street in front of a bridal shop. In its large window, there is a mannequin wearing a beautiful and regal wedding gown. The mannequin has no protruding breasts and no head. In just these few minutes, Sara's face has grown very sad.

She says:

"Let's go shopping."

"Shopping for what?"

Sara points to the dress.

"What? Do you know how expensive these dresses are?"

"How do you know? How many times have you been married?"

"I can guess . . . What's more, I . . . to tell you the truth . . ."

"You have no money?"

Embarrassed, Dara nods.

"But we're not actually going to buy anything. We're just going to pretend. We'll act."

They enter the store. The middle-aged shop owner, who is wearing very heavy make-up, contrary to most Iranian shop owners, greets them with a smile.

Although it is forbidden for men to enter such stores, the shop owner pays little attention to Dara's shy and uneasy presence. She asks Sara:

"Are you the bride?"

"Yes."

"Oh! It's been a while since a bride this beautiful walked into my shop . . . What style are you looking for?"

She puts an English-language catalogue in front of Sara. ~~All the bare body parts of the models, including arms, legs and hair, have been obscured by a black Magic Marker.~~

I don't like to interrupt the progress of my story constantly to offer explanations. But it seems I have no choice. Some things, certain actions in Iran are so strange and outlandish that without explaining them it is impossible for an Iranian story to be well understood by non-Iranians. These explanations are also important for young Iranian readers because, for example, since the day an Iranian sixteen-year-old opened her eyes to the world, she has always seen fashion magazines with this same black Magic Marker treatment and she thinks that all magazines around the world look like this. Therefore, it must be said that:

For years after the revolution, importing foreign periodicals and books to Iran was banned. Then the government decided to allow a slight opening in the country's visual and scriptural contact with the world. Therefore, a special section was set up at all Customs offices to censor Western publications entering the country. Agents would carefully leaf through journals and magazines that travellers brought from overseas and insisted on passing through Customs – magazines such as *Burda*, which is very popular in Iran – and they would tear out pages with pictures of bare-limbed women and women not wearing proper Islamic dress and throw them in the waste bin. No matter how much a concerned traveller would plead that on the reverse side of an advertisement in *The New Yorker* or *Newsweek* or *National Geographic* there was an important article, no one would listen. Imagine how many hundreds of thousands of models, Hollywood stars and beautiful women in advertisements have been sent off to the waste bins of airports in Iran. Later, to prevent such mass executions, these same Customs departments invented a new technique. Very sticky sticky tape, purchased not from China where glues are as weak as spit, but from the West, was supplied to all Customs offices in huge quantities. At the sight of a bare arm or a pair of legs, the responsible agents would stick a piece of sticky tape on the limbs, and with a deftness that only Iranian handy-men possess, they would swiftly rip it off, and the mighty sticky tape would lift those arms or legs off the page of the magazine. But this method was time-consuming, and embodied a violence akin to Khosrow's actions toward Shirin's stepmother on the night of the nuptial consummation. At any rate, man was driven from heaven to earth so that he will forever have to invent. After a while, a new approach, which is this system of blacken-ing with permanent markers, was invented. The method was later perfected when markers were purchased from overseas that, while black-ening completely and mercilessly, compassionately did not leak through to the reverse side of the page.

I must confess that after years of longing to see a current issue of *The New Yorker*, as I hungrily leafed through one that a friend had brought from overseas, before reading the short story, I was tempted to see what lay beneath the black. I held the page up to the light, but I could see nothing of the legs on that model lounging on a sofa with two black ribbons cross-ing each other below the hem of her skirt in the vein of Japanese brush paintings. I didn't have the patience to try to wipe the ink off with water or nail-polish remover, but a friend who also liked *The New Yorker* told me that the black ink does not come off with either water or nail-polish remover.

In the past few years, because of soaring demand, several fashion mag-azines have been published in Iran. In these magazines, photographs of the latest fashions from Paris and New York are printed in their actual form, but instead of the model, who should be wearing the clothes, there is only a pencil sketch of a woman. The pencil-sketched woman is, of course, wearing a headscarf.

The magic pedlar of Tehran, contrary to the character in that beautiful cartoon who sketched in pencil and whatever he drew came to life, spe-cializes in transforming all real things into pencil sketches.

Sara, however, does not browse through that black-inked *Burda*, and playing the part of the most serious bride in the world, she says:

"We are planning to get married in five days. To be honest, it was a last-minute decision."

"You mean Mr Groom is all fired up?"

"Something like that . . . The day after the wedding we are flying to Paris."

The excited shop owner rubs her hands together.

"Oh, that is so romantic. Honeymoon in Paris. Nothing beats that . . . and with such a handsome man . . . You will shine in Paris."

Sara points to the dress on the mannequin in the window.

"Do you have that dress for me to try on?"

"As a matter of fact, we have one just your size."

Sara goes to the dressing room. This is the perfect opportunity for Dara to savour the bitter taste of Sara's tooth-shattering retort. Well, like many enlightened Iranian men, he is subconsciously ashamed of his own incompetence and inaction when, after the revolution, mothers, sisters, and wives, through coercion and by having drawing pins stabbed into their foreheads, were forced to wear headscarves and chadors, and year after year their human rights were taken away from them. And at this very moment, the stinging slap of a political inspiration lands on his ear. Dara discovers that during all the years that he and his generation fought for utopia in Iran, they were wrong, and that they should have fought instead for this small and basic right.

I am wondering whether this is Dara's own discovery or not, when, ~~flir-tatiously,~~ the shop owner turns to Dara and says:

"Sir! Do you realize what a beautiful and attractive bride you have?"

Embarrassed, Dara mumbles something. The shop owner points at him and laughs:

"Wow! It's been a while since a groom this shy walked into my shop. Lucky bride . . . ~~Let's see, do you know what to do on your wedding night?"~~

All of Dara's sweat is oozing out of his pores. ~~The shop owner looks Dara over. She moves closer, and aware that she is sending a whiff of the latest Chanel perfume to his nostrils, she plays with the top silver button on her coverall.~~

~~"If your bride shops from my store, as her bonus, come here alone on your wedding day. I have some magic American pills. I'll give you a few, and I promise on your wedding night your *sonbol* will not buckle even for a second . . . Have you ever heard of Viagra?"~~

As you may have surmised, *sonbol* is a colloquialism for the male organ, but in fact the word means "hyacinth". Now, I know that the majority of Western scientists only invent things that are needed in their own country, and if at this moment Dara had not gone dumb with embarrassment, or if

I was there in the shop with him, we would say to that lady shop owner:

First of all, most of us Iranian men not only have no need for Viagra, but we in fact need pills to relieve us of our perpetually raised *sonbol*s so that we can at last, peacefully, tend to more important tasks such as inventing things that our people really need. For example, a pill that would record a Western masterpiece such as *Lord Jim* on our memory, or a pill that would stimulate comprehension of Kandinsky's abstract art, or a pill that would infuse an understanding of the philosophical implications of Einstein's theory of relativity or quantum physics in the minds of us Middle Easterners so that we become less dogmatic. Or even a pill that would download Mr Microsoft's acumen and entrepreneurship onto the genius minds of our youth for them to understand that, instead of inventing ways to break Microsoft's software codes, they can develop software that breaks the ancient codes in the brains of us Iranians.

Sara, wearing one of the most beautiful Iranian wedding gowns, walks out of the dressing room. With a playfulness that all women possess, and fully aware of the answer to her own question, she ~~coquettishly swings her hips and~~ asks Dara:

"What do you think?"

~~**It is the first time Dara has seen Sara wearing anything other than a coverall.**~~

If at this very moment you were in Dara's place, facing all that forbidden beauty clad in a magnificent dress, what sentence would you speak at the first sight of your beloved's bare shoulders and cleavage nestled among lace flowers?

No words come out of Dara's mouth. He simply stares in awe. Sara turns to face the large mirror. Now they see themselves side by side. Dara discovers how ugly and shabby his clothes are. He pulls himself out of the mirror's reflection.

~~**The store lights reflect off Sara's young and radiant skin. Dara feels he has a fever and sweat trickles down his spine. He is dying to reach out and touch those shoulders. A gentle and delicate touch, with his trembling fingertips allowed only to move along the outer limits of that skin.**~~

Sara says:

"Come, take my hand so that we can walk like a bride and groom."

In the mirror, they watch their graceful walk together.

Then Sara smooths the satin folds of the dress ~~on her chest and stomach~~ and her eyes fall captive to ~~the longing look in~~ Dara's eyes.

What they say about the language of eyes being more compelling and intimate than the spoken word is not always and on all occasions true. It depends on the person and the circumstances. On a spring night, in a romantic restaurant in Paris where you can see the Eiffel *sonbol* from the window next to you, you may find yourself with a talkative woman, or an arrogant man who incessantly talks about his incredible financial feats, and while the candlelight shines in your beautiful eager eyes you look into your partner's eyes, and in those eyes you read nothing other than what is coming out of his or her mouth.

I mean, if you really want romance, instead of Paris, which sells anything and everything and even memories of Montparnasse to tourists, come to Tehran. Your optical romance begins the moment you leave the airport.

An even more important aspect of the dialogue of eyes is its speed. If hours of conversation are required to reach an end, all those words can be exchanged in a one-minute dialogue between eyes, and the man and woman can take each other's hand and, rivalling a final scene in a Charlie Chaplin movie, quickly and merrily walk down a road towards a bright horizon and their point and purpose.

Therefore, in their eye dialogue, Sara says:

Make up your mind! Do you have the courage to want me or not?

Dara forgets all the religious, moral and ideological ethics that have been hammered into his head since childhood and with his eyes he whimpers:

I do. I do. I want you.

What does "I want you" mean?

It means I want to kiss you.

Have you ever kissed?

No.

I haven't either . . . It doesn't matter, we'll practise with each other.

Definitely . . . And then I want to smell you. I will start with your hair and go all the way down to your toes. I will smell you and kiss you.

And then?

And then I might just fall and die at your feet.

No. You're not allowed. You can die any time you want to except then . . . Then what will you do?

What will you do?

I will sigh.

Then sigh, and I will devour your sigh.

Have you ever drunk alcohol?

Yes. It helps me be bold enough to do whatever I want with you.

No. Don't. You're not allowed to drink because you won't be able to see me clearly and then you'll fall asleep.

I will drink.

Then I will send an old woman to you in my place.

An old woman?

You are so stupid! Haven't you read Khosrow and Shirin?

I forgot.

Anyway . . . You are not allowed to get drunk.

I will get drunk so that I will see two of you. I will lay one Sara down on her back and one Sara down on her stomach.

Then?

Then with one hand I will stroke the front of your calf and with the other the back of your calf, and I will move my hands up.

Sara sighs.

I will keep sliding my hands up.

From deep within her soul Sara breathes the sigh of a one-thousand-and-one-year-old want.

Then what will you do?

Sara, I'm scared.

I will give you milk from my breasts so that you will grow up and stop being scared.

I will grow on your body. At that final moment of pleasure your thighs will press against my sides, and you will break me in two.

Then hurry up and do something.

Here?

No, stupid . . . Find somewhere.

But I'm not rich. I don't have a hideaway for my flings and escapades.

Find somewhere where we can be alone without being afraid.

Yes, I did say that eye dialogue develops rapidly, but not this rapidly. To communicate all these sentences, I would suspect that approximately five minutes will be required, with no blinking to punctuate the stream of glances with commas.

The now bored shop owner interrupts the two streams of ones and zeros flowing from their eyes with a cough and says:

"Miss Bride! Mr Groom! . . . Have you decided? Do you want the dress?"

Sara ~~winks at Dara and~~ laughs.

"I like it, but from what I see in the gentleman's eyes, he doesn't really like this dress. ~~He seems to prefer that I take it off.~~"

Dara says ignorantly:

"No, I like it. It's very nice."

And bashfully he tries to memorize every detail of the image of Sara in that dress.

The shop owner says:

"The dress looks like it was made for you. It really suits you, my dear."

"How much is it?"

Hearing the price of the dress, Dara is flabbergasted. He could live comfortably on that money for three years.

Sara asks:

"Why is it so expensive?"

"It's from Paris."

"The price doesn't matter. The gentleman will be paying for it . . . But . . ."

Sara searches for an excuse to end the game. No help comes from Dara.

"But what?"

"I want to think about it tonight . . . Is that a problem?"

The shop owner, now suspicious, says sulkily:

"What problem could there be, miss?"

"If I decide to take it, will you give me a discount?"

"If you're a buyer, I'll give you a discount."

Outside the shop Sara says:

"You were about to have a heart attack! You so-called film buff, with all the films you have seen, can't you act just a bit?"

THE ARABS ARE COMING

"I will make the tea tonight," Sara tells her mother as she puts the kettle on the stove in the kitchen. Like all the other ten o'clocks of all the other nights, her father, a retired employee of the Ministry of Culture and Islamic Guidance, with his mouth wide open, has fallen asleep in front of the television in the living room. For this nocturnal tea, mother and daughter have their own ritual. They spoon the tea leaves into the teapot, they add a few petals of dried bitter orange blossoms from Shiraz to make it more fragrant, and after adding hot water from the kettle, they remove the kettle's lid and stack the teapot on top of it for the tea to brew gently with the steam from the kettle. The perfume of tea and bitter orange blossoms permeates a house whose man is asleep. The two women sit at the kitchen table to drink their tea from small narrow-waisted tea glasses and for Sara to listen to her mother gossip and chatter. Sara, like many Iranian young people, shares very few of her private thoughts with her mother, but tonight she is looking for an excuse to ask an important question about her future. This afternoon, after stammering and agonizing for half an hour on the telephone, Dara has finally asked:

"I wanted to ask whether you think . . . If it is possible . . . I know that Sinbad – well-to-do Sinbad – has asked for your hand, but . . . I mean . . . would you some day agree to marry me?"

And Sara, instead of giving him a serious answer, has joked, "So you want to fall into that trap?" Sara's brainless father grunts in his sleep. Her mother, while gossiping about the neighbour's wife, who seems to have again received a severe beating from her husband because she had engaged in small talk with the gentleman next door, smirks and says,

"Your poor father is so tired today. He left home this morning pretending to go and sort out some problem with his pension. But I am sure he went to see his friend Haji Karim ~~and smoked opium. His breath reeked of it~~. I didn't have the heart to spoil his good mood tonight, but I'm going to really have a go at him tomorrow."

"Leave him alone. What other pleasure does poor Dad have in his life? Let him have his fun once every few months."

"~~With all our financial troubles, the last thing we need is for your father to end up an opium addict.~~ Don't you pay any attention, girl? Day after day everything is becoming more expensive, and your father's pittance of a pension stays the same."

The conversation is moving in a direction that Sara does not want. Very soon her mother will start talking about her daily domestic toils and will again repeat how she works miracles and with great skill, sacrifice and frugality runs the household on Father's small pension. But as soon as she starts, a cricket that has long been hiding in the house comes to Sara's aid.

Both women turn to Sara's father. The cricket's sound seems to be coming from his open mouth. Mother takes off one of her slippers. Armed with her weapon, in a voice thick with belligerence and bloodlust she says:

"I finally found it!"

And she quietly inches towards Sara's father.

But Sara knows the cricket is not there. During the days and nights of the past week, every time the cricket's chirping has exasperated them, they have traced its sound from room to room, and every time they have reached the spot where they thought it was hiding, they have heard it sing in another part of the house.

Slipper in hand and disappointed, Sara's mother returns.

"Were you really going to hit Father in the mouth with your slipper?"

"The number of ~~opium-addicted~~ snorers is rising in this country; I wouldn't be surprised if the crickets have got into it, too."

"But I think you are in love with Father, aren't you?"

Her mother is taken aback.

"In love? Why do you ask?"

"No reason. Were you in love with Father when you married him?"

"No. Your father was the second man who asked for my hand in marriage. I was twenty-three and an old maid, that's why I accepted so quickly."

Sara imagines the ceremony during which her father asked for her mother's hand. She sees her father, young, shy, sitting on a Polish chair in the living room of an old house. Next to him, his parents. Facing them, more sombre, her mother's parents state, one by one, the terms of marriage to their daughter. And Father's parents, one by one, haggle over the stipulations, hoping to reduce the amounts that would have to be paid to the parents as the bride price and to the bride as the marriage portion. At a precise time, which Mother's mother determines, Mother enters the room carrying a tray of small tea glasses. Her eyes cast down and more timid than Father, her hands tremble and cause the tea to spill. The trembling becomes more pronounced as she holds the tray in front of the future bridegroom and with nervous coquetry says, "Please have some tea." And the groom, with unsteady hands, takes a tea glass and saucer and sneaks a peek at the face of the bride his mother has chosen for him. From the very few photographs that her mother has of her youth, Sara knows that even in those days she did not possess any particular beauty. But she says:

"You were only twenty-three and very pretty, why do you say you were an old maid?"

"Yes, I was very pretty. But in those days, if a girl was not married by the time she turned twenty, she was considered an old maid and everyone thought something must be wrong with her if no one had asked for her hand."

"But tell me the truth, were you ever in love?"

Mother looks at Sara with surprise, and then, as if a stale and distant sorrow has reawakened in her heart, she looks over at her husband.

"Please don't be shy, Mother. Tell me. I'm your daughter. Tell me . . . You must have fallen in love at one time."

Mother, nervous that her husband may have woken up and can hear them, does not take her eyes off him and reluctantly nods.

"Who was he? A relative?"

Mother shakes her head.

"Was he a neighbour's son?"

She nods.

"Was he in love with you?"

Mother lowers her voice and says dolefully:

"He had no idea. He used to sneak out of their house at night and smoke out on the street so that his parents wouldn't see. I would see him from the window. The poor thing always had to put out his cigarette after the third or fourth puff because some neighbour would invariably show up in the alley."

"Well, why didn't you try to send him a message or something, for him to know you were in love with him?"

"It was no use. Their financial situation was . . . Well, it was very bad. His father used to dig wells. He had to leave school at fourteen and start helping his father."

"Don't you regret not having married him just because he was poor?"

The wrinkles of sorrow, which Sara had only then discovered, multiply on her mother's face.

"No. Your father was a government employee. In those days, unlike now, being a government employee was a great privilege – a good and steady income, social status . . . A few years after my marriage, I heard that the poor thing drowned in the pit of a well he was digging."

"What will you say if I fall in love with someone like that and want to marry him?"

The cricket's chirping can now be heard from every corner of the house. Mother, stunned, stares at Sara. The wrinkles on her face scream out *No!*

"Tell me the truth, girl! Have you made such a mistake?"

To calm her down, Sara laughs and says:

"No, Mother. I just said it. But tell me what you really feel from the bottom of your heart. What will you do if I fall in love with a penniless man?"

"I will never forgive you. You have a rich, handsome and distinguished suitor who many girls pine for. Don't spoil your luck. Don't ruin yourself and us. ~~Your suitor has promised your father a comfortable job with a good salary. You know if the situation in this country continues like this, by next year your father and I will have to~~

~~go begging on the street.~~ I will never forgive you. On the day of judgment I will stand in your way and I will tell God that this girl – you – ruined herself and us."

Tears begin to flow from Mother's eyes. For the first time in many years, Sara kisses her mother on the forehead and says:

"But Mother, you have never tasted happiness. Perhaps if you had married that boy . . . I don't know . . . perhaps . . . Your story is one of those old tales of poverty and, I guess, love . . . But I was only joking. Please don't worry."

Mother is still looking at Sara with suspicion and concern. The tea glass shakes in her hand, but there is no tea left in it to spill. Father wakes up with a start. As always, he quickly changes the television channel and before finding out what programme is on he falls asleep again and begins to snore, as if a cricket is stuck in his throat.

On this television programme, as on most television programmes in Iran, a clergyman is lecturing about the tenets of Islam.

"Doctors at the Medical Examiner's Office have sought the opinion of the head of the judiciary branch with respect to occasions when a judge rules for the hand of a person who has committed theft three times to be amputated. Can they, at the time of executing the judgment, inject the condemned with anaesthetics so that he does not suffer? The honourable head of the judiciary branch has responded no, because Islam decrees that the condemned must suffer for the crime he has committed. Therefore, sir, madam, know that if you commit theft for a third time, your hand will be cut off. If in the course of an argument you blind someone's eye, your punishment will be for your eye to be plucked out. If, God forbid, you come to blows with someone and injure his right testicle, you will have to compensate him with forty camels; and if you injure his left testicle, you will have to compensate him with fifty camels. Why? Why is the recompense for the left testicle more than that of the right testicle? Because according to sacred stories a child is produced from man's left testicle . . ."

Sara abandons her anxious mother with no anaesthetics and goes to her room on the second floor. She pulls the curtains aside and stares up at the full moon that shines for merry and tearful lovers alike. She is now certain that the cricket is hiding somewhere in her room. She whispers:

"Dara, you rascal! You let this cricket into our house."

And the moon, generously, eternally, shines for all lovers, for all crickets, ~~camels, severed testicles, stolen kisses, amputated arms and legs~~ and eyes, without prejudice.

Sara, looking out from the window beside which she has spent many hours waiting for Dara to appear, with that same old view of the street and the pavement on its far side, dwells on her future. She knows with all her being that she is not willing to repeat her mother's life, to let her youth and dreams be frittered away in the kitchen for the ideal and ambition of how best to feed the family, with only hardship on the kitcheny horizon. ~~This strong impulse for change and for attaining happiness and beauty is perhaps because of the headscarf that has been forcibly nailed to her head.~~

Still, Sara has not been able to make up her mind. Each time she thinks about marrying Dara, all the financial and political difficulties that await her flash before her eyes, and consequently she thinks of Sinbad, of all the help this wealthy man can offer her family, and what's more, she sees in herself a power as great as that of an Iranian nuclear bomb to change this man, to recreate him to her own liking. She sees herself with him in the capital cities of Europe, drunk on the beauties and joys that await her there, with all the things that she knows can only be attained with money and Western freedom. She sees herself dressed in the most stylish Parisian dresses, in cafés and restaurants that she has only seen in contraband films and has yearned for. She sees her unchained Eastern beauty being admired by men with a flair for women, and she sees how it lures their longing looks in the wake of its splendour. And she sees herself in a sexy bikini – something she has never experienced – lying on the golden sand of a non-Islamic beach; in her spine the pleasing sensation of the grains of sand surrendering to the weight of her round buttocks, and in her chest the pleasant wonder of the sun shining in between her breasts. And all the while, from the corner of her eye, she sees tanned hunks showing off their six solid abdominal muscles, and she delights in ignoring them . . . But suddenly she sees Dara's pleasant face. She imagines herself with him in a modest, rented room filled with the pleasures and desires that only true lovers can discover and abounding with the novelties that only love can inspire at night and in the mornings after.

Sara shrugs and whispers:

"How can I know what to do? Which one? I don't know. I have to find out which one wants me more for myself. I will think about it tomorrow . . . tomorrow . . ."

Whether she sees or does not see from the window of her room, an army of Arabs is advancing down the street. They set out one thousand four hundred years ago, and having conquered the capital city of the Sassanid Empire, they are on their way to occupy the wealthy land of Khorasan, the last province of Iran. Their white dishdashas and unsheathed curved-blade sabres shine with a neon glow in the silver light of this night's moon.

DAMASK ROSE'S STAMEN

On this same night, in the small living room of their house, Dara is sitting beside his mother on a thirty-year-old sofa and appears to be watching an Iranian film series on television. His mother likes these melodramatic programmes. During scenes in which a mother, wife or sister cries, she too readily cries. And she glances at her son and her tears flow even more freely.

But Dara, after a quarter of a century of watching these Islamic films in which mothers, wives and sisters appear in their hijab even at home, has still not grown accustomed to them and finds them shallow and insulting. He looks at his mother and observes her grey hair that at home, uninhibited, shines black and white and looks at the actress in the film whose bed must never be occupied by her husband even when the storyline sends her to go and sleep.

Dara's mother has turned down the volume on the television set as much as possible because its sound infuriates Dara's father, so much so that from his fortress he suddenly yells:

"Shut these lies up! Madam, why don't you understand? These things will make you more stupid . . . Turn it off!"

Dara's father is a defeated Communist. I know that at this point in the story you don't need to ask what "defeated Communist" means. You know better than I do. But you don't know this man's story. Then ask me, so that I, like Shahrazad the storyteller, can try to tell you.

Dara's father was a Communist even before the 1979 revolution, meaning during the Shah's regime. In those days, he was a high-ranking Customs officer at Mehrabad International Airport, an important position in which, with a little bit of moral and financial corruption, he could have demanded the heftiest bribes from importers of Western products to clear their merchandise through customs without collecting the requisite duties. However, from the condition of his house, the family's sole possession in that poor neighbourhood of Tehran, you can guess what label those bribe-taking, bribe-giving Iranians who deem themselves quite clever pinned on him.

Two years before the revolution, the secret police discovered that Dara's father was a Communist. They arrested him in front of his colleagues and took him to Evin Prison, Iran's most famous penitentiary. Evin Prison is similar to the Bastille but with two distinct differences. In a very modern way it is more terrifying and harrowing than the Bastille, and while the Bastille entered the annals of history and was shut down after the French Revolution, Tehran's Evin Prison was expanded following the Iranian revolution, and the number of its political prisoners and their torturing increased substantially.

When the revolution triumphed, when the Shah with tearful eyes was forced to leave the country, when the revolutionaries broke down the prison gates, Dara's father walked out of Evin Prison like a national hero. People cheered him, and one emotional Iranian hoisted him up on his shoulders, just like other emotional Iranians did with other prisoners, and carried him a long way. Then, because he had no money, he had to walk a long distance home. Of course, his wife and young boy too embraced him like a national hero. A month later, Dara's father, who was still a national hero, returned to his job, until six years later when he was again arrested for the crime of being a Communist and sent back to Evin Prison. This post-revolution Evin Prison was very different from what it was prior to the revolution. It was not even comparable to Guantánamo. In this prison, consistent with the constitutional law of the Islamic Republic, any form of torture is forbidden – the same way that the constitution forbids any form of censorship. However, when an interrogator determines that a political prisoner is not confessing as he should, he finds the prisoner guilty of lying, which is a crime in Islam, and sentences him to be whipped. Dara's father, on several occasions, had the pleasure of such floggings. His problem, however, was that he had nothing to confess. He was only a simple supporter of the Communist Party. Every Friday night he would find the party's newsletter in his front yard, and his task was to make copies of it in any way he could and to distribute the copies among others. His mistake was that he was using the photocopier at his office, an agency of the Islamic

Republic, to make copies of the Communist Party newsletter, and he did so in a country where almost every day, out on the streets, some group of demonstrators would chant "Death to the Communist who says there is no God."

A few months after the fall of the Berlin Wall, Dara's father was released from prison because for a Communist such as he, whose party had for almost half a century heeded the call of Big Brother and the Communist Party in the Soviet Union, no punishment or whipping was as bad as having to return home to learn that the world's Communist parties were one after the other regretting and denouncing their past Stalinesque ways. In other words, the wisest and cruellest punishment for Dara's father and others like him was to discover that all the years they had endured prison and torture, and all the years they had mourned the execution of their party's heroes and lamented their own survival, had almost overnight become worthless. Therefore, this time Dara's father returned home broken and dejected and not as a national hero, but as a man accused of having spied for the Soviet Union. He had been dismissed from his job and did not have a penny of income. The first thing he did was to find a fortress for himself in his house, and this fortress was nothing other than a small storage room on the first floor. In keeping with the habit he had developed at Evin Prison, he spread a blanket on the floor to sleep on, although the storage room was not large enough for him to sleep with his legs stretched out. Then he took a radio to this cell and started listening to Farsi news broadcasts on foreign radio stations such as Voice of America, Radio Israel, BBC, Radio France and others that had started the overseas-based opposition to Iran. Since the founding of the Islamic Republic of Iran, these stations had promised their listeners that this regime would fall in a matter of months; and the stations' listeners, at parties in homes that day by day had grown more similar to the palaces of the *One Thousand and One Nights*, or in homes that had day by day become more ramshackle, or on the benches in parks where the elderly sat, had repeated this news to one another until the present time in our story when Dara's father, after more than thirteen years in his Communist fortress, looks twenty years older than his sixty years of age.

Contrary to him, Dara's mother, who is a religious woman, has no interest in world politics and no interest in whether an Islamic regime, a monarchist regime or a Communist one rules in Iran. Every day she observes the seventeen segments of her requisite daily prayers, she fasts during the entire month of Ramadan, unbeknownst to her husband she saves a portion of the measly household income and gives it to the cleric at the neighbourhood mosque as her Islamic duty, and strives every day to cook the most delicious meal at the least cost for her husband and son.

Their meagre income comes from Dara's work painting houses and the small carpets his mother weaves. And every day, in her prayers, Dara's mother thanks God that their circumstances have not got any worse and that she still has her husband and son at home. So many Iranians have lost family members in the execution of those opposed to the Islamic Republic, in the war, in the bombings of Iranian cities by Iraq and . . . and . . . and there are many who have had their homes confiscated by the government.

Tonight, Dara's mother, after her protracted chore of daily cooking and after her evening prayers and expressions of gratitude to God, is sitting with her son to watch this evening's television series about a mother who has lost two sons to war. Because of Dara's father's sensitivity, she has kept the volume as low as possible. In this part of the film, the doorbell rings in the mother's house. The mother dons her chador and goes to the door. An elderly man dressed in a Revolutionary Guard uniform is standing at the door holding a box of pastries. He offers the box to the mother. Then he begins to deliver a lengthy speech about how God has been kind to the people of Iran by having bestowed upon them the gift of the Islamic Republic, and about how the iron hand of this holy regime, which will soon topple the tyrannical governments of the world and bring salvation to the people, is strengthened with the blood of its martyrs. Then he says:

"Sister, congratulations. Your son has been martyred at the front."

Hearing this news, the middle-aged woman who plays the part of a Party of God mother, with a smile on her lips and her eyes consciously or unconsciously somewhat tearful, rings the doorbell of the neighbouring homes to offer them pastries and to tell them that her third son too has been martyred.

From the corner of his eye Dara notices that his mother is watching him from the corner of her eye. He is not used to sharing his private thoughts with his mother, but tonight, for the first time, he is looking for an excuse to talk to her about the idea of marriage. Mother provides him with that excuse when she asks:

"Dara, I have noticed that you are very preoccupied these days. Has something happened?"

"No, nothing special."

"I'm a mother, I know when my son is happy or when he is sad, even when he is not in front of me. You have been very unhappy these days. Tell me. Are you involved in politics again? Don't go destroying yourself and us again!"

Dara's father shouts from his small fortress:

"Woman, what do you want from the boy? Leave him alone. He knows better than you and me."

Dara's mother lowers her voice and says:

"You see? He won't even let me watch a film in peace or have a simple conversation with my son. I have to be deaf and dumb in this house for him to be happy. God bless him, after eighty years his hearing is better than mine."

Ever since the start of their marriage, Dara's mother has been in the habit of adding twenty years to her husband's age.

~~Dara's father yells, "Madam! If you had been slapped around in prison as much as I was, by now you would either be completely deaf or you could even hear the cockroaches whisper."~~

~~And he turns up the volume on his radio.~~

Dara says:

"One of my old friends is getting married tomorrow night. I was wondering whether I should go or not."

He is lying. In fact, he has contrived this story after thinking for hours about how to bring up the subject of his desire to get married.

"Why shouldn't you go? You definitely should. You need to have some fun. God willing, your turn will come, too. I hope I will see you in your groom's suit before I die. At the end of all my daily prayers I pray for God to improve conditions in this country; I pray for your father and me to be freed from this misery and for you to find a high-paying job, to buy a house for yourself, to take your bride's hand, and to take her to your home."

Dara's father yells:

"Madam! You've spent a lifetime praying for these things and your God has shown us nothing but more of his wrath, the situation in this country has got worse. Don't you see? You pray for rain and we get floods, you pray in thanks and the earth quakes. Why won't you accept that something's not quite right here?"

Dara's mother, as is the habit of some Iranian women when they hear blasphemous words, bites the soft stretch of skin between her thumb and index finger and mimics spitting on it twice, and says:

"God forbid. May the devil's ear be deaf. Do you see how he reviles God? May God rain flames on the grave of he who planted the seed of these Communists who say there is no God."

She shouts:

"Sir! If it weren't for my prayers, you'd be long dead, you'd have rotted through a hundred shrouds by now."

Dara's father shouts back:

"Madam! Why can't you understand? Our poor son wants to talk about himself. He wants to know whether he can get married or not. This poor boy is being fooled, just like me. Son! According to the latest scientific research, only twenty per cent of the men in the world have brains, the rest have wives. But it doesn't matter if you want to ruin your life with your own hands the way I did. Go and be a fool! But for the love of God, marry someone who is neither a bourgeois nor like your mother. At least marry someone who has a few drops of Communist blood in her so that she will be patient and not too demanding, so that she'll come to this house and live with you in your room."

Dara's mother loses her temper.

"Sir! Are you suggesting that I was impatient and demanding? Who was it, during all those years you spent in prison, in the cold of winter and the heat of summer, who put her head down to sleep alone every night hoping for the day that you, sir, would walk through the door?"

"Madam, I was thrown in prison and suffered torture for trying to free this country from superstitions such as yours."

"Sir, you paid for your denial of God and your blasphemies. It is people like you who have brought this country to ruin. If you had any pride and honour you would think of your wife and child. For all these years that you have supposedly been the man of this house, you have not managed to bring in even a single penny. You just lie there day and night listening to that radio. I am the one who has kept you fed with the little I make and the pittance this boy brings home."

The yelling parents suddenly grow silent. It is the first time that such a frank and cruel exchange has taken place in this house. Dara gets up and shouts, "Stop it. It was my mistake. It was my mistake for saying that I want to go to a wedding."

With his eyes darker than ever, he pounds his fist on his thigh and heads for the stairs to go up to his room.

The television series has reached a scene in which the mother has washed her sons' gravestones with rose water and is now sitting beside the last grave talking to her last son.

"I miss you terribly, but I know that you are with your brothers and that you are happy together. I too am happy now that you are all in heaven. Now you have a stream of honey flowing on one side and a stream of milk on the other, and you are lying under a tree of whatever fruit you like, and whenever you want a piece of fruit a branch will bend down to you, it will come to you so that you won't have to reach up and pick the fruit. Now you each have seven thousand nymphs waiting for you in your castle in heaven . . ."

On the last step of the staircase Dara hears his parents crying. What's strange is that they sound so alike.

Dara, like all lovers in the world, sits beside the window in his room. His second-hand computer, next to the bedding spread on the floor, is turned off. He looks at the lighted windows across the street and sighs. He wants to think not of the seven thousand nymphs who could be waiting for him in heaven, but of his one nymph here on earth. The fight between his parents has once again brought home the dark reality of his life. They need his occasional income. Given their circumstances, can he bring into the house another mouth to feed? In the past few days he has created sentimental scenes of his marriage to Sara in his mind. In this very room, he has seen her as his wife, who says, If you want me to be a real wife to you, tonight you must kiss me a thousand and one times. He has seen himself offering Sara a single damask rose, which he then takes from her, plucks its petals, and spreads them on the bed, and with the stamen of the rose he caresses her neck. But tonight, with the slap in the face he has received from his parents' screams and sobs, he has realized that reality is far from his dreams and fantasies. He therefore starts to think of an invention or innovation that would make him rich, that would allow him to buy a large house in the most beautiful part of Tehran for his parents, so that when he is no longer worried about them, he can build a house for himself in one of the remaining walled gardens of the city and invite his Sara there.

But for now, the view he has of the world is that of a narrow dead-end alley in a poor neighbourhood where the houses are so tightly crammed together that their walls seem to be pushing against each other, perhaps to gain a few inches from the neighbour's property.

And in the alley, a one-horse cart rolls towards the street. Its load, hundreds of roses with their petals plucked and their yellow stamens shining like spears in the moonlight. The cart's wooden wheels roll over a half-singed wing.

A MAN WITH THREE WIVES

D ara has invited Sara at nightfall to his home. The occasion coincides with the publication of two chapters of this story in a literary magazine which has not yet been suspended. Since I am not experienced in writing such love stories, my intention was, before all else, to observe Mr Petrovich and the censorship department's reaction, and then to seek the opinion of my readers who are accustomed to the darkness and horror of my stories. The result was that the magazine received a warning from the Media Supervisory Committee at the Ministry of Culture and Islamic Guidance for having insulted the blessed territory of Tehran University, for having insulted the brothers of the Party of God, for having insulted the sacred slogan of freedom, for having insulted the image of the blessed Iranian woman, and for having indecently portrayed the revolution's second-generation young girls and future mothers of martyrs. With this warning, the number of the magazine's warnings reached the holy number of seven. In other words, the borderline beyond which the holy order of suspension will reach the hands of its editor-in-chief.

And the result of seeking readers' opinions was that some of them determined and spread the rumour that I, at the sacred age of fifty, have fallen in love and am creating a crude and vulgar scandal.

However, Dara's intentions for inviting Sara to his house have no apparent connection to any blessed affair. And I am so worried about my love story and my weaknesses in it that I cannot fathom why he has done such a thing.

Three days after the night of the row between Dara's parents over his going to a wedding, again while watching a television series, Dara has told his mother:

"One of my old schoolfriends wants to come over so that I can help her with her essay. Is that all right?"

His mother, with the glint of instinctive wisdom in her eyes, has stared at her son and her expression has soured.

"May the devil's ear be deaf, don't you ever do such a thing. The neighbours will see a strange girl coming and going in our house and they will start a thousand rumours. ~~Especially Mr Atta, who is in the Baseej volunteer militia. He will definitely report it and the agents will raid the house. With your political background, we'll get into a world of trouble.~~"

Dara's father has yelled out from his fortress:

"Leave him alone! Let him invite his girlfriend over. The boy is thirty-something years old and he still hasn't held a girl's hand. They torched the brothel district, they executed the madams and they produced a hundred times more prostitutes for themselves. How long can a penniless boy whose piss has frothed whack off? Dara! Can you hear me? Definitely invite her over. Tell me when she's coming and I'll send your mother to the mosque so she won't be home."

Dara's mother has been shocked and horrified by the crude words that had never before echoed off the ceiling of her house. The Iranian television series has reached the point when each of the three wives of a wealthy Muslim man has discovered that their husband has two other wives and they are trying to find one another. The climax of the series will come when the three women meet. Will they beat each other up? Will they sit together and weep? Or will they rip the louse's boxers off his arse and wrap them round his miserable head?

The interesting point about this series is that without the director and the censors at the state television station realizing, it alludes to one of God's wraths against a holy man. No, by "holy man" I don't mean one of the priests who have sexually abused children in church. In fact, I am referring to the case of the melting holy wee-wee of a venerable cleric who in one of the parliamentary elections in the Islamic Republic received the greatest number of votes from the province of Tehran.

Are you curious? Well, ask and I will tell you the story.

We first saw His Excellency on television in an educational programme on religion. Unlike many revered Iranian clerics, this gentleman had a kind face and smiling lips. He did not talk about the stoning of adulterers and the execution of apostates. The title of his programme was *Ethics at Home*. In his programme the gentleman would speak of spouses being kind to one another. He would advise women to try and understand their husbands and to be aware that when they come home from work they are tired, and because of difficulties at the workplace they may be in a foul mood. He would suggest that a woman can, by being pleasant and catering to her husband, let him know that he is not alone in this world and that he has her support and sympathy. On the other hand, he would advise a husband not to forget that his wife is his best friend and companion. "She is a flower in your house. Do not allow this precious flower to wilt. Be faithful to her and show her that she is the best woman you could find in this world. Do not look at her as a cook. Offer her presents, and if you cannot afford something expensive, one single flower is the best gift. Show her that in your eyes her beauty is eternal, and that you pray for her well-being in your daily prayers."

Thus, in television-watching households the gentleman became one of the best-loved and most famous faces. This popularity resulted in his election into the Islamic Parliament as the member with the greatest number of votes. And so it was, until suddenly, with no explanation, the esteemed gentleman's television programme was cancelled, and we no longer had any news of him at all. In other words, the gentleman disappeared. We Iranians were terribly eager to find out what had become of our kind cleric. Then, rumour about the *āftābeh* spread throughout the country.

Now the Western reader will ask me what *āftābeh* means.

Āftābeh is the Farsi word for one of the world's most indispensable objects. This instrument is very similar to the watering can Western ladies use to water their gardens, and we Muslims use it to wash the flowers of our body after relieving ourselves – which in my opinion is a more sanitary process than the tissuey Western method.

In any case, long after the disappearance of the kind cleric, rumour spread from mouth to mouth and reached me, too, that the gentleman, unbeknownst to his good wife, had taken partial advantage of his Islamic right to have four wives and had perpetrated the taking of a second wife. When his first wife found out, to exact revenge, she filled his *āftābeh* with sulphuric acid.

Dara, blushing and embarrassed, has mumbled:

"No. We were just going to study . . . Forget it. Don't argue."

And he has headed for the yard. ~~His father has yelled after him,~~
~~"Dara, you dimwit! Invite her. Go ahead and invite them over in pairs~~
~~so that you won't leave this world deprived like me."~~

Outside in the front yard, Dara has sat next to the flower bed and thought about his uncertain future, about Sara not having given him an answer to his proposal, about his financial difficulties should he ever get married and then, all by himself, he has come up with another narrative suspense. He has not sought my advice. Even if he had, I would not have been able to come up with anything. It was therefore his own unadulterated idea to invite Sara to their home at ten o'clock at night when his parents are asleep and to sit quietly with her here in this yard, or perhaps to even to sneak her up to his room. Just for an hour, or an hour and a half, no more, because Sara will have no excuse and no permission to spend the night away from home. After much mumbling he has told Sara about his plan and, contrary to his expectation, Sara has readily agreed. In fact, she herself has solved the problem of being out until midnight.

She has said, "I will say I am going to Jasmine's house to study and I will call a taxi to take me back home. The problem is, I can't leave home at nine o'clock at night pretending to want to go and study. I have to leave late in the afternoon and wait around somewhere until nine o'clock. I'll work it out. What will you do?"

"I will die waiting for you."

And I, instead of all this, will write in my story:

Dara, sitting next to the flower bed, has come to the conclusion that he must make greater sacrifices for his family, and if today he is beset by poverty and despair, it is only because he has not sacrificed enough, and that if at some point he manages to suppress his desires and yearnings, the day will come when the world's positive energies will come to his aid and he will have the means to get married.

Contrary to this idiotic sentence that can only come from the pen of a writer who has been chewed to the bone by censorship, it is now nine o'clock at night. This afternoon, Dara bought seven sacred stems of damask rose and hid them in a corner of the house. Before Sara arrives, he will pluck their petals and spread them in a circle in the shelter of the jasmine bush, so that he can sit his Sara down in a floral circle. He has tested the various locations in the front garden from the vantage point of the windows of the flat across the alley and has found the best spot. Yes, the jasmine bush will hide them from the neighbours' probing eyes.

Dara spreads the petals in a circle the diameter of Sara's backside, and with his heart pounding like that of a captive sparrow, he opens the front door and peeps out at the end of the alley. It is too early for Sara to arrive. He drinks a glass of water and returns to the front door. Five minutes later, when for the third time he opens the front door and looks down the alley, he hears Mr Atta's voice.

"How are you, brother?"

Dara looks up, and across the alley he sees Brother Atta's head and torso in the window of his flat. The second-floor window has a full view of the entire alley and key sections of Dara's house.

"Not bad, Brother Atta. How are you?"

"Thank God, I'm well. What's new?"

"Nothing."

"I saw you constantly coming to the door, I thought something bad may have happened."

"No. Do we always have to expect bad news? I was just bored and came to the door. It seems you're bored, too."

"No. A pious man is never bored. He has his God to talk to."

"Then I should say goodbye and let you talk to your God."

Dara has sensed that Brother Atta has grown suspicious, but he can't control his anger. He slams the front door shut and goes back into the house. The familiar voice of the Farsi-speaking radio announcer on Voice of America flows from the fortress of an Iranian Communist, but the light in the kitchen is turned off and Mother has gone up to her bedroom on the second floor. The primary danger has been removed. The minute he sees his son, Dara's father says:

"In this world you are either a winner or a loser. Sometimes, deep in your heart, you are glad that you are a loser, and sometimes deep in your heart you are sad that you are a winner. I mean, it's all one big pile of crap. Do you understand?"

"Yes, Father. Don't you want to sleep?"

"I have no sleep. But I'll sleep if you want me to."

The sound of the radio is silenced. Father, with his knees bent by sheer force of habit, lies down on the floor of his fortress. In keeping with solitary confinement regulations, the light in his fortress must stay on. Dara, sitting on the thirty-year-old sofa, not knowing why, asks his first intimate, and un-self-censored question of his father.

"Father. Have you ever been happy in your life?"

"In this crap life there are times when you think you are happy with the things you have done, even in a solitary cell, and there are times when you have doubts and you think you are unhappy. But then the time comes when you wonder what being happy really means. I pray to God you never come to ask this question. It's really bad . . . Goodnight, son."

Two minutes later the snoring begins. Dara can't tell whether this is natural snoring or whether his clever father is pretending to be asleep. It is 9.40 p.m. Dara drinks another glass of water. He cannot resist the temptation of going to the front door. At 9.44 p.m. he crosses the front garden, opens the door and looks down the alley to where Sara should appear.

Brother Atta, having materialized at his window again, says:

"Brother Dara, it seems you really are bored tonight."

"What can I say, Brother Atta. It seems you too are really bored to have glued yourself to the window."

"No, brother. My duties include guarding this alley and people's homes."

The residents of the alley all know that three nights a week Brother Atta serves in the neighbourhood Baseej volunteer militia and that at police checkpoints along the streets in the area, he stops cars with a Kalashnikov, smells the drivers' breath to make sure they haven't been drinking, searches the car boots and under the seats in case they have stashed bottles of spirits or narcotic drugs there, and if there are any women in the cars he interrogates them to see how they are related to the driver.

Dara quips, "Brother Atta, go and have a good night's sleep. I seem to have insomnia tonight. I'll guard the street."

Brother Atta laughs out loud and says:

"There are people in this country who are waiting for me and my brothers to fall asleep so that they can uproot us and Islam. But because I know you have repented of your past sins, I'll believe you. I'm off to bed."

He shuts the window and draws the curtains.

It is 9.53 p.m. Dara thinks, Another seven minutes . . . In another seven minutes Sara will be here ... Oh God! At last Sara and I, alone together ... Is it really possible?

He glances up at the window of Brother Atta's flat. He thinks he sees a shadow at the edge of the curtain. He thinks that perhaps it is the shadow of a statue. At 9.55 p.m. it occurs to him that it is impossible for Brother Atta to have a statue in his apartment because fervent Muslims consider statues and paintings of people to be forbidden. And the shadow behind the curtain moves ... "It's him. He's keeping an eye on me. That scoundrel!"

Dara goes back into the garden and slams his fist into the wall. Everything is falling apart. If Atta sees Sara sneaking into their house he will definitely report it and the patrols will raid the house. Dara looks at his bleeding knuckles. He must do something. It is 9.58 p.m. In a moment of madness and rage he walks towards the front door to go out and shout up at Brother Atta's window those words that he must shout out. But at the last moment – I don't know whether it came from me or from his own Iranian intelligence – he shuts his mouth. He walks to the end of the alley. There, he paces up and down like a caged wolf until six minutes past ten, when Sara climbs out of a taxi.

"The situation's a bit complicated. Our nosy neighbour is standing at the window spying. Please go for a walk around the streets here and come back in half an hour."

Sara agrees. Dara returns home and turns out all the lights so that perhaps Brother Atta's mind will be put at ease and he'll go to bed. From the edge of the drawn curtain in his room Dara keeps an eye on the drawn curtain in Atta's room. There doesn't seem to be a shadow behind it. At 10.30 p.m. he quietly opens the front door. Brother Atta's shadow appears behind the curtain. Dara again walks to the end of the alley. At 10.35 p.m. Sara returns.

"Well?"

Dara has no energy or words left to speak. All he can manage is:

"The guy . . . He is still at the window."

"At least ten cars stopped and solicited me in the half-hour I was walking around. Do you know what torture that is for a girl like me?"

Dara pounds his other, uninjured fist against the wall. The sound of skin splitting and blood spurting out is as loud as the sound of the army of Arab ghosts returning from their conquest of Khorasan, bringing with them a plunder of gold and jewels equal to all the riches of Arabia.

The vertebrae along Dara's spinal cord are splintering. He pleads:

"Can you . . . another half an hour . . . the guy will finally sleep . . . half an hour . . ."

Sara raises her hand to slap his face. I grab her wrist. She brings her face close to his, and into Dara's breath she growls:

"You are treating me like a prostitute. You will make a prostitute of me."

To Dara, the sound of the door slamming shut on the first taxi that arrives is like that slap in the face he did not receive.

Brother Atta's shadow is still behind the window. But to him, the sound of the front door of Dara's house slamming shut is not at all like a slap in the face.

And Dara's father mutters in his sleep:

"Ah . . . h . . . h . . . h! My wasted life, those prisons and tortures! Was it all a mistake, Comrade Gorbachev?"

MIRDAMAD AVENUE

Sara is sitting in one of the classrooms in the Department of Literature at Tehran University and appears to be listening to the professor. The boys are sitting in the front rows, and the girls are occupying the seats at the back of the classroom. The professor is discussing a poem by the poet who died six hundred years ago. Sara inspects the backs of the boys' heads one by one and selects the one that resembles Dara's head to look at. A week has passed since the night when she went as far as the perilous frontier of Dara's house, and during this time she has neither replied to his emails nor answered his nightly phone calls. Ever since she saw Shirin bleeding, resentment and fear of men has lingered in her mind. But on the other hand, she finds their scent and ruggedness enticing. From the back, the head of the boy sitting in the first seat of the second row is very similar to Dara's head, and Sara now feels she misses him terribly. The words "You will make a prostitute of me" keep echoing in her mind. This sentence that she has spoken to Dara somehow seems erotic to her. That night, after leaving Dara, she had felt wet while riding in the taxi. The taxi driver, looking at her constantly in the rear-view mirror, had fondled himself.

In the classroom, the boy whose head resembles Dara's head, as if he has felt the weight of Sara's eyes, suddenly turns around and smiles at her. He has a large, long Arab nose and sloping Mongol eyes. Sara turns to the window. The smog over Tehran is so thick that it is hard to tell whether it's sunny or cloudy. Sara smells a mixture of ambergris and sandalwood rising from her body and she imagines herself as a prostitute. The professor is saying:

"The key point in this poet's work is the term 'boy-servant'. His depictions of the boy-servant's beauties and the fact that from the desire of copulating with him the poet has no sleep and no appetite, should not mislead you. All his poems have profound mystical significance. The poet's lover is in fact his bridge to God. He is in love with God, not with a boy-servant with fuzz scarcely sprouting above his lips. The fact that the poet has composed many verses describing this fuzz is actually an allusion to the freshness and the coming-of-age of his love for God . . ."

The only image Sara has of prostitution is that of the women she has seen on certain streets in Tehran who ignore taxis and old cars, but the moment an expensive car brakes in front of them they stick their head in the window and, after a brief conversation, quickly jump into the back of the car and leave. Sara imagines herself standing on Mirdamad Avenue – an avenue like the Champs-Élysées in Paris, with some of the most expensive boutiques in Tehran. The first passing car to brake in front of her is that same taxi.

The driver shouts:

"If you have an empty house, hop in, you hot piece of arse."

Sara walks a few steps away from the taxi. A late-model BMW pulls up in front of her. Sara, in her titillating fantasy of being a prostitute, sticks her head in the car window. Sinbad is at the wheel, and Dara is sitting next to him. They offer her lascivious grins.

And the professor is saying:

"See how beautifully the poet has described the seven stages of love in this poem. In the desert he has lost the caravan of camels; he has lost his shoes too, and now he is walking barefoot. The desert thorns pierce his feet, and he is gratified by this torture. It is not important for him whether he reaches his mystical destination. What's important for him is to walk in the desert towards his beloved for as long as he can. The thorns are a symbol of the agonies we must endure in this material world until we reach God and arrive in heaven."

Sara does not get into the BMW. She kicks the car door and shouts:

"You piece of rubbish!"

In her mind she has imagined herself sandwiched between Dara and Sinbad. One from behind, one from the front, so that they will later switch places. Of course, up to this moment in the story, Sara has never watched a pornographic film and does not know how she has managed to conjure up such an image. The boy whose head resembles Dara's has again turned round and is smiling at her. He has Afghan teeth. Sara impulsively raises her hand to ask a question.

"Do you have a question, sister?"

"Yes. Why do we only study works from a thousand years ago in the Department of Literature? Why can't we also study something from Iran's contemporary literature?"

"What do you mean by Iran's contemporary literature?"

"For example, *The Blind Owl*."

"Sister, you call *The Blind Owl* literature? Such rubbish is not literature. You want me to put aside the beauties of our mystic literature and have you study works that are nothing more than sexual depravity, surrender to the West and promotion of ungodliness? You want to relinquish the beauties of the language of our literature and read ridiculous prose full of errors – prose called the contemporary literature of Iran? The people you students know as today's writers and poets fall into three groups. They are either spies for the West, drug addicts or homosexuals. It is every Muslim's duty to spill the blood of such people. Reading their writings is a capital sin. Reading their drivel will lead you astray. You will burn with these poets, with these so-called writers, in hell's inferno."

Now Sara, in her imagination, sets out along Mirdamad Avenue. She sees herself free to be a prostitute or a boy-servant or a woman who will scream at stupid Iranian men:

"Damn all your political slogans. When you wanted to be modern, you beat us over the head for us to take off our chadors, and when you found religion you beat us over the head for us to cover ourselves with chadors. Damn you! I will walk down Mirdamad Avenue any way I like. All you know is how to start revolutions and coups d'état. I will walk down this street and you, in your dilapidated cars or your expensive cars, stop in front of me because you want me only as a prostitute. To hell with you. I'll walk wherever I want."

I don't know how these rallying cries have ignited in the mind of my story's Sara. I have never in my life had the courage so bluntly and openly to plant such thoughts in the mind of one of my stories' characters. I am sure Mr Petrovich will go crazy if he reads Sara's thoughts. First, he will forbid his sister and mother from frequenting Mirdamad Avenue, and second, he will do his utmost for the government to pass a law so that no Iranian woman will have the right to step onto this fashionable street.

The boy whose head resembles Dara's again turns round and smiles at Sara. She notices that his eyes have changed from dark Mongol eyes to un-Eastern blue eyes. A sort of icy, English blue. Sara glares at him with such venom that the boy realizes he has to turn round and to allow only the back of his head to be seen by her. The professor is explaining that for the final exam everyone has to memorize seventy verses of an ode by the poet who died six hundred years ago and that they will have to write them down on their exam paper. Sara wants to walk out in protest, but she is not brave enough. Yet now she knows that she is after all brave enough to answer Dara's phone call or email tonight.

Meanwhile, Mirdamad Avenue is empty of Sara's presence, and the prostitutes whose numbers are increasing daily are walking along its pavements. The moment they are certain that the patrol cars from the Campaign Against Social Corruption are not nearby, they will step onto the street and quickly get into the first expensive car that stops for them.

And the mysterious scents of the perfumes that have been brought to Iran's empires by way of the Silk Road wander the streets of Tehran searching for a nose that likes them.

A COBRA AT THE WINDOW

At night, house windows in many cities around the world look alike, their curtains and the shadows behind those curtains. Yet there are cities where the windows are not only unlike those anywhere else, but at night bear no resemblance to their daytime appearance. Tehran is one of these cities. For Dara, the most marvellous moments come during his nightly study of windows whose curtains are often drawn. He likes to discover those with a gentle light shining through their colourful curtains, and to imagine poetic scenes of the tender deeds of the homeowners.

Tonight, on his way back from work, he has found three such windows. But there is something particularly special about the third one. Its rich, brown velvety curtains have given it an aristocratic air . . . ~~It has somehow reminded him of the windows of the lovemaking house of Anna Karenina and her lover.~~ Today he finished painting a house and collected his pay. When he arrives home, he will put three-quarters of it next to their old television set for his mother, and he will go up to his room proud that he has been a good son to his family. So now, until he reaches home, he can watch the windows and bear the welcome weight of his pride, that same pride which over the past week he has repeatedly broken. Time and again he has emailed Sara and not received a reply, and then, going against the promise he has made to himself, ~~and despite his fear of wiretapping,~~ he has repeatedly called Sara's house. Contrary to other nights, instead of Sara, her father has answered the telephone, and when he has heard Dara's silence on the other end of the line, he has showered this crank caller with the worst obscenities.

~~And Dara's imagination enters the house through the velvet~~

~~curtains and sees a man and a woman who, without any fear, with all the freedom in this world and the nether world, are kissing each other.~~

How do they kiss in Dara's imagination?

I know you expect me as a writer to introduce a new method of kissing to you with my storytelling inventiveness. But I can't, because before this story all the kissing schemes have been written and shown in stories and films. Even, for example, when the man is hanging upside down from the ceiling and the woman has her feet planted on the ground. Therefore you will not find any new manner of kissing in this story other than that same old clumsy way Adam kissed when his lips accidentally brushed against Eve's and he discovered that there is something to this act. This kissing style is completely in tune with Dara's personality because, as you know, he has never kissed any lips.

Therefore, despite all the cinematic kisses he has seen, he pictures that man and woman's kiss behind the window in the same way that his lips' imagination picture it. A fig-flavoured Adam and Eve kiss in Tehran.

I am terribly sleepy. I feel like my head is about to explode. I have wasted three entire hours trying to find a new method of kissing, and now dawn is near. In about two hours, Iranian sparrows, unaware of all the bombs, terrorists, kisses, Anna Kareninas, Saras and Petroviches, will start chirping in the bitter orange trees. I know that splashing cold water on my face will no longer force sleep to leave my eyes, and my lips sting because I have bitten them so much. I must allow my eyes to take a nap.

Dara, with tired arms that no longer have the strength to bear the burden of a paintbrush for even a single stroke on a wall, yet proud of the weight of the money in his pocket, walks into a narrow alley that is a shortcut to his home. Halfway down the alley he senses a phantom following him. A powerful, ruthless and terrifying phantom. A phantom that can destroy any creature with the wave of an arm. Terrified, Dara turns and looks behind him, but there is no one there. The alley is in one of the old neighbourhoods of Tehran that, with the passage of time, has become home to the poor. The two-hundred-year-old houses along its winding path have tall brick walls surrounding their yards, and the spectre of two-hundred-year-old eucalyptus and locust trees looms above them. The windows of the houses are dark. The alley is crowded with old shadows. Dara walks faster. Now he can clearly hear the phantom's footsteps. Again he stops abruptly and looks back. The

sound of his pursuer's footsteps also stops. Dara feels his legs weakening. His instincts cry out for him to run but he doesn't have the power. And suddenly, he sees the glint of a dagger like the silver flash of a cobra's strike . . .

No, this won't do. Let's leave this chapter entirely unread. I don't understand why I have dragged Dara down that terrifying alley, and I don't know why that phantom is following him. My only guess is that the phantom is a professional thief who has somehow learned that Dara has his wages in his pocket and he therefore wants to kill him and take his money. Ridiculous! I don't need such a chapter in my love story. Please go ahead and delete this chapter that only a novice writer could perpetrate.

THE HASHASHIN IN TEHRAN

O
n this cloudy day in Tehran, those people who have enough
leisure time to take occasional notice of the sky will observe the
flight of a bittern above the city. The bittern is a bird that lives
in northern Iran, far from Tehran, alongside lakes and swamps and its presence in Tehran, which has neither lakes nor swamps, is very unusual.
According to villagers who live up north, along the coast of the Caspian
Sea, the world's largest lake, the bittern is a mourning bird. It always cries,
and if it does ever sing, its song only denotes suffering and separation.
Therefore, if you and I or one of the residents of Tehran see this bird flying
in the sky above the city, we should expect an ominous event. Perhaps
today, in one of the city squares, before hundreds of eyes, they have hung
someone from a crane to teach people a lesson. Perhaps in a different
square they have cut off the right hand and left leg of a thief, or perhaps
in Evin Prison a student prisoner, after suffering four months in solitary
confinement, has been forced to confess before television cameras that he
was paid by the CIA to instigate anti-government demonstrations. I don't
know whether this bittern is aware of these incidents or not. All I know is
that it will fly over Tehran until the sun finally sets.

**Dara is lost in one of the suburbs of Tehran. This morning a stranger
has called him and said that he was given his telephone number by
someone whose house Dara had painted, and because he was told that
Dara is an honest and conscientious painter, he would like to hire him
to paint his newly constructed house. This is how Dara has always
found work. A former client who has been pleased with his painting
has given his address or telephone number to someone else. But this
time he has been walking around this poor neighbourhood since three
in the afternoon, and he cannot find his way to the stranger's house. He**

has asked many people for directions, and each person has sent him down a different path. He has wandered down dirt roads lined with small, humble houses, and now that the sun is setting over Tehran, from a winding alley he has suddenly arrived at one of the wastelands where the city's refuse is dumped and incinerated.

Dara walks towards the mounds of waste. Smoke billows from them. Smoke from waste is a blend of all the world's darknesses. And this smoke that rises from the bowels and peaks of the tall mounds of refuse has, like a fog, dimmed and darkened the air. Suddenly, from the heart of the darkness of this foul-smelling vapour, a man wearing a black burnoose appears. He has pulled the burnoose's hood so low on his brow that his face cannot be seen. Or perhaps he has concealed his face with a dark scarf. With an unwavering gait the man walks towards Dara. Dara thinks he is imagining this phantom that belongs to centuries ago. He asks himself, "Who is this guy? Why am I seeing such a thing?" And the man with stonelike strides, with clusters of smoke accompanying him, walks towards him. Dara whispers, "Something is at hand. Why is he walking towards me like that?" The man in the hooded burnoose is now one step away from him, and it is in this one-step distance that Dara sees the glint in the man's eyes and the flash of the dagger that has emerged from his sleeve. The dagger, with the swiftness of a cobra's strike, slashes through Dara's jugular. The man, as if he has merely swatted a fly from around his face, walks away. In his wake, blood gushes from Dara's neck, and in the final moment of his life he learns the answer to the final question of his life. That phantom was none other than one of the Hashashin – a member of the Order of the Assassins founded in the eleventh century by Hassan Sabbah. A bittern hovers above the wasteland; smoke from the mounds of garbage gather around Dara and hide him from the eyes of the world.

No, no . . . Not again.

Tonight, when I turned on my computer to continue writing my novel, I realized that last night I wrote this scene. What is going on? I have no recollection at all of having written such a scene. Why did I kill the central character of my story right in the middle of the novel? And in such weak prose. I had no such intention. On the contrary, I have been meaning to write a tender love story without any gloom and darkness. Am I Dara's murderous phantom? How is that possible? The problem is that, unlike the

Hashashin, I don't believe that if I kill someone I will go to heaven. These people belonged to a secret sect who, from the eleventh to the thirteenth century, assassinated important people in Islamic lands, including one of Iran's most famous ministers and even the Patriarch of Jerusalem during the Crusades. I cannot believe that in the corners of the mind of someone like me, someone who has been in touch with the arts all his life, a murderer of the Hashashin ilk could lie in wait.

On the other hand, I am somehow taken with the notion of one of the Hashashin appearing in twenty-first-century Tehran. Not because these people have been the inspiration for terrorist groups and even suicide bombers in our times, but because the presence of this olden-days phantom with his face concealed could perhaps be appealing to my readers.

Therefore I will not delete this chapter. Instead, I will rewrite its last sentences in the following manner.

With a flick of his wrist the phantom of the assassin whisks the hidden dagger out from the sleeve of his burnoose. The vapour of the joy and sorrow of release from this world rises from him. Dara sees the glint of hatred for his own and the others' existence in the phantom's eyes and hears the wail of the dagger that rises to his murder. In such horrifying circumstances, anyone else would have frozen and the dagger would have slashed through his jugular, but ~~the quick thinking that comes from years of being a political activist and~~ the hundreds of action movies he has seen save Dara, and he leaps back. And then, conforming to an Iranian proverb, he has two legs, he borrows two more and runs. But the phantom, as if he too has borrowed two additional legs, chases him. Dara passes between two smouldering mounds of rubbish. He runs behind the truck that is dumping the city's new waste and rams into three boys who are nervously collecting plastic containers from among the rubbish. The boys are each thrown to a different side. ~~Together all three shout, "Fuck your sister and mother."~~ Ignoring them, Dara runs towards the nearest houses he can see through the thick smoke. Still he feels the phantom's heavy gait behind him. He runs into a narrow alley. He is hoping that by being among people the phantom will disappear. But halfway down the alley he turns and looks behind and sees the phantom still chasing him. At the greatest speed he can muster, Dara runs through the barefoot boys playing soccer and past their obscenities; the phantom runs, too. He passes by the women sitting

in front of the steel doors of their homes gossiping. He is gasping for air. ~~He runs past a wall with the graffiti~~ ~~DAMN THE FOREFATHERS OF HE WHO PISSES~~ ~~HERE, and past the yellow and brown urine stains on the wall and the~~ ~~ground that somehow resemble Pollock's paintings; the phantom, too.~~ His lungs are stiffening, but the Hashashin phantom, as if he is now standing on a flying carpet, steady and steadfast, is behind him. At the end of his energy, Dara is rescued ~~by the Islamic Republic~~. He sees a long queue of men and women outside a grocer's shop and throws himself in the middle of it. People start shouting in protest.

"Hey, get to the back of the queue!"

"Get out!"

"Hey, someone get this bloke out!"

And the phantom passes by. Well, he is right to do so. At no time in history has a member of the Hashashin ever assassinated a man in such a setting. These queues are remnants of the protracted Iran-Iraq War. During the war, because the price of rice, meat and cooking lard was rising daily, the government had distributed coupons among the people, and every so often on the radio and television they would announce the number on one of the coupons, which could then be used to buy a few kilos of rice or half a kilo of cooking lard at subsidized prices; and holding their coupons, people would queue up in front of designated stores. Long after the war, as year after year a greater number of Iranians unknowingly plunge below the poverty line, occasionally the government continues to announce the number on one of these coupons for the purchase of a few kilos of rice or frozen beef from Australia, and this makes people very happy.

Objections against Dara, who has jumped the queue continue, and he barks back:

"For God's sake, I don't even have a coupon."

"Then get out of the queue."

Dara, still bent over with his hands on his knees trying to catch his breath, moves slightly to the side.

The third person ahead of him, ignoring the incident farther back, says to another man:

"Do you see what's become of us? Our country is sitting on a sea of oil, and we have to queue like beggars for five or six hours for a handful of rice."

The second person ahead of Dara, who looks like he too is disgruntled, but who also looks like he is sure the third person in the queue is an agent of the secret police who wants to identify the disgruntled, says:

"Brother, we must endure until the revolution achieves its goals. We must punch America hard in the mouth. Our queuing up is a hard punch in the mouth of the Great Satan, Britain, France, Germany, Russia, Israel and everyone else."

The fourth person in the queue, who also looks disgruntled, but who seems to have realized that the second person ahead of Dara is a staunch member of the Party of God, says:

"Yes, our Party of God brother is absolutely right. We must make sacrifices to save the world."

Someone from the middle of the queue yells:

"Hey! Are you going to get out of the queue or not?"

Dara straightens his back and says:

"Sir! I'm not queuing. I am not even a human being to queue."

LIKE A FLY

"Someone is trying to kill me."

"What do you mean?"

"I mean, I'm supposed to get killed . . . and don't think I'm afraid. To tell you the truth, in a way I want to be freed from this horrible life. But before I die, I want to know why they are trying to slice my vein."

"Don't torture me like this. Tell me what has happened."

Sara's eyes, after having shed two tears, have grown narrow and misty.

They are sitting in a park on two benches facing each other. When there is no one walking along the pathway between them, they talk, and every time a passer-by draws near, they turn away from each other like two strangers.

Dara says:

"If I am to die because of you, it will be the best way to die."

"Don't you dare die for me. Tell me what has happened!"

"I have no enemies; I mean, to be honest, I am too much of a nobody for someone even to want to be my enemy . . . During the past two days I have thought a lot about it, and I have come to the conclusion that my only enemy is your suitor. Other than he, no one stands to gain from my death. Why did you give him my address and telephone number?"

"Sinbad doesn't even know you exist."

"Great! What good fortune! ~~But this guy you are keeping on the back burner belongs to a powerful group. They can find out about everything. They can do whatever they want. Why do you want to get me killed?~~ Just tell me to get lost and I will."

"Stop yelling! For God's sake, lower your voice. The Sinbad I know would never do such a thing. He is a good man. No . . . not Sinbad . . . It's impossible. ~~Maybe they are trying to kill you because of your political past."~~

"~~No, that's impossible. I've been living like a sheep for years. All I do is paint houses. I'm not involved in any political activities at all. They know this very well. Even if they do want to get rid of me, they can do it much more easily and expertly.~~ Who would want to kill a nobody like me?"

"Don't talk about my Dara like this. My Dara is a great man."

"As great as your nice Mr Sinbad?"

"You are being jealous. I don't believe this story you are fabricating. You and I don't need to make up such stories. We are together. Why don't you understand?"

"I am starting to understand what togetherness means, but I will not allow your Sinbad to swat me like a fly. I will kill him."

A man approaches them. Sara turns away. Dara too turns away. The man seems to be crazy. ~~His walk somehow resembles dancing.~~ He is singing, "When at night I hold the image of you in my arms, at dawn the scent of flowers rises from my bed . . ."

He looks at Sara and Dara, laughs out loud, and says:

"You devils! I've caught you red-handed. Be careful! You're not as smart as you think."

He walks away.

Sara, trying desperately to keep her voice down, says:

"I'm begging you, be careful. Don't torture me like this."

"You don't want to be tortured, but you love torturing."

"Shut up! You're showing me a side of you that I have never seen."

"It is what it is . . . Will you marry me?"

"I don't want to marry anyone. You men are all idiots. You only think about yourselves."

"You are lying. You want to sell yourself to rich Mr Sinbad."

"Is that what you really think of me? Selling myself?"

"I don't care any more. I'll kill him – not because he's going to be your husband, but because he wants to get rid of me. Give me his address."

Sara's eyes have grown even narrower. She frees herself from the bench and before leaving, says:

"You have gone mad with jealousy. You shouldn't do this."

"I'll kill him before he kills me."

"The hell you will. You are going crazy."

Sara walks away. Behind her, Dara, who has started walking in the opposite direction, yells:

"You have driven me crazy."

And his shout resonates among the weeping willows and maple trees.

DAVĀLPĀ

I have tried to dissuade Dara from what he is planning, but I have been no match for him. I see clearly how my love story is moving in a direction that I never intended. The story is falling apart. The characters are each playing to a different tune without being able collectively to create symphonic harmony. I have to think of something. I have to do something.

The key point is that Dara cannot be allowed to kill Sinbad. He has to give me time to find out who is trying to murder him. But this brainless boy will not listen to me. Yes, clearly he is blinded by jealousy. I have never in my life felt this weak writing a story, and as far as I can tell, Dara has never felt this powerful. He cannot understand that right now a man named Petrovich is delighting in the fact that this story is being mired in shit. Therefore

Some nights, without telling Sara, Dara prowls the streets around her house. He knows that one of these nights Sinbad will come to visit, and the only solution he has come up with is to find him here and to exact his revenge. He has a screwdriver in his pocket and has often imagined that, in the vein of Hollywood movies that teach the people of the world all methods of murder and assassination, he will stab this innocent object into the base of Sinbad's throat with all his might, and he will give it a few sideways twists to really tear up everything in his head.

I say:

"With what you are intending to do, you will only make the enemies of Iranian literature happy. Let's think together and help each other write a new and beautiful love scene for you and Sara, one that has never been written in any novel. In our country, blood is shed day and night; hatred and animosity are constantly advertised; people are at each other's throats and want to delete each other. I mean, censor each other. You and I should not fall into this trap. We must do something different. Let's put our heads together and come up with something beautiful to do . . ."

"I am really fed up. I have to kill him."

I can understand that after years of tolerating oppression, humiliation, pain and suffocation, now, like an infected cyst, rage has burst open in Dara's soul and leaked its poison into his blood, driving him insane. This is just the point dictators fail to understand, and even if they do, they have no alternative but to increase the ranks of their torturers and censors, until the day when the insanity of revolution floods the streets and burns and kills.

Dust from the passage of the Afghan troops who have gone to the conquest and looting of Isfahan lingers in the air and gently rains down on the city's rooftops.

I tell Dara:

"But the Dara I have written and created sentence by sentence cannot commit murder. He is peaceful and loves mankind. He has learned from art and prison that the first rule of being human is to do no harm unto others. His talent in life is forgiveness and shunning violence."

Dara grabs my throat. He shoves me back and slams me against the wall of his room. For the first time I realize how strong his right arm has become as a result of painting walls and ceilings. In my face he shouts:

"You shouldn't have written me like this. You shouldn't have written me as browbeaten and pathetic. You wrote me as an earthworm. You wrote me so that no matter what they do to me, all I can do is squirm and bear the pain. You wrote me like this to pass your story through censorship. I don't want to be written as an earthworm, so that even when they cut it in two it turns into two earthworms. You are my murderer too, for having written me as so utterly miserable. All the torment and misery there is you have written for me. You are no different to the torturer who would flog me so that I would concede there is a God. I want to write my own murder."

From the pressure of Dara's powerful grip my air passage is constricted. Yet I struggle to say:

"Dara, this is just a story."

He squeezes my throat even harder and growls:

"Even in your story the likes of Sinbad have pilfered this country's oil

229

money, they have taken all that me and my kind ever had, and I have just kept silent. What else do I have for them to take other than Sara? And her, too, he wants to take from me. I will not let him."

In his eyes there is a wildness that I have never seen in my mind's eye. He releases my throat. He turns his back to me and still growls:

"In my mind I have often whipped that interrogator who used to order them to flog me. You haven't had the guts to write this. You haven't even had the guts to write bluntly and openly about the wounds on the soles of my feet. You have not written how the feet swell, and the interrogator forces you to walk for the blood to circulate back into your body so that he can again whip your soles with a cable. And you are so proud of being a writer. To hell with your writing. To hell with all your words . . ."

Dara takes refuge in the corner of his room; he sits with his back to me, rests his head on his knees and weeps. Ashamed, I walk out. On the first floor, I pass by his father's fortress. As is his tendency, he is talking to someone in his sleep. I can't understand what he is saying, but I want him to say: The fuckers didn't tell us not to pull the bowstring.

I pass by the jasmine bush in its nocturnal sleep in the flower bed of Dara's house. At his window, Brother Atta is observing my exit. From the end of the alley I think I see a burnoose-clad phantom at the head of the alley, but when I arrive there the street is empty of phantoms and humans. From near and far I hear a drumming sound – *tak, tak, tak, tak*. I don't understand what is causing it, and I am in no mood to investigate. Dara has broken my heart with his broken heart. Now I wish I were worthy enough for one of the Hashashin to play one note of his dagger on my jugular. At midnight in my office in Shiraz, I see myself aimlessly wandering along the dimly lit streets of Tehran. I am angry at Dara, but deep in my heart I know he is right. Only now am I starting to understand how great his love for Sara is. Far greater than my story-writer's imagination and images of my loves.

And on Tehran's streets, the farther north I go the more beautiful the streets and the more plentiful the trees become, and the more concentrated the drumming sound – *tak, tak, tak*. I can't understand what is happening. Windows open one by one, and people look out to see where the noise is coming from. Doors open one by one, and sleepy men in grubby wrinkled pyjamas walk out. They turn their ears in the direction from which the nearest *tak, tak, tak* is coming, and then from a location even closer, in the opposite direction, another *tak, tak, tak* starts and they turn their ears to that side. Then, dazed and confused, they stare at one another.

Someone says:

"Sır! I think America has launched an attack."

Another replies:

"Sir, America doesn't attack with *tak, taks*. Their bombs come suddenly, like an earthquake, and pulverize all that we have."

Someone else says:

"If America hasn't attacked, then this is a new plot by our own government; tomorrow either fuel or bread will be more expensive."

The drumming sounds have a strange reverberation; one can't tell from which direction they are coming. They echo off the walls of the city's houses and grow more intense. I see members of the Baseej volunteer militia and the Revolutionary Guard Corps hastily stationing themselves at intersections and setting up checkpoint barricades. They arm their Kalashnikovs and ready them to be fired.

A man whose large belly is sticking out from his pyjamas, with the long hair around his navel swept in one direction like algae in street gutters, says:

"What if it's Judgment Day?"

Another replies:

"Sir, it seems you have a few screws loose. In religious stories it is said that on Judgment Day, Gabriel will blow his horn so loudly that we will all go deaf, and the sun will come so close that human brains will start to boil. What does this *tak, tak* in the middle of the night have to do with Judgment Day?"

I cannot say that they are frightened. Since the days when Saddam Hussein would aim Scud missiles at our cities, and suddenly three or four houses in our neighbourhood would explode, and their bricks together with the flesh of their occupants would fly at our windows, and after the dust had settled we would see a deep crater instead of those houses, we Iranians are no longer all that afraid of bombardments. I cannot say that they are shocked either. During the thirty-odd years since the revolution, we Iranians have seen and heard so many strange things that if, from the skies of our cities earthworms pour instead of rain, rather than being shocked, we will argue whether this is a new conspiracy by the British or the Americans or our own government, and then we will return to our homes to find individual solutions – scientific and non-scientific – to protect our houses from earthworms.

Now the *tak, tak, taks* are coming from every corner of Tehran. At a police checkpoint at an intersection, the Baseej militiamen, who are angry at not having found the source of the noise, stop cars, drag the drivers out and with the butts of their Kalashnikovs smash their car stereos. I assume by now the aggressive anti-riot police have surrounded all the university dormitories in Tehran. And still the *tak, tak, taks* reverberate in the streets and echo everywhere.

I have reached Liberty Street, that same place where Dara for the first time showed himself to Sara, and I arrive at the narrow tree-lined Sixteenth of Āzar Street. I like this street very much. Thirty years ago, when I was a student at Tehran University, taking a stroll down this street was very comforting to me, especially in the autumn when maple and sycamore leaves carpeted its pavements. Long ago and before the Islamic Revolution, on a sixth of December, Mr Nixon travelled to Iran as Vice-president of the United States. At Tehran University, students demonstrated against American imperialism, and the army attacked the university and killed three students. University students and political activists named this day University Students' Day, and every year on the sixteenth of Āzar there were demonstrations and protests against the Shah's regime. The students would break the windows of college buildings, and the university guards would attack them. They would beat them up and arrest some of them, and in jail they would flog them or sodomize them with Coca-Cola bottles. They would then release them so that on the next sixteenth of Āzar the students could break even more windows. However, after the revolution, the Islamic Republic's regime executed so many students and political oppositionists every day that no one could name a particular day for a particular occasion. Therefore, all our days became the sixteenth of Āzar, meaning all our days became days on which a group of people were killed for freedom. The masterwork of the Islamic Republic was that it eradicated the importance of occasions. I, therefore, walk along Sixteenth of Āzar Street, and the sycamore leaves that have dried like tortured hands are crushed beneath my untortured feet. Suddenly I hear a sound – the sound of the wings of a bird landing on a tree. I look up at the leafless branches, I don't see anything but I instantly hear the drumming with a six-eighths time signature

– the rhythm of commonplace Iranian songs – *tak tak, tak tak tak* . . . It is nothing strange, just a woodpecker. It is this, that's what it all was: woodpeckers. After years during which no city resident ever heard a woodpecker peck a tree, they have attacked Tehran's trees, tens of thousands of them, and they are hammering away at the dry tree barks to extract worms and wake people up.

When they discover the source of the noise, the Baseej militiamen aim their Kalashnikovs at the upper branches of the trees and shoot. But the woodpeckers are greater in number than their bullets, and the never-ending *tak, tak, taks* echo in the city of Tehran.

Dara, prowling around Sara's house, mutters:

"What have I ever done to Sinbad? I know they will finally squash me like an insect. It's better that I take my revenge on one of them before I am snuffed out."

He walks and walks ~~and the minutes of the nights pass slowly, more slowly than the drops of vodka dripping from a home-made still into a bottle.~~ **And the more nights and the more hours he walks around Sara's house, the greater his rage and hatred become.**

I shout:

"Dara, go home! You are ruining everything. I am a censored writer. I can easily delete you from my novel if I choose. I'll send you down a street, and suddenly a truck will crash into you and you will die."

He doesn't hear me, and he walks. I regret my own words. I realize that I too have easily contemplated murder.

At last, one night, around ten o'clock, when Dara in his continuous back-and-forth is near Sara's house, the front door opens and a man walks out.

Dara vents:

"I finally have him."

He walks faster to catch up with the man.

I yell:

"No, Dara! Don't!"

The man heads down the street. Dara follows him and in the darkest corner of the street claws at his hair from behind and puts the screwdriver at the base of his throat.

"You murderer, I will kill you."

Contrary to his expectations, his prey is a feeble creature with no

resistance in his muscles. Still Dara presses the screwdriver against the soft skin under the man's throat, but the moment he feels skin tearing he unconsciously eases the pressure. Terrified sounds burst out of the man's mouth.

Dara roars in his ear:

"Why do you want to kill me, ~~you fucker~~?"

The man is shaking violently.

"How much have you paid them to kill me, Mr Sinbad?"

The man moans:

"Ha . . . Ha . . . Haji . . ."

The weakness and terror of his prey make Dara angrier and more fearless. Contrary to the murder plot he has time and again imagined, still standing behind the man he locks his arm around his neck and presses the screwdriver against his left ribs so that its blade nestles in the soft skin between the two ribs closest to the man's heart. The man has started rasping.

"Now do you understand what dying feels like?"

From the man's larynx diarrhoea-like sounds spurt out. From among those broken syllables Dara only understands:

"I . . . I . . . Ha . . . Haj . . . Haji Ka . . ."

And Dara's prey faints. Despite his scrawny body, the man's mass now weighs heavily on Dara's arm. Dara releases him. The man falls to the ground. A car drives by, and in the light of its headlights Dara realizes that he has hunted a skinny old man whose mouth has foamed from fright; he is convulsing and instead of blood, urine is spreading on the pavement. Dara runs. He runs past Sara's house. He throws the screwdriver at the front door and runs for several miles. He runs until he runs out of breath. Drenched in sweat, he takes cover in a dark corner. One hundred feet away, the flashing lights of several police cars are just the shock he needs. The cars have surrounded a house and police officers are dragging handcuffed girls and boys out, and while slapping and kicking them they are throwing them into the police cars. Clearly, they have discovered a night-time revelry.

Dara changes his route, and like a sensible young labourer, heads home. He is only now realizing what he was on the verge of doing.

He moans:

"Oh God, I was about to kill a man. I was so blinded by jealousy that I was about to kill a man. Sara, what have you done to me? What sort of an animal have I turned into?"

The closer he gets to his house, the more terrified he becomes of himself. And the closer he gets to the southern part of Tehran, the smaller, humbler and more tightly crammed the houses become. There is a slice of moon in the sky, but it doesn't bear the moon's customary complexions. It resembles the wrinkled remnant of a burst balloon.

Finally, Dara leaves behind the streets with their streetlamps lit and those with their lightbulbs burned out and arrives at his neighbourhood. At the corner of the last intersection a man calls out to him. He is sitting on the ground, leaning against the traffic light. In a weary voice he pleads:

"Young man! May God grant you long life. Help me. Carry me on your back to the other side of the street."

In the green glow of the traffic light the man's legs can be seen. Skinny and long, boneless, twisted around each other and seemingly completely crippled. The lights turn red. Dara says:

"Tonight when everything is a nightmare, the last thing I need is you . . . Get lost!"

Terrified, he quickly crosses the street and thanks God that he had a storytelling grandmother who had told him the tale of the Davālpā.

In Iranian fables, Davālpā was a creature with two long legs, like two long strips of leather, who would sit on riverbanks and beg passers-by to hoist him up on their back and carry him to the other side of the river. If a passer-by pitied this seemingly crippled man and lifted him onto his back, the two strips of leather would quickly wrap around his neck and torso and for the rest of his life he would be forced to carry the Davālpā wherever he wanted to go.

Dara opens the front door of his house and before going in looks down the alley. He thinks he sees a phantom draped in a black burnoose standing there.

Dara decides not to go out in the dark of night and not to frequent secluded areas in the light of day and, as of tomorrow, to leave his house only when he has made sure the phantom is nowhere nearby. But times will come when he, despite all caution, will be caught off

guard by the phantom of the assassin, and he will escape. Until at last, defeated and worn by the pursuits and escapes, he will whisper:

"You want to kill me? Go ahead, kill me. ~~To my right ball!~~"

Transferring anger and frustration to one's testicles is an Iranian expression that basically translates into "I don't give a fuck." This manner of capitulating and no longer caring happens not only to fictional characters but most likely to everyone in real life, too. For example, at some point in time you suspect that your telephone is being tapped. Well, during the first few months you will be quite nervous and cautious. You will not talk about politics with your friends on the telephone, and the minute one of them starts to tell you the latest joke about the country's president you will quickly change the subject, and if you live in a country like Iran, you will never call to order black market films or alcohol. In fact, the sound of your telephone ringing will start to pierce your ears like a thorn. And this is only if you are an average person. If you are a political activist, there will be far greater precautions and self-censorships. The interesting point, however, is that after a few months or a year, depending on your emotional state and your personal tenacity, you will gradually grow accustomed to the person in charge of tapping your telephone. Little by little you will feel that he is a member of your family and an even greater confidant of your secrets. Sometimes you will perhaps talk to him indirectly during your telephone conversations, or tease him with a joke. It is in this same manner that one gets used to the fear of being followed and the threat of being killed. At some point, one finally transfers this fear to an anatomical organ, which would vary depending on one's culture, and then together with that anatomical organ one goes prancing down the street.

And Mr Petrovich will say:

"What do you mean by bringing that assassin and Davālpā into your novel? You have planted these synbols in your story to suggest that there are terrorists in Iran, and that there are creatures here that once they climb up on people's backs they will never climb down again. Is that right?"

I will say:

"You are wrong. First of all, it is 'symbols' and not 'synbols'. Second, these are Dara's nightmares. Dara is going mad; these are his horrific illusions. Is going insane allowed in our country? It is not a crime, is it? Is it?"

Mr Petrovich will stare into my eyes to read what's left of my thoughts.

I feel tired. My back is too burdened for my knees to carry, and my throat is too tight to breathe. I wish I could be alone somewhere – away even from the eyes of Sara and Dara – to pour out this ill-omened saltiness that burns my eyes. But even if I were in the middle of a desert between Shiraz and Tehran, Dara on my right and Sara on my left would stand waiting, staring at me. And all I know is that I must not come to my knees before their eyes.

THE FREEDOM OF INSANITY

I magine you live in a country where you are not even free to be insane. It's frightening. I know. Imagine you are a twentysomething-year-old girl and mentally disabled. During the day – because your family wants to be rid of you – you go out, and in the streets of one of Iran's northern towns, you wander around. There are men who with instinctive shrewdness realize that you are mentally disabled, and with an ice-cream cone they lure you under a stairway and they empty themselves inside you. And you enjoy it a little as you eat your ice cream. Then you are arrested, and the judge sentences you to death. You don't understand what is going on. One day they take you from the prison to the town square, and you see that a crowd has gathered there for you. You are happy that so many people are there just for you, and you try to smile at them to show them that you are happy to see them. But before they can see your smile, an officer pulls a bag over your head and you no longer see anything, not even the face of the last man who emptied himself inside you. And all you feel is the coarseness of the rope around your neck. Then all you want is the sweetness and chill of ice cream, and you feel that your air passage is constricted and you are vomiting. You are happy you are vomiting. You try to laugh. But the rope that has tightened around your neck pulls you up using a crane; it doesn't allow you to laugh; it only allows your lips to contort in an ugly way. If you are lucky, because of the weight of your body your neck will break and you feel no pain. But if the rope has not properly lodged around your neck, you have to suffer for a few minutes until you find relief. And the men who have emptied themselves inside you, and who are surely among the onlookers, are perhaps gratified by watching your body's convulsions as it hangs from the noose . . .

I too am looking on as my love story is being hung. I am beginning to understand that I have deleted so many scenes and replaced them with new ones, and I have choked and stifled so many sentences, that my novel – the information that I must offer the reader – is no longer coherent. I know I have no right to give in. I have no right to go insane. To save my novel, Dara must be wise and call Sara and say:

"I have to apologize to you."

"For what?"

"Don't ask, just accept my apology. Forgive me."

"What have you done?"

"What I almost did. Don't ask me what I was about to do. Will you help me?"

"Yes, yes. Just tell me what has happened. What do I have to do?"

"Just help me be the man I was on the first day you saw me. I don't want to be . . . I don't want to be a murderer. Why do you all want me to be a murderer? Help me!"

~~Dara's sobs are like nails piercing the ears of those who tap the telephones of lovers.~~

And I am ashamed of myself for having unknowingly and unintentionally sent an assassin into my novel to kill this innocent man. Given my guilty conscience, Sara has no other choice than to say:

"Very well, my darling, I won't ask any questions. Just tell me what to do."

"You are wiser than me, think of something, do something, so that we can start again."

The good fortune or misfortune of lovers is that they quickly forget their good fortunes or misfortunes.

CRIME AND PUNISHMENT

At one o'clock in the morning, in the heart of the desert, when *The Moon Is Down* and the sky allows the stars – the sight of which is the lot of us earthlings – to tell their stories without fear, I climb out of my car. The road is deserted. The Milky Way stretches all the way behind a mountainous terrain on the horizon. I hear the wind stir in the thornbushes. I can now confidently say that it is wintertime. The chill of the desert forces sleep out of my head, and I can wake Dara up too for him to stare at the ceiling and with eyes wide open to see his Sara. I like my midnights of solitude on the desert roads of Iran. I have driven two hundred and fifty miles to arrive here, and I still have another three hundred miles to go before I reach Tehran, where tomorrow afternoon I will start my story-writing workshop at *Karnameh* magazine. It is forbidden for writers such as me to teach at literature departments in universities in Iran. But sixty young people have registered for my workshop, which is being held in the offices of a privately owned magazine. They are very eager to become story writers.

A large blue meteor burns in the sky and disappears on the northern horizon. The wind blows from the heart of the desert and brings the sound of camels' bells from a caravan carrying silk that on this night, hundreds of years ago, was approaching the Shah Abbas caravanserai . . .

I have to go so that I can arrive at my friend's house before the maddening morning rush hour of Tehran and sleep for a few hours.

But at 6.45 in the morning, as I enter the city limits, I come to a full stop behind a logjam of traffic. In the distance I can see the marble white of the Freedom Tower. This beautiful structure was built years before the revolution as a symbol of Tehran. In those days it was called Shahyad, which means "in memory of the king". Naturally, it was renamed after the revolution. Tehran's sky is strangely clear of smoke and smog, and its ultramarine blue tempts one to fall in love, provided that the hundreds of drivers lift their hands off their useless horns, stop glaring at the drivers of the cars next to them as if they were responsible for the traffic jam and play the CD or cassette tape of a banned romantic song that they have hidden somewhere in their car

I and the sparrows of the house have grown accustomed to seeing you,
In the hopes of seeing you we take wing from our nest . . .

I know that this sentimental hope is hardly possible. Many of those drivers have a gruelling day ahead of them. They are troubled by their continuing descent into poverty, stressed by work hours filled with conflicts with colleagues and clients and tired of the fact that, after the end of their workday at one of the many government offices, they have either to go to their second job or pick up passengers in their twenty-year-old cars and drive them around until late at night, just so that they can perhaps come up with tomorrow's expenses. Then let them blow their horns and blow their horns. No one moves even a foot forward, which is very strange. One hour, two hours pass. Even stranger is that there are no cars coming from the opposite direction, either. By now everyone has turned off their engines, lifted their hands off the horns and with that unquestioning and unique Iranian patience, they wait. Something unusual must have happened up ahead. I see excited people on the street going in that direction. I lock the car doors and follow them. A mile farther up, I reach a large crowd circling around something. Contrary to Iranian customs in such large crowds, the people are utterly silent. They are neither pushing and shoving to move farther up, nor are they making snide remarks and calling one another names. As though the sun has dawned, from over each other's shoulders they peer at the centre of the circle where the shimmer of a turquoise hue can be seen. I make my way through the crowd. They are so mysteriously quiet that I don't dare ask what has happened. Stranger still, the moment my elbow touches them, with no anger or resistance they make way for me to move farther up. I have steadily entered the halo of an unfamiliar scent. It is a natural fragrance that without the aggressive pretences of artificial perfumes, and without intending to, has spread and fused with the turquoise hue . . .

Suddenly, I come face to face with it. Right at the exit ramp for Mehrabad International Airport, it is sprawled out across the coarse and scarred asphalt from one side of the boulevard to the other, like a massive hill that has appeared overnight. Its turquoise colour has a calming, rippling, neonlike glow. It is as if a huge flame burns inside it. The crowd, without the twinge of curiosity, having surrendered to the magnificence of that presence, stands staring at it from a distance that respects its boundaries. The only sound that can be heard comes from the walkie-talkies of police officers and plain-clothes detectives. Their commanding officers shout, asking what is happening there, and they receive no answers. No one dares move forward to touch that turquoise whale lying on its stomach and facing the mountain range of northern Tehran. With a seemingly natural calm, it has spread its large fins on the asphalt, its eyes are open with no indication of life or death and, as in all whales, the line of an eternal smile is etched across its face. Freshness and the vigour of life radiate from its skin, but on the highest point of its middle there is a patch where layers of coral, oysters and the shells of unnamed sea creatures have turned into stone in such a way that colourful plants from sea gardens and jasmine bushes will grow, or have grown, among them.

Now I realize that the unfamiliar scent that has flooded my body with a sense of delirium and intoxication is the scent of ambergris. My knees weaken. A huge Chinook helicopter hovers over the whale. But we all know that this helicopter that can easily move tanks is powerless before that contentedly lazing mass on Tehran's asphalt. All it can do is irritate us and the whale with the wind from its propellers and its ear-splitting noise.

I want to sit down. And from this unfamiliar temptation, all of us who have circled around, one by one, quietly sit down, even the police who normally disperse any unauthorized gathering with the force of their batons and tongue-lashings.

Mr Petrovich will think, I must get myself to the ministry as quickly as possible to report to the director so that he can immediately instruct all newspapers and news agencies not to write a single sentence and not to broadcast a single word about the sudden appearance of this strange creature in Tehran . . .

That afternoon I start my story-writing workshop. To the one hundred and twenty eyes staring into my eyes I say:

"My advice to you is, if you can live in Iran for a few days without thinking of a story, if you can live a few days without the temptation to write, then take pity on yourselves and don't come to this workshop again. Throw the dark dream of becoming a writer in Iran in the waste-paper basket at your house and go and look for a comfortable life, carefree and happy . . . But if you cannot live for one day without writing one sentence, if without writing you cannot sleep, if you are in love and you don't know who you are in love with, then welcome to the prestigious world of the Iranian story."

One of the girls starts to read her story. A story about the shadow of a man behind the curtain in a woman's house. The woman pulls the curtain aside, but there is no one there. Yet fear persists in the house and in the story because the woman knows, and we know, that the shadow will return.

Many words flutter around in my head in critique and analysis of the story. I wait impatiently for others to express their opinions so that my turn will come to speak. Suddenly my eyes lock on to a pair of familiar eyes at the farthest corner of the classroom. Mysterious and sharp, they stare at me. I am sure they were not there before. I forget everything I wanted to say about the underlying layers of a good story. Instead, I say:

"It's a good story. But let's remember that every good story needs rewriting, too. Like an emerald, one can cut and polish it over and over again. Perhaps it would have been better if every writer had the ambition to write a single story in his lifetime and worked on this one story until the final moment of his life."

I add:

"That's enough for today . . ."

But Mr Petrovich raises his hand to speak. Seeing the stunned look in my eyes, all eyes turn to that corner of the classroom.

"May I speak simply as someone who is interested in stories?"

"Sir, you need no permission."

"I wanted to ask why you, who truly are a good teacher, did not talk about the underlying layers of the story that was read. I think you censored yourself so that this young lady writer doesn't get into trouble."

I don't know how to respond. He continues:

"It seems the woman in the story is terrified when at night she sees the shadow of a man behind the curtains in her bedroom. But in my opinion, the shadow is in fact a reflection of the woman's hidden desires. The story wants to suggest that in the mind of every woman there is a hidden man, and the shadow of that sin appears behind the curtains in her bedroom. I think this story is an insult to all decent women. If the writer herself has the shadow of a man behind the curtains in her bedroom, she should not attribute her own sinful desires to other women as well."

I say:

"Sir, you're going too fast. First of all, the story only tells us that a man's shadow is behind the curtain. There is no mention of a bedroom . . ."

"Sir! What sort of a comment is that? You are either trying to fool me, or you don't know anything about story-writing. Any reader can discern that those curtains are bedroom curtains. Shadows don't appear behind living-room curtains, and even if they did, the lady of the house would grab a broom and beat it against the curtain so much that the shadow would regret ever having appeared."

I say:

"The workshop has ended. For the next session, read Kafka's *The Trial* so that we can discuss it."

I gather my papers from the desk.

I walk out of the building, and I am surprised to see snowflakes. I am sure that when I was driving over to the magazine's offices, the sky showed no signs of clouds or snow. But snowflakes, without a doubt, are falling. I see the dark shadow of Mr Petrovich a short distance away. He is standing there smoking a cigarette, waiting for me. I start walking. He asks:

"Aren't you going to get into your car?"

"No. I want to walk a little. I really like the snow."

He joins me. I don't want him to learn the whereabouts of my friend's house where I am spending the night. I randomly pick a direction and start to walk.

"How was my critique of that woman's story?"

"It was interesting. I am surprised you don't teach a creative-writing course."

"I am thinking about it. Frankly, given all the years I have spent reading stories by you Iranian writers, and plenty of translations of foreign novels and short stories, I think I know stories and novels better than any of you."

"I congratulate you."

The snow has quickly emptied the streets of pedestrians. The snowflakes, although large, are very light. They float around us.

"How is your story coming along?"

"I'm stuck at the next-to-last scene."

"Are you waiting for inspiration?"

"Inspiration doesn't deem the likes of me deserving. It comes looking for you."

"But I want you to be able to write an Islamic love story. And if it happens to be postmodern, then all the better. In other words, for everything in it to be all muddled and confused and yet for it to criticize modernism, which incites sin. Don't forget, we take no issue with postmodernism. After all, it promotes a return to tradition."

"In any case, regardless of whether my story is traditional, modern or postmodern, it is all getting very convoluted."

I turn onto another street. The pavement is so deserted that seeing a frail man walk towards us is somehow comforting. He is carrying a leather bag. His back is bent, and he is so drowned in thought that it seems he doesn't see us. Just as he walks past us I recognize him. He is none other than Hooshang Golshiri, that same great contemporary writer I mentioned before. He has played an important role in my life as a writer, and I shout happily:

"Mr Golshiri!"

In the light of the streetlamp his face looks tired and old. He seems to be straining his memory to remember me. Then in a cheerless voice he says:

"I didn't recognize you! Your hair has turned so white . . . Is it snow?"

I shake my head.

"No, it turns white despite the snow."

He pulls a handwritten manuscript out of his briefcase and hands it to me.

"I have discovered a brilliant young writer. Read."

As if he has just then noticed Mr Petrovich, he says:

"I see you are walking with Mr Petrovich!"

I stammer:

"The gentleman is walking with me. You know . . . He graced my story-writing workshop tonight."

The glint of his usual humour and cleverness comes alive in his eyes. He turns to Mr Petrovich.

"My dear sir, what news of my *Prince Ehtejab* and *Christine and Kid*?"

His voice sounds young.

Mr Petrovich says:

"What's the rush, Mr Golshiri? Your books are a bit complicated, and it takes time to scrutinize them."

Golshiri's masterpieces have been waiting for a publishing permit for some twenty-seven years. He says:

"I'm in no hurry. I was going from Prince Ehtejab's house to Christine's house. They constantly ask when they are going to be published, and I have no answer for them. Will you be at your office tomorrow for Morad to come and pay his respects?"

Morad is one of the characters in Golshiri's *Prince Ehtejab*. Every time he comes to visit the prince he brings news of the death of one of the prince's relatives, until the end of the novel when he brings the prince news of the prince's own death.

"Why Morad? You should come yourself. We'll have some tea and chat. Perhaps we can even reach a compromise."

"No, Morad doesn't know how to make an appointment. Christine . . . What if Christine comes? Will you give her an appointment?"

Christine is a pleasant English lady who in Golshiri's novel falls in love with an Iranian writer in Isfahan. Frightened, Mr Petrovich holds his arms out to shield himself.

"No, no . . . Absolutely not . . . Never . . . No."

"Are you afraid your colleagues will suspect you of being a British spy?"

"Precisely."

Throughout the dialogue between Mr Petrovich and Golshiri, I am tempted to sneak away and escape to my car. Golshiri knows how to talk to Mr Petrovich more effectively than I can. From the very first day when the censorship machine started, Golshiri announced that he would not change or delete a single word in his stories, and as a result, most of his books have not received a publishing permit. I take a step back. Mr Petrovich has his back to me. Two steps, three steps. I keep walking backwards. I wave to Golshiri, and . . . I head for my car. I am cold. The floating snowflakes get into my eyes; they seem to be acidic; they burn my eyes. I keep wiping away my tears, it doesn't help, again the burning snowflakes . . . I remember Hooshang Golshiri, not having seen his new novel published and reprinted, died several years ago . . . I am very cold.

In a computer chat Sara asks Dara:

"Is it snowing in your neighbourhood, too?"

"Probably less than it is in yours."

"The weather was so nice. How come it suddenly started to snow?"

"I don't know. I like the snow."

Sara sighs.

"Me too. I wish we could go for a walk together in this snow."

"It would be beautiful. We would walk together and look at our footprints on the snow. ~~I would take your hand to warm you~~ . . . To me, love only means creating beauty."

After their last ungratifying rendezvous, they waver between love and anger.

Sara says:

"But I have still not forgiven you."

"I know. I can tell from the tone of your voice. What do I have to do?"

"Well . . . I can't leave the house this late at night . . . Why don't you go out? Go out on this beautiful night and walk for me, too. Imagine I am next to you."

"These days, because of that guy who's been following me, I don't go out that much."

"You mean you won't take a risk for me? What sort of a man in love are you?"

"Is that what you want? You want me to risk my life for the sake of imagining you?"

"What if I do? So far, you have only bragged about love. But you have never proved your love to me."

Dara doesn't hear Sara's playful giggle.

"Fine, I'll go out."

"Are you telling me the truth?"

"You'll see. Maybe I will finally be freed from this love."

"Dara, I was joking!"

But Dara pays no attention to these last words, and turns off his computer to go out and prove to Sara the sincerity of his love.

While Sara sends Dara out to walk in the snow and to look at his footprints, I am racing towards my car hoping to save myself from this night.

Heads made of fog float in the air. I try not to run into them. I keep thinking I am going the wrong way. On the opposite pavement a few *shahneh*s are dragging away the poet who died seven hundred years ago. One of them, trailing behind, is carrying a goblet and a decanter – the evidence.

Mr Petrovich is standing on the other side of my car smoking a cigarette.

"Did you buy this car recently?"

"Yes. For years I have wanted a new car that I can travel in with peace of mind."

"Did you buy it with the royalties from your last book?"

We both burst into laughter. We both know that in Iran, even a well-established writer can at most buy a car tyre with his royalties.

"It's a nice colour . . . Someone has scratched it with a knife on this side. Have you seen it?"

I walk over to the other side of the car. Yes, there is a scratch from one end of the car to the other.

"There are jealous people everywhere."

"Yes, there are."

I open the car door.

"I really have to go now. I've just remembered that I've got to pick up a friend who's waiting for me in the street. The poor thing has probably turned into a snowman standing there staring at his footprints in the snow."

"I'm not stopping you. I just wanted to ask you a question."

My heart sinks. In Iran, a single question can turn a person's life upside down. Mr Petrovich, with those same eyes that can read the mind of his counterpart, stares into my snow-covered eyes. The car keys are stuck to my fingers like a lump of ice.

"Do you recall a hunchback midget in any of the stories you have read?"

"No . . . Not at all . . . Why?"

"Don't be quick to answer. Think."

A purple fog cluster passes over my shoulder.

"I don't know . . . Maybe . . . As far as I can remember there is a hunchback midget in one of the tales of *One Thousand and One Nights*. Why?"

In the fluorescent light of the streetlamp I can clearly discern Mr Petrovich's frightening look of mistrust. Again I ask:

"Why?"

"It's not important. I just wanted to say that I never forget the kindness of people who send gifts to my office."

I jump in my car, shift into four-wheel drive and speed through the snow-covered streets of Tehran. It is one in the morning and too late for me to go to the friend with whom I was supposed to stay that night. I have to find a cheap motel; I have very little money in my pocket. A piece of carpet, the size of the palm of my hand, flies into the windscreen and stubbornly sticks to it. The windscreen wipers get caught behind it. Even now its shades of azure and indigo are distinct. I increase the speed of the wipers. The piece of carpet goes flying into the street.

In the south part of town I pass a young man walking alone in the snow. I don't have much time; at this hour of the night even the motels close their doors. I leave the young man to continue his walk with the warmth of his heart and the heat of his imagination, and once in a while to turn back and look at his trail on the snow and see two sets of footprints that end at his feet.

Finally I find a motel. I take my duffel bag and quickly walk to the front door. It is closed. I have no choice. I have to knock. A surly old woman opens the door. Her withered face is heavily made-up. Her gums and the few teeth she has are black.

In a hoarse voice she wheezes:

"What do you want?"

"Madam, why would anyone knock on a motel door . . . Do you have a room?"

"If you have money, come in."

I follow her into a long hallway, the doors on either side all closed. The end of the hallway is drowned in darkness. We reach the reception desk. It takes up half the width of the hallway. The narcotic whiff of opium is percolating from somewhere. The old woman walks behind the rotting wooden desk calloused with grime from the hands of thousands of travellers. She pushes a large, old notebook in front of me for me to write down my information. I blow away the fragments of broken moth wings from the page, and as I write my first name, last name, point of departure, destination and purpose of travel in the columns of the notebook, my eyes catch a glimpse of the entries made by the last guest at the motel.

Mr P. . . .

I freeze. The date entered is ten years ago. Suspicious, I look up at the old woman. She exposes her sparse black teeth to me with a smile. I don't know why, but from that very first moment her face and comportment have seemed familiar to me . . . She rubs her thumb and two fingers together, gesturing for money. I take the crumpled notes out of my pocket and throw them on the reception desk. Patiently she flattens them out and counts them. I am still staring at her, trying to remember where I have seen her before. She snarls:

"It's too little . . . Give me more."

She holds her hand up to my eyes and again gestures for money.

"How much does a motel room cost?"

"It's snowing outside, isn't it? Do you mean to tell me it's not snowing?"

"But that's all I have."

I follow the path of her gaze. My watch . . . I bought it only recently. I put the watch in front of her.

"I'll hold it as a pawn. If you bring the money in seven days, it will be yours again. Otherwise it's mine."

She hands me a rusty key and points to the end of the dark hallway.

"The toilet is there."

"I don't need it at the moment."

"Any time you've no money but you've got some pricey piece, come and see me. As you are such a polite and well-mannered man, I'll charge you less interest than I charge others."

She looks me over.

"Do you have a cigarette?"

I take two cigarettes out of my pack. She lights one up. After a deep puff she smiles coyly and says:

"It's a cold night. If you need anything else, don't be shy . . . All right?"

"All right."

I lie down on the grime-encrusted bed. I am very cold. I pull the blanket that smells of a traveller from ten years ago over me. Hard as I try to imagine why the old woman's face and mannerisms are familiar to me and grow even more familiar, nothing comes to mind. I try to lull myself to sleep by thinking about the love story I am writing. Sara is asleep. Dara, if he has not fallen prey to that assassin, must have turned into a snowman by now. And suddenly I feel sterile. I cannot think of anything for my story's next scene . . .

I try to see the beautiful sleeping Sara on a beautiful bed in Dara's imagination, to see her plump half-open lips that seem to have just been released from a kiss, to see her chest as it rises and falls with every breath . . .

And, with an ancient squeak, the door gently opens.

THE SNOW QUEEN OF TEHRAN

I t seems that we, together with Dara, must close our eyes to all the danger and go for a stroll. **Sara, who has sent Dara out for a solitary walk in Tehran's falling snow, is now suffering from a guilty conscience. She thinks, I sent the poor boy out in the cold and the snow, so now I shouldn't sleep either until it is inspired to me that he has returned home. Several times she splashes cold water on her face. At three in the morning, after the final rinsing of sleep from her eyes, she returns to her room and looks out the window. Suddenly all the chill of the water evaporates from her face. Outside, on the pavement across the street, there is a white ghost wearing a layer of snow from head to toe. Sara would recognize Dara even under an avalanche. This is the first time she has caught him in front of her bedroom window. Dara is standing there like a snowman.**

Around one thousand years ago, in an epic legend in verse called *Shahnameh* (*The Book of Kings*) – which, if written in any land other than Iran, its fame and influence would today far surpass that of *The Iliad* and *The Odyssey* – a story was composed about the love of an Iranian hero named Zal for the daughter of the ruler of Kabul, which Westerners are now familiar with because of the mad actions of the Taliban. This Iranian mythic hero was born with hair as white as snow. Well, one night Zal stands beneath his beloved's bedroom window, and his beloved lets her long tresses hang from the second- or third-floor window. Then Zal takes that most beautiful and magnificent rope and climbs up to her bedroom.

Sara wants to cry out:

Oh! What are you doing out there in the cold? You will catch pneu-monia, ~~darling~~.

But she is scared of waking her parents and the neighbours. She

252

thinks she must somehow share in the cold that her beloved is suffering. Therefore . . .

Sara flings her bedroom window open and shakes her head so that the strands of her hair like thousands of ropes fly free. She takes off her shirt for the cold to invade her body too and for her nakedness to warm her beloved standing out there in the pitiless cold. For centuries, however, my wretched Dara, unlike Khosrow, has been deprived of seeing such warming scenes and I of writing them.

Ask, then, How will you write this hot scene? For me to write

Sara flings her bedroom window open. All her suppressed emotions cry out for her to share in her beloved's suffering. The snow is a cold cloak clinging to Dara's body, and she is selfishly warm in her clothes. The wind beats against her; from the cuff of her sleeves and the collar of her shirt it licks at her arms, her neck. She longs to be on a snow-covered plain, alone, unseen, free. She sees herself on a snow-covered plain. The warmth of her being gradually melts away her clothes. She is inspired to give the truth of her existence to the nature from which it was born and she . . . The snowy wind beats against her; it turns her shoulders into ice and fills the hollow at the base of her throat with snow. And the hands of the Snow Queen touch those hills for which the Farsi language has no words . . . The snow covering Dara's body gently melts . . .

At the sight of the Snow Queen, Dara's eyes, ~~the eyes of that young virgin,~~ **have opened wide. He crosses the street, and in front of Sara's house, with thoughts for which the Farsi language has no words, he stands staring up at the bright window . . . Time for him has stopped.** How many minutes go by? He doesn't know, and neither do I. **The snow is quickly turning Sara's body into ice,** ~~yet she feels her nipples burning, pink steam rises from them.~~ **After some time, Dara comes to himself and realizes that he is torturing his beloved. He tries with hand gestures to tell her she will catch cold. But Sara misunderstands.** ~~She thinks Dara is asking her to take off her bra as well. She reaches back and undoes that clasp that no man in the world likes. Dara feels his eyes burning, black smoke will rise from them.~~ **Like a statue he stands staring up at the window that has opened onto all the anguish and all the denial he has suffered since puberty.**

On that street, neither he nor Sara see the return of the Mongol

army from their capture and razing of the splendid city of Rey. They take with them thousands of captives to shoulder the loot and the spoils. The jingling of gold echoes in the streets of Tehran. A snowflake sits on Dara's lips. He licks it away. It tastes sweet. Without turning his eyes away from that window, he opens his hand to catch a few snowflakes. He tastes them. No, it was not a fantasy. The snowflakes are as sweet as ice cream. Sara reaches her hand out of the window and the snowflakes rush towards it. Dara is utterly drained. To stop himself from falling he leans his hand against the wall of Sara's house. A tall wall, like all walls around Iranian houses, that to stop thieves from entering is crowned with a steel grate and arrowheads that make this house, like most Iranian houses, look like a cage. Staring up at the window, Dara feels that the bricks of Sara's house are soft and delicate to the touch. He starts stroking them. The bricks transmit a pleasant sensation to his hand. No, you are mistaken; he is so decent that it has not occurred to him to climb the wall and get himself into Sara's room. He looks at the bricks he has stroked and feels he wants to embrace that wall with all the strength in his arms. He stands with his body pressing against the wall and lifts his head up to convey this feeling somehow to Sara. But Sara has disappeared from the window, and the light in her room is turned off.

Dara thinks:

You little devil!

He jumps at the touch of a hand on his shoulder. Happy, he turns around to find Sara there, but instead he sees a police officer brandishing a gun.

In fact, Sara had seen the police car approaching from down the street and had turned out the light just in time. The police officer brusquely asks:

"What are you doing?"

Dara, stammering, tells the truth.

"I was stroking the wall."

The officer laughs and turns to his partner, who is sitting behind the wheel of the police car.

"Did you hear that? The gentleman was stroking the wall."

Dara starts to laugh, too. The police officer, whose large stomach is bouncing up and down from laughter, says:

"You must have held it in your arms, too."

Dara laughs and nods. The officer tells his partner:

"Did you hear that? He hugged his wall."

The officer in the police car pounds his fist on the steering wheel and chortles. Now all three are laughing. To add to the camaraderie, Dara runs his hand over the wall, but a stiff slap lands on his ear. The snow flies off his hair. The officer has quickly turned serious.

"You scoundrel, you wanted to climb up the wall and rob the house."

Dara, his hand on his burning cheek, shakes his head. With a quick kick the officer throws Dara to the ground and cuffs his hands behind him. Sara, from the darkness of her room, sees the officer throw Dara, head first, into the police car. Then the revolving lights disappear at the end of the street.

Sara knows that tonight at the police station Dara will be slapped many times so that he will confess to having intended to break into their home, and she knows that tomorrow too he is likely to be slapped even more so that he will confess to previous thefts. She slumps down next to the window and weeps.

Not much time remains until the sun dawns on the high and low rooftops of Tehran. The tawny dust of shattered earthen casks of wine pours down from the sky.

"CANARIES ROASTED ON A FIRE
OF LILIES AND JASMINES . . ."
(*Ahmad Shamlu*)

S inbad is standing in front of the mirror in his house, trimming his beard, when he hears the telephone ring. Sara's troubled and trembling voice frightens him. This is the first time Sara has called his home.

She says:

"I need your help. Please come."

"What's wrong, Sara? But . . . Certainly . . . I will leave right away . . . Where should I come?"

At fifteen minutes past nine Tehran time Sinbad enters the same Internet café where Sara and Dara had taken refuge on the first day they met. Sara, the only customer in the café, is sitting in a corner. Her face is pale and her eyes are red from crying. She seems to have lost a lot of weight in only a few hours. Sinbad, with a lover's concern, sits across from her.

"I was so scared when I heard your voice. I thought something must have happened to your mother or father . . . You know I will help you in any way I can. Tell me what has happened."

Sara, worn out and choking back her tears, asks:

"Are you willing to help me without asking any questions?"

Sinbad stares at her sunken eyes. He is an intelligent and experienced man. Sara, noticing his hesitation, pleads:

"Please help me . . . But don't ask any questions."

Sinbad looks around. It is the first time he has stepped into such a café.

256

"Do you come here often?"

Tears roll down Sara's face. She knows that if the police find out that Dara has served time as a political prisoner, the poor boy will face the greatest ordeal of his life.

She sobs;

"Don't ask anything . . . Just help me . . . and I will marry you with no conditions."

Sinbad orders a tea.

Two women police officers clad in black chadors and armed with batons wander around the café. They are seasoned enough to tell from Sinbad's appearance that he is one of them and do not bother this brother.

At five o'clock that afternoon Dara is dragged out of the temporary holding cell at the police station. To protect Sara, he has confessed to having intended to rob her family's house and, under all methods of coercion, he has repeated that it was the first time in his life he had attempted theft.

He is taken to the police captain's office and there, for the first time, Dara sees Sinbad, and Sinbad sees Dara. The police captain explains that Mr Sinbad, a very influential and highly respected gentleman, has vouched for him and offered explanations that have convinced him that Dara had not intended to rob that house. The captain adds that although the police sometimes treat suspects harshly, which at times is necessary, they are generally kind-hearted men and know when to forgive because they can tell when a criminal deeply regrets his actions and will not repeat his offence . . . The captain puts a pledge form in front of Dara for him to sign. In this letter of repentance no mention is made of Dara's offence; it is only stated that he regrets his unlawful actions and swears never again to commit a crime. Dara signs the form.

Then, in a fatherly tone, the police captain says:

"Young man, you are free. Go home and don't ever think of committing a crime."

Dara leaves the station. Out on the street there is no sign of last night's snow. Numb, exhausted and humiliated, he repeats Lorca's famous poem in his mind: "At five in the afternoon. It was exactly five in the afternoon. A boy brought the white sheet at five in the afternoon . . . The rest was death, and death alone at five in the afternoon," and a few steps away from the police station he runs out of the energy that was keeping him on his feet. His knees buckle. He sits down on the pavement and leans against the wall. His eyes see the world in a blur and the passers-by as dark shadows . . . A few minutes later, he senses a man standing over him. Then the man, who like himself seems to lack the energy to go on, sits down next to him.

"Thank you."

He hears no answer.

He remembers Sinbad's face from the police station. A man with a handsome beard who looked sad and defeated and avoided looking at him.

"You saved me. Thank you."

"You should thank Sara. She saved you."

Sinbad too sounds tired and humiliated.

Dara says out loud:

"At five in the afternoon. It was exactly five in the afternoon . . ."

"How long have you known Sara?"

"A long time. But she only got to know me recently."

"Does she love you?"

"I don't know . . . but I am in love with her."

Sinbad snaps:

"What kind of a man in love are you that you don't know whether your beloved loves you or not . . . Are you stupid?"

"I must be. I'm really stupid. But this is the first time I've fallen in love."

"Every person falls in love only once. Do you so-called intellectuals fall in love as often as you go to the toilet?"

Sinbad sounds like he has a lump in his throat. Dara feels he shares a pain with this man and can therefore be sincere and take that Iranian mask off his face. He asks:

"Are you in love with Sara, too?"

"I was, until this morning."

"I see! When a person falls in love, being freed from that love is not in his control. Do you fall in love as often as you go to the toilet?"

"You're right. But today I saw how much Sara loves you . . . When I promised her that I would help you, I made a deal with myself that this will be the last time I ever trust a woman . . . Sara promised she would marry me if I saved you."

At this point in my love story, Dara speaks the wisest sentence he will ever utter in his life.

Enraged, Dara pounds his head against the wall and says:

"Sir! When you fall in love with a woman, you have to ~~say screw everything,~~ forget about everything you have ever trusted, had faith in and were certain of."

After these words were spoken on some street in this world, the two men turn to each other; both see the world in a blur.

"You sent someone to kill me."

"To kill you?"

"Yes."

On Sinbad's face sorrow gives way to the power of ridicule.

"It looks like the police punched you really hard in the head!"

"Yes. But I'm not crazy."

"You are. First of all, you are not someone I would want dead. Second, until today dear Miss Sara had kept it a secret from me that she has a lover like you hanging around."

Just now Dara hears the voice of a second man sitting next to him.

"I also have a talisman for hatred and freedom from love."

Powerless, Dara rests his head on his knees so that no one will see his tears. And he hears Sinbad's dejected voice:

"How much do you want for your talisman?"

"For you, one hundred and one gold coins."

"That's a lot of money . . . What guarantee do I have that it will work?"

"As soon as I hand it to you, you will be free from all the love there is. You can pay me then."

"Will you accept a cheque?"

"Everyone will accept a cheque from you, Mr Sinbad, even American companies that sell Internet filters."

"Then get the talisman while I write the cheque."

The world remains a blur before Dara's eyes. He wants to sleep, right there where he sits, for one thousand and one years and to wake up again in his childhood. His heavy eyelids close . . . Some time later, he wakes up from the pressure of Sinbad's hand on his shoulder.

"I'm leaving. Sara will never see me again . . . Don't think I'm into making grand sacrifices and playing such loony lovers' games. No. I just don't want to have a woman at home whose thoughts are with another man. Do you get it?"

"Yes."

The fingers resting on Dara's shoulder press down gently.

"Take care of that girl."

And Sinbad, for the time being, exits this love story without knowing that at this moment of exit he is perhaps for ever freed from the torture of constantly having to trim his beard.

Dara is struggling to stand up and return home so that he can free his parents from worry. He hears the magic seller's voice.

"A talisman to be free from love and hate, for you, only one cigarette . . . Do you have a cigarette?"

Dara stands up.

"I don't. Even if I did, I wouldn't give one to you."

"Do you want me to give one to you?"

"Do you have one?"

A hand puts a lit cigarette between his index and middle fingers.

Mr Petrovich will say:

"I didn't like this scene at all. You are saying that a man like Sinbad has left the field wide open for a good-for-nothing former Communist and film pedlar. It is not believable at all. You breach those same principles of realism that you preach. Sinbad is far stronger than this."

I will say:

"Well, I too am saying that Sinbad is very strong."

"You are a weak writer because you haven't grasped the psychology of your story's characters. In my opinion, Sinbad should fight to the death."

"Well, he is fighting."

"With whom?"

"With himself."

"Why are you talking nonsense? As if it's the civil war in Iraq? As if he has nothing better to do than to fight with himself?"

"Is it because the Iraqis have nothing better to do that they are fighting among themselves?"

"You were not supposed to talk politics."

" . . . "

"And if you ever do talk about a civil war, it had better be about the American Civil War."

"Anyway, I can't change this segment of my story."

"Why?"

"Because my story's character made his decision all by himself. Sinbad's action was really not part of the plot. He made the decision independently and acted on it."

"If you are right, then why does your story's Dara not make a sensible decision and do something right for a change?"

"For example?"

"For example, a loser like him who has repeatedly made mistakes in life, has screwed up plenty and has even troubled the police should finally get wise to life."

"You mean personal evolution?"

"No . . . I mean suicide."

ASSASSIN'S ALLEY

Cautiously, Dara pokes his head out of the front door of his house and checks the alley to see if anyone is lying in ambush for him. There appears to be no sign of the Hashashin phantom. He walks out. But the most dangerous place is the entrance to the dead-end alley where the assassin could be hiding round the left or right corner so that he can slash through Dara's jugular the instant he steps into the street. To avoid being caught off guard from either the left or the right, Dara chooses the centre of the alley as his path. At the head of the alley he quickly glances in each direction, and when he has made sure that no dagger is waiting for him there, with hasty steps he heads down the street.

Dara would not have left the house if he didn't have to. But today he has to pick up the down payment for painting a store so that he can buy the paint. The street doesn't have its usual character. People are rushing towards the west end of the street. Dara asks the neighbourhood bird seller, who is pulling down the blinds in his shop, what is going on. He learns that a young man accused of drinking is going to be whipped in the square. For fifty years the bird seller has been selling lovebirds, canaries and doves to the locals. Dara asks him whether he too is going to the square to watch.

The old man looks down the street with disgust and says:

"No. I'm going home to stop my wife in case she is tempted to go."

And he sets out in the opposite direction from the rest of the people. Dara follows him with his eyes and suddenly sees the assassin. Still with steely determination, possessed, he is walking towards him. Dara starts to run. He turns into the first alley, then into the next. The alleys in this old neighbourhood, all lined with small two-hundred-year-old houses whose bricks have become blackened with soot, lead into one another like a labyrinth. Each time Dara is forced to slow down to catch his breath, he looks back and sees the assassin, showing no sign of fatigue or shortness of breath, still chasing after him. Dara is familiar with this neighbourhood, but in one of his backward glances he mistakenly runs into a dead-end alley, and by the time he realizes his mistake, it is too late. He doesn't see the assassin's dark face, but he suspects that from the satisfaction of having trapped his prey, there is now a smile on his lips. The alley is the haunt of hashish and opium dealers. Five men, three of whom are clearly addicts and the other two thugs, are standing and squatting here and there.

At the dead end, Dara desperately looks around for a means of escape, and the only thing that comes to his mind is to go and stand next to the burliest drug dealer. The assassin, perforce, stops a few steps away.

Dara's heart is beating like the heart of a sparrow captive in the hands of a ~~horny~~ man. The alley is rife with the smell of opium percolating from the houses. The drug dealer, who has a few scars on his face and neck and whose attitude clearly indicates he is the local ringleader, asks Dara:

"What do you want?"

"What do you have?"

"You're new to this?"

"Yes."

"We have opium and hashish."

"I want hashish. How much is it?"

The man points to one of his underlings squatting next to the wall and says:

"I'll give you five grams for five thousand tumans."

It is right now that a shrewd inspiration must come to innocent, naive Dara.

Dara points to the assassin and says:

"But he's selling at three thousand tumans."

This is the most cunning comment one can make in the drug-dealer's alley. In other words, there is new competition on your turf cutting in on your market. The thug whistles, and immediately one of the addicts who appeared to be napping gets up and at a gesture from his boss, with his hand in his pocket – meaning with his knife at the ready – he walks towards the assassin. But before he can utter the first word of a threat, the assassin's knee jabs him in the chest, and the instant he keels over in pain, the powerful blow of the assassin's elbow pins his scrawny neck to the assassin's knee. The man falls. But a few moments later, the assassin finds himself surrounded by four knife-wielding men. The thugs of Tehran are far better skilled than Borges's thugs. With his dagger, the assassin slashes the face and chest of two of them, but the man who had fallen to the ground with a stab of his knife renders the Achilles tendon in the assassin's right foot useless. Blood gushes out of the assassin's ankle; he leans against the wall to hold himself up but he can't. Besieged by four knives, he falls down on his knees. Dara finds the most opportune moment to escape. And he can rest assured that this assassin can no longer pursue him.

Stunned, I look at this Dara who is walking out of the dead-end alley, and I feel the blade of a knife against my Achilles tendon.

THE WEDDING

A month has passed since the incident of Dara's arrest. During this time he has refused to see Sara. Not because he didn't want to, but because he felt humiliated. All his male pride and all the dignity that he had constructed word by word in the eyes of his beloved were destroyed on that snowy night when, right in front of Sara's eyes, the police had thrown him in the car head first and, worse, when his rival had come to his rescue. However, during this month, in the course of their few computer chats and telephone conversations, Sara with her female wisdom has tried to heal the wounds of humiliation and help Dara put them behind him. In the past week, she has discovered the best cure: irony.

"You were so strong and intelligent. You told the truth and the police didn't believe you. The poor policemen hear so many lies from offenders that even when someone tells them the truth they don't believe him. Think about it. If you had said anything else, the police would have grown suspicious of our house and arrested me, too . . . Oh, it could have been so much worse . . . You humiliated yourself to save my reputation. And when you humiliated yourself you realized you really loved me . . . We should thank God the police arrested you, otherwise you would have got drunk watching me. The way your wild eyes were staring at me like the devil, when you wanted to break a hole in the wall . . . Well, more than a hole. You could have brought the wall down like Superman, broken the door and entered the house. Imagine, my poor father, my faint-hearted mother, they would have woken up to see an overheated Superman in their house. Who knows, on that dark night, in the condition you were in, you could have gone after my mother by mistake, just like Khosrow."

One of woman's many talents is that they know how to correct or erase a man's memory. Therefore, by the end of his month-long seclusion, Dara too can laugh at that night's escapades. But this is not the subject of this chapter.

Then ask me, What is supposed to happen in this chapter?

For me to write:

Sara and Dara attend a wedding celebration in one of those Iranian gardens that are world-renowned for their beauty. The *One Thousand and One Nights* beauty of some of them is because they have been planted and fashioned with much labour, and just like a mirage, suddenly in a valley or in between mountain walls or on barren desert terrain, a green haven has thrived from the miracle of a spring. The regular cohabitants of these gardens are often opium-addicted gardeners, a couple of night-singing nightingales and rosebushes along a narrow stream, the overflow of which quenches the earth.

In Tehran, in the foothills of the Alborz Mountains, there used to be thousands of these gardens. However, during the past few decades many were deliberately left to dry, and in their place all manner of high-rise buildings have sprouted from the earth.

Sara's cousin's wedding is being held in one of the remaining gardens. Sara has managed to give Dara an invitation. They are both happy that they will be in a beautiful garden together.

However, they will not be able to talk or to sit next to each other.

You will doubtless ask why.

First of all, in a place where a horde of her uncles, aunts and relatives are gathered, Sara cannot casually sit with her boyfriend. The moment they see her with that boy they will start making up rumours which will circulate from mouth to mouth, and week after week and month after month they will become more exaggerated until Sara gains fame among one and all as a ruined girl. The other reason is that at post-revolution Iranian weddings, the men's and women's sections are separate and the two groups cannot under any circumstances commingle. In cities, weddings are normally held in catering halls that have separate men's and women's sections. Couples say goodbye to each other at the door and go to their own special section. Ever since traditional Iranian music has been to some extent allowed, there is music in these halls, but not very lively music with pop rhythm and a beat that would drive Iranians to

involuntarily gyrate their hips. Now and then, in between pieces of traditional music, inadvertently or intentionally, epic anthems that are relics of
the years of war are also played – anthems with themes of picking up
arms and heading for the battlefields and spilling blood or shedding one's
own blood on the earth. Men, sombre and typically surly, sit on chairs
lined up in rows and eat pastry and fruit and talk about politics, the daily
increase in the price of goods, the value of the dollar, the billion-dollar
embezzlements in government departments, an imminent attack by the
United States and the horrifying increase in the number of drug addicts,
and their discussions are often spiced with jokes about government leaders and the revolution.

"Sir! You are clueless. Given the country's present situation, by next
year bread too will become scarce, just like the days of World War Two
when the British occupied Iran."

"Who cares if we don't have bread to eat. Sir, our honour has been lost!
Poor Iranian girls are being exported to Dubai by the hundreds to become
prostitutes for the Arabs."

"They say America is going to attack Iran in the next two or three
months; we'll be saved."

"Sir, you are being naive! This regime is itself American."

"No, sir! The British brought this regime to power."

Women, in their own section, are by far more energetic and cheerful.
They have taken off their coveralls and chadors or headscarves and,
dressed in brightly coloured, sleeveless and open-neck dresses, they fly
like a flock of restless sparrows from one side to the other. They laugh,
they chitchat, sometimes they gossip, and some of the frisky ones finally
find a way, even if for a few seconds, to be seen from the men's section.
Yet almost eighty per cent of the attendees, for lack of any other activity or
entertainment, constantly glance at their watches waiting for the dinner
hour. On enormous tables, large trays of colourful Iranian food are laid
out, and with the announcement of "Dinner is served," guests storm the
tables, which in a matter of minutes look like wheat fields after a locust
attack.

But the story of weddings in private gardens is an entirely different
one. If the bride's or the groom's family own one of these gardens, they
will hold the wedding ceremony there on a beautiful night – of course, in
a semi-clandestine manner, away from the eyes of the patrols from the

Campaign Against Social Corruption. Although the gardens of Iran still do not have separate men's and women's sections, Iranian families have grown so accustomed to the separation of sexes that men automatically move to one side and women to the other. If the garden is distant enough from the city, usually one of the underground bands will be invited to liven up the event with wistful songs from the past.

By the time Dara enters the garden, almost all the guests have arrived. He is nervous because he doesn't know what to say if someone asks him whether he is related to the groom or the bride. He can't very well say, I am the bride's cousin's boyfriend, because it is quite possible that instead of rice and kebab he would feast on a good beating. Given that it is wintertime, a large tarpaulin tent has been set up in the tree-less section of the garden, and here and there gas heaters are ready to heat the space. Inside the tent, a crystal-clear stream with Iranian murmurings ripples between the rows of chairs, and the various entries and exits are decorated with lights and flowers. The weather is not cold, and the guests are flowing back and forth between the garden and the tent. Dara has found a secluded corner and is sitting there alone. Every so often, hoping to see Sara, he steals a peek at the section where the women are gathered. Sara told him she would be wearing one of the most beautiful dresses in her life ~~just for him~~. But no matter how often he peeks across the stream, he sees no sign of her. He is so preoccupied with thoughts of Sara that he seldom thinks of that assassin. Only once in a while, in his mind, he sees the moment when the assassin tried to remain standing on his good leg, and yet he fell to the ground. Dara no longer thinks of his own instant of shrewd wisdom, which rose from somewhere deep in his subconscious – and led him to accuse the Hashashin assassin of selling hashish – because love has the power to bring forgetfulness to one's conscience.

An old man whose face and frailty speak of years of opium abuse, ~~tottering in a way that screams of him having downed one or two glasses of vodka in a secret spot in the garden,~~ passes in front of him. A few steps away, he stops, turns round and stares at Dara. Dara nervously smiles ~~and pretends to be busy watching the airs and antics of the male singer, who has plucked his eyebrows and is wearing a sequined shirt. Staggering~~, the old man sits down next to him. With a sly smile on his lips, ~~in a delirious and drunken voice~~ he says:

"Well, well, what a polite and respectable young man. Are you from the bride's family?"

Dara politely says no. The old man continues to stare at him.

"I like you. ~~With this fine-looking face, if you were any other young man, girls would be romping and rollicking all around you, but~~ I see that you, refined young man, have come to sit in this corner all by yourself, polite and timid, and you're not making mischief. Oh, what can I say of our youth today? My heart bleeds. ~~Case in point, my own son. The one singing. Look at the idiot. He's made himself up like a woman, all dressed in tight clothes. Watch how he wriggles his arse . . . . But you, polite young man . . . . I really like you.~~ What is your name?"

"Dara."

Dara is sweating under the vulgar gawping of the old man. There is a cut under his throat that has not healed. Dara feels he has seen the old man before, but hard as he tries he cannot remember where.

~~"Would you like a glass of home-made arrack?"~~

~~"No, thank you."~~

~~The old man lays his hand intimately on Dara's thigh.~~

~~"Don't ever stand on ceremony with me. See there, behind the trees, they've made a cosy nook for drinkers like us. If you like, we can go and wet our whistles."~~

~~"You've had enough for both of us. Thank you."~~

~~"But it just doesn't taste right without you."~~

~~Dara ignores the old man's comment. He looks around desperately, hoping to see Sara and silently plead for help.~~

~~On the other side of the stream, women and girls have started dancing to the singer's new song.~~ The old man hiccups and says:

"You polite and clean-cut young man, are you from the groom's family?"

"Yes."

"How are you related?"

"I'm a friend."

"I wish my son had friends like you. The louse. All his friends are just like him; ~~those pretty boys,~~ they won't sit with me for even a minute to chat so that I stop feeling so lonely."

And he hiccups. ~~Dara politely lifts the old man's hand off his thigh. The old man smiles drunkenly.~~

~~"You devil! Don't be cruel."~~

Dara shifts one seat away from him, but the old man slides over to the seat next to him.

"You're shy, too! Oh, how I love shy young men."

A man with his mouth stuffed with pastry walks by. The old man, in the Iranian custom of expressing friendship and respect, puts his hand on his chest and half rises from his seat.

"Yours truly Mr Kaaji."

Mr Kaaji, with bits and pieces of pastry flying out of his mouth, warmly greets the old man.

"My dear Mr Kaaji, you know how fond I am of you and how much I respect you and your revered family."

Kaaji too puts his hand on his chest and, as a gesture of respect, bows slightly.

"I will most definitely come to visit you and to pay my respects."

He walks away. The old man whispers, "You see this guy, Kaaji? He is ~~a vile bastard,~~ a scoundrel. Until just ten years ago, he and his wife lived in a rented room. ~~Then, I don't know how, he managed to push his way into some government office, and now he steals by the billions. He has sent his wife and kids to Canada, has two temporary wives in two separate houses and he's living it up.~~ I can't stand him, I really can't stand him. I don't want to look at his evil face even for a second."

Witnessing this sort of Iranian hypocrisy always makes Dara angry. The blade of the assassin's dagger flashes in his mind. In moments of sorrow he misses that Hashashin phantom, and is perhaps sorry that he failed in his mission.

There is still no sign of Sara. Dara is thinking of leaving. In fact, at the bride's request, Sara has ended up being a bridesmaid and has gone to the hair salon with the bride. There, the bride and her entourage are subjected to the world's most extreme make-up. At a designated hour, the groom, in a car decked with flowers, followed by a few other cars packed with friends and relatives, appears in front of the salon. The bride, covered with a white chador ~~so that no one on the street sees her sleeveless dress and bare shoulders,~~ is deposited in the groom's car, and the caravan, horns blowing, travels through the streets and heads for the wedding venue.

From the sound of the women's cheers and ululations, Dara learns of the bride and groom's arrival. ~~The band plays the old wedding song.~~ An old, joyous melody rises from the leafless branches of the trees. And Dara sees his beautiful Sara. ~~She is wearing a body-hugging white dress with silver threads~~ running through ~~the fabric. Her round, inviting shoulders and slightly plump arms shine mercilessly. Her skirt comes up to her knees, and Dara catches sight of Sara's calves. Their elongated muscles are just wide enough for a man's hands to wrap partially around them as they gently move over their curve, and then they gradually taper down to the tops of her ankles, just enough for a man's thumb and middle finger to circle around their fragile slenderness. For an instant, Dara sees the image of Sara's thighs circled around his body and the gentle gliding of those cool calves along the back of his scorching legs. He shakes his head to throw out that shameless image.~~

~~From the subtle movement of Sara's breasts the silver strands of her dress sparkle, and Dara discovers that a woman's waist is narrowed halfway between the width of her shoulders and the breadth of her hips for a man's hands to embrace and complete it.~~ Sara suddenly swings her head round halfway, ~~the bounty of her hair swells, moves away from her face,~~ and her eyes find Dara sitting in the corner. She smiles at him secretly and glides towards her mother.

Now you know very well that there is absolutely nothing I can do to stop the scissors of censorship from cutting off Sara's breasts, calves and waist. I therefore have to write the self-censored sentences in the following manner.

Dara sees his beautiful Sara. He sees the projection of her two crystalline collarbones that curve and end as handles of two crystal goblets. Sara's arms are like icicles against which the moonlight shines as they dangle beside two curved impressions . . .

No, even I get a chill from this icy illustration. I am tempted to liken the surfacing of Sara's beauties to the clichéd surfacing of a bikini-clad Ursula Andress from the sea in *Dr No*, but Mr Petrovich has most likely seen this film. On the other hand, I really don't want to turn my story into a still life by a gluttonous painter and write about two trembling pomegranates and compare Sara's fair skin to peeled almonds and describe the sudden protrusion of her behind as an apple. Perhaps I can write

The trees are jolted from their winter sleep and unleash a neigh of desire. Sculpted flesh moves among them.

No. I don't like these butcheresque metaphors either. I will write:

In seasonless paradise, a silver snake coils around two slender columns carved in marble and slithers up. It steals over a spring of honey and arrives at two concave curves. It moves higher still and chafes its icy scales against two white flames with crimson tips, and then, with its heat-seeking tongue, it moves the single pearl of a necklace aside and licks that soft, small hollow beneath.

No, I don't like this either.

Sara saunters over to the stream to be more clearly in Dara's view. The reflection of the multicoloured lights shimmers on the water. In that mercurial mirror, from the blending of the greens, azures and indigos, a new colour has emerged in the world. ~~It reflects on the paleness of Sara's arms and shoulders, and an even fresher colour is composed . . .~~

Unlike me, who wants to reveal Sara's beauties to my readers, **Dara does not want other men to see ~~the bareness of~~ Sara's ~~body~~. In fact, he is even angry at her for wearing this dress.**

A girl walks by and obstinately smiles at him. Embarrassed, Dara looks down. The old man shouts:

"Did you see? Did you see how that tramp was flirting with you? Damn these young girls who lead our innocent young men astray."

Dara is tired of secretly watching Sara. He gets up to move to the spot closest to her. Sara sees him approaching. She bites her lower lip, signalling *no*. Dara is only a few steps away. Sara turns her back to him and starts talking to a man standing alone by the stream and watching the water flow by. Dara feels as though one of those idle tent heaters has been turned on in his body and is burning at full flame. He recognizes the man with the tired face and sagging shoulders. Dr Farhad, his head hanging down, every so often raises his eyes and glances into Sara's bright eyes, and then, feeling uneasy, he turns away.

He asks:

"Where have I seen you before?"

"At the hospital. Do you remember when you operated on Shirin and stitched her up? I was standing next to her."

"Yes, yes. Now I remember. It was so shocking."

Standing close by, Dara pretends to be busy watching the water flow by in the stream.

Now you probably want to ask why all the characters in this story stare at that stream.

First of all, in a desert country such as Iran, a stream is one of the most beautiful sights to behold. Second, in a country where office workers' productivity is all of twenty minutes in an eight-hour workday, listening to the murmur of water and watching it flow by is a much-needed form of mental and physical rest and relaxation, especially since all of us know by heart, and persistently remind each other of, that famous half-couplet by one of our greatest poets from seven hundred years ago:

Sit beside the stream and watch life flow by.

Therefore, in my realistic story, it is natural and must be plausible for my characters not to move from beside that stream.

Sara says:

"Doctor, I am surprised to see you here."

"To tell you the truth, I don't like wedding parties all that much. But the bride's father is my mother's maternal cousin, and I was duty bound to come. You must be here with your family or your husband."

"I don't have a husband."

Dara coughs. Sara glances at his angry eyes ~~and twirls a lock of her hair around her finger.~~

"Doctor, today girls in Iran are not like they were in the past, they don't marry the first man who asks for their hand. They are very selective. Until they have weighed all their options, until they are sure that the man declaring his love truly wants their happiness and not his own, they don't fall into the marriage trap. How about you? You must be here with your girlfriend or your wife."

The doctor blushes.

"No, I'm alone. I haven't had time for girlfriends, and I don't have time to spend with a fiancée."

All he has courage for is to look into Sara's eyes for five seconds.

"One of these days you will find a girl of your liking, a girl who will value your noble and selfless character and you will live a happy life."

The doctor seems to be frantically searching his mind for an appropriate sentence to speak. His mouth has remained open, and he cannot find one. Sara smiles at his innocence and timidity.

The doctor whimpers:

"I hope so . . . Loneliness is very . . . Loneliness is really . . . These days I have come to realize how very lonely I am . . ."

~~And he turns his deprived Iranian eyes away from the sight of Sara's cleavage.~~

"A lot of girls in this town can only dream of becoming your wife . . . By the way, in case I'm ever ill, where is your office?"

The doctor digs nervously into his pocket, twice dropping his briefcase, until at last he produces a business card and offers it to Sara. Then, unglued and confused, he walks out of the tent . . . Dara returns to his seat. He takes an orange and squeezes it in his fist. The juice spews out from between his fingers.

~~The old man says:~~

~~"That is exactly how you are squeezing my heart."~~

~~The garden singer starts belting out an Iranian rap song, a product of Los Angeles.~~

~~"I said, wiggle your hips and shake your boobs. You said, I'll wiggle my hips and shake the world . . ."~~

~~The women start to dance. A short distance away, young girls and boys make up their own group. Two guys, with their heads and necks on the ground and their legs up in the air, start spinning like break-dancers.~~

Mr Petrovich will ask:

"Can you hear the racket of vulgar music and dancing and snapping fingers coming from somewhere?"

I will answer:

"No. Rest easy. The people in town are all asleep. The houses are quiet; the windows are shut; the curtains are drawn. Innocence, like a spring breeze, is blowing through the streets and alleys and the angels are yawning."

A girl grabs Sara by the hand and drags her into the crowd of dancing boys and girls. Sara reluctantly moves her hands and hips and then slowly backs away from the group and settles for watching their harmless merriment. Given that they rarely have such opportunities, the girls and boys are dancing so feverishly that it seems they have entered a contest to release tormenting energy.

The old man points to Sara.

"Check out that cute missy. Don't buy into the way she stands there looking so timid. It's obvious she wants to dance, but she's playing coy so that they take her hand and pull her to the centre of the crowd. Once there, she'll turn into a ball of fire. I know these women like the back of my hand. Don't ever trust their appearance or the words that come out of their mouths. Reverse them."

Dara sees Sara's profile, and in that profile he sees no sign of joy. It seems that this Sara, contrary to a few minutes ago when she was flirting with Dr Farhad, is now the same Sara who had stood in front of Tehran University with DEATH TO FREEDOM, DEATH TO CAPTIVITY. The old man points to Sara's legs.

"See how slender her ankles are. My late father taught me that women with slender ankles have really tight holes, and those who have thick ankles have really ample goods, thick-lipped and puffy. This big."

He holds the palms of his hands together in front of Dara's eyes.

Again Dara drags himself one seat away from him. His heart aches. Watching other people dance and be merry has always made him sad. It reminds him of the happiness he has not had and the fact that he doesn't know, and has not learned, how and in what he will find his happiness. With every year that goes by, he grows more certain that we Iranians are a nation of grief and sorrow. We don't know happiness at all, and at times when we do exhibit happiness, we are in fact only pretending.

Watching the girls and boys dance reminds Dara of his neighbour's two daughters. They were identical twins. After the revolution, one of them joined the Party of God and the other became a Communist. When the police raided their house to arrest the Communist sister, the Party of God sister pretended to be her. In prison, they had put her in a closed coffin for three months so that she would give up her Marxist Communist denial of God and repent. Five years later when she was released, she no longer resembled her twin, and her sister had broken ties with the leftist faction and had spent those years praying and asking God to return her sister to the family alive. Years later, the twins disappeared. For a long time no one had any news of them, until we heard that in Istanbul, in front of the UN refugee agency, in protest against Europe's hypocritical policies towards Iran, hand in hand the two had set themselves on fire . . .

Dara scolds himself for not leaving, but he doesn't have the will to go, nor does he have the will not to look at Sara, and his eyes continue to invite her to his side.

Sara, holding two small plates filled with pastries, walks towards him. She offers the first plate to the old man. The old man says:

"I adore you, my darling girl, no one gave me a thought except you who are like a daughter to me."

Sara bends down and holds the second plate in front of Dara. As soon as he reaches out to take the plate from her, Sara whispers:

"The minute you see me talking to a man the ugliest doubts come to your mind."

And a single teardrop falls on the pastries.

Dara gives his plate to the old man and follows the stream to the darkness at the end of the garden. ~~He sees the shadow of a young girl and boy kissing. Hearing his footsteps, they separate and turn their backs to him.~~ Some distance away, Dara leans against a tree and lights a cigarette. Surprised at how Sara has seen the serpents of jealousy in his eyes, he dwells on the uncertain future of his relationship with her. He feels their love is travelling a course over which he has no control. Lighting his second cigarette, in the glow of the flame he sees Sara standing in front of him; he reaches his hand out towards her shoulder. Sara pulls back. Dara, still leaning against the tree, slides himself down to the ground. The scratches the tree bark leaves on his back are soothing to him.

He says:

"I am only now realizing that I don't really know you. You are not the Sara I knew. I am so confused."

"Because, selfishly, you have always wanted me to be the way you have imagined me in your mind. The only person who ever saw me as I really am was that poet who peddled books. Go back to the party; I want to dance for you."

And she starts to walk against the current of the stream. A few minutes later, Dara lights his third cigarette. The coquettish giggle of a girl emanates from somewhere in the darkness of the garden. Dara thinks that if Sara truly loves him, she will give him that handwritten book. He throws the half-smoked cigarette in the stream. In the dark, he doesn't see that on the water, every so often, a damask rose floats by. That same flower that our grandmothers would tell us fables about: a beast falls in love with a beautiful girl, kidnaps her, and takes her to his garden. Whenever he needs to leave the garden, to make sure the girl does not escape, he cuts off her head and hangs it on a tree. The girl's blood drips into a stream, and each drop turns into a damask rose, until the young man who is to kill the beast and save the girl sees the flowers and traces them back to the garden. Dara returns to the party and sits where he had sat before. The bride and the groom are mingling with the guests and exchanging pleasantries with them. Dara imagines Sara in the wedding dress she had tried on in that store and sees himself in that groom's place holding her hand. In their winter sleep, the trees convey their *One Thousand and One Nights*-ish fantasies to one another on a cool breeze.

Suddenly they hear the sound of china plates breaking.

The singer has thrown the microphone aside, and leaping towards one of the tent exits he has knocked over the table laden with trays of pastries. The female drummer too has thrown down her sticks and, following the singer, leaps towards the darkness of the garden. The poor guitarist, who has an electric guitar slung around his neck, cannot rid himself of the wires and falls down. It is only then that everyone notices the green-uniformed patrols from the Campaign Against Social Corruption who have suddenly appeared at the entrance to the tent. One of them grabs the guitarist by the back of his neck and pushes him face down onto the ground. The three others chase after the two fugitive musicians. Screaming, the women and girls run towards the villa in the garden.

The old man laments:

"Oh dear! This is bad. The bastards are . . ."

The agent who has arrested the guitarist is now smashing the man's guitar with his feet. The three other agents return empty-handed. Men who have been drinking, looking pale, hide in the corners. Others, including the groom, his parents and other relatives, gather round two of the agents. One by one they plead for them to turn a blind eye to the party and not to spoil that joyous occasion. The old man takes a cucumber from the fruit tray and, thinking that it will get rid of the smell of alcohol on his breath, nervously bites into it.

Then he rubs his hands together and says:

"The way the groom is begging, he's only going to make matters worse. This is a job for me. You, young man, don't go anywhere until I negotiate with them and come back."

He stands up and immediately starts to stagger. He straightens his back, takes a deep breath, swallows the bitter end of the cucumber and bravely heads towards the agents. By the time he reaches them, he is walking perfectly straight. He shouts:

"Well! Well! I smell the scent of rose water from the battlegrounds of truth against the unrighteous."

He breaks through the crowd gathered around the agents, opens his arms, embraces the ranking officer and lays a few sopping kisses on the man's cheeks.

"Welcome! You honour us. Mr Kaaji, bring some pastries for our brothers . . . Gentlemen! Gentlemen! These brothers are only doing their job. We must not argue with them . . . Someone go after those foppish musicians and bring them back. They should pledge to our brother right here that they will never repeat such abomination . . . Mr Kaaji, did you bring the pastries?"

The ranking officer is looking at the old man with suspicion. The old man kisses another officer on both shoulders.

"Excellent! I feel alive again. Brothers, don't you recognize me?"

The officers look at each other and shake their heads.

"Huh! Really! It's obvious you brothers are new to the job. All the brothers at the Campaign Against Social Corruption, from the lowest-ranking all the way up to the commanders, know yours truly, and know all about my revolutionary deeds before the revolution. Everyone present here knows that I have donated all my wealth to buy homes for the brothers of the revolution. If you don't believe me, ask your base commander, Colonel Salman. Every week, he and I walk barefoot to Friday prayers. I am devoted to all the brothers of the revolution. I am Haji Karim . . . Who went after that damned singer and his musician?"

With the air of a commander he points to a few young men.

"You, you and you, go and find those two and bring them back here."

There is such authority in his voice that the three young men obediently run towards the garden. The others, wide-eyed and open-mouthed at the old man's performance, stand around staring. He just about forces each one of the agents to take a plate of pastries and sits them down on chairs. Little by little he has quelled their anger at seeing the decadent party. All of a sudden, the old man kicks the drum, and while trying to extract his foot from its middle, he slyly goes on to say that he himself will take command of the party, he will not allow the women to come out of the villa without their heads covered, he will get rid of the musical para-phernalia and even if they don't find the singer and his friend tonight, tomorrow he will himself deliver them, hands tied, to the revolutionary brothers. In old Iranian tradition, he plucks a strand of his beard and puts it in the palm of the commander's hand as guarantee of his promise. Half an hour later, the agents have lost their harsh and brusque expressions. They amicably explain that they do not like disrupting such joyous gath-erings, but that some families really carry things too far.

The incident is coming to a happy end, and the old man is walking the agents to the garden gates when the ranking officer's two-way radio comes on. He reports that Haji Karim has pledged and attested for everyone at the party and that they are returning to the base . . .

The shout of the base commander blasts out:

"Who the hell is Haji Karim?"

"Colonel! Haji Karim, your friend. He says all the brothers know him . . . The guy you walk barefoot to Friday prayers with."

And only he grasps the implication of his commanding officer's shouts. And only the old man grasps the implication of the ranking officer's furi-ous glare.

The officers arrest the phony Haji Karim, the guitarist, the father of the bride, the bride and the groom and take them all away.

~~The guests, dumbstruck, flop down on the chairs. No one has the energy to talk and no one knows what to do.~~ Now the gentle one-thousand-and-one-year-old rippling of the stream can be clearly heard. Dara chooses his path so as to walk past Sara. He inhales her scent and whispers:

"Goodbye."

Sara mumbles:

"I'm sorry."

Dara walks towards the garden gates. Suddenly, like a miracle in Tehran, high above the broken-hearted, ~~graveyard-like~~ silence ~~of the people,~~ high above the glow of the colourful lamps that now seem unsightly, ~~and high above a broken guitar,~~ the familiar song of a night-singing nightingale rises from somewhere in the garden. A nightingale that in this season of cold should not be in the garden, a nightingale that in a thousand verses of Iranian poetry, in the hours of darkness, for the love of a red rose and in sorrow of its separation from it, has forever sung and will forever sing.

"AT DAWN THE SCENT OF FLOWERS
FROM MY BED . . ."

The next scene of our story begins in Dara's house.

Dara's parents have gone away for three days. ~~In Iran, this is a golden opportunity.~~ Therefore, after much mumbling, stage-setting and pangs of conscience and shame, Dara has invited Sara to his house. And Sara, after much mumbling and pangs of conscience and shame, has accepted his invitation. But she has repeatedly insisted:

"Only for half an hour. Just to sit and have a cup of tea together, and then I will leave. Only half an hour."

In fact, after the incident on that snowy night, they have become more cautious and conservative. In other words, more intelligent. Mr Petrovich will like my last sentence. Of course, to get to know each other better and to protect their pure and chaste love, they would have preferred to go for a walk in a beautiful park in northern Tehran.

Our story's two lovers have discussed and planned extensively the method by which Sara will approach the front door and the manner in which she will quickly enter. Like two urban guerrillas hunted by the secret police, they have tried to foresee all the unforeseeable incidents and problems that could arise. In truth, their greatest fear is of nosy neighbours who know Dara's parents are away, and if they see a girl entering the house, they will immediately conclude that soon, none other than the sin of fornication will be committed in that house. It is likely that Brother Atta will call one of the many bureaus of the Campaign Against Social Corruption and request that their agents come as quickly as possible before a sin is committed under that city's sky. If the agents are delayed or are negligent, Atta, who believes himself responsible for all of

Iran's sexual organs, will bombard them with telephone calls until they finally raid the house and arrest the two guilty parties.

As planned, Dara has left the front door ajar five minutes before the designated time. At nine in the morning Sara, looking petrified, enters Dara's house. She dashes past the jasmine bush in the front garden and throws herself into the building.

Mr Petrovich tolerates this scene, hoping that at the end of my novel the guilty characters will suffer such remorse, misery and ruin that my story will at least take on a morally educational aspect and that it becomes a lesson to boys and girls who, according to an old Iranian proverb, are like cotton and fire and if left alone, will destroy not only themselves but their house and home as well. Perhaps I, too, as a writer who for years has written under government censorship and cultural censorship of the people of my land, will subconsciously arrange a dark ending full of repentance and shame for my protagonist and antagonist so that my story receives a publishing permit. Anyway, as far as I can remember, with the exception of a few old stories, for centuries all Iranian love stories, in verse or prose, have ended with the parting of the two lovers, the laughter of death and the sneer of Satan.

In the house, Dara takes Sara to his room. He has carpeted Sara's path from the front door all the way to the middle of his room with flower petals . . . Sara, looking pale, leans against the wall. Dara, from the corner of the drawn curtain, inspects the houses across the street to see if anyone, from the corner of a drawn curtain, is inspecting their house. Both their hearts are beating wildly and are about to explode.

Sara wants to ask, Are you sure no one comes to your house unannounced? But she doesn't, because if I write this sentence, Mr Petrovich will ask, What do they want to do that they are scared of someone turning up unexpectedly? Even if he doesn't ask this question, he will become more acutely sensitive towards my story's characters.

Dara offers Sara something to drink.

A real drink, of course, not the kind he has gulped down two glasses of since this morning.

Sara is still gasping for air. She takes the handwritten book of *Khosrow and Shirin* out of her handbag and throws it down in front of Dara.

"I used to leaf through it every day. I really liked it. But it is of no use to me any more."

"Why not?"

"Look at it!"

Dara opens the book. All the bright, vibrant colours of the miniatures and illuminations have faded. A dark shadow has spread over the unveiled and exposed hair, arms and legs of the women, and it seems a coarse eraser has scraped and smudged certain words and sentences. The book's pages reek of mould. Dara throws it aside. He wants to speak that sentence which most Iranian men are accustomed to telling their wife, lover, sister or mother, I told you so. But he keeps his silence. He doesn't smirk either. He only says:

"Thank you for coming."

Sara moans:

"What have I done? I shouldn't have come."

Now Sara's eyes are brimming with tears. Dara, without asking, knows why his beloved is in tears.

Ask me what Mr Petrovich thinks of this scene, and I will say, He has now fully engaged all his faculties and his sixth sense as well.

I will therefore write:

There is no strength left in their knees. Sara in this corner of the room, and Dara in that corner of the room, cower down . . .

In a trembling voice Sara asks:

"Why?"

This "why" that Sara has asked is a historic "why" that reveals itself not only in our literature, which is fraught with longing, sorrow and partings, but even in our folk songs. My favourite folk song, awash with sadness and desire, is

> *The breeze that comes from your tresses,*
> *is to me more pleasing than the scent of hyacinth.*
> *When at night I hold the image of you in my arms,*
> *at dawn the scent of flowers rises from my bed . . .*

We Iranians seem never to tire of these poems and songs.

The "why" that Sara has asked is the "why" that forlorn lovers in the land of Iran have for centuries asked the land of Iran. And none of the great Iranian thinkers and intellectuals – who the world has yet to discover – has ever taken the trouble to find an answer to this question.

An old song is playing on Dara's dilapidated stereo. The singer laments, "When at night I hold the image of you in my arms . . . At dawn . . ." And Sara and Dara, each in a corner of the room, sit staring into each other's tearful eyes.

You may have noticed that since Sara's entrance into the room, I have not written that she has removed her headscarf, and I will not write that from fear she is wet with perspiration and that she has unbuttoned her coverall, and I will not write what a sheer and low-cut camisole she is wearing under it. The Iranian reader knows very well what some Iranian girls wear under their coveralls. Sara runs her fingers through the hair that has fallen loose on her forehead and combs it back. Dara sees her underarm and the pale shadow of its shaven hair. The musky scent of her underarm floats in the room.

But to inform the reader of how Dara has panicked at the sight of all that beauty within his reach, and how with his eyes he is devouring the abundance of Sara's long black hair, I will write a few sentences in a stream of consciousness with images of a cold and dark winter night when wind and thunder, like evil ghosts, knock on doors and windows and a marble statue trembles in the house.

Then I will write:

Dara and Sara's hearts beat like the hearts of two caged sparrows in a magnificent tale. Not only from fear of being discovered and disgraced, ~~but also from the flight of their sparrowlike fancies to those acts that can be performed in private~~ . . .

I hate likening a rapidly beating heart to the heart of a sparrow because I think it is an old cliché. But at this point in my story, other than such a simile, I cannot think of a more creative sentence, and both you and Mr Petrovich know why. Truth be told, in this scene my heart too is beating like the heart of a caged sparrow, because I want Sara and Dara, after a thirty-minute silent conversation with their eyes, to exchange a smile. Then I want Dara to get up, walk over and sit next to Sara, and I want them to kiss. The very first kiss of their lives – clumsy, scared, drenched with saliva and yet unforgettable for the rest of their lives. But in their souls a force stronger than the desire for a kiss has awakened. A force that numbs and weakens them, that through all the nightmares they have had, threatens them and brings them tidings of terrifying punishment.

Sara, ~~hating her own and her lover's fears,~~ with a quick kick throws

her sandals to the other side of the room. One of the sandals lands in front of Dara. Dara picks it up. He touches it and . . . ~~smells it, kisses it.~~

I am sure the kissing of the sandal will not receive a publishing permit, and I am forced to resort to ancient metaphors of Iranian literature and to seek the assistance of Omar Khayyám. Although Khayyám was the greatest mathematician of his time, he preferred to sit beside the stream in his garden and, with one eye on life flowing by and the other on his jug of wine, compose quatrains about the death of lovers and beauties and the transformation of their bodies into dust, about jug-makers who make jugs from that dust, and about lovers and beauties who sit beside the stream and drink wine from those jugs. Thus, Khayyám's dusty ecosystem comes to my aid and I write:

Dust from the sole of that sandal on Dara's hands . . . He rubs that dust, which heralds divine unity, between his fingers . . . The chill that dawns in the body of the dead creeps onto his hands. The ~~lustful~~ words ready in his mind to be spoken to Sara become words etched on gravestones. He tastes the dust. It tastes sharp~~, it tastes of Shiraz wine~~. All the paths and places on which Sara has walked and all the gardens and riverbanks of life, all are within this dust and all will someday return to this dust and unite with the dust of Khayyám's sandals, and a stream will flow over that dust and from it plants will grow and a lover, ignorant of the glaring eyes of death, will sit beside that stream and write an ode to the eternal beauties of his beloved.

Mr Petrovich will quite likely appreciate this piece because it will make the readers think of death and hell. But this segment could also be written like this:

Dara kisses the sole of Sara's sandal. The dust has the sharp taste of the old wines of Shiraz in earthen decanters that the *shahneh*s have broken and offered to the parched earth.

Two veins on Sara's ankles, the rivers Tigris and Euphrates, that have taught the agony of man's separation from man to the silver flamingos . . . Two violet veins that on the peak of the ankles come together and flow ~~to that place where all the torments and joys of man are born~~ . . .

Sara does not hear Dara's stream of consciousness, but having seen his caress and passionate kiss on her sandal, she sighs, a sigh that I am afraid Mr Petrovich will hear from the white between the lines of my story.

Sara says:

"Well, why are you sitting so far away? Come closer."

Dara, who is in an unnatural state from having tasted the dust of the broken earthen decanters of wine and the plants along the riverbank, like a tame and harmless sheep moves towards Sara on all fours. This is the first time in Sara's life that a man with fire in his eyes, with a breath scented with wine and a tongue tainted with death, moves towards her like this – like a sheep that can quickly transform into a wolf. Stronger and saltier still, sweat seeps from her pores. As he approaches his prey, the sheeplike wolf glares at the fresh and succulent flesh on Sara's shoulders in which virgin blood flows.

In the depths of Sara's ears, the voices of mothers, grandmothers and aunts rise like the dead on the day of resurrection – a day that lasts three hundred thousand days – all the words of wisdom and words of warning that from childhood until a few days ago have been spoken in her ears.

"My girl, don't you ever let the boys touch your flower! If one of them says let me see your flower, quickly come and tell me so that I can cut off his ear."

"My girl, you are ten years old now, you shouldn't be playing with the neighbour's boys."

"Sara, if God forbid one of the boys in the neighbourhood ever asks you to go to some quiet corner with him, don't you be fooled. You will be ruined for the rest of your life, and on Judgment Day God will punish you. In hell guilty women and girls are hung by their breasts from hooks and roasted on fire."

"Sara, you are grown-up now, you shouldn't go to the door in short sleeves."

"Sara, your uncle Javad is a letch, don't wear skirts when he comes over to our house."

"My girl, now that you will be going to the university on your own, you have to be very careful. Don't forget that men only want one thing from women. No matter how many nice things they say, the minute they get what they came for, they will throw you away like a used tissue. No matter how many promises they make, they will never marry you because they think a girl who gives herself to them before marriage does not deserve to be their wife."

"You see these men? They're all wolves. Some of them in sheep's skin, some of them in dog's skin, some even in mouse's skin, they know a thousand different ploys and poems. The moment they learn what type of man you like, they will become that man. You will end up in a brothel."

"Sara, don't be duped by the lewd boys and girls at the university who fool you and say let's go to the cinema, let's go for some ice cream. One ice cream and you'll be disgraced in this town. My girl, be very careful. Don't bring shame to yourself and to your family."

But that wolf that was once called Dara, guised in mouse's skin, has now moved close to Sara. She can hear the mouse's uneven breaths and senses the heat of his body against her own. She sees a drop of sweat fall onto the floor from Dara's temple.

Dust wails, ~~wine froths in one-thousand-year-old earthen decanters~~ **. . . Sara's heart grows heavier from one moment to the next. Its beating slows . . .**

Mr Petrovich will say:

"Wait! What is going on? There seem to be things happening in your story that I can't see. There seem to be unseemly things going on in between these three dots. Why has Sara's heart slowed down?"

"Sir! Your instincts don't always tell you the truth. There is nothing going on. Dara is still rubbing the dust from the sole of Sara's sandal between his fingers. And Sara's heart, like everyone else's, sometimes beats fast, sometimes slow. You yourself have read in stories that when some sexual encounter is about to take place the characters' hearts beat faster . . . Read the next sentence and see how Sara fouls things up for Dara."

Sara says:

"You look like a wolf."

Dara, ~~a few feet away from Sara, freezes in his place and~~ **in a trembling voice says:**

"I think I look like a miserable dog."

~~"No, I prefer you to look like a wolf . . . Come!"~~

Dara at last crosses *The Longest Yard* and sitting next to Sara leans against the wall. Now their bare forearms touch. Sara strokes Dara's cheek with her fingertip.

"You've cut your face. Was your hand shaking while you shaved this morning?"

"Yes. But you prefer a bearded man."

"Leave your jealousy for some other time."

That morning's trembling has again started in Dara's body. Its cause is nothing but the first amorous touch of a woman's delicate hand against his face. With a courage that he had not known he possessed, Dara takes Sara's hand. The sweat on their palms combine. They look at their hands resting one in the other.

And Sara sees the stain of turquoise paint on the edge of Dara's nail.

Behind the curtains covering the window of that room, a turquoise sky with no winged horse and no flying carpet stretches towards Tehran's eastern horizon, toward Khayyám's city of Neyshabur where beautiful Iranian turquoise beneath the earth dreams of becoming a gem on the beautiful fingers of an Iranian girl~~, fingers that now ache from the pressure of a lover's hand~~. Sara ~~returns the pressure of Dara's hand in kind and~~ says:

"Gentle!"

Mr Petrovich will say:

"What happened? What did Sara say? What is Dara doing? What if this cunning guy has gone after Sara?"

I will say:

"I don't think so. Perhaps to release his emotional stress he is squeezing Sara's sandal in his fist and Sara is afraid that her sandal will break in two."

Sara raises Dara's hand to her lips and kisses the finger that bears the turquoise stain. A kiss so silent that neither Mr Petrovich nor even I can hear. From the touch of Sara's lips against his skin, a hellish roar echoes in Dara's ears. He is tongue-tied, and no word or action comes to his mind. Sara, with eyes closed and lips half opened, rests her head against the wall. Dara is still dwelling on the scorch of that kiss on his finger. All the turquoise mines of Neyshabur seem to have caved in under his nail and the injured miners are screaming for help . . .

I nudge him. "Stupid boy! What are you waiting for? This poor girl has come as far as she can. It's your turn to make a move. See how her lips are ready and waiting? Do something, you dimwit. Hurry! Women's patience doesn't last as long as a shot of vodka."

Dara turns to Sara. ~~He sees her proportionately plump arms waiting for the pressure of his arms and the empty place of his broad hands on the curves of her shoulders.~~ He looks at the black stain on Sara's misty, rose-coloured lower lip, the fruit of biting her lips in fear~~, and at the~~

~~white skin beneath her freshly plucked eyebrows~~. And at last, staring at her closed eyes, he opens his lips.

"Death to freedom, death to captivity , , , what you had written on your sign . . . It was very strange. What did you mean by it?"

Sara lifts her head from its resting place against the wall. ~~She opens her eyes that had been closed to the fantasy of a kiss.~~ She grins.

"I was inspired . . ."

This is the wisest and most ironic response that can come from the lips of an Iranian woman. From the days when the most magnificent Iranian women were carried to harems of seven hundred in covered palanquins mounted on camels, until today when a lady defender of human rights in Iran receives the Nobel Peace Prize after having endured years of persecution and threats, and unlike her, an Iranian woman amasses such wealth in the United States that she buys a ticket on the Russian spacecraft taxi and becomes the first woman tourist in outer space, no such inspiration has ever come to an Iranian woman.

Sara, continuing her mysterious comment, says:

"I am tired. I am very, very tired."

It is now that the spark of love is ignited. Right at this very moment when that mystifying look awakens in Sara's eyes. A look that has gleamed in the eyes of wine-bearers in forbidden taverns of seven hundred years ago, that has gleamed in the eyes of freedom-loving women burning under the hot-iron torture of the secret police, that has gleamed in the eyes of a mother who has received the bones of a son martyred at war, that will gleam in the eyes of the young girl who will someday write the most beautiful Iranian love story.

Tell me:

You seem to be an absent-minded writer! Didn't you write earlier that this spark of love had already ignited?

And I will say:

Why don't you pay attention? I am not talking about Dara's spark of love. I am talking about Mr Petrovich's spark of love. He is now staring into those noble Oriental eyes that my prose fails to describe. His heart is beating like the heart of a sparrow held captive in a fist. But you are right when you say I am an absent-minded writer. I was not at all aware that, throughout this unimaginative story, Mr Petrovich's imagination of Sara has been extremely active. And now, with every ounce of his emotions, he feels he has fallen in love with this girl. This girl who is neither lewd nor saintly.

Mr Petrovich says:

"Please take Sara out of this womanizer's house. Send her home! I myself will send Sinbad to China to buy pencils."

"But sir, that won't do! What about my story's plot?"

"Then I forbid you to allow Dara's hand to touch her."

"Sir, even if I wanted to, this Dara is so clumsy and confused that he is not capable of doing anything. I am sure he now wants to go on and on about a few days ago when he painted a house turquoise."

"That is very good. In my opinion, you have written a successful and refined love story that may receive a publishing permit . . . Except . . . except, I have one problem."

"What problem?"

"Well, if somehow I wanted to meet Sara, I don't know what I would have to do . . . Ever since I read segments of your story, she has attracted my attention. Don't think I have wicked intentions. I want to ask for her hand in marriage. Rest assured that I can make her happy . . . Can you think of a way for us to meet somewhere?"

"No . . . If you wanted, for example, to meet Anna Karenina, I could perhaps find a way, but . . ."

"Who is Anna Karenina? Is she like Sara?"

"She's better than Sara. I can't say she is very beautiful, but she has a certain charm that would bring any man to his knees. Perhaps you can censor the segment where she falls in love and stop her from committing suicide."

"No . . . And you call yourself a writer? Don't you know that when a man like me falls in love he has eyes for no other woman?"

"I wish you had told me sooner. I think I should write a novel about you and your love story."

"By the time you write that novel, delinquent boys like Dara will have ruined Sara . . . But I have an idea. Tell me what you think about it. Write that Sara drops the handkerchief Dara has given to her somewhere near the Ministry of Culture and Islamic Guidance, maybe even in front of my office so that no one else will see it. I will pick it up and run after her. I will say, Miss, is this your handkerchief? . . . She sees me. She thanks me. Then I will say, Miss, you deserve much more than such a handkerchief. You should have a handkerchief woven of gold with pearls along its edges. This way I open up a conversation with her."

It is here that I remember Dara's notorious handkerchief. In traditional Iranian weddings it was customary at the end of the evening, while festivities were still under way in the house, to send the bride and groom hand in hand to a room known as the *hejleh,* or the nuptial chamber. There, an old woman would stand waiting behind the door. After the groom had conquered the bastion of the bride, he would deliver a handkerchief stained with the blood of her virginity to the old woman. She would in turn display the handkerchief before the guests, and joyous screams and shouts would rise because the test of the bride's purity had been proudly and successfully performed. Of course, a bride whose hymen was for example circumferential or vertical and produced no blood, would on this night be either murdered or disgraced before one and all and dispatched to her parents' house. Now you have discovered the hidden significance of the complicated symbol of my story, and now you understand why Mr Petrovich is so sensitive about this handkerchief.

And the word "blood" reminds me of that assassin who wanted to release Dara's blood from his jugular. I shout:

"Then it was you who sent that assassin to kill Dara!"

Mr Petrovich raises his index finger to his nose, suggesting that I lower my voice.

"You are accusing an official of the holy government of the Islamic Republic of assassinating his opponents. I will pretend I did not hear what you said."

Then with an air of authority he says:

"The longer Sara and Dara stay together, the greater the danger threatening your story. Find a solution quickly; otherwise, get the fancy of publishing a love story out of your head."

I say:

"You call this a love story? Or a . . .? Look at what has become of my hopes and dreams. Every single bone in this story is broken. Every single one of its chapters has gone to a wasteland around Tehran, those same places where they burn rubbish. Perhaps I should have just strangled Sara like Desdemona at the very start and put us all out of our misery."

He says:

"I think it has turned out to be a nice, educational story! Now put your creativity to work so that Sara ends up loathing Dara."

His eyes have regained their frightening glint of shrewdness.

"Don't force me to take action myself. Get Sara out of that house of sin."

I no longer have any energy or passion to write. I have to take to my grave the dream of putting that enchanting period at the end of a good love story.

I say:

"Sir, don't kid yourself! It's too late. In the process of writing this story, I have again come to the conclusion that writing a love story with a happy ending is not in the destiny of writers of my generation . . . and my work on this story is done. I no longer have any control over it or its characters."

"What do you mean? Why are you talking nonsense? Start writing."

"Your Excellency, I can't! I have been completely scissored out of this story. I'm done in . . ."

Ask me:

How?

So that to you and to Mr Petrovich I say:

"Listen! Sara wants to speak for herself."

Sara tells Dara:

"In that flower bed in your front garden . . . That jasmine bush . . ."

"Yes, I have been meaning to prune it, but I haven't had the time."

"No, don't . . . To allow a plant the freedom to spread throughout the garden is beautiful."

Dara and I, and Mr Petrovich, look at Sara's beautiful sentence in awe. Sara stares at the two violet veins on her ankle. She strokes them with her fingertip and rubs her tired ankle.

Then, as though she has suddenly remembered something, her eyes widen; she freezes.

"What's wrong, Sara? What happened?"

"When I walked into the garden, the first thing I saw was that jasmine bush . . . To be honest, it frightened me. Now I realize that it seemed as if a pair of terrifying eyes were looking at me from inside the bush."

"That's impossible . . . There is no one in the house except you and me."

"But I am sure I saw it. Maybe when you left the front door open someone came in and hid in the bush."

Dara, with his heart beating out of his chest, from the corner of his bedroom curtain looks at the jasmine bush. His eyes are wide with fear. It seems there is something in its branches.

Later, when terrified he runs to the garden, there he will see the corpse of a hunchback midget staring at the front door of the house . . .

And all I know is that before it is too late, as fast as possible, even if with a flying carpet, I must get to my house and lock the door from the inside . . .